Julie Roberts has been writing since she was fifteen years old, spending hours filling pages with adventures in wild jungles, ancient castles, Cornish smugglers' coves, capturing foreign spies and outwitting aliens from space.

Now, she writes Romantic Historical novels set in the Georgian/Regency era. She is also a member of the Romantic Novelists' Association, and at their Golden Anniversary Conference, was thrilled to achieve third place in the Elizabeth Goudge annual writing award.

Find Julie on Twitter **@julieoroberts**, Facebook **/julierobertsauthor**, or visit her website at **www.julieroberts.me.uk**

By Julie Roberts

Regency Marriage Laws series
The Hidden Legacy
Dangerous Masquerade
A Tangle of Secrets
A Tainted Marriage

A Tainted Marriage

Julie ROBERTS

ACCENT

First published in 2020
by HEADLINE ACCENT
An imprint of HEADLINE PUBLISHING GROUP

1

Cataloguing in Publication Data is available from the British Library

ISBN 978 1 7861 5980 9

Typeset in 10.5/13pt Bembo Std by Jouve (UK), Milton Keynes

Printed and bound in Great Britain by Clays Ltd, Elcograf S.p.A.

HEADLINE PUBLISHING GROUP
An Hachette UK Company
Carmelite House
50 Victoria Embankment
London EC4Y 0DZ

www.headline.co.uk
www.hachette.co.uk

A Tainted Marriage

Chapter One

April 1815

Alexander Kilbraith, fourth Earl of Rossmore, entered Lord Synclare's home. He was late. Giving his cloak and hat to a footman he made his way to the ballroom. He paused in the doorway and was challenged by the babble of voices and high-pitched laughter that rose up to meet the chandeliers. In contrast, the kaleidoscopic colours, pastel and brilliant, made by the ladies' gowns swirling in and out of their gentlemen's dark attire was a pleasing sight.

The Season had started with the usual rush of invitations from hopeful mamas wishing to secure the best matrimonial match for their daughters. He was in their eyes the most eligible man in the room, offering both title and wealth, but had avoided all attempts to trap him. His reputation as determinedly single enabled him to come and enjoy these evenings without watching every word and gesture he made.

When the music stopped he noticed Lady Crowmarsh, or more specifically, the dark-haired woman standing next to her. She was not one of the London *ton*, her dress not to this Season's fashion, but he was curious to know how such a beautiful woman had escaped his notice at any of the other balls he had been obliged to attend.

He walked towards them, nodding his acknowledgements as he threaded his way through the throng of guests. 'Lady Crowmarsh.' He raised the elder woman's gloved hand to his lips, 'Pray, introduce me to your new acquaintance.'

Fluttering her fan to cool the flush that had come to her cheeks, she replied, 'Lord Rossmore, we are honoured. May I present my niece, Miss Matthews.'

Grey eyes fringed with dark lashes looked into his. 'Lord Rossmore,' and she dipped a curtsey.

Rossmore was aware of the tightness in his shoulders, a shyness he could not remember since a young man. 'May I request a dance?'

'I am about to be claimed for the next. Shall we say the one after?'

He bowed and stepped aside as a young dandy arrived at his elbow. A throb pounded in his temple and he had to admit to a touch of chagrin that he had to wait in line for her. He did not recognise the young buck, but it pleased him to see it was the cotillion, a dance that gave little personal contact. It did, however, give him time to see how she lowered her gaze when she honoured her partner, smile as she enjoyed the dance, and finally be escorted back to her aunt.

Now she was his and he led her forward to dance the waltz. He laid his gloved hand on the back of her satin gown and his pulse beat faster, his throat gone dry. To get his nerves under control he asked, 'Your aunt has never spoken of you?' that sounded as though she should have.

'I live most of the year in the country. My father does not hold a residence in London. His last visit was for my coming-out season. I always stay with my aunt and Lord Crowmarsh when in Town. This hectic lifestyle does not go well with me, my lord.'

'May I ask the purpose of this visit?' What was wrong with him? That was an impertinent question to ask.

'I needed a change of scenery. Aunt Matilda, as always, was kind enough to offer her hospitality for a few weeks.'

He decided to give up talking and let the music sweep them into the twirling dance and the pleasure of exploring his feelings. She was comfortable in his arms and her figure youthful, given she was well past her coming-out. And her scent was like a summer meadow. He pulled her a little closer. Then out of nowhere his next thought stunned him – he wanted to sweep her away to a place where no one would find them. When the music stopped he grasped her arm, towing her with unwarranted haste back to her aunt.

Rossmore could see confusion pass over her face. 'Thank you, Miss Matthews.' He nodded and bowed to Lady Crowmarsh. 'Good-night.'

He did not slow his step until he reached his coach.

Rossmore entered his Grosvenor Square house in a state of agitation, thrusting his cloak and hat into his butler's arms. 'You may go to bed, Saunders, I shall not require anything else.' He walked into his study, closing the door firmly, the sound echoing round the hall.

He walked directly to a small table and a decanter of brandy, pouring a full glass. He loosened his neck cloth, sat down in a winged chair by the fire and looked up at the portrait of his late wife, Liddy, hanging above the fireplace.

Life had been calm and orderly until a few hours ago. Yet one look at Miss Matthews, one waltz with her, he was now thinking only of how much he wanted her. Ten years he had been a widower and in all that time no woman had come near to making his heart hammer with such a wild erratic beat. He had vowed never to marry again. Never to have another wife, who could die in his arms after bearing him a son, an heir who had died within minutes of his birth. He never wanted to be left with that ravaging grief again.

So what was happening? What was making him even think about another woman? The implications of having feelings went against his vow.

With no heir, his half-brother Geoffrey would inherit the title, the estates and the wealth Rossmore had worked hard to increase since his father's death. He and Geoffrey rarely saw each other, a mutual arrangement that suited them both, but of late, Geoffrey's reputation and reckless lifestyle had become the gossip of every club in Town. His gambling habits were wild, and those jackals he called friends encouraged him to higher stakes for their own gain.

So where did it leave him? With the responsibility of seeing that the Kilbraith legacy did not get squandered or cheated away in the hell-hole taverns his brother had succumbed to.

His beautiful young wife filled his mind as she always did when he needed comfort. There had been so much joy when she told him she was with child; her sweet kisses as she lay in his arms as he touched her soft skin when her confinement restrained their passion. Liddy's portrait had been his constant reminder of her death. But circumstances had changed and it was time to fulfil his duty. Miss Matthews was the lady who was prising open the corner of his heart.

Grace woke with her mind full of Lord Rossmore. His behaviour last night verged on an insult. He had appeared out of nowhere, asked for an introduction and requested she dance with him. Swept her into a waltz, poked his nose into her personal visit and then dragged her, yes, dragged her, back to Aunt Matilda and left. Her aunt smoothed over any embarrassment by sitting down next to her dear friend, Lady Gilmore, and asking a footman to fetch a glass of wine. Yet none of this could diminish how his hand had been firm on her back, guiding her expertly round the floor; never once did they falter.

She remembered how tall he was and his green eyes below that copper-coloured hair. He took her back to a time when she was young and full of expectations. Back to Simon, her gallant officer who had intended to make her his wife. Was this what attracted her? The same colour hair and eyes? Only partly – she found Rossmore's arms made her feel safe, somewhere she would like to be again. Would he wish it too? Time would tell; perhaps he would visit today.

A light knock and her maid, Esther, came in carrying a tray. She put it on a table near the window and pulled back the curtains.

'Good morning, miss.'

'Good morning, Esther. I shall eat my breakfast by the window; it looks such a lovely day.'

'Very well, miss.' She curtsied and left.

Grace lay back and wondered what Lord Rossmore was doing. Did he breakfast in his bedchamber or was he an early riser who liked to read *The Times* before settling into his daily tasks?

Although tea was the choice of many ladies, she preferred coffee, and the enticing aroma made her throw back the counterpane and get up.

Last night's music seeped into her memory and she raised her arms, placing her hand on the imaginary Rossmore's shoulder, her other hand in his and waltzed with him, dipping to the one-two-three beat as her bare feet danced across the carpet. She remembered how his arm had tightened and drawn her closer as they circled the ballroom, her cheeks burning with the thrill of his daredevil disregard of propriety. The sound of the door opening caught her off guard and she stopped, not knowing quite what to do.

But Esther was too excited to notice any unusual behaviour. 'Miss, I have a note from Lord Rossmore! His footman will wait for a reply.'

Grace took his lordship's letter. She broke the seal, couldn't believe her thoughts were coming true. 'Esther, Lord Rossmore wants to visit at four o'clock. What am I to say?' She sat down at her desk. 'Please, pour me a cup of coffee, I need to fortify my nerves.'

Grace drank it without stopping. 'Please, another.'

Then she took a deep breath and wrote a reply and agreed to four o'clock. 'Please, take this to Reeves for his lordship's footman.'

By the time Esther returned, Grace had abandoned any thought of eating. 'I must go and tell Aunt Matilda. She may not like being disturbed before the noon hour, but she would never forgive me if I didn't tell her at once.'

Grace pulled on a robe over her nightgown and left, hurrying along the landing to her aunt's room. She knocked and a maid opened the door and let her in.

5

Matilda Crowmarsh was sitting in bed, a white nightcap askew on her grey hair, with her breakfast tray in front of her. 'What is all the noise and fuss, Grace? The house sounded as if a coach and horses were on the loose.'

Grace sat on the edge of her aunt's bed, not able to hold back her news. 'I've received a note from Lord Rossmore, asking if he might visit this afternoon at four o'clock.' Her throat suddenly went dry and butterflies fluttered in her belly. 'I'm so nervous, it was all just a dream last night, but this morning . . . he wants to come and see me? A Miss Nobody from the country?'

Aunt Matilda's round, plump face creased from forehead to chin with smiles. 'You replied yes, Grace?'

'Of course, Aunt, it would be the height of bad manners to refuse.'

'We must have tea. Tell Cook to get the Wedgwood china out and to bake one of her best cakes. Grace, I had no idea you made such an impression on him. I must send notes to everyone, especially Lady Grant. She has been trying to offload that pudding of a daughter to any lord with sufficient income to keep her. This is her second season, you know.'

Grace was beginning to feel like a prized spaniel, to be shown off to every envious lady in the land. 'Aunt, I would prefer it if we kept this to ourselves. He might not come and then what would you feel like?'

'Not come! He has requested to come. But, perhaps you are right. We will still have the Wedgwood. Find your prettiest gown and have Esther dust extra powder on your face. Daylight is so much harsher than candlelight. That country air has put an unwanted tinge to your face. Oh, I can't believe it, Lord Rossmore in my home.'

Grace watched the minute hand of the ornate urn-shaped mantle clock tick towards four o'clock.

Esther had dressed her hair leaving a trio of ringlets falling over her left shoulder, allowing her mother's silver locket full glory above the scooped neckline of a white-and-pink, flower-patterned muslin afternoon gown. She hoped Lord Rossmore would not think her overly presented, sitting in a chair beside her aunt, who had chosen the sofa as her strategic position to conduct this ritual of afternoon visiting.

Grace clasped her hands together in her lap. 'I'm trembling all over. How long do you think he will stay?'

'The customary one half-hour. Grace, do not fret, I am quite able to serve tea and converse with him. Just follow my lead and keep smiling, dear, you look far too pensive.'

The clock chimed.

As if this were a signal, the door opened.

'Lord Rossmore, m'lady.' The butler stepped aside. Rossmore walked in and Grace's heart skipped a beat. He was pure elegance. A white neck cloth emphasised his copper hair that touched the collar of his dark brown coat, and fawn-coloured trousers completed the aristocratic persona of Alexander Kilbraith.

He bowed to Lady Crowmarsh.

Turning, he bowed to Grace. 'Good afternoon. It is delightful to be in the company of two beautiful ladies.'

'We are honoured to have you visit us. Please, be seated. You will take tea?' Matilda Crowmarsh was the height of politeness as she waved him to a chair placed opposite her niece.

Grace's tongue froze in the presence of the earl. Nothing sensible came into her head of what to say to him. So she lowered her gaze and waited for Aunt Matilda to lead the conversation.

However, it was Rossmore who asked, 'As you live mostly in the country, Miss Matthews, do you ride?'

At the mention of horses, Grace was on more familiar ground and answered, 'Yes, I do. I have a chestnut mare and there is no happier moment in my life than riding her across the meadows, through the woods and along the cliff tops.'

'And where is this wild race that you take?'

'In the county of Dorset, I ride above Whitecliffs Bay.' Grace suddenly found it almost an agony to be sitting in the drawing room encased by deep blue walls and heavy maroon velvet drapes, while outside the windows the fresh spring air beckoned to her. 'London is very crowded, do you not think so?'

'Indeed it is. But if I may be permitted, I should like to show you at least the greenery of Hyde Park along Rotten Row in my carriage.'

Lady Crowmarsh beamed, her gaze going from his lordship to her niece. 'Oh, the parade on a warm afternoon is the greatest of pleasure, sir. In my young days it was *the* place to be. *Everyone* of note is there, especially in the Season.' She offered his lordship a small tea plate and then Cook's superb fruit cake.

Grace hid a smile behind her hand. Lord Rossmore did not seem the type of man who spent his time with the delicacies of afternoon tea. But she had to admire his deference to Aunt Matilda.

The clock ticked, the minutes passing much quicker than Grace expected as they partook of their refreshments. Then her aunt returned to the subject of horses.

'I hear that Lord Newton has bought a matching pair of greys. What is your opinion of them, my lord?'

'A good pair, madam, but a little too young, as yet. They will need a great deal of training before they are ready for a race against mine.'

'Horses seem to be something you admire, as does my niece.' She gave a wave of her hand. 'It is quite comforting to know you have a common interest.'

Grace swallowed hard. Goodness, what was her aunt doing, match-making? Lord Rossmore had the reputation of being the most unattainable lord in England.

'Oh, I shall not be staying much longer, Aunt.' Grace's cheeks were red with embarrassment as Lord Rossmore raised his brows. 'I have a need to go home, my father—'

'Then you will accompany me tomorrow afternoon in my carriage. We seem to have a settled spell of good weather. I will call at three o'clock.'

He was not asking. It was a statement which expected no refusal.

Lady Crowmarsh puffed up her ample bosom and nodded her agreement. 'Until tomorrow, my lord, Miss Matthews will accept, of course.' She rang a small hand bell, an indication that the visit was at an end, and the butler immediately opened the door.

'Will you show his lordship out, Reeves.'

Grace fumed. She had been a pawn in a chess game, a game that both her aunt, and Lord Rossmore, knew how to play. As she calmed down, the contradiction was she really didn't object.

The following morning, Grace was in a state of panic.

'We need to select a gown for my outing. I will bathe first, then you must help me, Esther, it has to be absolutely the right one. Hurry now.'

By mid-morning, Grace had pulled nearly every walking-out gown from her wardrobe and cast it aside.

'I can't decide.' She sat on the bed. 'What do you think, Esther?'

Her maid pulled a pale green gown embroidered with white daisies and matching cape from the discarded pile. 'I think this one. The colour suits you well, and I can ringlet your hair for that little feathered hat you bought last week.'

'Um, you could be right. I don't want to look like a girl newly out in Society. It's no good giving him the wrong impression. I'm well past frivolous frills and ribbons in my hair.'

Esther raised her eyebrows. 'Not a dowager lady, either,' she muttered as she hurried away to prepare the gown.

With the outfit settled upon, Grace went down to her lonely lunch. Aunt Matilda did not usually leave her suite until the early afternoon. But today she was in the dining room and bubbling with pride.

'Rossmore's invitation is extraordinary, Grace. I cannot believe he has finally come out of hiding. We shall be invited to every Society ball for the rest of the Season, and may have to turn some down. This is wonderful. I will have to order new gowns, so will you.'

Grace, sitting down at the table, replied, 'Really, Aunt, it is just a drive in his carriage. Surely, Society is not going to have the vapours.' She took a small piece of pie and started to eat.

'I despair of you, Grace. This country living of yours is addling your brain. It is *Rossmore* we are speaking of, not some lowly lord. He's an earl. Oh, I am all of a flutter.' And she drank deeply of a glass of wine by her plate.

Grace continued eating and let Aunt Matilda talk away, who was so thrilled she didn't even notice when Grace made no replies. And when she tasted a blackberry preserve tart her voice rose to almost a panic. 'I cannot eat another morsel. Madame Du Val will tut-tut if I have widened but an inch.'

Matilda waved to the footman, signalling she was ready to leave the room and he opened the door. 'I will see you after your drive, Grace. Oh! I cannot wait for your return.' She left the dining room in a flurry of excitement.

Grace sighed, wishing she were anywhere else but in London; gossip was the last thing she wanted. But she would present herself as perfect as was possible. It was a small repayment to Aunt Matilda for offering her home and hospitality.

Five minutes to three o'clock, Grace waited by the window in the small salon off the hall. She was still not sure about her choice of dress. When she had put it on and seen her reflection in the long mirror, she couldn't make up her mind if she looked like an over-dressed governess or not. But there hadn't been time to reconsider.

The clock chimed three.

Within the minute an open carriage pulled up in front of the house. Suddenly she was full of trepidation as she watched Lord Rossmore step out and then heard the front door open. She was tempted to go out into the hall and forestall having him announced, but while she was debating the option, the door opened and Reeves showed his lordship in.

He bowed. 'Good afternoon, Miss Matthews. I see you are ready.'

Grace curtsied. 'Good afternoon, sir. One of my peculiarities, I am always punctual.'

'Then let us depart.' He came forward and held out his arm. 'To the park, madam.'

Grace placed her hand on the sleeve of his dark blue coat; their colour matching was excellent. She hoped this would apply to their characters.

Rossmore's coachman drove with ease and manoeuvred around the hustle and bustle on the roads. When they entered the park he slowed the pair of greys to a walk.

'On such a lovely day we shall enjoy the sunshine, Miss Matthews. You are looking exquisite, that colour suits you.'

Grace sighed; was it a habit of his to make such personal remarks? 'Thank you, sir. I must admit I was a little unsure. London society demands such high standards.' And she silently thanked Esther.

'Would you prefer to ride?' The carriage slowed to a stop in the shade. 'It is far easier to see the sights of the park from the saddle.'

Grace looked about her. It had become almost a nose-to-tail procession, and those on horseback were much better equipped. 'Yes, I would. I love to be free and able to ride across the countryside. That is why I spend most of my time there. London has a restricting atmosphere.'

'Then tomorrow I will bring you a mount and we shall find the countryside for you.'

Yesterday she had been nervous, in awe of him. But today her natural feelings of being in control of her own life surfaced. His commanding attitude made her bristle. 'You are assuming quite a lot, sir. For one, I might decide that I do not wish to ride with you, and two, perhaps I have another engagement.'

'Ah. A little peculiarity of mine, I'm afraid. I'm used to commanding and getting my way.' His smile took away any rudeness and he leaned over and took her hand. 'Will you please ride with me tomorrow, Miss Matthews?'

Grace looked down at his gloved hand and although she could not feel the warmth of his fingers, his touch was firm and strong. She had no engagements and she did not want any other. They were only recently acquainted, but she sensed that he was a man she could relate to. He smiled, and she accepted that being a widower for such a long time he had drifted into a pattern of set ways. As she had, and there, at least, was something else they had in common.

'Thank you. I would like to join you.'

'Shall we say two o'clock? Our ride will be longer than today.'

The greys responded to the coachman's tap of the reins and he coaxed them smoothly through a gap.

Everywhere she looked, ladies were dressed for the spring weather. Parasols shaded fair complexions and colourful gowns. Riding-habits vied for dominance over the jackets and hats of the gentlemen. She glanced at Rossmore again, his copper hair in the sunshine gleamed, and she approved of the way it curled just below his ear. His profile was lean, strong and capable. He should be a military man, but an earl had many responsibilities to manage and that would be his first call of duty.

Grace was brought out of her thoughts as a rider came alongside. A strikingly beautiful woman, in a flamboyant red riding-habit, fair hair under a perky hat, smiled at Lord Rossmore.

'Alex, it's wonderful to see you out in the park. Willy is behind talking to some stuffy old duke, but I was sure it was you.'

'Isabelle. One can always depend on your sharp eyesight. May I present Miss Matthews.' He turned to Grace. 'This is Lady Wainwright, my cousin's adorable wife. Our drive will be all over town by midnight.'

'Really, Alex, that's not fair. I can see a dozen heads turning in your direction. That you are out is enough to set their tongues wagging.' Her horse snorted and she laughed. 'Even Crispen agrees. My apologies, Miss Matthews, but you will be the only topic worth talking about tonight.'

Grace didn't know what to say to such a comment – her name on everyone's lips by tonight? Heat flared in her cheeks, spread over her face.

Fortunately, Rossmore came to her rescue. 'Shame on you,

Isabelle, for that outrageous remark. To make up for giving Miss Matthews such a frightening expectation, you may invite us to visit the day after tomorrow.'

Isabelle nodded. 'Done.' She leaned forward and held out her hand to Grace. 'We will be the best of friends, Miss Matthews, and I shall make sure my husband stays home to meet you.'

'Thank you, Lady Wainwright.'

With a light tap of her whip, the lady turned her horse and rode away.

Good grief, was there no end to this man's assumption: a carriage ride today, horse riding tomorrow and a visit the next day! Society would be holding its breath expecting an announcement.

'Sir, I must remind you that making arrangements for me are somewhat unorthodox. We have no connections . . . no . . .' Grace swallowed, frustration swept through her and she ended with, 'I would like to be asked.'

Lord Rossmore smiled. 'Will you come?'

She found him irresistible and her discomfort vanished. Surely there was no harm in visiting Lady Wainwright? At least they would be chaperoned within her home. 'Oh, very well, I should like to see this cousin of yours. If he is more polite, perhaps I shall ask him to take you in hand.'

Laughing, he replied, 'Willy has been trying for years with little success. The carriages are leaving. I think it time I returned you to your aunt.'

'Yes, it is becoming a little chilly now.' And Grace settled back to enjoy the homeward ride.

The greys slowed as they turned into Berkeley Square and stopped outside the terraced town house.

Grace waited for Rossmore to help her from the carriage and escort her into the hall. 'Thank you for this afternoon. It is my first outing in the park since coming to stay with my aunt.'

'I hope, then, that I can be the one to show you all of your first sightings of the Season. I will bring a horse for you tomorrow at two o'clock.'

Her immediate thought was: *come at dawn, sir, I need the fresh air and open space*. She said, 'Thank you. I shall be punctual, of course.'

He bowed and a smile curved his lips. 'Then until tomorrow, Miss Matthews.'

He left, leaving Grace unsure of what she had let herself in for. She would think about it later. Right now, Aunt Matilda was waiting for her in the drawing room full of anticipation.

Chapter Two

Lord Rossmore inspected the two horses saddled in his mews yard. 'A good pair, indeed. But I think the chestnut would suit my lady better.' He took hold of the reins and patted the mare's neck. 'You look to have the same spirit. You'll make her a worthy mount.'

'There's no better this side of Westminster, my lord.'

'I have the fullest confidence in you, Burns. And should the mare please my lady, keep her brushed and ready.'

Rossmore gave over the horse to his groom and mounted his own stallion. If he was to get to Berkeley Square at two o'clock he must leave now. He wanted to test her peculiarity – a woman on time two days running? Hah!

The clock was chiming as he entered the hall and Grace was coming down the stairs, pulling on a pair of gloves. She was aptly named, her grace and manner encompassing a beauty any man would want to possess. With each step her plum-coloured riding habit showed every curve and he knew she could compete with any of the *ton*.

'Good afternoon, Miss Matthews.'

'Good afternoon, Lord Rossmore. Do I detect a note of surprise? No matter, I am so glad we are riding, I couldn't abide sitting in a carriage on such a glorious day.'

She reached him and Alex took her hand and lifted it to his lips. He could smell her floral scent and his pulse pounded a little harder. Hell, he was acting like some beau in his first flutter of love.

'And I have the perfect mount for you. Come, let us be off.'

Outside the groom that would accompany them handed him the chestnut's reins.

'Will she do, Miss Matthews?'

'Sir, she is beautiful and so similar to my own mare, who is named Chestnut. It is a great reminder to me of Whitecliffs. You have an excellent eye for a horse. Oh, do let us get going. I can't wait to see how she handles.'

Yes, he knew his horses and it seemed, this woman.

Alex cupped his hands and tossed Grace up onto the saddle. The groom placed a mounting box for Alex and within a few minutes they were riding out of the square.

Alex directed Grace along the roads that took them past homes of the growing *nouveau riche*, many of whom were traders and had made their fortunes from the steam-powered factories or sailing ships bringing tea from China.

He watched her gently steer the mare without jerking the bit and command by voice rather than the whip. She could handle the horse well and he relaxed. He had feared it a rash offer yesterday promising her an out-of-town tour. He stayed silent, content to let Grace concentrate on both the road and horse.

When they reached the less-populated area she commented, 'I must commend you on your knowledge of Town, my lord. Do you travel this way often? What is this part called?'

'This is called Kensington. There are times when I travel this way and on to Chelsea for business.'

'What a strange name, Chelsea. One would expect that village to be near the sea. Is there any significance to it?'

Rossmore didn't want to explain why he visited this part of town. Prize boxing bouts were not suitable conversation for a lady's ears. Instead he answered, 'It's Old English for "landing place on a river for chalk or limestone".'

'I cannot see any connection. But I do not wish to delve too deeply. I want nothing to spoil my afternoon.'

'That is my intention. Soon we will turn onto open common land and you will be able to ride to your heart's desire, and let your

16

horse fly.' Each spurred their mounts into a trot and Alex steered them onto the open heathland beyond.

Grace's delight fuelled an enthusiasm in him he had not thought possible for years and was inflaming a new energy in him. Life had become stale and controlled. He had drifted from year to year, following the seasons like a puppet, ruled by social customs. Should he point a finger at Geoffrey for what was happening to him? Could he really make a new start? Become a whole man again? *Marry Grace?*

He followed her, the ground firm under his horse's hooves, and the lush green of the common a backdrop to both horse and her flowing riding habit as she let the mare increase its speed. Her laughter carried back to him on the breeze, and although she sat side-saddle she jumped over a fallen tree with ease. He urged his horse to go faster, wanting to be beside her. In that moment of exhilaration his years of loneliness were pushed into the past. There were no ifs and buts; he yearned to feel young again, live again a full life with Grace. It was madness – he had known her one evening and two days – but it didn't matter. He wanted her with him, beside him when he lay in bed. Dance with her at every ball they were invited to. No matter what had started his fever, he would not throw away this chance to break out of the prison he had created from the moment Liddy died.

Finally, she stopped in the shade of a tree. He dismounted and held his arms out to help her down.

Her cheeks were flushed. 'Sir, that was almost as good as riding the cliff tops. I would like to come again.'

Rossmore put his hands on her waist. He could feel her panting from the ride. As he lifted her down, he felt her heartbeat. It matched his own thunderous drumming and he pulled her close. 'I will bring you every day, if that is your wish.'

He watched, unsure of how she would react, but her grey eyes, full of excitement, looked steadily into his. Nothing could stop his desire to kiss her and he held her gaze, touched her lips with an exploration of taste and wonder. Then he drew her even closer and parted her lips, deepening his kiss.

She didn't move when he let her go. 'Should I apologise for that?'

'No. It is what we both wanted. Needed, I think. My life has been lonely of late.' She laughed softly. 'I think I am beginning to see myself as the old maid past her prime.'

Alex could have shouted hallelujah. Instead, he pulled her further under the tree's leafy foliage and its darker shadow, shielding them from the groom and kissed her again.

Grace stepped away and shivered. 'This is all happening a little fast, sir. I am considered by many as left on the shelf, but there are standards to be observed. I cannot allow any scandal that would bring my aunt and Lord Crowmarsh into disrepute. We should not do this again.'

Alex knew she was right. But she had thrown him into a state of impatience. 'Grace, there is a new energy in me. A desire I have denied since losing my wife. I don't want to spend the rest of my life without you. What I'm saying is that you are weaving a path to my heart, a love that could grow strong between us. A few moments ago your lips told me that is so.' He studied her face, saw the uncertainty in her eyes, but she did not look away.

'Aunt Matilda has spoken to me of your tragic loss. I do not think I want to fight your late wife's memory for your affections—'

'No, this is not what I meant. Liddy and I were young, and yes, very much in love. We had only a year together and her death was the darkest moment of my life. But I want to live again and I want it to be with you.' He took her hands and raised them to his lips and kissed each gloved palm. 'I have never been surer about anything. Perhaps my years alone have meant I was waiting to find you?'

Alex pulled her close. 'Will you marry me, Grace?' The words tumbled out so unexpectedly he couldn't believe he had said them.

Grace pulled away, her hands pressing on his chest. 'Marry you? Sir, I think you have gone a little mad.'

But there was determination in his eyes. This was no flippant gesture.

Her pulse hammered. What he asked seemed unthinkable, yet

18

the memory of how pleasing his hold had been when they danced, how her heart teased her senses. Could she love this man? His kiss, the taste of him, his arms holding her close, was she brave enough to take the risk?

The answer came without hesitation, 'Yes!' She wanted to share her dreams with him. 'My lord, are we both mad?'

'Mad, maybe. We have a life to live, Grace, and many years to make up. We could wait a month. The banns need to be read in church. You need that time to have a wedding gown made. And I want the most beautiful bride of the Season standing beside me when we make our vows.'

'Lord Rossmore, please, a moment, you rush me too fast . . . we seem compatible, could be—'

He cut in, 'Could be man and wife. Then no one can gossip.'

He was rolling her along on a wave of optimism. And it could work, if they both locked away the past, opened their hearts to accept a new life.

'Very well, I accept,' she said in a low tone, almost a whisper.

Rossmore pulled her close. She lowered her gaze, suddenly shy as he said, 'Thank you, my dear. We shall do well together.'

Grace went to her bedchamber immediately Lord Rossmore returned her to Berkeley Square. She paced the room. Within the hour, his note requesting an audience with Lord Crowmarsh would arrive. Then his request of formally asking for her hand in marriage. What had she been thinking? She hadn't, that was obvious. A marriage in four weeks! She would send a letter now and say it was all a mistake and that they needed time to acquaint themselves with each other.

One of her dislikes was morning visits. She preferred reading on a rainy day or riding with the sun warming her face, the wind touching her hair. What did he do? By his own admission he avoided social events as much as possible. That would suit her well. He also had a vast knowledge of horses. And riding was her greatest pleasure.

Grace stopped at the window. The daylight was fading and in Berkeley Square's communal garden the Plane trees, which in the morning were individual beauties, would soon become dark silhouettes. Rossmore's strong features came to her mind. Could she, over time, nurture a deep and enduring love for him? She would have a home to manage, God willing become a mother to their children. They both had a chance of a new life. It all rested on her decision now, on this moment. A letter could end it all. She closed her eyes: a dance, a carriage ride and an exhilarating race across a common – could one know a person in so short a time? No, of course not, but did she want a future with only loneliness and sorrow dogging her days? Her answer had been pledged on a warm afternoon under the shade of a tree. He was willing. Then so was she.

Her uncle could start the negotiations on behalf of her father. It was little more than a formality.

Grace had never been close to her father. He was a man who had kept his family at a distance. A cold and austere master and since her mother's death she stayed with him only occasionally. She spent her time at Solitaire House, at Whitecliffs Bay, interspersed with visiting relatives and friends. The last time she had seen her father was at Christmas. She had been faced with the news that he had taken to his bed with the rheumatics. In fact, he was a recluse inside Woodford Hall who hadn't ventured beyond Dorchester in years. He had complained about every meal put before him, or the fires were too hot or he was abandoned and left to freeze. And the estate manager was an incompetent fool, even though she had seen reports to the contrary. She wondered why the house staff stayed, but they were all aging themselves; new work would not be easy to find.

Grace turned away from the window and her thoughts returned to Solitaire House. Although it was part of her father's holdings, he rarely went there and never would now. He had given her mother an allowance to maintain the property and allowed them to stay there whenever they chose. When her mother died, her father had extended the arrangement to her.

She rang the bell and when Esther arrived said, 'I'm ready to change for this evening. We are staying at home, so perhaps a less formal gown.'

Bathed and dressed, Grace studied her reflection in the long mirror. Outwardly she appeared serene in a lavender silk dinner gown. Inwardly her thoughts were like a see-saw; she was balanced on the pivot, one step either way could result in disaster or happiness. It wasn't too late to send him a letter if she wrote it now telling him to cancel any plans of a betrothal. She went to her writing desk and sitting down pulled a sheet of paper from the drawer. The blank page stared back at her.

After all her deliberation earlier, why was she still torturing herself with doubt?

She had left it too long to attract a virile bachelor – he would want a young beauty walking beside him. That left a widower with young children. The future was mapped clear – spinster or a marriage of convenience. At least, she had chosen Rossmore. She picked up the sheet of paper and put it back in the drawer.

Grace was startled by a knock on her door and Aunt Matilda came in. She was triumphant.

'Grace, I have heard from Crowmarsh that Lord Rossmore has asked to speak with him this evening. I am so very pleased for you, my dear. Who would have thought such a match would be made this Season? We are to have an earl in the family. Your father will be relieved. Maybe this news will help him endure his rheumatics more tolerably.' She sat down in the chair by the fireplace. 'How do you feel?'

'I'm stunned, frightened and jubilant. I want to cry, laugh, and, most certainly, hide away from the gossiping *ton*, who will tittle-tattle morn till night. I can hardly believe it. I don't think I will until Lord Rossmore arrives later.'

'He is coming after dinner. We will wait in the drawing room. Everything will be dealt with according to custom. Come, let us go and have a sherry. I think we both need some form of stimulant.'

Grace wiped away a tear slipping down her cheek. She *was* happy, *really* she was. So why was she crying?

Lord Rossmore arrived at nine o'clock and he was immediately taken into her uncle's study.

Grace waited with Aunt Matilda in the drawing room, each twisting their handkerchiefs and listening to the clock tick. Grace couldn't stand the tension any longer. She got up from the sofa and walked round the room. 'What are they talking about?'

'Oh, there is much to discuss, things that need not bother us. I know my father kept Crowmarsh in his study three hours. But, of course, I was the eldest of four daughters, so I expect by the time it was little Elsie's turn, it only took an hour.'

'Yes. You only had sons. He hasn't had any practice.'

'Perhaps we should have another glass of sherry. It is after all a special occasion.'

The sherry came and they sipped it and then continued to sit and twist their handkerchiefs.

The clock chimed eleven.

Grace studied her aunt. All her visits in the past had given her many happy memories. For all her grandeur, her aunt was homely and pleasing to be with. She appeared to be reading a book, yet she didn't turn any pages. How could she calmly sit there not knowing what was going on?

'Aunt, can we play a hand or two of whist? This waiting is intolerable.'

'If you think that would help, of course.'

After twenty minutes, Grace put her cards on the table. 'I think twisting handkerchiefs is easier. Shall we return to our seats?'

'Yes, my dear. Staring at pages is less stressful.'

Five minutes to midnight the door opened. Lord Crowmarsh walked in with a light step considering his ample girth. And despite his age he still had a head of blond curls. Rossmore followed, looking as though he had won the biggest prize of his life.

Lady Crowmarsh beamed and let out a sigh.

Grace stood up. So much had happened on this day – she had wakened a spinster, had a proposal of marriage in the afternoon and was betrothed before midnight. It was all too much and for a moment she thought she would disgrace herself by fainting.

'Grace, my dear, Rossmore and I have made a settlement. I will have my solicitor prepare the papers and go to see your father for his signature. He will, I know, be delighted. He has expressed on past occasions his desire to see you wed before he dies. The announcement will be made tomorrow.' He held out his hands and she went to him. He kissed her cheek.

'Thank you, Uncle, for everything.'

Rossmore stepped forward and bowed to Lady Crowmarsh. 'You have been very patient, my lady. From tomorrow the *ton* will enjoy every moment until Grace and I are wed.'

'And I shall enjoy all the attention they devote to me. This is my first wedding in this house. A moment to be cherished, sir, three sons do not require much planning.'

Crowmarsh turned to Rossmore. 'Take Grace into the morning room, man. I expect you have a few words to say.'

'Thank you, sir.' He offered his arm to Grace and escorted her out of the room.

So this is how it was done – she had no say in anything. A bargain struck as though she were a sack of potatoes to be sold off.

In the morning room there were a few candles alight, just enough to see by. Grace waited, trying to sort her emotions into order.

'Well, my dear, we are officially betrothed.' He stepped towards her. 'I think we are now entitled to kiss, formally.' There was a light tone to his voice and he tipped her chin up with his finger. 'Halfway there.' He touched her lips with his and kissed her with a tenderness that broke the anxiety that engulfed her. Her mind cleared, there were no more doubts, she was ready to take the step of marriage.

Chapter Three

The following afternoon Lord Rossmore escorted Grace into Lord Wainwright's house in Portman Square. A door opened off the spacious marble-floored hall and Willy came out.

He bowed. 'Welcome to our home, Miss Matthews.'

Grace curtsied and Rossmore removed his hat and gave it to the footman.

'Willy, Isabelle has trained you well, thank you for being here this afternoon.'

'Now would I dare displease my lady of the house?'

Rossmore shook his head. 'Not if you value your life.'

As the banter subsided, they entered the room Willy had come from.

'Good afternoon, Miss Matthews.' Isabelle waited beside a rose-coloured, brocade sofa. 'And to you, Alex, it has been a long time since you last visited me. But Willy keeps me well informed, especially after you and he have been at White's on those gentlemen-only gossip nights.'

'Shame on you, Isabelle, Miss Matthews will think I am a gambling, drinking rogue.' Rossmore turned to Grace. 'Such words are overly exaggerated. Those days belong to my youth. Willy, I need your support.'

Isabelle waved her hand towards the two men. 'Gentlemen, please, enough of this frivolity. Come, Miss Matthews, please be seated and let us get back to normality.'

Grace sat down in the chair offered. The three relatives were so at ease with each other, she was not sure what was expected of her. But it did give her the opportunity to take in the beautiful cherrywood tables, ivory brocade walls and the chandelier that was reflecting the sun's rays through one of the two French windows.

Isabelle sat on the sofa. Her pink-coloured muslin gown was of a shade that very much complemented her blonde hair and hazel-coloured eyes.

'I am so glad that we arranged this informal tea party, Miss Matthews, it's the only way to get Alex out in Society during the day. You are definitely a good tonic for him.' She turned to face Alex. 'Do you agree, sir?'

'Yes, I do.' He made a point of clearing his throat. 'In fact, this has turned out to be a most opportune time to start the party off. Miss Matthews and I are to be married.'

Both host and hostess gaped.

Alex slapped his cousin on the back. 'Surprised?'

'Betrothed! But you can't be, I mean, you've only just become acquainted . . . I mean, after all these years? Good God, man, at last!' He gripped Alex's hand and pumped it up and down. 'I am mightily glad to hear it.' He went to Grace and bowed. 'A double dose of best wishes to you, Miss Matthews. When is the wedding day?'

Alex spoke before Grace could answer. 'Four weeks from today.'

Shocked at his announcement her brain ceased to work. The only thing she did comprehend was that her face heated to boiling point and she was angry. How could he have declared their betrothal in such a bold manner? Did he think she was just a specimen to be paraded on show?

Taking a deep breath she spoke before he could do any more damage. 'My lord is a little too assuming; in four weeks, yes, but we have not discussed the details.'

Isabelle, who was sitting speechless, got up and went over and joined Willy.

'May I offer my felicitations, Miss Matthews. I am surprised, like Willy, but I do wish you much happiness for the future.'

Alex came and offered his hand and Grace stood up. At least she was now on a level footing with them all. 'Thank you, Lady Wainwright. Lord Rossmore does not seem to understand that our betrothal has been an unexpected announcement to all. It has quite put my aunt, Lady Crowmarsh, into a state of nervous excitement and she calls for her salts every time she thinks of all the arrangements to be made.'

'Will the wedding be in London or at your father's estate or . . . ?'

Grace could see Lady Wainwright was floundering. Rossmore had given no thought to the proprieties of their betrothal. 'My father is very ill and unable to attend. My uncle, Lord Crowmarsh, will stand for him.'

Grace gave her over-zealous betrothed a meaningful look that said – *you presume too much, sir; I want a say in this*. But he chose to ignore her and said, 'I think we will be wed in Berkshire at Rossmore Manor. The estate is at its best in the late spring.'

'Sir! Please, no more.' Grace waved her hand at him. 'You are running too fast for me. Let us return to the purpose of our visit. It is not only my aunt who will be requiring the salts if we continue at this pace.'

'Oh, I think this calls for champagne, don't you, Alex?'

'I certainly do, Willy. Perhaps the ladies would like to continue with their tea until you have organised the wine?'

'We will. Miss Matthews has need of the stimulant as much as I do.' Lady Wainwright held out her hand, inviting Grace to return to her seat.

Willy rang the bell and the butler came in. 'A bottle of my best champagne, Lawson, Lord Rossmore and Miss Matthews are betrothed; make sure it is the best in the cellar.'

'And will you serve tea now, *before* we celebrate.' Isabelle's tone indicated her requirement as mistress of the house took precedence.

'Well, Willy, that is surely the most effective way to spread the news. Even Lawson will be hard pressed to keep quiet.' Lady Wainwright shook her head in despair. 'I'm sorry, Miss Matthews, are you going out this evening?'

26

Grace nodded, 'Yes, we are going to Lord Maynard's residence. I understand it is a *petite boule*, although my aunt has said that Lady Maynard rarely does anything on a small scale.'

'Then be prepared for an evening of jealous mamas, nosey chaperones and wide-eyed young ladies, who will want to know how you achieved the impossible and captured the elusive Earl of Rossmore. You may even be suspected of witchcraft and magic.'

Isabelle's light-hearted banter eased the awkward moment.

Grace sipped her tea that had been served. This afternoon was proving to show how single-minded Alex could be and she wondered what other embarrassments might occur before tomorrow's dawn light rose over the horizon.

With a measured lapse of time Lawson reappeared with a tray of crystal glasses and a bottle of the celebratory wine.

Alex took her hand and she stood up next to him. Her heart beat like a drum, for she had not been the centre of attention for many, many years.

'I hope this is not too overwhelming for you, my dear, but it's how Society reacts to unexpected and exciting news.' Rossmore tucked her hand through the crook of his arm and led her to a table where Willy was pouring the champagne into four glasses.

Isabelle handed her a glass and kissed her cheek. 'I hope you are ready for a month of shopping, balls and exhaustion.'

Willy raised his glass, 'To the Earl and future Countess of Rossmore. Our best wishes for your happiness together.'

Grace trembled and her hand wasn't quite steady as she sipped the wine. The pale liquid fizzed and bubbles rose in her glass. She looked at Rossmore, and saw a strange look in his eyes that she couldn't quite read. It disturbed her. Was he having second thoughts? Should she ask him if there was something wrong? But here in his cousin's home was not the time for a discussion on betrothals.

'Come on, Alex, a kiss for your bride-to-be.'

Instantly, his expression changed and she saw him smile. 'Shall we indulge them?' He took the glass from her hand and put both glasses on the table, drawing her towards him. 'Willy is a stickler for romance.' His lips touched hers for a brief moment and then he drew back.

'There, Lord Wainwright, our betrothal is publicly sealed.'

Lady Wainwright touched Grace's arm. 'Come and sit down on the sofa and take a moment to revive your senses.'

Grace appreciated Isabelle Wainwright's thoughtfulness and sensed Alex's unorthodox manner had not entirely pleased his hostess.

'If you and your aunt would not consider it an intrusion, I would so like to help. There is a mountain of organising to do.'

'Thank you. I'm sure we will need all the help we can get. My aunt only had sons to deal with and although she is looking forward to this occasion, I would not wish her to become so exhausted she does not enjoy the day. As soon as we have the details, I will speak with you.'

Grace's new found acquaintance clapped her hands with delight. 'Oh, we will have a marvellous time.'

Grace wasn't so sure. She had lain awake for hours last night worrying about her marriage, about what she should tell him, something he might not be able to forgive. Why hadn't she refused his proposal until she had thought it through? Now his hasty words openly announcing they would wed in four weeks gave her little time to allow him the chance to reconsider. It was something she couldn't even confide to Lady Wainwright.

She looked over at the two men, sensed their close friendship as they studied a report in *The Times*. She looked around the pleasantly furnished room and knew this was how she wanted her home to be, full of life and happy memories.

There was plenty of time to talk to him before any formal plans were made.

Rossmore was escorting Grace to their first Society evening as a betrothed couple, and she did not know what to wear. She dithered, discarding each gown as unsuitable. What would the *ton* be expecting? If what Lady Wainwright said was true, she would be the centre of their scrutiny and gossip.

'Oh, Esther, you must think me quite impossible to deal with, but I can't choose, will you?'

Esther took a pale lemon, watered silk gown from amongst those scattered on the bed and held it up. 'This one, it's just right for you, youthful *and* mature. Isn't that what you want to be?'

She wondered if that was how Rossmore saw her. Which made her further wonder what he really wanted from their marriage? What was it that had made him ask her, when all those first-Season beauties would be more pliable than she would ever be? But she answered, 'Yes, it is. I don't know how you put up with me, Esther. The next month is going to be hectic. I shall see you have a present; would you like a new dress?'

'Oh, you know I wouldn't leave you. But a new Sunday dress! That would be lovely. Thank you.'

'That is very reassuring, Esther. And you are going to start earning it now, because I have it on good authority that every pair of eyes will be on me tonight. I put my curly strands into your capable hands. Polite Society will be reporting on every dark ringlet you twist.' Grace sat down at her dressing table and looked in the mirror. Her complexion was fair, if a little coloured from the country air, her nose was average and high cheekbones gave good structure to an oval face. Acceptable, she concluded, for a spinster of twenty-eight years. Whatever the comments, she would have to do. Anyway, his lordship had chosen her from all the others.

'Well, Esther, you have three hours to make me the envy of Society.'

Rossmore waited in the drawing room for Grace to come down. He was about to do what he had been avoiding for years, be called the *Catch of the Season*. But he was old enough to handle any witty remarks, or snide ones which would come from some of the young bucks.

The door opened and Grace came in. He had thought her

beautiful when they first met, but now she brought a lump to his throat. The dress was cut low and her full breasts in the high fitting bodice allowed the skirt to fall to her satin shoes.

The desire to pull her to him was almost a pain, but instead, he gave a deep bow. 'My lady, you look delightful. I shall have no chance of a dance on your card, except the privilege of the first waltz.'

'Thank you, my lord. It is going to be a long night.'

'Before we go I have something for you.' He took a small box from his pocket and opened it. A ring, with an emerald central stone and small diamonds embedded into the gold band, sparkled on a black velvet cushion. 'This has been the Rossmore gift since my great-grandfather set the family tradition three generations ago, that each countess should be given this circle of precious stones in her betrothal ring. I hope I have judged your finger correctly.'

He lifted Grace's left hand onto his palm and slipped her long glove off and placed the ring on her third finger. 'A perfect fit, and our half-way step to marriage.' She was trembling and he realised he had ignited a moment of surprise in her. It thrilled him to think that he could make her so aware of what lay ahead for them. He continued to hold her hand, waiting for her reply.

'My lord, I don't know what to say. I have never seen such a beautiful ring. It is truly a gift I shall treasure forever. But how did you have it crafted in such a short time?'

'Our jewellers have one deposited in their vaults in readiness for the next Countess Rossmore. My ancestors proved as impatient as I, and I am happy to continue the tradition.' He drew her into his arms. 'There is something we need to address. Stop calling me sir, my lord or Lord Rossmore, when we are private. My name is Alexander, but my family call me Alex. Grace, is there anything wrong? I detect uncertainty in your eyes.'

'No. I have called you Alex in my mind, but to speak it aloud?'

'Is it so difficult?'

She took a deep breath then said, 'Alexander Kilbraith, my husband-to-be.'

'Perfect. Now we can truly seal our betrothal.' He touched her lips gently with his. 'Now any fears you have will melt away.'

Outside the entrance to Lord Maynard's house the burning flares presented a touch of grandeur. Inside the hall, footmen waited to take cloaks and hats. Lord and Lady Maynard waited beyond.

'Lord and Lady Crowmarsh, we are delighted to welcome you this evening.'

'It is a pleasure as always, Maynard. You are aware my niece and Lord Rossmore are recently betrothed and I have invited him to join us this evening.'

Lady Maynard immediately dipped a curtsey and said, 'It is an honour, Lord Rossmore, and our felicitations to you and Miss Matthews.'

'Thank you. We will not linger, Lady Maynard, you have guests still arriving.'

The Crowmarsh party passed on to the room prepared for the evening. It was not huge but sufficiently large enough for a *petite boule*. As if a ripple of awareness spread across the guests present, talking stopped and each turned to the doorway. The silence was profound. Rossmore held out his arm and Grace placed her gloved fingers on his sleeve.

'Smile, Grace, it will only be this one occasion that our entrance to a ballroom will be so daunting. By tomorrow they will have another unsuspecting soul to gossip about.'

'I will hold you to that declaration, Alex. May we please walk on and break this absurdity that verges on bad manners.'

The moment broke as Alex led Grace into the crowd. She thought of Isabelle's words earlier that afternoon, *witchcraft and magic*. If only she had such power, she and Alex could disappear in a puff of smoke.

Lord Crowmarsh took the lead to where two unoccupied chairs were placed near the dancing area.

'Be seated, my dear, I foresee that a glass of wine will calm your nerves. And you also, Grace?' Two heads nodded in unison.

Grace looked at Alex. She had thought when they first met he had the stance of a military man, and at the moment he could well be compared with a general, his authority apparent when a young buck approached from the side towards her.

'The answer is no, Mr Blackburn, my betrothed is about to take refreshment. And the answer remains no for the rest of this evening.'

The young man's face reddened from fringe to chin. 'But my lord, this is a celebratory evening. Miss Matthews is the belle of the ball.'

'Quite so. And her first dance will be with me.'

Accepting defeat, Blackburn retreated to a group of other young hopefuls.

Crowmarsh returned and Grace accepted her glass of wine. 'Thank you, Uncle. After this stimulant I shall be ready to dance the night away.'

'Then I leave you in Rossmore's protection. Matilda, I am pleased to say, is far more experienced in dealing with these social intrigues. And when I disappear to the gaming room, her friends will swarm like bees around her.'

'Do not listen to his chatter, Grace. We will be triumphant this evening and the *ton* will have plenty to gossip about in their drawing rooms tomorrow.' She raised her glass in a salute.

Alex had to stand aside while the lords of the realm filled Grace's dance card. But he had written his name for the first waltz.

'This is our dance, Grace.' He led her forward into the throng of dancers. Taking her in his arms he said, 'My one chance to hold you to me. Does your heart beat as fast as mine?'

'You are very forward, sir . . .'

'Stop being so prim, Miss Matthews. I want every man to envy me. Know that any thought of seduction with you will result in a duel. Illegal as it may be.'

'Really, Alex, you chase off a young buck; then demand I accept your advances. The next four weeks are going to prove quite adventurous.'

'Do you not wish to feel young again, Grace? I do, so be warned, my love.'

The music began and Alex swept her into a twirling dance, pushing aside thoughts of Liddy. He had made a decision when he asked Lord Crowmarsh for Grace's hand in marriage. She was now his future and he pulled her closer.

'It's way past two o'clock and I'm very tired, Esther. If every ball is going to be like this, I shall not arrive at the altar at all, but be confined to my bed.' Grace waved to the door. 'Anything else can wait until morning, away with you and sleep well.'

Esther yawned behind her hand. 'Thank you, miss. I'm so pleased your evening went well, goodnight.'

For all her tiredness, Grace felt restless and walked round the room. The evening had truly been a success. She fingered the pale lemon, watered silk gown hanging on the outside of the wardrobe. It had been a perfect camouflage for her inner nervousness. Her aunt had shielded her from those she considered not worthy of conversation and Alex had not left her unattended, except when she danced with those marked on her card, but even so it had been a stressful evening.

She sat on the side of the bed and smoothed her cotton nightgown across her thighs. A month from now she would be waiting like this for Alex to join her. A shiver of apprehension ran down her back.

She lay down and pulled the covers up to her chin, closed her eyes and thought about how he had held her close as they waltzed, caring nothing about the propriety of such an action. It had been both a moment of fear and exhilaration rolled into one as they circled the ballroom floor. Then after supper he had taken her in his arms again for a second waltz. When the music stopped he had whispered in her ear, 'I want you to myself, can we not disappear?' She had blushed like a young girl, delighted at such an outrageous comment and then saw the devilment in his eyes. She mouthed, 'No,' and he had smiled and led her back to Aunt Matilda.

These recollections made Grace laugh out loud and she hid under the sheet. These were the moments she would remember, not the constant flow of the *ton* almost fighting each other for an introduction, for the betrothed of Lord Rossmore needed a military blockade to stave off Polite Society.

Memories did not tire her brain and sleep was useless. It was only when the morning light showed through a crack in the drawn drapes that she relaxed and slept.

It seemed nothing more than a moment later that bright sunlight flooded her bedchamber. The aroma of coffee tempted her to open her eyes and she saw Esther standing by the side of the bed.

'It's just past the noon hour. I thought it time to bring you a breakfast tray.'

'Breakfast! You should have awakened me earlier, Esther. But you're right, I do need something to entice me out of bed.' She sat up and let the woman place the tray on her thighs. 'Thank you. Will you please give a message to my aunt that I shall rest now and join her this afternoon in her sitting room?'

'Yes, miss. There have been lots of notes delivered for you.'

The excitement in Esther's voice made Grace recall her annoyance at the *ton*.

Grace opened the twentieth note and sighed. 'How are we going to cope with all these invitations, Aunt Matilda? Most are from households I do not recognise. Who is Lady Hollingworth?'

Matilda laid her circular needlepoint frame on her lap. 'I believe a cousin, once removed, on Lord Crowmarsh's side. We haven't seen them since her marriage and that was at least ten years ago. Don't fret too much, Grace, you can decline many of them. It is the wedding guest list that always causes a problem. Those we have to leave off must be on your betrothal ball list, and that will dispense with the outer circle of relatives and acquaintances.'

Grace looked out of the window at the small rear garden and wished she could be sitting out there, instead of at a table spread with notepaper. What poppycock that a lady should not sit in the sun. However, to pander to convention there was a shady spot with a wicker table and chairs.

34

'I shall speak with Alex later about that. He suggested the service take place at Rossmore Manor, his estate in Berkshire. Would that cause a problem?' She gazed at the blue sky and thought of her garden at Solitaire House.

'That is a little presumptuous of him, but it would reduce the guest list having a wedding outside of London. What do you want, Grace?'

'Me! I haven't given it any thought.' Alex had swept her along with his announcement and since then there had been little time to consider any arrangements. 'I assume the church would have been built to hold only a small congregation? I think he is correct, Rossmore Manor would be perfect. I shall agree with him on this and find out how many guests we can invite.'

The more Grace thought about it, an idea formed in her mind. He had chosen the wedding venue; she would propose their honeymoon to be at Solitaire House at Whitecliffs Bay.

She sighed again; the longer she dallied the longer this would all take. It was her duty to reply and once done she could concentrate on the wedding plans.

An hour later, Grace stretched her back. 'I think it's time for tea, Aunt. The footman can deliver the replies while we replenish our constitutions.' She got up and rang the bell. 'Will attending all these social functions tire you too much?'

'Not at all. If any more notes arrive we can make the excuse that you are engaged in your wedding preparations. Everything will be well, my dear. I may not have had any daughters, but I do know how to decline unwanted invitations.'

Grace thought she would have to watch how her aunt handled this situation for it would prove a valuable lesson in her dealings with Alex.

Chapter Four

Matilda Crowmarsh stopped just inside Grace's open bedchamber door. 'Are you ready to leave, Grace?'

'Yes, Aunt. Esther left an hour ago for Kilbraith House.'

'Oh! What a betrothal ball this is going to be. With Lady Wainwright's invaluable experience of her wedding a few months ago, we have, Grace, in two weeks organised a ball that Society will talk about for the rest of the Season. It was extremely gracious of Rossmore to allow us to hold it at Grosvenor Square. This house would not have served to accommodate the number of guests we need to placate those who are not being invited to Rossmore Manor for the wedding.'

'You have a very wicked side to you, Aunt, but true, we have not upset Society. All will have been associated one way or another with the earl.'

'Strategy, Grace, is something you will have to master once you are married.'

'I have a good tutor in you. Be prepared to teach your niece everything you know.'

'There's plenty of time for that. Come now, or we will be late.'

They arrived in Grosvenor Square mid-afternoon and were helped from the coach by Alex.

'Welcome to Kilbraith House, Grace. Saunders is very nervous about meeting you. He has been with us since before I was born, but I know you will deal with him in your usual gracious manner.'

His smile and warm words eased the apprehension she too

experienced about meeting a household that had not known a mistress for ten years. 'Thank you. I will do my best to create a good impression.'

Inside, Grace was astonished to find a large square hall, the floor tiled with black-and-white chequered marble and family portraits hanging on the walls. Surpassing this it was the black-iron, scrolled staircase that led up to the first floor that held her attention. Alex stopped before an elderly man.

'This is Saunders, who is in charge of the household. He will attend to anything you require today for the house preparations, and when we are in residence.' Alex made the formal introduction sound very intimidating. Life in London was so different to her carefree days in the country.

'Good afternoon, miss. Welcome to Kilbraith House.'

'Good afternoon, Saunders. I'm sure we shall fare well together.'

He bowed and turned to the woman next in line. 'This is Mrs Fielding, the housekeeper. She will deal with any domestic requests for you and your guests. Next is Mrs Coals, the cook, and beyond the footmen and maids.'

Grace nodded in turn and felt a sudden panic overcome her. She was going to be in charge of a London town house. Her father had never taken a residence in Town, always preferring the country lifestyle. She had accompanied her mother to visit Aunt Matilda and old friends from time to time, but had never bothered her head about running such a house. She paused a moment to calm her nerves. A hopeful thought passed through her mind; Saunders must be an exceptional butler and would not appreciate her interference in his domain. Everything would be well; it couldn't be so very different from Solitaire House – just bigger!

Alex turned to Lady Crowmarsh. 'Welcome to Kilbraith House. Should you require anything, Saunders is available to you. Mrs Fielding will show you to your bedchamber.'

'Thank you. May I ask that Saunders gives me a tour of the ballroom and where we will receive our guests?'

'Of course.' He looked back at the butler. 'Saunders, I leave Lady Crowmarsh with you.'

Far away in her domestic thoughts, Grace didn't hear Alex speaking until he stepped towards her.

'. . . I asked if you would like to take a tour of the house.'

'Yes, that would be wonderful. Are you sure you have time, my lord?'

Alex's lips twitched, but his reply was very formal. 'I have an hour. Sufficient for today. But as the house is full of florists, musicians and cooks, let us escape to the garden, at least there I know little is to be done.' He nodded his dismissal and the staff hurried away in all directions.

'We can go out through the morning room, Miss Matthews, and that we can regard as a small portion of the house inspected.'

Such correctness almost made Grace laugh out loud. She knew exactly what Alex would be about once they reached a secluded part of the garden. 'Thank you, my lord. This is most kind of you.'

Alex wasted little time in showing her the yellow decorated room and they were out in the garden almost at a run.

Like most town houses, the garden was moderate in size, yet a haven of serenity: an oval lawn surrounded by rose bushes, shrubs and a sheltered corner with a white-painted table and chairs to sit and read or enjoy afternoon tea.

'I feel like a naughty boy again. I wanted to shock Saunders by calling you Grace and touching your arm. Come here, behind this shrubbery.' He stepped off the path and pulled Grace against him. 'Why did I say a month? I should have got a special licence and we could have been married in a week.'

'And have every gossip in Town declaring you had compromised me and were forced to marry. Think, sir, what that would have meant for me.'

'Oh, Grace. This betrothal ball is driving me mad. Put my ludicrous words down to a moment of insanity. But I do demand a kiss.'

Grace surrendered without protest. They were both now

38

constantly in the hub of Society, that even one stolen kiss was a precious gift.

'When we are at Solitaire House, things will be so different, Alex. The house is very small compared to this and only Mr and Mrs Gillett are resident servants. There are two rooms in the attic for Esther and Miles. We will have so much freedom. There must be a hundred words, but I can't explain how wonderful it is.'

'Then I await such a glorious liberty with joy. Let us continue our tour. I think the upper rooms will be far quieter.'

Grace sat at the dressing table in the bedchamber she was to occupy on her return from their honeymoon. Reflected in the mirror was pale pink floral wallpaper, and the velvet curtains reminded her of wild mint. She tilted her head slightly and saw the large canopied bed. Although it was only two weeks to the wedding, this is where she and Alex would spend their nights. She looked from the mirror to the connecting door to his room. It seemed overly large and somehow menacing, but that was a silly notion. Time was racing by and there were so many things still to do. But once tonight was over she had decided to decline any more invitations that weren't already in her diary.

There was a light tap on the door and Isabelle Wainwright came in. 'Alex is waiting downstairs, Grace, with your aunt and Lord Crowmarsh.'

Grace stood up.

'You look lovely, my dear. Gold satin suits your colouring. Are you ready?'

'I suppose so, Isabelle. A hundred guests to entertain. I fear I shall not be able to speak to them all.'

'Oh, don't worry about that. It is the attendance that is important, so that they can recite endlessly that they were here. Alex has made them very happy and negates any snub about not being asked to the wedding at Rossmore Manor.'

'You make it sound all so . . . so . . . like two cats fighting over a mouse.'

Isabelle laughed. 'That is exactly right. Polite Society expressed to perfection. Come, my dear, it is time for you to be inspected.'

Grace walked to the door. 'As you say, let battle begin.'

Grace's legs ached and she wondered how her aunt managed to look so fresh and sparkling after nearly two hours greeting their guests.

Alex sighed. 'Are they finally coming to an end? This is the first space I have seen.'

'It will only be the late comers now, my lord. Perhaps we can leave them to be announced as they arrive?' asked Lady Crowmarsh, and there was a hopeful tone to her question.

'An excellent suggestion, please take your leave and rest awhile.'

Grace was just going to say she would like a glass of lemonade when she saw two more guests arriving. She noticed that Alex had also seen them, but there was a tension in his manner, and she wondered why the sight of the latecomers had affected him.

Then the announcement: 'The Honourable Geoffrey Kilbraith and Mrs Kilbraith.'

Grace waited beside Alex, spellbound by the likeness of the two brothers.

'Geoffrey.' Alex nodded and then turned to his brother's wife. 'Rachel. I am delighted that you are here. I feared your confinement would prevent you travelling.'

'Had it been to any other occasion, then yes, I would not have risked the journey. But on such an event, how could I not.'

Grace saw that the woman was with child and waited for her to finish her greeting with Alex.

'Miss Matthews, may I present my brother, Geoffrey Kilbraith, and his wife, Rachel?'

'I am delighted to meet you both. Lord and Lady Crowmarsh have just gone to partake of a little refreshment. Would you like to sit down, Mrs Kilbraith?'

'Thank you, Miss Matthews, I would, somewhere quiet and in a corner. I shall enjoy watching and having the opportunity to catch up on all the Town gossip from my acquaintances. Living at Hawthorn Hall is lovely; but I miss their companionship and chatter.'

Alex offered his arm to Rachel. 'A quiet corner it shall be.'

Grace looked at Geoffrey, wondering what was amiss between the brothers. Obviously something of a personal nature; their coolness to each other was quite marked.

Turning to her, Geoffrey asked, 'Shall we join the mêlée, Miss Matthews?'

'Sir, I would hardly call the occasion of your brother's betrothal celebration such a brutal word. I hope our guests do not sink to brawling with each other before night is done!'

'My apologies, madam; I did not mean to offend.' He held out his arm and Grace placed her hand lightly on it. 'Shall we join my wife?'

They found Rachel sipping lemonade and talking with Isabelle and Aunt Matilda.

'Miss Matthews, what a moment of joy this is. We will not be staying long, Geoffrey has another engagement, but I am staying in London tomorrow and returning to Hawthorn Hall the day after. Would you and Alex come to tea at our town house?'

'Yes, of course. Tomorrow at four o'clock?'

'Perfect. Please do not let me keep you from your duties. I can still remember how hectic life is before one's wedding.'

'I agree, Rachel,' Isabelle chirped in. 'I shall take advantage of you this evening and sit and gossip until you leave. Off you go, Grace. Enjoy your moment.'

Aunt Matilda got up. 'Yes, I have my duties too, goodbye, Mrs Kilbraith.'

Grace looked at the gowns, at the array of bird feathers and spring flowers intertwined in the ladies' coiffure. Ruby and emerald necklaces provided a splash of contrasting colour amongst the stiffened white neck cloths, shirts and dark evening attire. And such splendour was set against the pale oatmeal-coloured walls and urns of evergreen boughs with clusters of daffodils boasting spring was here. The lighting subdued with little candlelight other than from the chandeliers. Footmen dressed in deep red uniforms weaved between the guests, offering glasses of champagne balanced on silver trays.

Alex was walking towards her, a smile now on his face, his eyes locked with hers, wooing her, telling her how much he wanted her. Her throat tightened and unshed tears came to her eyes. Everything was so perfect, too perfect perhaps, for she had not found the moment to tell him, or explain her secret.

He took two glasses of champagne from a passing footman and gave her one. 'A toast to the most beautiful woman in this room.' He tapped her glass and sipped. Grace couldn't break away from his gaze, and all the noise faded as she lifted the glass to her lips, tasted the liquid in her mouth like his kiss.

'To us, Alex,' she whispered and together they moved into the crowd to circulate and entertain their guests.

Grace woke from a deep sleep. For a moment the softness of the feather mattress made her think of a fluffy summer cloud. The bed was wider than she had ever slept in, the thick cotton, mint-coloured drapes unnecessary now that winter had passed. The room was twice the size of the one she had in Berkeley Square.

Although she often disapproved of Alex's forthright ways, his endearing wish that her bedchamber be redecorated to her liking before she arrived at Kilbraith House for their betrothal ball had been added to her preparation list. The decorator had been a polite elderly man who, with just a few words of advice, left Berkeley Square with her wallpaper and drapes choices, promising his lordship's timetable of one week would be achieved.

Now she lay content, and counted on the wall over the mantelshelf how many sprigs of her chosen pink roses were blooming amongst green leaves. A delight that would banish away wet dreary days when her future life was spent in London. The sound of sparks flared from a burning log in the grate, which was warming every corner of the room, meaning a maid had come in earlier while she was sleeping. There were two windows. A deep pink brocade chaise longue was placed before the nearest so she could rest, read and look at the private central garden of Grosvenor Square. Two winged chairs were set beside the fireplace, covered in the same mint cotton of the bed drapes. The most beautiful piece of furniture was the cherry-wood writing table placed before the second window. The luxury was beyond anything she had ever seen, and there was still space for her to dance.

Grace threw back the covers and stepped onto soft carpet. Alex had been extremely generous in ensuring her comfort. And she would make full use of it today and indulge herself with breakfast in bed, and reading the latest *La Belle Assemblée* magazine.

Come four o'clock, Alex and Grace arrived at his brother's residence in Lincoln's Inn Fields. They were shown into the drawing room where Rachel sat on a high-backed, armless chair, embroidering a motif on a baby gown. She immediately put it aside, saying, 'Welcome to my home, Miss Matthews, and to you, Alex.'

He went forward and took her hand. 'Thank you. You seem none the worse for your outing last night.'

'Oh, it would take a lot more than a delightful evening of entertainment and gossip to upset my constitution. Four children romping about Hawthorn Hall has quite prepared me for a hectic life.'

Grace waited, thinking how well Rachel was coping with her situation. Would she be as capable in the years ahead? She looked round the room. It was not large but tastefully decorated with a touch of warmth in the gold and blue furnishings.

'Come and sit on this comfortable chair next to me, Miss Matthews, and tell me all about your wedding plans for I shall not travel to Rossmore. The doctor tells me I have about another three months to wait but the thought of producing my fifth child in some sordid inn is not something to be contemplated.'

Grace sat on the offered chair and said, 'I shall be delighted, Mrs Kilbraith. As you know we are being married at Alex's estate in Berkshire and then honeymooning in Dorset.' She glanced towards her future husband where he stood looking out of the window and with no comment from him continued, 'The guest list is quite small, that is why we held a ball last night. Aunt Matilda is a brilliant strategist when it comes to handling the ladies of Polite Society. She has satisfied everyone and assures me I will be accepted without any backlash by the *ton*.'

The door opened and several tea trays were brought in.

'Thank you, Harris. I'll ring if I need anything more.' The butler signalled the footmen to leave and closed the door.

'Are you joining us, Alex? If you are wondering where Geoffrey is, he went out an hour ago, but promised to be back before you left.'

'I shall think it an honour if he does return. I'm sorry, Rachel, that was an ungracious remark and tea will quench my thirst far more than Geoffrey's wine.'

Grace was curious, but more to the point, concerned, as to what the aggravation between the brothers could be. Alex seemed to have a suppressed anger towards him, which she found disturbing and manners did not allow her to inquire why. She had asked Alex about his parents, but he seemed reluctant to talk about them. Of course, his mother and father were dead, but his step-mother was alive, yet she had not been presented to her.

She sighed. This was not the time to be pondering Alex's behaviour. Likewise when she had asked him to tell her about Liddy he had shaken his head without answering. It was all very mysterious.

'Do you take sugar, Miss Matthews?'

'No, thank you.'

'Alex, will you please put Miss Matthews' tea on her side table?' He did as he was bid and then sat on a chair.

'And will you indulge me with the honour of calling you Grace? We will be sisters once the wedding ceremony seals your marriage.'

'Oh, I should so like that, Rachel.'

'Thank you, sister-to-be. Now, tell me of your wedding plans so far. If my fifth child is another boy, I will despair of ever having a daughter to wed.'

'My aunt and I have been most fortunate in that Lady Wainwright offered her support for which I am most grateful. Once Aunt Matilda and I had finalised the betrothal ball guest list, Isabelle took over and released us to concentrate on planning the wedding. All the invitations have been sent and the replies have flown in. With no refusals, Rachel, our worries are mostly over. Rossmore Manor's house staff has been given detailed instructions. Isabelle and Aunt Matilda are travelling down a few days before our wedding. This has left my aunt and me the luxury of choosing my bridal gown and trousseau. And as we are honeymooning in Dorset at Solitaire House, our clothing trunks will be waiting for us on our arrival. Alex and I will only need our travelling attire at Rossmore. It has all been most civilised. My panic over organising a wedding in four weeks was quite unnecessary.'

'You must come and visit me at Hawthorn Hall when you are settled back in London. There is plenty of room, please do not feel you would be intruding. Geoffrey prefers town life. He finds the solitude of country residence very depressing.'

'Oh, I must disagree with him. It is the most wonderful place to be. Thank you, I will write as soon as we are prepared to start visiting.'

Rachel's warmth and goodwill settled well with Grace and she hoped her relationship with Rachel, and her children, would draw the brothers closer. 'And when you are able to travel again, we will welcome you and your family at Rossmore Manor.'

Grace glanced at Alex. He had gone into his silent mood again which was beginning to trouble her. 'Does this arrangement meet with your approval, Alex?'

He stirred, raising his head to meet her gaze. 'Yes, my dear, Rachel is always welcome at my country estate. And I have so much fun teaching the boys to fish in the summer months. Likewise Rachel will not let us forget our all-day picnics farther afield.'

'It will not be this summer, Alex, but next year, all circumstances being well, I will let the boys loose on you with pleasure. Would you like more tea, Grace?'

45

'Yes, please. This arrangement makes me feel part of the Kilbraith family already. We must make a family gathering to include Lord and Lady Crowmarsh, Isabelle and Willy. And may we include your step-mother, Alex?'

'Mother remarried, Grace, and now lives in Italy. She suffers with the rheumatics, not even the English summer can tempt her to return. You have by now received her apology for not attending our wedding?'

'No, Aunt Matilda would have informed me had she received a communication of such importance. Letters that have to cross the Channel can sometimes be delayed. If you are so sure she will not come, perhaps in the autumn we can go to visit her.'

'As you wish.'

Grace took this as closing the subject; another family mystery?

'It appears Geoffrey will not be joining us today, Rachel. Grace and I have a soirée to attend this evening. I wish you a safe and pleasant journey home.'

Grace took her cue and went over to Rachel. Taking her hand she bent and gave her a kiss on the cheek. 'We will soon be sisters and must write frequently with our news and gossip.'

'Thank you, Grace, I will indeed correspond with you. Goodbye. Alex, will you pull the cord, Harris will show you out.'

Alex and Grace were announced as they entered Lord Fryer's reception salon, the ladies' voices ringing louder than the masculine laughter.

Lady Fryer swept forward, her heavy brocade gown not hiding the ample girth of her hips, and her words were tinged with an Irish lilt. 'Alex, my best wishes to you and Miss Matthews. Welcome to our concert evening. I have engaged the splendid soprano, Gertrude Lang, in honour of your betrothal.'

Alex bowed. 'This will be an evening to remember, Catherine. May I introduce my betrothed, Grace? I am sure our years of friendship will allow you both, privately, to converse on first names.'

Grace curtsied. 'Thank you, Alex. Good evening, Lady Fryer.'

'Good evening, Miss Matthews.' There was a chuckle in her voice as she continued. 'Let me introduce you to my husband, who has the habit of disappearing into the flock of gentlemen when I need him most.'

Grace glanced at Alex and he nodded. 'I leave you in Catherine's welcoming embrace.'

This left her following her hostess towards the *flock of gentlemen.*

An hour later, Grace freed herself from the attentions of the other guests and found a corner close to the open French window. Alex came over and said quietly, 'It is very hot in here; shall we go into the garden?'

'Will that not be considered bad mannered? Lady Fryer made it clear, as a very close friend of yours, this evening is in honour of us.'

'Catherine is very lax on protocol. The young bucks will be leaving soon for the taverns. Then we can return for the formal entertainment.' He tucked her arm into the crook of his and led her out on to the terrace.

The chill air after the warmth of the house made Grace shiver. 'Maybe this was not such a good idea. Spring evenings can be somewhat unpredictable.'

'There is a summerhouse. I'm sure we shall find that a much more enjoyable place to sit.' Alex slipped her hand into his and led her down a shallow flight of steps onto a path that curved round a central lawn. Placed in the centre was a marble nymph, totally naked, pouring water from an urn into a circular pond.

'An outlandish statue, I'm afraid. Fryer has quite a liking for the classics.'

'If I were to go into a state of faint every time I saw such an artefact, I would have to hide in my bedchamber and never come out.'

'I am pleased to hear such a statement. A fainting wife would be quite tiresome to deal with.' Not letting go of her hand they followed lighted torches along the path until a Roman-style temple, complete with columns and more nymphs, came into view.

Alex opened the door and the Roman design continued inside with a low velvet couch partially covered by a gold cloth next to a marble table. They were the only furnishings, very much intended for an intimate tryst for two lovers.

'Sir, this is not what I had imagined. Have you been here before?'

Alex closed the door. 'I haven't had you to myself since we were at Kensington. Propriety may have to be observed, Grace, but you cannot ban me from kissing you.' He stepped forward and wrapped her into the warmth of his body, taking away the evening chill.

'No, I do not want that either, but this is a little too . . .' she turned her head and looked at the couch, '. . . naughty?'

Without a word Alex lifted her and laid her down, then sat close. 'Desire and want flare hot, Grace, but I will agree with you, this is perhaps not the place to indulge in our first lovemaking.'

'Oh.' Unexpected disappointment ran through her. In that moment when he laid her down she had wanted him to take her, to release the passions that had been building inside her. But if she did, what would the outcome be? Common sense told her this was not the time, and definitely not in their host's garden temple.

'Do I detect regret?'

Grace could feel her face go hot and her wicked heartbeat betray what she really wanted. Instead, she smiled. 'I think we both feel that.' She touched his cheek with her palm and leaned forward. 'Kiss me, Alex, and then I have many questions for you about our wedding plans.'

He gently kissed her mouth, but that only teased her need and turned his into a volcano. She raised her arms, circling them round his neck, felt his hand cup her breast as he pulled her into him. His hands slid round her waist and he crushed her into his chest and she felt the thunderous hammering of his heart as their passions flared.

The sound of voices made Alex draw away. 'There are others

close, my love. I do not think this is perhaps the place for us to talk. And Catherine's soprano will soon be entertaining us for the rest of the evening.'

Grace nodded, but she didn't want to leave. She was beginning to realise that the companionship of relatives could never be a substitute for the closeness of being held, kissed and loved.

Chapter Five

Twelve days later Grace had her first glimpse of Rossmore Manor as the coach rounded a curve in the long drive. She turned to her husband-to-be sitting beside her. 'Oh, Alex, the house is magnificent. Look how the windows gleam in the sunlight, like gold nuggets in the red brick. It's beautiful.'

'Thank you, Grace. I was sure you would love it, as I do. There won't be much time to give you a tour of the estate, but we'll take a short ride tomorrow morning before our guests arrive.' A moment later the coach stopped at the portico steps.

The front door opened and Saunders came out looking flushed, with a bombardment of noise following him. 'Everything is in order, my lord. There is just a little difference of opinion as to where Lady Crowmarsh requires the flowers.'

Aunt Matilda and Isabelle had journeyed to the estate three days earlier, allowing Grace and Alex a more leisurely pace.

'I'm sure you have it under control, Saunders. Miss Matthews' room is ready?'

'Yes, my lord. Everything is complete above the main stairs. I have taken the liberty of delaying the introduction of the staff to Miss Matthews until later.'

Grace saw Alex nod, but there was also a twitching of his lips; obviously Aunt Matilda was proving to be a challenge for the butler.

Alex held out his arm. 'Welcome to Rossmore. May I escort you in and have the pleasure of conducting you to your room myself? We must leave the busy workers to finish their tasks.'

'Thank you. But I must speak with Aunt and Isabelle a moment. Then we may proceed.'

Inside, Grace stopped. 'Oh, this is so spacious and the skylight wonderful, Alex. There is so much room and you have a wooden floor instead of marble. I see you like the less formal here in your country estate.'

Muttered words of frustration came from somewhere to her left. 'Indulge me a few moments, Alex; one of my helpers may be in there.' Without waiting for his answer, she disappeared into the drawing room calling, 'Aunt Matilda, Isabelle, I'm here.' Sunlight flooded in through the French windows onto the gold-coloured brocade upholstery. She turned in a circle, taking in the abundance of flowers filling every corner of the room.

Isabelle was kneeling on the floor. 'I've dropped my scissors. I was just trimming the leaves that are spoiling the oval shape of the roses. Oh, here they are.' Picking them up, she stood and hurried forward, holding her arms wide. 'Thank goodness you're here. We need a calming presence and a pot of tea.' She looked across at Alex standing in the doorway. 'Good afternoon, Alex, will you ring the bell, please?'

'Good afternoon, Isabelle.' He pulled the bell-cord beside the fireplace. 'I shall sit and await tea,' he muttered, and sat down in a winged chair.

Grace's calm evaporated. 'Where is Aunt Matilda? Oh, I should have come with you, there is so much to do. What can I do to help?'

'Nothing, all is finished for today. Matilda will be here in a moment, she's checking the final menu with Cook.'

As if summoned, Matilda Crowmarsh came into the room looking dishevelled, but with a satisfied smile on her face. 'Grace, this is perfect timing. Tea is on the way. Did you have a good journey?'

Grace went to her aunt and hugged her close. 'Yes, very much so, thank you. Isabelle tells me all is ready.'

'That is so, and tomorrow we will have a morning of rest. Then your guests will be arriving in the afternoon. We will serve an informal buffet dinner for six o'clock in the Orangery. This will

51

leave the house free for the final preparations and your wedding Saturday morning.'

Alex abandoned his chair. 'Good afternoon, Lady Crowmarsh. You look a little tired but very happy. I can only take this as a sign you have enjoyed planning your niece's wedding. And thank you for not opposing my wish that Grace travel with me from London today.'

'Good afternoon, my lord. As I said a month ago, Grace has become a daughter to me. What more could I ask for?'

The arrival of Saunders with a footman carrying the tea tray halted all talk and everyone found a seat to enjoy their refreshments.

An hour later, Alex escorted Grace up the wide stairs and along a corridor. He opened the door to a bedchamber. 'This is your private room, Grace, decorated in pink and green as at Kilbraith House.'

Grace walked in and immediately the spacious room was a haven of tranquillity from the scurrying servants, harassed florists and Aunt Matilda who had taken on the overwhelming task of organising her wedding.

'Do you like it?'

'It's perfect. Thank you.'

A breeze through the open window moved the curtain and Grace glimpsed the parkland and heard the birds calling in their clear sweet voices. Sight and sound flowed through her like a soothing balm.

Alex stepped into the room and pushed the door shut with his foot. Two steps brought him to her and he pulled her into his arms. 'This is our last moment alone. Our last kiss before we are man and wife.' Grace lifted her face to him, waiting for his lips to touch hers. When they did his passion swept away all that she should be saying to him before they stood together in the church.

Alex drew away and smiled. 'I would like to stay, but we do not want to start a frenzy of gossip among the household.'

'Away with you, Lord Rossmore, you are quite shameless. Go

and give a word of praise to Saunders; Aunt Matilda can be quite forceful at times.'

Alex bowed. 'As you wish, my lady.' He left, closing the door.

Through the diamond-shaped, leaded panes of her window Grace watched the dawn light rising through a pale mist over the parkland. This was her wedding day and behind her the ornate gold clock ticked each minute nearer to when she would become the Countess of Rossmore. These quiet moments to herself would soon be broken with maids and footmen taking laden breakfast trays to the thirty guests slumbering in their beds.

The house yesterday afternoon had been in turmoil with travelling trunks piling higher and higher in the hall. How could so much clothing be required for so short a visit? Aunt Matilda had plans to stay the week, and had invited some of her close friends to remain and keep her company, but the majority of guests had only been invited to stay two nights.

The bedchamber was furnished very much the same as at Kilbraith House, but with the luxury of her own bathing room. This she was looking forward to using after Esther had brought her coffee and toast. Grace got back into bed. She would not leave this room until the carriage arrived to take her to the church.

Esther smoothed a final strand of hair into place. She had changed Grace from a sleepy-eyed woman into a beautiful bride.

'If only we could paint you on canvas as you are at this moment.' Esther's voice broke on a sob. 'I shall always remember you looking like this. So calm and happy.' She took a handkerchief from her pocket and wiped her eyes. 'I will go and tell Lady Crowmarsh and Lady Wainwright you are ready.'

'Thank you, Esther. You have become a much-trusted friend over the years, and I hope that will continue. Now off with you to the church. At least you will be one face that I recognise among the congregation.'

In a few minutes Aunt Matilda opened the door and came in.

Grace had never seen her aunt so regal, as she was in a lace over turquoise silk gown. And to complete her grandeur a peacock's feather was woven into her silver-grey hair.

'My dear, you are the most beautiful bride I have ever seen. Madame Du Val has excelled in her creation. And the emeralds, you will be the envy of every lady in the church.'

'Thank you. The necklace is a surprise after Alex has already given me the Rossmore betrothal ring. But I will treasure this more, because it is from him and not a symbol of his heritage.'

'Men are quite a mystery at times, Grace.' Aunt Matilda touched the circular necklace lying below the pale skin of her throat. 'Crow-marsh gave me this on our wedding eve. It is Tibetan Turquoise. He said he wanted to give me something the other ladies of the *ton* would not dream of wearing. And to me, it is a love gift, and irreplaceable.'

'I hope my life with Alex will be as happy. We . . .'

The reminiscing was interrupted when Isabelle arrived.

'My goodness, I am outshone in such finery. Matilda, my dear, you look exquisite.' She turned to Grace. 'And every gentleman — bachelor or wedded — will be casting daggers at the unattainable earl, who has now taken such a beauty for his bride.'

'Isabelle, you have such wicked thoughts.' Grace waved her hand. 'Willy should take you in hand.'

'A little late for that, for I am his heart's love forever.' She twirled. 'Do you like my gown?'

'Pale blue satin is so your colour, Isabelle. And your sapphire necklace; does it have a special meaning for you?'

Happiness and laughter faded from Isabelle like the sun hiding behind a cloud. She sat on the chaise longue and clasped her fingers together. 'They were my mother's. Papa gave them to me when she died. I was only ten years old, but he said I was to lock them away until I was grown up. This is only the second time I have worn them; first when I married Willy and today.' She sighed deeply and looked up. 'No more sadness, this is a celebration day for my lovely almost-to-be cousin. Matilda, I think it is time for us to be leaving for the church.'

54

'Yes. Crowmarsh is ready, Grace. He will call for you when the carriage arrives.'

'Thank you, both, for all that you have taken on and arranged in such a short time. Now enjoy the day and I will see you later.'

In the quietness of her bedchamber Grace watched the clock tick away the minutes. In less than an hour she would marry Alex.

From the moment they had met he had swept her into a courtship that had been three days and their betrothal one month. Now, at the eleventh hour, she was frightened that the final step into matrimony would be a disaster for both of them. She looked at her image in the mirror – at the ivory silk gown flowing softly over her body, the sleeves touching her wrists. Esther had coiffured her dark hair to hold a delicate circle of diamonds her uncle had given her for a wedding gift.

In contrast, the emerald necklace that Alex had given her yesterday evening was set exactly the same as her ring. He had come into her bedchamber through the connecting door to his room. The next time they came back into this house he would have the right to come to her whenever he pleased.

A knock on the door told her the carriage had arrived. She picked up the posy of spring flowers. It was too late for second thoughts.

The Reverend Tilbury, his prayer book open and balanced on his palms, waited on the altar step in the estate's private church. The Earl of Rossmore, attired in a tailored black coat and trousers, his pristine white neck cloth folded to perfection, signified the man of position and wealth. Behind him seated in the oak pews were the guests Lady Crowmarsh had invited from London to reside in his country home.

He turned as the organ music began to play. Lord Crowmarsh was leading Grace down the aisle towards him, but he didn't see her, it was Liddy who was coming to him. He had vowed never to marry again and had held his faith, until Grace set his pulse hammering.

The music stopped. Grace was standing beside him. Her grey eyes gazed into his, searching, seemingly asking him a question.

The rector was calling the congregation to prayer. It was too late for second thoughts.

Grace sat beside Alex in the centre of the long dining table. The room was filled with the hum of voices giving her an excuse to sit without speaking. The wedding breakfast was an endless parade of dishes. She wanted this over. Her greatest wish was for time alone, time to collect her thoughts before she journeyed to Solitaire House for the honeymoon.

'You are very quiet, Grace, are you all right?' Alex leaned towards her and took her hand. Despite the warmth of the day her fingers were unnaturally cold.

'I feel a little tired, that's all. You will agree it has been a very hectic four weeks.'

'And, my dear, you feel a little sad? I'm sorry your father was not well enough to leave his bed to come.'

'Do not worry about my father. I'm sure he was more than happy to relinquish his role to Lord Crowmarsh. And from experience I know Aunt Matilda has little patience with her brother. She was delighted to organise our wedding day.'

He lifted her hand to his lips, lightly kissed the Rossmore wedding ring. 'Once we are at Whitecliffs, the sea air will revive you. For now, we have a duty to our guests.'

In the drawing room Grace and Alex circulated, and became separated as she stopped to speak to the fashionable ladies from London.

'Lady Maynard, I hope you are enjoying our day, and I am so pleased you will be staying on with my aunt. The parkland presents so many delightful carriage outings.'

'My dear, Rossmore's generous invitation to his guests to extend their visit will, I am sure, give Matilda much joy.'

Grace moved on to the country ladies who stood apart. They were strangers to her and their conversations were merely polite salutations and each agreeing to visit when she was residing at Rossmore Manor.

Aunt Matilda walked in through the open double doors from the garden and came towards her. 'Are you coping, my dear? The wedding reception can be the most stressful part of the day. But you have satisfied our London guests. I admire how you have not missed one lady in this room. I will entertain our guests from now on. It is time for you to change into your travelling gown. Go with Isabelle and rest a while.'

Grace looked round the room for Alex but he had joined the gentlemen and was engaged in deep discussion.

This was her opportunity to escape and she looked for Isabelle Wainwright, easily recognisable with her blonde hair piled high with blue ribbons threaded and cascading to her shoulders. She saw her standing by the door. They had, without any difficulty, developed a companionable friendship. She went over to her. 'Will you come and sit with me while I change? I have a memento for you of today.'

'Grace, thank you. I'll tell Willy where we are and he can prise Alex away from discussing wheat fields and cows. Landowners seem to have nothing else to talk about except business and money.'

In her bedchamber, Grace looked at her wedding ring. She had vowed before God to love, honour and obey a man she barely knew. She would be sleeping in his bed tonight and any other night he wished. Marital love was her duty, but could she become deeply, emotionally, *in love* with him? What she had allowed herself to feel before now was a layer of love that could have been broken – ended. Now, there was no end. Were the few common interests they shared enough for a lifetime together?

The door opened and Isabelle came in. 'Oh, you are not changing. Shall I call your maid?'

'Please. The bell-cord is by the bed. Esther will be hovering; this is her big day as well as mine. She won't be content until I am attired to perfection and she sends me off in a flood of tears. I don't know what I would do without her.'

Isabelle pulled the cord and sat on the edge of the bed. 'How are you?'

'A little shocked. This should be the happiest day of my life, but somehow it isn't. I don't mean that I regret marrying Alex. It's because too much has happened in only four weeks. But, when Alex and I arrive at Whitecliffs, it will be heaven. We will have space to breathe and time to get to know each other better. So, no more doldrums, I mustn't spoil Esther's day.'

Grace opened her dressing-table drawer and took out a box. She gave it to Isabelle. 'Thank you for all your help, and a little present for you to remember this day.'

Isabelle lifted the lid. 'Grace! A diamond horseshoe, it's beautiful. Thank you, my dear, so very much.'

'It has a double meaning. For the day we met in the park and you invited me to tea, and the superstition for good luck.'

Isabelle's eyes watered. 'Yes.' She took it out and went to the mirror and pinned it to her gown. 'I wish you happiness, Grace. You will give Alex time to adjust; he's been on his own a long time. He still blames himself for Liddy's death, which I know is wrong of him, but . . .'

'But he's had ten years to grieve and I hope we can make a veritable life together. I have wondered about being a second wife – will I become jealous of Liddy – but Alex and I must come to terms with it all. It's a challenge for us to build our lives on.'

Isabelle turned to Grace and gave her a hug, 'He will love you, Grace, I know he will.'

'And I shall love him.'

The door opened and Esther came in. 'Time to change, m'lady, are you ready?'

'Yes, Esther. We mustn't keep his lordship waiting too long.'

Lord William Wainwright, Alex's cousin, had been his closest friend since boyhood. Both were of similar height, but Willy's hair was as dark as a moonless night beside Alex's glowing copper. Willy touched his arm and drew Alex from the group of gentlemen. 'Grace has gone to change.' He lowered his tone. 'You are a lucky man to have found Grace. I know it's impertinent of me to

58

say, but let the past go, Alex. I wish you both a long and happy life.'

Alex did not answer immediately, then said, 'Thank you, Willy.'

Holding hands, Grace and Alex ran down the portico steps in the early afternoon sunshine, the ladies throwing flower petals as they weaved their way through the laughing and cheering guests to their coach. And they did not stop waving until the coach drove out of sight.

Grace felt the pressures of the day fall away as she watched the sunlight sporadically flash across her pelisse as they drove through a beech wood on the Wiltshire road. She was disappointed their journey would be broken by an overnight stop, but they could not make the distance to Solitaire House today unless the wedding had been at dawn. This would have suited her, but probably not her guests. The thought of lords and ladies rising while the sky was dark conjured up amusing scenes in her mind.

'That's the first smile I've seen on your face today,' Alex commented.

'I had not realised one's own wedding could be such a nervous experience.'

'Then it was a good decision to have it in the country and not London. We should have been obliged to ask many more guests.'

'We have not agreed on how long we are to stay at Solitaire?'

'There is no hurry to return. I know you have been looking forward to this visit; let us not make a date.'

'Thank you, my lord.'

'Grace! Will you stop calling me "my lord"? I thought we agreed that in private we call each other by our given name?'

'Yes, but I find it . . . difficult . . . sometimes.'

Alex sighed, making no adverse comment, only said, 'Rest awhile for now, it's quite some way before we reach the inn for our overnight stop.'

She leaned back against the padded seat and closed her eyes. The tension in her shoulders eased and the silence lulled her to sleep.

59

The shouting of voices woke her. They were at the coaching inn and Alex was coming out of the doorway with the innkeeper. The coachman opened the door and Alex offered his hand to help her out. 'Everything is ready, Grace. Your room is upstairs to the rear; I thought that would be quieter for you.'

Grace thought she misheard – her room? Inside she followed the innkeeper's wife up a narrow flight of stairs and was shown into a small bedchamber. It was sufficient for the one night, although the single log burning in the grate gave little cheer to the room. The valise that Esther had packed for this stopover was on the bed. Alex had said he did not need Miles, his valet, for one night. She had thought to do the same. Now what had been a kindness to Esther might turn out to have been a foolish gesture for her.

'His Lordship has ordered dinner in an hour in the private room downstairs, milady. My gal will be up to help you soon.' The woman bobbed a curtsey and left.

When the innkeeper's daughter arrived, Grace thought her much too young to know how to dress a lady and dismissed her. Why change her gown? The effort would be quite wasted sitting in an inn. She opened the valise and took out her nightgown and laid it on the bed. Her toiletries were very minimal, a hairbrush, comb, soap and her own towel. Esther had insisted on that, declaring any item washed in river water was quite unsuitable to touch her mistress' skin.

At the appointed time, Grace went downstairs to a small square parlour with one table set for two. In contrast to her meagre fire upstairs, the welcoming warmth from several large logs recently stoked into life were sending sparks shooting up the chimney.

Alex was waiting. 'The innkeeper has only ale, spirits or wine. I have taken the liberty of ordering wine.'

'A good choice, sir, I prefer wine.'

He poured a glass from the pitcher.

There was a tension about him that she didn't understand. Was he nervous? That should be her; weren't all brides supposed to be so on their wedding night? Was he thinking about Liddy? Surely he would not do that to her, especially tonight. Hadn't he told her he needed to make a new life? Unheeded, a spark of chagrin flared. To hide her thoughts she said, 'A pleasant parlour, my lord, far more comfortable than my room. Did they not have a larger one?'

'We had travelled far enough for today. The inn at the next town would have taken another hour's travel. I shall ask the inn-keeper for something larger for you.'

Alex started for the door, but Grace stopped him. 'No. It's only for one night.'

He took her hands. 'You are cold, come to the fire and warm them.'

This was the first time he had lovingly touched her since leaving Rossmore Manor, if she disregarded his polite moments of helping her in and out of the coach.

'Are you alright, Alex? Is there anything—'

'No.' His interruption was sharp. He pulled her towards him. 'No, Grace.' He stroked his finger down her cheek. 'The inn is small, but you were tired and I thought it best to stop here.'

Grace sighed. 'I'm hungry, let us eat.'

Alex pulled a chair from the table for her to sit and then sat opposite. They ate the roast beef and potatoes in silence until Grace asked, 'How is your room?' He didn't look up. A pain stabbed her temple. The only sounds were the fire and the ticking of a clock.

Without warning, Alex said, 'You were tired before we left Rossmore. I do not wish to be called a heartless husband, so perhaps you would like to retire after dinner?'

Grace smiled across at him, 'Yes, if that is what you want. I would like a little fruit first to refresh my palate; the meat was a little heavy for a lady's digestion. Perhaps something we can share?'

'If you so wish. Would you like an apple?'

'Yes, please.'

Alex rang the bell and the innkeeper's daughter came in. 'Lady Rossmore would like a bowl of fruit.'

'We only got apples, sir.'

'Excellent.'

The girl returned a few minutes later and Alex chose a large red apple and cut it in half, giving Grace a share.

The sun had set and the night sky turned the room into a cocoon of glowing red firelight. It was warm and she wanted to be in Alex's arms, feel his lips on hers. They had waited, observing propriety to the full, except of course those stolen moments of opportunity. She looked at the table space between them and it seemed like a moat that shouldn't be crossed. Alex made no attempt to move. What was happening? Should she take the first step? 'If you will excuse me, I shall go to my chamber.'

Alex got up and took her arm. 'I . . . I'll accompany you.'

She climbed the stairs, conscious of Alex just behind. Along the passageway she stopped at the second door and reached for the latch but he covered her hand with his.

'It has been a strenuous day for us both. Goodnight, Grace, sleep well.' He leaned forward and kissed her forehead, then retraced his steps downstairs.

Grace watched him go, more confused than ever by his behaviour. She opened the door and went in. The room seemed to have shrunk, the bed grown in size, their wedding bed, the feather mattress overly wide, the counterpane folded back, leaving the eiderdown and sheet readied for two lovers to slide in. When they arrived at Rossmore Manor, there had been passion between them, a longing for this night.

What was wrong?

The humiliation of Esther witnessing her now, abandoned in this room was unthinkable. Heat burned her cheeks and tears splashed onto her wedding ring. Suddenly, that Esther and Miles had travelled independently, with instructions to make their own night's stop-over, was a blessing.

She hadn't told him her secret, so what had she done to make him reject her?

Chapter Six

Grace woke to the sound of knocking. She felt muzzy, her temple throbbed and her eyes hurt. Where was she? The strange room pressed in on all sides and her heart pounded.

The door opened and the young serving girl came in with a tray. 'Good mornin', your ladyship.' She bobbed a curtsey. 'His lordship asked for your breakfast to be brought up to you. Do you need me to stay and 'elp? Your coach will be ready to leave in an hour.'

Grace looked at the girl's flushed face: she was more nervous than last night. 'No. Please come back in thirty minutes. Has his lordship eaten?'

'Yes. He is gone to the stables.'

'Please tell him I will be ready within the hour.'

Was this a dream? Was she really married and abandoned inside of a day? The ring on her finger told her otherwise and reminded her why her head ached so. She had lain awake till the early hours, her thoughts repeatedly going over the weeks before their wedding. Friendship had grown into companionship and then . . . ? She threw back the covers and got up, poured a cup of tea and sat on the bed. What should she be feeling at this moment? She should be a new wife lying beside her husband. Their desires and passions having drawn them together, fulfilling their marital vows. His words of a new beginning were all a sham, a sham betrothal, a sham wedding. She had expected, wanted, to truly be a wife to Alex, and this brought her full circle back to last night – he had not desired her.

★

Grace saw Alex step forward from the waiting coach. He took her hand and raised it to his lips. 'Good morning, Grace. I hope this early start has not over-taxed you? I thought you would want to arrive at Solitaire House as early as possible.'

Grace snatched her hand away, and lowered her gaze. How could he pretend such endearing consideration for her wellbeing? Renewed anger flared and was released through her burning cheeks. She had married a man who had walked away, and by his absence, refused to consummate their marriage.

'Good morning, my lord. It is most thoughtful, for I am eager to reach our journey's end.'

Alex held out his hand to help her into the coach.

Grace glanced around the courtyard. Jenkins, their coachman, was holding the horses steady, waiting for her and Alex to enter the coach. Several lady travellers were standing together, and one in particular was whispering behind her gloved hand. She and Alex were obviously providing entertainment. To refuse her husband's help could add gossip to her chagrin. She placed her gloved hand in his. Sitting in the farthest corner, Grace hoped Alex would give her the courtesy of doing likewise when he got in. She could not bear for him to touch her and the throbbing in her temple had spread across her forehead.

After a while, the rhythm of the ride eased her taut muscles, only to be replaced with the inside temperature rising with the midday sun. With each minute Grace became overly warm, but she would not unbutton her pelisse and draw Alex's attention to her person. Instead she looked through the window at the green and lush countryside and concentrated on the passing fields dotted with lambs. The coach journeyed on through a woodland copse, and as the sun found its way through new-leafed trees she saw blue-bells ripple from pastel mauve to dark purple. White stitchwort and yellow dandelions sprinkled the hedgerows.

Grace turned her head to look across at Alex and saw that he was staring at her.

'Would you like to stop at the next inn? Perhaps eat a light meal?' His voice sounded strained.

'That would be pleasant; my back is beginning to feel rather stiff. A short walk would be acceptable.' Her answer was as stilted as his question. He opened the hatch and spoke to the coachman. The atmosphere was like a blanket, wrapping each in their designated space. She did not understand why everything was going wrong. It was his fault. Where was the tenderness he had shown, the words that made her feel cherished, touches that signalled she was right in agreeing to marry him? It seemed the last twenty-four hours raised nothing but questions.

At that moment the coach pulled into the courtyard of an inn.

Grace followed Alex around the side of the thatched building to a grassed garden. Sitting on a wooden bench she watched the clear water of a stream dance over grey pebbles and silvery fish flash in and out of the weed. She heard footsteps on the paved path and looking round saw Alex striding towards her. Today he was wearing a change of clothing. The sunlight made his hair look more bronze than copper, the cut of his jacket emphasised his broad shoulders and the tight breeches and polished boots made him seem even taller. What spell had he cast over her that she had allowed herself to be persuaded into marriage?

'The innkeeper will bring a table and we will eat outside.' Sitting next to her he continued, 'It is a beautiful day to be arriving at the sea. You look pale, Grace, is the journey too much for you?'

'Sir, I am not one of those fainting pansies that flutter around London. Have you forgotten that I have lived most of my life in the country? It is nothing for me to walk five miles.' She could not control her anger. 'Will you be able to keep up with me when we climb the high cliffs behind Solitaire? It is not my custom to be taken in a carriage everywhere, I prefer to ride, let the wind take my hair every which way.' Grace stood up and walked to the stream, her nerves coiled tight straining for release.

'Your spirit is returning, Grace, that is good, I was beginning to wonder if we had made a mistake.'

'Made a mistake, sir? I do not understand your meaning. I am now your wife; perhaps you are the one who has made the error, Alex. You seem not to know what your role as a husband means.' She was trembling, incensed by his words. Tears welled and she fumbled in her reticule for a handkerchief only to be swung round to face him.

'I am the master, the one who decides what you will do, where you will go. This house may be your father's, Grace, but when I am there I will be in charge.'

This was something Grace had not given any thought to. Solitaire had always been her domain, but marriage changed everything. The angry words that sprang to her lips were never said as Alex pulled her towards him and kissed her with the passion she had known. She sensed his frustration as he pulled her into his body so that she could feel his need. Feel him lift her into him and rock them. She wanted to hit him, scratch him, do anything but give in to the desire that she too felt. In seconds they had gone from insults to passion . . . the cough that came from behind Alex made them step apart like guilty lovers caught indiscreet at the wrong moment.

The innkeeper was grinning. 'Shall I serve now, m'lord, or later?'

Alex shielded Grace behind him. 'Now, if you please. We still have some miles to travel.'

Grace sat in her corner pretending to be asleep. She peeped to look at Alex. The meal together had been awkward and neither had looked at the other, or spoken a single word. They had departed in the same fractious atmosphere as they had arrived.

A half-hour later the coach turned south from the Dorchester road and the lanes narrowed. The coach swayed from side to side as the wheels slipped off pointed fragments of rocks embedded in the hardened soil. Their speed slowed to a crawl.

Grace looked out of the coach window. She couldn't keep her

excitement from showing much longer. They were now travelling on the elevated countryside that would enable her to see White-cliffs Bay within the next few minutes. The coach rounded a curve and started to descend and she saw nestled between two headlands the traders' buildings and fishermen's cottages that lined the descending dirt road that ended alongside Smugglers Inn.

Picturesque, as always, boats lay anchored out in the calm waters. Half-a-dozen horse-drawn carts stood waiting on beach boards for the fishing boats bringing in their catch on the incoming tide. As the coach passed the church, Grace made a wish – she hoped they would be able to restart their honeymoon anew tonight.

Her excitement doubled. She was almost there. The waiting was a torment, but in a few minutes Solitaire House would come into view.

Then she could see it, sheltered in the woodland halfway up the hillside. A family house, all the day rooms on the ground floor. There were only four bedchambers, another small room used for bathing, but this hardly mattered, there were rarely any visitors. The servants' rooms were in the attic and the old retainers who cared for the house had rooms off the kitchen. Beyond the garden, high hedging separated the coach house and stables from the house.

A few minutes later, the coach circled round the blacksmith's forge and an involuntary cry left her lips, all the friction between them forgotten. 'Alex, we're here. Look, isn't it the most perfect setting you have ever seen?'

The house was a dwarf compared to Rossmore, but she didn't care, this was the only pleasure her father had ever given her. But-terflies fluttered low in her belly and a triumphant thrill rose up. It happened every time the square, red-brick building came into view; it was the panacea she needed.

As the coach slowed, Alex twisted to look out. 'You sound as though you are home, Grace. I look forward to our stay.'

Grace didn't hear his remark or wait for the coach door to be opened, but turned the handle and jumped down, running up the steps to where Mrs Gillett was waiting.

'Welcome home, Miss Grace.'

'Gillie, I'm here at last. The coach ride has taken forever. Oh, I can't wait to see the garden. Has Gillett been looking after my flowers? Have you made me scones for tea?' Grace hugged the plump, white-haired woman.

'Yes, to everything, m'lady.'

Then she moved away from Grace and curtsied to Alex. 'Welcome to Solitaire House, m'lord.'

'Thank you, Mrs Gillett.'

Alex stopped in the hall and turned to Grace.

'Well, my dear, we're finally here at your Solitaire House. I'm sure you're eager to show me around. It won't take as long as Rossmore, but I think we will enjoy our stay. I can call from the hall and reach you wherever you are.' He took her hand. 'Shall we begin with my study?'

Through the open doorway she could see a large desk placed where her own delicate Sheraton had stood.

'His lordship sent instructions that he required a study. There wasn't anywhere else, Miss Grace. Gillett put your desk in the small sitting room.' Mrs Gillett's cheeks deepened to crimson and apprehension showed in her eyes.

'That's quite all right, Gillie. I intend to spend much of my time out of doors on this visit.' She looked at Alex, saying, 'I see you have taken over my writing room. So perhaps we should start there.' Grace loved this room, because the French windows gave a view of the garden, but a gentleman needed a study, so be it. 'Your desk looks a little out of place amongst my feminine chairs and cushions.'

'That will not be a problem. Most of my post will only be the urgent papers that I have to sign. My agent will handle the daily correspondence. I don't mean to ban you from here, Grace, but I do need somewhere private for myself.'

Grace nodded. This was one concession she had to make. The house could not grow another room. 'Let us move on. It's nearly teatime.'

The ground floor did not take long. There was only the drawing room, dining room and small sitting room that Alex would want to know about. They came back into the hall as Mrs Gillett was coming down the stairs.

'Your rooms are ready. His lordship's man and your maid arrived earlier and are unpacking. When would you like tea?'

'In half-an-hour and in the garden, please, Gillie.'

Grace started to walk up the stairs, expecting Alex to follow, but he had gone into his newly acquired study and closed the door. Was this to be a pattern, shutting her out? She went on up the stairs and entered the bedchamber she had taken over when her mother died.

Esther was hanging dresses in the wardrobe and she turned and curtsied. 'Good afternoon, m'lady. Did you have a good journey? This is the last of the unpacking. Mr Gillett will store the trunks in the coach house.'

'As always, Esther, the last few miles are the most uncomfortable. When I have washed my face and hands, and you have tied my hair, I shall be presentable for his lordship. After Gillie's scones and tea I shall enjoy wandering in the garden and seeing what Gillett has produced this spring. And, Esther, you must go to the kitchen and find out all the latest gossip. Then you can tell me all while I dress for dinner.'

'Oh m'lady, you know nothing interesting happens in these parts. Murder, robbery and mayhem is for the cities.'

'Rubbish, this coast is perfect for spies and smuggling. I'll bet you a farthing his lordship will send Miles into the village on the same errand. Ply Gillie with some London gossip and she'll reciprocate.'

Grace stood on the top step leading to the circular sunken garden. Lilac, yellow broom, bluebells and marguerites were in flower. Rose bushes, showing a profusion of buds, covered the banking like spectators in Rome's Coliseum. A table and two chairs waited for the gladiators in the shade of a tree cast by the afternoon sun.

69

Into the stillness came the sound of bumblebees, as they flew from flower to flower, and the distant cry of gulls, reminding her that the sea was only a short distance away.

Grace felt a presence and Alex came to stand behind her.

'Is this what you have been longing for, Grace? Perhaps I too, will find this tranquillity beneficial to my mind. Mrs Gillett is bringing the tray, shall we be seated?'

'I take tea here every afternoon, weather permitting. Perhaps I can entice you to join me sometimes whilst we are here?'

Taking her hand he led her to a garden chair. 'Is that an invitation or command, Lady Rossmore?'

'Both, I think, Lord Rossmore.'

They ate like two children at a party, every crumb cleared from their plates.

'Mrs Gillett has surpassed her usual tea. Those scones piled high with cream and preserves were the best I have ever tasted.'

Alex smiled at her as he picked up his cup. 'I will have correspondence from London each day, but if it pleases you, I will try to join you for tea.'

'It is no matter. Perhaps I shall not be here *every* day. I walk and ride a lot when I am visiting the area.' A niggle of irritation passed through her: was it really necessary for him to have business documents delivered here? This was supposed to be a time for them. 'Is that why you disappeared into *my writing room* as soon as we arrived?'

'My commitments are far more pressing than your gossiping letters. I am the one who has the responsibilities, Grace. Solitaire is your playhouse.'

'My what!' Irritation turned to anger. 'Do I need to repeat myself, Alex? I am not feeble-minded and weak like so many of my gender. Fawning behind scented handkerchiefs and swooning to attract attention is for the young miss, just out of the schoolroom, encouraged by their mothers to trap the young bucks. Pray remember, you are years older now than when your wife was alive.'

Alex froze.

The two gladiators stared at each other, their weapons about to be drawn.

'Never compare my Liddy to frivolous kittens who have not yet been weaned.'

'And do not compare me with tabbies that have nothing to do all day but gossip and fan their way through Society.'

'I will repeat. I am the one in charge, the provider for the present and the future Rossmores to come.'

'Is that reference to *your* heir or brother Geoffrey's?'

Alex stood up, pushed the chair backwards with such force that it toppled to the ground. His face was thunderous and he banged his fist down on to the table, spilling tea from the cups. 'That is something only time will tell. But God forgive me for letting this marriage . . .' He closed his mouth, pressing his lips together until they were a thin line.

'Say it, Alex. Say to me what you couldn't last night.'

He took a step backwards, opened his mouth to speak, but no words came out. Turning, he strode back to the house, leaving Grace, for the second time, watching teardrops splash onto her wedding ring.

She shouldn't have brought Liddy's name up. Her tongue just ran away with the words. Was his late wife going to be a ghost that stood between them? Isabelle had said he needed time. Did that mean in the bedchamber?

Esther's slim, wiry figure darted about the bedchamber preparing her mistress's evening clothes and she chattered happily about the local gossip.

'Mrs Gillett says that the smuggling along the coast has increased, but the Excise men rarely catch anyone. The Mayor's daughter has run off with a sergeant in the Hussar Regiment and a Norwegian sea captain has taken the big house coming into the village.' She paused to take a breath. 'Old Tom Morgan has said the weather is set fine for the next month and his son Ben is to marry Daisy Walters on midsummer's day. Will you still be here then, m'lady?'

'I asked for gossip, but what a variety, Esther. I don't know how long we are staying. His lordship has been kind enough to leave that decision open.' Grace pondered on this thought. The expectation of having her honeymoon here at Solitaire where they could enjoy the sea air was rapidly losing its appeal, if Alex was going to continue in his present mood. Their quarrel in the garden proved to be a torturous exercise, one she did not wish to repeat at dinner.

Alex had the adjoining bedchamber, but there was no sign of him as Grace descended the stairs wearing a blue silk gown cut low with a curved neckline. She had not worn any jewellery, thinking her soft curves would tempt any man, even her husband, should he deem to make an appearance before bedtime.

It was customary to dine at six o'clock when Grace was at Solitaire. Alex was not in the drawing room. She went to the window, her gaze on the grass slope running down to the road, but her mind was elsewhere. What was he doing? It wasn't her fault that Liddy had died, yet he seemed to have brought her presence with him. Her breathing quickened and tears flooded her eyes. How could he do this to her? Grace heard the door open and knew Alex had come in. She could not turn to him, she felt like the intruder, the one who should not be here. Yet Solitaire was her haven, where she always found comfort and peace.

'Grace, I'm sorry. I didn't mean to upset you this afternoon. Can we try to have dinner without any more harsh words?'

Still not turning, she said, 'We must try, Alex, this is not a good start to our marriage.' The sound of liquid being poured made her glance over her shoulder and she saw him down the golden nectar in one gulp. 'Brandy is not the answer to our woes. But perhaps you could pour me a small glass, then we can both go in to dinner better tempered than we are now.'

Her forthright comment appeared to astonish him, but he did as he was bid and, having refilled his own glass, walked over to her. Handing her the glass, he raised his own. 'To our future together, Grace.'

Grace studied the handsome man attired in evening clothes. He was a head taller than she and his green eyes looked sad, but his scent reminded her of how dashing he could be. He had a charm that coaxed, a determination bordering on forcefulness, which had swept her into marriage to make her his wife. She must give him time. Time heals everything. She, of all people, knew that. Raising her eyes and looking directly into his, she answered, 'To our future . . . husband.'

Dinner started well. Mrs Gillett had laid two settings at one end of the twelve-seat table and the closeness helped ease their troubles of the day.

'This is most unusual, Grace. Saunders would tut-tut for a week if he could see us.'

'Solitaire is not run like your London home. It's something Mother insisted on and I have continued in the same way. I don't intend to change it either.' The edge in her voice made it plain that this was her house, her rules, even if he did confiscate her writing room and declare he was master when in residence. This thought dampened her spirits and she placed her knife and fork on the plate, her appetite gone.

'Grace?'

'Yes?'

'Perhaps this was not such a good idea to come to your doll's house. I do not want to take over, but you must realise that when I am here, I *will* undertake the responsibilities of the master.'

Grace could feel her anger resurfacing. She wanted to shout at him, but knew it would only cause another confrontation. Perhaps they should declare war lines, with a no-man's land in between. 'That is something I had not envisaged when we decided to come. I am very possessive of Solitaire. You cannot understand how a woman feels to own nothing. I need to adjust to our new arrangement.'

There was little else to be said.

'I do not want a dessert, sir.'

'Nor I. It has been a clear sunny day, the daylight lingers. Would you show me beyond the garden? I believe a spot of sea air will do both of us good.'

From the main garden a flight of steps disappeared into the wood behind the house and continued with a dirt path that climbed upwards.

Grace led the way. 'Apart from cutting out any dead or weather-damaged trees I have instructed Gillett that the wood be left to nature.'

'You have a strong belief in conservation, Grace? Do you have any particular reason?'

'I have read in several journals many botanists' views about our flora and fauna, the habitat of our wild birds.'

Grace turned and looked back towards the house. 'The trees are now leafing well, but on a misty day in winter the view from here is shadowy, mysterious, more like a drawing in charcoal than a spring watercolour.'

'That is a very poetic description. But I appreciate what you describe. When I am in residence at Rossmore Manor during the autumn and the trees are turning russet, the myriad of copper and yellows, it is as though I am seeing the parkland in oils. You have inspired me to have the artist Turner capture such a scene. Would you like that, Grace?'

'Yes, I would, Alex. Thank you.'

'Do you realise this is the first time you have called me Alex without stumbling over the etiquette of my title.' He reached for her hand and linked their fingers together. 'Thank you, my dear. Shall we continue our exploration?'

Walking on through the trees they came to where the path forked. Grace led Alex to the right. The gentle rising path changed to a narrow steep track. Grass verges kept the new growth of ferns and bushes back as they climbed. Grace looked over her shoulder. 'Gillett keeps this clear for me, so your clothes should not be soiled.'

'What do you think I do when I am at Rossmore, Grace? Sit in the house all day? Let me tell you I am on the go morn till night. Bosworth is a fine estate manager, but I like to make the decisions where my farms and land are concerned. Looking after the wellbeing and livelihood of my tenants means I get a good return on my investments.'

As he finished speaking they emerged onto a grass headland and before them the ocean was deep blue and the horizon a dark line against a skein of pale yellow tinged with red.

Grace walked close to the edge and looked down. Waves crashed against the rocks and beat a thunderous roar every few seconds. The noise was deafening. 'The tide is fully in,' she called to Alex, as he came to place his arm round her waist.

'You dare the elements, standing this close to the edge; come back, Grace.'

'Why? Does it make you giddy to look down? I have come to stand here since I was a child to watch the sea, the sunsets, the storms, the gulls soaring. Oh Alex, I feel free here.' She turned to him, expecting that he would step back, but he didn't and they were now so close she could feel his breath on her cheek.

'My senses do not go reeling with the height. It is you that will tip me over the edge with your scent.' He took one step back and pulled Grace with him.

She experienced again the desire, the same wanting, that she had known earlier that day by the garden stream. Alex was drawing her into him, letting her know that his own desire was melding them together. He lowered his head and she tilted her face so that his lips could taste her own. It was the gentle brushing of his tongue along her lower lip that made her open them, let his tongue brush along her teeth, feel the tip explore her own and then she was lost in an abandoned kiss that she never wanted to end.

Then he was pushing her away. A sweat beaded his forehead. 'I can't . . . I vowed . . . come, Grace, it is time to return.'

Grace heard the words, but did not move. 'Alex, please, you cannot treat me like this. I am your wife now – what do you want of me?'

His face had gone white. He was looking at her as though she were a stranger – and at that moment she knew – all he could see was Liddy.

'Not now, Grace, I can't ...' He turned and started walking back.

Grace did not follow. She could not compete with a ghost.

She watched the light fade, the sky become black velvet sprinkled with diamonds and the tide pulling away from the jagged rocks by the moon's never-ending cycle of time. She turned and walked back along the descending path, so familiar that every protruding stone and twisted tree root was avoided as she returned to Solitaire House. To lie awake, thinking, crying, for a husband who had put a wall between them as they made their vows at the altar.

Chapter Seven

Grace had been sitting on the drawing-room window seat all morning. The weather matched her mood: grey, oppressive and miserable. 'Is this rain never going to stop? I feel the cramps starting in my legs.' She rubbed the back of her calf muscles with vicious strokes.

They had been at Solitaire for three days, and whenever she and Alex were in the same room one could cut the atmosphere with a knife. He spent most of his day in her confiscated study and she was beginning to understand that Alex intended to continue in this mode. She picked up her book, flipped the pages and muttered, 'I'm becoming like a dormouse, wrapping my nest around me, fearful of what's outside.' She got up from the seat and rang the bell. She was going out regardless of the wet.

Alex saw Grace walk across the garden to the steps that led up into the woods.

She wore a heavy cloak with the hood pulled low across her face. The sight made him curse out loud. 'You are a fiend, not fit to be called a man. Damn you, Alexander Kilbraith, to the bottom of hell!'

Go after her, his heart said, but his feet remained unmoving.

Grace climbed the steps from the garden into the wood. Rain found its way through the leaves and dropped onto her dark blue, hooded cloak. Mud, like soft glue, tried to take her boots from her feet and she gave up trying to keep her hems from staining as she followed the path and took the left-hand track that went down. It was difficult and her feet slipped several times until the woodland thinned into grassland and she came to a planked platform, offering a place to rest. Treading warily on down a flight of wooden steps, Grace lifted her skirts and stepped onto the beach.

The wet shingle was dark grey and shelved down to sand mixed with fine grit, but felt firm under her tread. Grace walked and lifted her face to the sky, letting the blown droplets mingle with the tears on her cheeks. At last the bottled-up emotions could be expressed; she could cry, letting out sobs that the confinement of Solitaire would not permit. The gulls soared; she wanted their freedom to fly away from what was likely to be a life of despair if Alex could not let go of the past. Till death us do part sounded romantic, but the reality would be harsh if one looked into the future. Grace wiped away her tears with the palm of her hand; she would not let this happen, she would fight for that future – somehow.

The rain was easing and the tide was out. She walked looking down; there were often unusual stones to collect and she needed something to brighten her day. So it was a surprise when a pair of boots appeared before her. Her gaze travelled upwards to dark pantaloons, a blue naval jacket, then a rugged face and fair hair. A pair of blue eyes held an inquiring expression.

In an accented voice he asked, 'A silver coin for your thoughts, madam?'

'Oh! I . . . I didn't see you.' Grace stepped back, conscious of being on the beach alone. She should have brought Esther with her, but she hadn't wanted company; besides, she had walked this beach a hundred times without meeting anyone.

'Captain Hugo Olsen.' He tried to click his heels together and bow, but the sand squeezed between his ankles and the sound came out as a plop. 'My apologies, I am better suited to the deck of a ship.'

Grace smiled, her fear receding. 'Lady Rossmore.' Their introduction was totally improper without a chaperone present. But she was not in any mood for the trivialities of the *ton*; in fact she felt a rebellion her Aunt Matilda would swoon over. 'You have the house at the top of the village?'

'News travels like fire swept by the wind, I only moved in this past week.'

'You will find gossip the main occupation of the local ladies, so I warn you, Captain Olsen, keep your affairs close to your chest if you don't want the whole county of Dorset to know.'

'Thank you, Lady Rossmore. I do not have the returned pleasure of knowing where you live?'

'At Solitaire House, just below the cliff top.' Grace could have bitten her tongue out. Alex would not be pleased to know she had been conversing with a stranger, albeit a near neighbour. 'I must go, Captain.' She turned to retrace her steps, but he followed and walked beside her.

'I meant no offence. Please, do not think me a rogue in speaking to you. Perhaps I may call on you one day?'

'I think not. Lord Rossmore is not receiving guests at the moment, good day to you, sir.'

This time he stopped and nodded his head, 'Good day to you, Lady Rossmore.'

The rain had stopped and a weak sun was drying the sand. Grace forced her feet to pace out her steps rhythmically, but she wanted to run and it felt like miles before she reached the wooden steps. Stepping up each tread slowly, her heartbeat steadied. Damn the restraint her sex was under! He had seemed polite enough, yet had she been seen Alex would be furious.

She rested on the platform and looked back at the sea. It was cresting with white foaming waves as far as she could see. Great swells brought in the surf that crept up the sand; the tide had turned. The captain had appeared out of nowhere, although she had been busy looking for stones. He was certainly a handsome man. A strange place to rent a house; Whitecliffs had no harbour big enough for a ship. She would get Esther to do her kitchen gossiping again. He was intriguing – had she become so bored that another man could interest her? On her honeymoon!

When she stepped onto the path rivulets of water made the climb treacherous and she slipped several times. The lower inches of her cloak and dress changed to the colour of the mud. Her gloved hands, grasping for the outcrops of stone, became sore and not until she reached the steps leading down into the garden, did she rest.

Mrs Gillett was at the kitchen table, a bowl in front of her, her hands kneading the mixture within. At the sight of Grace a frown creased her forehead. 'What have you been up to, Miss Grace? Good lord, you're soaking wet! And the mud! Where have you been?'

'Gillie, please, no questions. I need to go to my bedchamber. Will you ask Esther to come at once and get Gillett to fill a bath?' Grace kept her gaze down; now was not the time for her old nurse's lectures. 'Is his lordship in the study?' She refused to call it *his*.

'I do not know where his lordship is.'

This news wasn't what she wanted to hear. A roving Alex might mean he could have seen her. She needed to get out of her soiled clothes.

The hall was empty. Grace saw that the study door was ajar, but not enough for her to see if Alex was inside. Leaving a trail of muddy footprints, she ran up the stairs and along the corridor to her room. Inside, leaning against the door she felt her heart pounding and waited until it slowed. Moving away, she was untying her cloak when the adjoining door burst open.

'Where the hell have you been? You were missing at luncheon and Esther said—' Alex broke his stride and stopped. 'Grace! What has happened, are you hurt?'

She knew she looked bedraggled and the hood had not protected her head. A glance in the mirror showed that the combs had fallen out and her dark hair hung in waves about her face. There was no way of hiding her muddy clothes. 'The path to the beach has become slippery . . . and so . . .'

Alex walked towards her with measured strides. 'Am I hearing you correctly? You have been down to the beach?' His tone was soft, nothing more than a whisper. 'On a day like this, when you could have fallen and broken your neck!' His voice gained volume. 'Do you wish to make me a widower before I have become your husband?' He pulled Grace to him. 'Is it revenge?'

Grace looked up at him. There was concern in his eyes and around his lips a white line was etched into his skin. She could feel him holding in his anger, which was more violent than the situation demanded. 'I . . . I felt like a caged animal, restless. Solitaire has never done this to me before. I needed space . . . space to breathe. The beach . . .' She paused; pride would not let her tell him she needed space to cry. As the impact of his words sank in, so did their meaning. Had she deliberately put herself at risk? Was her hurt so deep that the hidden pain had become revenge that made her do such an irresponsible act in weather like this? 'I'm sorry, Alex, it was thoughtless of me.'

Her admission seemed to release the tautness in his body. He pushed her cloak from her shoulders and let it fall to the floor, then cradled her in his arms and kissed her wet hair, slid kisses down her temple, her cheek, finally to her mouth. Grace could feel his warmth chasing her coldness away and she surrendered her lips to him, with abandonment and joy. This was the Alex she knew and wanted.

There was a knock on the door, it opened, then closed.

Alex lifted her into his arms and carried her to the bed. He wrapped her in the counterpane and with his forefinger stroked her lips. 'My need for you is great, but now is not the time, my love. Esther is waiting outside. When you are refreshed, sleep awhile. I will see you at dinner.'

Grace wanted him, wanted her husband. Every time they seemed to find the moment, something or someone came between them. She watched him go out through the door, signalling Esther in. Was she ever to become a proper wife?

Grace decided to wear Alex's wedding present to her, the emerald necklace. It hung low into the curvature of her neckline and the pale grey satin gown shimmered like liquid silver.

Alex waited for her at the bottom of the stairs. 'You look beautiful, Grace. I take it your escapade has not harmed you?' He held out his hand as she stepped down into the hall.

'No, Alex, when living here a little mud and rain has never hurt me. Being Lady Rossmore does not make that any different.' That outburst was unnecessary, but her nerves were not as placid as her countenance suggested.

'I will not let you anger me tonight, Grace. I have decided our dinner and evening will be pleasantly spent. Your independence will be put aside and I shall act the perfect gentleman.' With that, he offered his arm and they went into the drawing room.

Dinner passed with light chatter, but Alex did demand Grace recount to him a full report of her beach adventure. She retold it in truth, except for meeting the unexpected Captain Olsen. This she decided was best kept as her little secret.

They retired to the drawing room and Alex offered her a game of backgammon.

'My point, I've won.' Grace clapped her hands. 'You owe me five guineas. I will take your note if you do not have the coinage, sir.'

'You show a fine hand at the game. Next time we will do the cards; how is your whist?'

'You'll have to wait to find out.' Grace held out her hand. 'Your IOU, which I will hold until after our card game.' Grace felt happy, young and even a little light-headed. Gillett had served a fine wine at dinner and she had not refused when Alex refilled her glass a third time. Unable to stifle a yawn, she said, 'Time for bed, my lord.' It came out so brazen she blushed. 'I mean . . . it is time for me to retire.'

Alex laughed out loud. 'Is that your command or invitation, my lady scarlet cheeks?' And he got up and went to move her chair. 'Your boudoir awaits, madam.' He put his hand under Grace's elbow and they left the drawing room. With each step Grace felt she was moving towards her destiny, but a glance at Alex's face told her otherwise. At her door, he tried to smile, but the effect was false and he cleared his throat before speaking. 'I have an urgent communication that must go to London at dawn. I . . .'

'It's alright, Alex, I will wait.' She opened her door and went inside.

Hours after Esther had left Grace lay looking at the canopy. She could just make out the floral pattern with the moonlight coming in the window. Alex had come back up the stairs some time ago and all movement inside his room had ceased. Was he lying awake like her? How did men's minds work? Maybe she could find a book to tell her? These questions flew out of her mind as their connecting door opened and closed.

This is what she had been waiting for, yet her heart pounded, each beat rising to her throat as Alex came towards her. His copper hair seemed to be the only part of him that had colour, as though he were a ghost shrouded in an opaque grey robe. He sat down on the edge of the bed and took her hand in his and lifted it to his lips. Between soft kisses he said, 'I am here, Grace, to fulfil my vow made before God, but I carry a heavy heart with me. My greed may be your death and I could not . . .'

'Alex . . . please, my love, don't blame only yourself for what we both want.'

'It may be so, but I have killed one woman, I am afraid that . . . I could not continue to live if it happened again.'

'Dark thoughts are not wise. We must all hope for God's mercy.'

Grace saw the tears running down his face and pulled him down to her. She found his lips and tasted the wetness as she kissed him and he clung to her.

The reversal of roles happened seamlessly. He threw back the covers, Grace feeling his hands grasp her hips, slide the nightdress upwards, past her waist, past her breasts and over her head. Body oil softened her pale, naked skin, allowing his hands to glide around her nipples. They hardened with each passing. His fingers kneaded her breasts and when he let go, Grace felt a chill to her skin as he tore at the buttons of his robe, throwing it away, for he too was naked underneath. This time his fingers kneaded her ribs, her waist. His hands lifted her hips and he bent his head and kissed her abdomen, slid kisses down into the heat of her. Grace was on fire; he could bring her to this point of hunger in just a few moments. She looked at him, his manhood was erect and she gloried in the fact that this man was hers, she was his. The past was the past; all she wanted was his fulfilment inside her. 'Alex, love me now!' she cried, as he lowered himself onto her.

Then everything went wrong.

He called out, 'No. I vowed.' His hardness softened and he rolled away from her.

Grace didn't know what to do, what to say. She reached for him, but he shouted out savagely, 'Get away from me.'

'Alex, don't say such things.'

Grace felt degraded. What did he mean? That he *couldn't* love her? Then Liddy came into her mind. Her worst fear was coming to fruition. She slipped off the bed and pulled her nightdress back on. Then she handed Alex his robe. 'I think you should go back to your own room.' Grace tried to hold back her tears, but they slipped down her cheeks.

Pushing his arms into the sleeves of his robe, Alex walked over to the connecting door. Before opening it Grace watched him take a deep breath. 'We will talk tomorrow.' Then he was gone.

After hours of sobbing into her pillow, Grace fell asleep. When she woke up her eyes hurt and she had a headache. How was she going to face Alex, knowing he didn't want her? Staying in bed wouldn't solve the problem, but Grace didn't want to get up, either. As she lay in a state of gloom, a knock sounded at the door and Esther came in.

Her maid looked flustered. 'His lordship said I was to bring your breakfast at nine. And give you this letter.'

Grace took the letter and indicated for the tray to be put onto a table by the window. 'Thank you, Esther, you may go.'

Alex's writing was distinct. Large, rounded and, as always, with his seal on the flap. She didn't know whether to open it first or have a cup of coffee. Perhaps the hot liquid would reinforce her nerve, for she feared what words were inside.

Even after the coffee, she could not bring herself to open it. She had been married seven days; surely he was not dissolving their marriage? She slid her finger under the seal and broke it.

Grace,

As I indicated last night, I had an urgent message to go to London. I have decided to go myself. Please continue to stay at Solitaire for as long as you wish.

Alex.

No endearments. No regrets. Dumped in Dorset for as long as she wished!

The fire of passion that she had felt last night was turned into a fire of fury.

Solitaire might be her refuge, but no one told her how long to stay. As Grace tore the letter into shreds, she whispered, 'I'll leave when *I* say so – today, tomorrow or maybe never, Alexander Peter Kilbraith.'

Alex couldn't remember the last time he had been so tired and bone weary. After two days' riding, to make matters worse, his horse had gone lame just before reaching Hammersmith. A busy innkeeper in the hamlet promised him a fast replacement, at an extortionate price.

Waiting in the private parlour, he sat staring into a tankard of ale and cursing himself for his cowardice. How could he have said such words to her? He couldn't face her; his shame was overwhelming. Although it had been dark outside, he had called Gillett to acquire him two horses from the blacksmith's stables in the village. As the dawn light filtered through a veil of mist he had left Solitaire House with his man, Miles. The servant grumbling a tale of woe because the luggage coach had been sent back to Rossmore

Manor and wailing he was a very poor horseman. But Alex could not have left Grace without the coach and Jenkins. Once back at Kilbraith House, he had Grace's coach, horses and her man, Benton, for his use.

A thought ran through his mind, lifting his mood for a moment; his wife's mare, Chestnut, still had two very handsome grey geldings for company.

Finishing the ale, he found Miles and left.

By mid-afternoon they arrived at Kilbraith House in Grosvenor Square. Alex hammered on the front door.

It was opened by Saunders, the butler. He stepped back and spluttered, 'Your lordship, we were not expecting you. Is something wrong?'

Alex made straight for the stairs. 'Have a bath made ready immediately and send up something to eat and a bottle of brandy.' The curt order matched Alex's stern face. Only when he had discarded his riding clothes did he regret his entrance.

A footman arrived with a tray and told him his bath would be ready in ten minutes.

'Tell Miles that I shall not need his assistance until later. I wish to take a leisurely bath and rest before dressing.'

When the door closed, Alex went to the window and looked down onto the Square and his thoughts went back to Solitaire. Again he cursed himself for not facing his wife with the honesty she deserved. How could he expect her to understand? She had said that everything had happened so fast, their courtship, betrothal and marriage. What had made him rush into it without stopping to think through the consequences? He wanted an heir, but not in exchange for Grace's life. Willy had said let the past go, but it was not that simple.

It all came full circle to Geoffrey, who would inherit. Alex shuddered. There was four years between them and in appearance they could have been twins: the copper hair, build and height, it was uncanny. But there the similarities ended. Alex, like generations before him, had worked hard to protect and strengthen the

Kilbraith name and lands. His responsibilities for their estates lay in far more than bricks and mortar, grass and trees. The livelihoods of his workers and tenant farmers depended on good management. He would not see it squandered and lost forever in Geoffrey's hands. It was a mystery where his brother's ways came from; he must be a throwback to a distant ancestor. Alex despised Geoffrey for the way he treated Rachel. She seemed to mean nothing to him and his gambling was like a disease that gnawed away his common sense. It was a bleak outlook for the future.

The water was hot and felt good. He leaned his head back on the rim and closed his eyes and immediately Grace filled his mind. She was laughing and happy a month ago when they danced together, walked in the park and planned their honeymoon. He should have realised then that she wanted a full and satisfying life with him *and* his children. Why had he been so blind? Why hadn't he stopped it then? Because it was not possible, a betrothal was not broken once sealed.

So, what was he going to do? For now, nothing. Grace was out of reach at Solitaire, out of temptation's way.

Chapter Eight

The Honourable Geoffrey Kilbraith threw down his quill and slammed the ledger closed. He got up and went to the window that overlooked Lincoln's Inn Fields. He drummed his fingers on the sill – how was he going to make ends meet until the end of the month? Alex was the first born and inherited the title, lands and money. Geoffrey resented being the half-brother, even though Alex made him a generous allowance; increased it each time Rachel produced another child. Luckily it would go up again soon; a fifth was on the way. He would have to speak to Harris about reducing the staff, including telling Mrs Vance to cut back on the housekeeping. Of course, Lucille would have to remain in her rooms at Chelsea. That was one essential he was not prepared to give up.

He heard a tap on the door and Harris announced that Sir Quentin Baines had arrived.

'Show him in, Harris.'

Geoffrey resented Quentin. He was a dandy, a man whose only concern in life was his fashionable wardrobe. His doting mother gave him money every time he took to tears and wept in her lap, like a dewy-eyed spaniel. But he was good for a loan and that's what Geoffrey wanted today.

Quentin came in dabbing his face with a silk square. 'Good day, Geoffrey. It is a fine afternoon for a trot in the park. Will you call your man to saddle up?'

Geoffrey forced a smile. 'I have a little business to do with you first.' He waved him to a chair. 'I'm a little short until my allowance arrives. I know I can rely on your good nature to help me out.' A trickle of sweat ran down his spine as Quentin's face sobered.

'Bit difficult this month, Geoff, Mother has gone to the country. No one else to tap, I'm afraid.'

'Hell, Quentin, I can't ask Alex. He's on his honeymoon somewhere by the sea, Whitecliffs, wherever that might be.'

'How was the wedding?'

'I didn't go. Aging brides and country yokels are not to my taste.'

Quentin grinned. 'How lucky I am to be Mama's only son and heir. What about your mother?'

'No. The last time I asked for a loan, she said I should be more responsible and think about my family. Moaned for over half-an-hour about why I hadn't been born more sensible like my father.'

'What about Lucille?'

'Good God, man, ask my mistress for a loan!'

'Get her to pawn those trinkets you keep giving her.'

'Please, Quentin. Just enough to cover my gambling notes. My reputation is at stake.'

'Give me the notes; let me see what you owe.'

Geoffrey opened his desk drawer and took out several sheets and handed them over.

'You're definitely having a run of bad luck. Alright, just these, don't come begging again this month. Now call for your horse.'

Rachel Kilbraith eased herself up from the sofa; she must remember to sit on the ladder-backed high chair from now on. With each confinement she found herself banished to Hawthorn Hall, the country estate that Alex had given to Geoffrey when their father died. It had several farms, woodland and a lake that she walked to each afternoon. The swans were nesting and she felt a warming towards them. Mutual maternal instinct, she thought. Perhaps it would be a girl this time; she so wanted that special bond for herself that she had when her mother was alive. She pulled the bell-cord; Nurse could bring the boys and she would sit and watch them playing until tea was served.

The afternoon was warm, without a breeze and the lake reflected the reeds like a mirror.

Rachel sat on a seat with fifteen-month-old Phillip on her lap. He was the only one who looked like her, with his oval face, blue eyes and blond hair. She hoped he would not have her slender frame, which was easily hurt, especially when Geoffrey crushed her beneath him.

Five-year-old Thomas, her eldest, stood by the lake, watching the swans. 'Why does the swan have to sit on her eggs all the time?'

'Because birds do,' said Nurse Thompson.

'Nursey, that's no answer. You don't know; I'll ask Mother.'

Rachel heard the exchange of words and sighed. Thomas was the image of Geoffrey, in looks and mannerisms: petulant and impatient. He came and stood before her. 'Why does a swan sit on her eggs, Mother?'

'To keep them warm until they hatch. Then later the baby cygnets cuddle up under her to keep warm.'

Thomas pondered the answer. 'I'll tell Nursey, so she will remember next year.'

Rachel watched Nurse Thompson sitting on the grass supervising Charles and Henry throwing a small, soft ball back and forth to each other. The nurse was a gentle-mannered woman who came from the Welsh Valleys and her lilting accent was never raised in anger against her children. She was a treasure indeed, and Rachel hoped she would be content to remain employed by her for a long, long time.

Rachel shivered. She compared herself with the swan. Four boys and increasing yearly, and only twenty-six years old. Could she cope with it? The swan managed. Did nature favour the wild-life over humans?

She called out, 'Nurse Thompson, I'm going back to rest. Please take Phillip.' It was time to go inside to her ladder-backed high chair and enjoy Cook's fruit cake and tea.

*

In the late afternoon, Geoffrey's coach drew up in front of Hawthorn Hall. He waited for a footman to open the door. He felt irritable and out of sorts. Country life was not for him.

Rachel was coming down the steps, flustered as usual. Why couldn't she behave like a lady of the *ton*? And these constant confinements were driving him mad. It seemed he only had to touch her in bed and she was off again.

'Geoffrey dear, we were not expecting you, is anything wrong?'

'Of course not. Can't the owner visit his estate? Have Jessop get my rooms ready. I will be in my study until dinner time.'

He made no attempt to touch Rachel and she stepped back as he passed. Then he slammed the study door shut.

He slumped into the chair behind his desk. Things were going from bad to worse. He had lost heavily on cards last night, which left him no option but to flee, until he could secure a loan to pay up. To console himself, he had visited Lucille. What she had told him plunged him into the pit of hell. She was with child. He had accused her of bedding with others and she had become hysterical, clinging to him, crying and begging him to believe her. It was his and only his. Rubbish, he had been with her for several years, why now? No, he would not accept it. He would cancel payment on the rooms; let her new lover pay the bills. This gave him a sense of triumph, a saving to cover his gambling notes.

His thoughts turned to Alex. Everything was easy for him. A straightforward life, no money troubles, no demanding children – a new wife to warm his bed.

An heir to steal what should be his!

Geoffrey jumped from the chair and paced up and down. It would all be his if Alex had not married. It could all be his if . . .

Geoffrey sat back down and closed his eyes to think.

The following day and with a hefty loan secured from a lowlife, shifty, money-lending rogue in his baggage, Geoffrey returned to London.

★

Geoffrey waited hidden while his coachman knocked on Lucille's door. He was arriving unannounced, the thought at the back of his mind to catch her out with her new lover.

The coach door opened. 'Miss Lucille is at home.'

He got out, the thought of catching her out replaced by a smug satisfaction she was waiting for him.

Lucille looked different. Then he realised that she had the growing shape of Rachel and this infuriated him. 'How far are you gone, trollop?'

'No matter what you say, Geoffrey, this child is yours.'

Lucille tilted her chin and her oval face, fair hair and blue eyes reminded him of someone from long ago. 'Pity there is no way to prove it.'

'Have you never thought that what we have means more to me than money and trinkets? That I haven't wanted anyone but you, since we met? Do you love no one, Geoffrey, but yourself? How I pity your wife and children.'

'Be careful what you say, Lucille. I am here, sitting on a chair that I pay for. Perhaps you can be used to my advantage. I had in mind to stop seeing you, but . . . as always you bring a heat to my body that needs to be quenched. Come here, you will not cringe from me with the excuse of harming your child.'

She went and sat on his lap, her lips trailing kisses up his cheek, into his copper hair. 'You won't leave me, will you, Geoffrey? It is too late for me to seek out a crone to rid me of this, but I will see that it's never here when you call.'

'It had better be so. Now I want the reward I am due. You cost me a fair sum, one I can't afford, but I cannot be without you. Undress me slowly . . . I have a lot of thinking to do.'

Several hours later, Geoffrey entered his club. He had come looking for Sir Quentin Baines, finding him in the reading room, hidden behind *The Times* newspaper.

'How's the shipping world? You haven't lost a ship, I hope. Damn costly business to be in, good dark earth is much safer.'

Geoffrey sat in the chair opposite. He felt strained, and his remark to Quentin was false and unnecessary.

'What's the trouble this time?'

'Nothing, can't a friend be jovial?'

'That's not a joke, Geoffrey. Ships lost at sea never are.'

'Sorry, old man.'

'What do you owe money for this time?'

'Money! Why do you always think I'm in debt? No, I have a thought I want to talk over with you. I'll treat you to a first-rate meal and a romp at Madame Chastain's, if you promise to keep what I tell you a secret.'

'My lips are sealed. Lead on.'

Outside, Geoffrey waved Quentin into the waiting hackney. This was something else that was costing money – using public coaches for his clandestine meetings.

The private room at Chastain's was a red cavern. Crimson drapes hid the windows and the wallpaper was decorated with Chinese dragons that danced in and out of the shadows cast by the flickering candlelight. The tablecloth reflected gold and made the two men's faces look like masks.

Geoffrey did not speak until the serving wench left. 'Quentin, now that Alex has married I will be pushed aside when he has an heir. His celibacy has been my trump card to the earldom. Now, within the year, I shall be nothing. Oh, he will continue my allowance, but it is not enough. I was sure he wouldn't marry again. This woman must have wound him round her little finger. She's a Miss Nobody!' He slammed his hand on the table. 'The earldom and its wealth belongs to me.'

'That is not so, Geoffrey. You know a second son only inherits if there's no heir.'

'*I know that*. But he's waited *ten years*. Good God, man, I need his money. I've been dreaming of it for so long, I can't lose it now.'

'Well, I can't see any solution. You'll have to make your estate more profitable. Spend more time at Hawthorn Hall and get to work with your manager.'

'I would die if I had to be there more than a few weeks. Society is where I belong. No. I have been thinking. We need to separate them.'

'How?'

'Plague him with Liddy's memories. He said he would never marry again. He blames himself for her death, the fool.' Geoffrey picked up his wine and downed the full glassful. 'He's back in London now.'

'It's a tricky set up, Geoffrey, but well worth the effort. Do you know why Alex is back?'

'I hear that it's urgent business. How long he intends to stay I do not know. I have someone, shall I call him Mr X, who has a lever to prise them apart. We need to work fast. Can I rely on you to be my string puller?'

'It sounds like a lot of rushing around, not quite my style . . . but it would help relieve my boredom until I join Mama in the country.'

Geoffrey held out his hand. 'A gentleman's agreement.'

Quentin hesitated.

Geoffrey extended his arm further across the table. 'To the end of boredom.'

Quentin accepted Geoffrey's handshake.

Alex flipped the pages of *The Times*, irritated by the concerto of snuffles, whistles and wheezy gurgles coming from the aged snoozers occupying most of the chairs in the lounge at White's.

Willy Wainwright came into the room and stopped next to his chair.

'Alex! Back already?'

'No, I'm a ghost.'

'Bit sharp tongued for a newly married man. I would still expect you to be away tucked up cosy with your bride. What have you done with her, left her weeping into her pillow for your love?'

Alex could feel his skin prickle with guilt. How close Willy was to the truth. 'I have urgent business that I could not leave to my agent.' The lie sat like bile in his stomach, but he was not prepared to say anything, even to his closest friend.

'I'd have to be near bankrupt to abandon Isabelle. Good grief, man, it's only just over a week since you were wed.'

'That's the reason I'm here in person, extra family responsibilities. I can't take any risks, Willy.'

Willy sat down in the chair opposite. Although first cousins, his bone structure was heavier and his complexion darker than Alex's. Frown lines creased his forehead. 'Alex, I know . . .'

'No, you don't. Leave it be, Willy. Tell me, how is Isabelle?'

At the mention of his wife's name, Willy brightened and a grin split his face, 'The greatest news you could ever want to hear. I'm going to be a father by Christmas.'

Alex's hearing dulled. Willy was chatting away, but he couldn't hear what was being said. His world was being dominated by breeding women – Rachel, Isabelle, Grace, if he succumbed to his desires. He stood up, looked around – where was the door, he needed to get out into the street, into the fresh air.

'What's the matter? Where are you going? Alex!'

Willy's answer was his retreating back.

Alex walked down one street, along another, round corners. His life was turned upside down. He prided himself on his ability to cope with emergencies, other people's predicaments, but his own – well, he was beginning to realise they were a complicated puzzle he needed a magician to sort out. One thing was clear. He couldn't hide in London forever.

Alex finally returned to his club for dinner and spent the evening until midnight playing whist with three other lonely old lords. Pocketing his winnings he asked for his cloak and left.

His coach was the only one still outside and he told his coachman to drive to Westminster Bridge. The streets were quiet, the *ton* not yet ready to leave their dancing and games until the dawn. At the bridge he got out and walked to the centre point and leaned against the side, watched the dark water swirl beneath on its way to the sea. He heard the sound of dipping paddles and whispered voices, but no boat could be seen under the starlit sky. Alex hadn't felt this hollow ache in years. That was because he had hardened his heart to any pleasures since Liddy's death. Work had been his playmate, morning, noon and night. But he had found a companionship with Grace, even a kind of love. Now he had wrecked her life; chained her to a marriage that he could not fulfil unless he let his guilt go. Willy had been right; he must move on and embrace his future with Grace. He straightened up to his full height, squared his shoulders, his mind made up. He would return to Whitecliffs, talk to Grace and start again.

Alex woke with a start. Something had happened. All was quiet, but he got out of bed and put on his robe. A scratching noise sounded on the door. Opening it, the corridor was dark and empty, but a light was fading down the stairs. Alex went back and took the single candlestick from the mantel-shelf and lit the wick from the embers in the fireplace. His bare feet made no sound as he descended the stairs. The study door was ajar and Alex could hear the voice of a girl. Pushing it wider, he moved into the room. The light from the candle only illuminated the circle around him, but out of the darkness a whisper filled the room, 'Alex, how can you desert me, our vows were for life.'

'What is going on? Come forward.'

'I cannot, my life is now in the darkness of eternity. I will wait for you, till we can be together again.'

'Stop this nonsense, come out now!' Alex swung the candle high above his head as he moved forward and the portrait of Liddy filled the light. 'No more tricks.' He moved back to the door. 'There's no way out. This is the only exit.'

Alex shouted, 'Saunders! Saunders, wake up.' There was no response. Grabbing a candle branch from a side table, he hurled it into the hall, heard the ear-piercing crash as it landed on the marble floor. Alex stood in the doorway; convinced he had the culprit trapped. Minutes later, Saunders, his nightshirt covered by his jacket, came from below stairs.

'My lord, what is happening?'

'We have an intruder hiding in my study. Bring more light; hurry, man, and get the footmen to the hall.'

Alex knew a lone female could not overpower him, so he relaxed his stance, but remained guarding the doorway.

Fifteen minutes later a dozen candle branches filled the room. No one was found.

Saunders returned. 'My lord, every corner of the house has been searched. There is no person, female or otherwise here. However, the intrusion can be explained by the fact that the boot boy and the key to the basement door are gone. I can only assume he let the intruder in. I have a footman staying in the kitchen and will have the lock changed in the morning.'

'Very well, Saunders. Go back to bed.'

Alex went into his study. He poured a brandy and sat down in the chair opposite the portrait. 'I won't believe you are here, Liddy.' The silence lulled him into memories that were his secrets alone. Deep in his subconscious he saw Liddy, young, laughing, sewing baby clothes, smiling at him. Then she was fading into a mist, growing smaller and smaller. He shouted, 'Come back, don't leave me, where is my son?'

His next recollection was the sun crawling over the treetops through the window, warming his face. For a moment he couldn't remember where he was and then felt the ache in his back where he lay twisted in the chair. His shirt was damp, clinging to his chest and his face was wet with tears. In the morning light, Liddy's portrait looked more faded than usual. Alex cursed. How could he go to Grace with such turmoil in his mind?

Chapter Nine

Grace had heard nothing from Alex since his return to London. She knew his urgent business was an excuse, but it served well for Mrs Gillett and Esther. He was, after all, Lord Rossmore, a man with many commercial investments.

She had cried all that first day and hid in the wood above the house, so that no one should see how wretched she was. Her eyes had hurt and she knew they were red and puffy. Walking had been difficult through the undergrowth and when her legs tired she sat on a fallen tree trunk and bent with her face in her hands, which made her back ache. Thirst had finally driven her back to the house.

What was to become of her? Would she be kept out of the way, banished to the country estate? Her immediate reaction had been to go to London and confront him with their dilemma. Then the thought of gossip flying round the drawing rooms cooled her temper. He had decided to let their marriage simmer in the pot of uncertainty. Until she heard from him she would live at Solitaire.

Life settled into a routine. The weather was warm and the sea calm. Allowing for the tides, Grace walked along the beach, sometimes taking Esther, but mostly alone, her thoughts running wild asking why he was doing this to her? This fuelled her anger against him and, knowing he would disapprove, she deliberately went out alone, riding her horse, Chestnut, over the headlands. She rarely went inland, although the fields were green with corn, heralding the harvest to come. The lowing cry of the cows, bereft of their calves saddened her; it was too much like her own feelings.

This morning, Grace had abandoned her hat and the wind whipped her dark hair behind her like the mane of the horse she rode across the cliff tops towards the village. Reaching the road, Captain Olsen's house came into view. It stood solid and square, the red brick acting like a guardian over the village cottages. A family house, three floors high. She had never met its owner and now it was rented to the tall, blond-haired Norwegian. He must be very lonely in such a large establishment. As though her thoughts came to life, the captain appeared at the door.

'Lady Rossmore, good morning.' He raised his hat and waved it at her. 'A fine mount you have there.' Not waiting for an acknow-ledgement, he walked down the steep path and stood in the road.

Grace had no option but to rein Chestnut in and the horse snorted and sidled as she pulled it under control. 'Good morning, Captain Olsen. That is a foolish action, sir, to step in front of a trotting horse. Do you not value your life?'

'It is a risk worth taking, if it will promote our acquaintance.'

'A bold comment, Captain; I will put it down to you being a foreigner.'

He looked up, a flash of anger in his eyes.

Grace felt her cheeks burn, for she was beginning to like the unconventional sea captain. 'You speak English very well, my compliments to you.'

'Your King George has much to answer for, madam. My Eng-lish is a necessity. I seek only your company for a short while. Is it permissible to ask you to walk with me in the village?'

This was becoming awkward; being seen with him in a public place could cause embarrassment for Alex. This thought sent her temper soaring, something she found difficult to control of late. There was one rule for him – yet another for her.

'You may, sir, walk with me to where I will continue my ride over the downs.' Olsen held up his hands to help her dismount. 'Thank you, Captain.'

He took hold of the reins. 'It is I who must do the thanking, Lady Rossmore.' He stepped beside Grace and led the mare into the village, its hooves kicking up puffs of dust on the dirt road. Grace saw several women out shopping and knew by the way they nodded their heads that whispered words were being said about her and the newcomer. To overcome her discomfiture, Grace stopped at a window and looked at the display of fishing tackle. 'Tell me, Captain Olsen, do you have such contraptions on your ship?'

'No, ma'am. My ship and cargo has no need for dangling nets or lines. My cook does well enough with the supplies we take on board from the harbours. Salt pork and potatoes make a good meal for me.'

'Why are you not with your ship, Captain? I must admit I find it strange that a seagoing man is living in a house – on the land.'

There was a bitter sound in Olsen's voice when he replied, 'She's in for repairs at Weymouth. We were caught by a storm. I should not be in England, but home in Norway. It is costing me dearly, both in time and money.'

Grace could see his anger and it changed his manner into something she was not sure she liked. 'I'm sorry to hear that.' She moved away and walked on. When the Captain came alongside her a few seconds later, his attitude had changed back to the charming man she had encountered on the beach.

'May I offer you some refreshment before you continue your ride?'

Grace looked at him. 'Refreshment? I do not understand you, sir.'

'At the inn, madam; it is a warm day, a little ale to quench your thirst.'

'Are you quite mad, sir? A lady does not go into an inn with a stranger.'

'Oh. So I'm a stranger now. You deign to speak to me on the beach and walk with me along the road, but refuse my offer of refreshment. I do not understand the mannerism of the English.'

Grace had not meant to be rude, but he was totally untutored in his ways.

'I'm sorry, Captain Olsen. The *ton* of London Society does not allow such liberties.'

'But you are not in London, madam.'

That was true. Grace always felt freer here in Whitecliffs, like a girl of the country, not a lady of the restrictive city. Who was there to tittle-tattle, except those she had seen whispering earlier? They never went outside the county, let alone visit London. And they certainly wouldn't be included in the drawing rooms of Society. Again, her rebellion surfaced and before she could think through the consequences, she said, 'Very well, Captain. Shall we see what the good innkeeper has to offer?'

Seated in the Smugglers Inn parlour under the low ceiling, Grace thought the Captain's large body appeared to fill the room. Luckily there were no other occupants and now that she had time to reflect, she knew this was wrong.

'Would you like ale, madam?'

Grace kept her gaze lowered. She was aware of his eyes looking at her deep green riding dress. She blessed the design, with its high-buttoned neckline. This rebellious reaction to Alex was putting her in a compromising position, one she needed to end now. 'No, thank you. I must go . . . this was not a good idea.' In her haste to rise, she knocked the table and the Captain's big hands clutched the edge to steady it. Lord, she was making things worse; the innkeeper's wife was nodding her head and smirking.

'Please, wait.' Captain Olsen started to rise from his chair.

Grace ignored him and rushed out of the door. She was attempting to mount Chestnut by the time he arrived.

'Allow me to help, Lady Rossmore.' His words were harsh and sarcastic as he cupped his hands for her booted foot. 'You cannot flee until you are in the saddle.'

This was beyond endurance. More gossip to be spread around, but she needed his assistance. No way was she going to raise her skirt, but by not doing so, her toe caught in the hem and she toppled into Captain Olsen's arms. Grace smelt the tang of soap, felt the cloth of his coat brush against her cheek and his strong arms steady her. Then hold her away.

'This is more than I bargained for.' There was no warmth to his tone. 'Your foot, Lady Rossmore, if you please.'

Grace was tongue-tied, flustered and wanted to die. She stepped back and without looking at him, placed her foot into his hands.

From the saddle, she managed a smile. 'Thank you.'

'For the non-refreshment or the . . .'

Grace kicked Chestnut's flank into moving; she didn't want to hear the rest of his words.

It rained for two days.

Grace had not been out of the house, using the time to write letters she did not want to send. Pretending to Isabelle Wainwright that everything was well, for she would know from Willy that Alex was back in London – alone! She was concerned about Rachel. Geoffrey had declined their wedding invitation, saying it would be too taxing for Rachel's delicate health. A proven excuse, one Rachel had voiced when she and Alex had visited her the day after their betrothal ball. Then there was Aunt Matilda. Here was a lady who did not mince her words and if she thought there was trouble between Alex and herself, firecrackers would be sparking long before the fifth of November. To keep her aunt in the loop of deception her words were minimal, happy and content with staying in Dorset. She just hoped Aunt Matilda and Alex did not meet face to face. Although society manners would not allow fractious words spoken between them.

A shaft of sunlight pierced the window and Grace saw that the grey rain clouds were breaking. She could go out at last. Running across the hall into the study and opening the glass door into the garden, she stood breathing in the air. Not caring for the damage the wet grass would do to her shoes and dress, she went down the steps into the sunken garden. With each second the sun strengthened and the flower petals dripped raindrops like tears.

Grace was so lonely. This was not a self-imposed exile, but one forced on her by Alex. She didn't know if she could endure his silence much longer.

There was a movement behind her.

'Here's a letter for you, Miss Grace. Not from London, though.' Mrs Gillett's tone reflected her disapproval of his lordship's absence, although not a word of criticism passed her lips.

'Thank you, Gillie.'

The seal was embossed with a ship and Grace had a premonition of the sender. The invitation was, indeed, from Captain Olsen, inviting her to his card evening tomorrow. Obviously, it would include other people from the area, but she hesitated to accept such a blatant disrespect of her position without Alex.

She would go riding, think about it, but she knew the answer would be no.

Grace wasn't really sure how she had come to be in Captain Olsen's house. Then her subconscious voiced the word – liar. Her resolve to decline his invitation went out of the window last evening when she sat eating a lone dinner at Solitaire. Alex's refusal to even write a letter was paining her deeper and deeper. Could a heart break in two? This in turn made her angry and she had written her acceptance and sent Gillett immediately to deliver it.

The drawing room's dark red, embossed walls spoke of an older occupant before the Captain, since he had not been in residence long enough to have it refurbished. Two card tables were set between the heavy oak furniture, leaving little room to move around and pipe smoke circled to the high ceiling, cloaking the cobwebs that hung in the corners.

'You make an excellent partner, Lady Rossmore,' said the Reverend Clive. 'We will go home with a few extra guineas to spend.' He gave Captain Olsen a brilliant smile. 'Your loss, Captain, my wife is too much of a nervous player. I can see through her bluffs every time.'

The gathering, besides the Clives, included Mr Donald Patterson, Mr Peter Brawn and their wives. Both gentlemen connected with shipping. The evening had passed pleasantly enough, but Grace had been conscious of Hugo Olsen's eyes on her.

'Your winnings, my Lady Rossmore.' Captain Olsen was holding out three golden guineas. 'A fair exchange, for such charming company all evening.'

Grace blushed. She was not *his*; she was Alex's wife, albeit in name only. But words to contradict him would only give Mary Clive tattle to repeat. 'Thank you, Captain.' Holding out her gloved hand, she kept her fingers straight, but he wrapped his hand around them and dropped the coins into her palm, closing her fingers. He held them, his eyes locked to hers, forcing her to be the first to look away.

'Captain Olsen!' Mary Clive's shocked voice made Grace snatch her hand away.

'Mrs Clive?' The Captain's fair brows arched.

Mary Clive rose from her seat, now flustered at her exclamation. 'Thank you for a delightful evening. Come, Reverend, it is time we were gone!'

Grace also rose and made to follow them.

The Reverend turned. 'Lady Rossmore, is your coachman bringing the carriage for you?'

'Yes, thank you. He has been waiting outside all evening.'

Grace saw the smug look on Mary Clive's face. They would be the talk of the village after church tomorrow.

Captain Olsen did not attend church.

The small rectangular stone building seated only thirty parishioners.

Grace sat in the pew reserved for her when she was at Solitaire, with Esther and Mr and Mrs Gillett on either side. The absence of Alex emphasised his desertion, not only to her, but to the whole village. There seemed to be more worshippers than usual and she became aware that those who had not arrived early were standing on both sides.

104

Halfway through the service she saw the Reverend Clive's eyes on her while he preached on the loyalty and devotion of family life. The ladies of the congregation could not miss his stare, and no doubt Mary Clive had been busy tittle-tattling long before the service started.

It was an overlong sermon and when Grace came out into the sunshine the first person she saw was Captain Olsen walking towards her. He never broke his pace as he acknowledged and smiled at the families he passed.

'Good day, Grace. You are a flower of perfection, in your pink dress.'

Grace could not believe her ears. What was the man trying to do? Ruin her reputation completely? 'Captain Olsen, this has gone far enough. You will not call me by my given name and I will not allow you to comment on my attire.' Her voice, growing louder with each word, caused all conversation around her to cease. Every face was turned in their direction.

'Please accept my sincere apologies, Lady Rossmore. Put it down to the old sea dog in me. I seldom have the pleasure of female company when aboard my ship.'

Grace's face became crimson. 'Esther, please ask Gillett to call the coach, immediately.' Without a word to the Captain, she walked away along the path to the lych-gate As she arrived Jenkins slowed the horses and Gillet opened the coach door.

The short drive was unbearable and both Mrs Gillett and Esther kept their gazes lowered, seeming to find their gloves of great interest.

As soon as Gillett had opened the front door, Grace left the coach, and running up the steps did not stop until she was in her bedchamber. Anger, pride and a near hatred for Alex overwhelmed her and she burst into tears. Great sobs burst in her throat and she marched like a military guard up and down the room. She knew she would be sick if she didn't control her feelings. Then her thoughts turned to Alex. There he was in London, amidst his cronies, wining and dining, gambling into the early hours, drunk and asleep until noon. The only sure thing was that he was not bedding a mistress. This thought made her laugh, but turned into a gurgling sound, as she started to cry again. To hell with how her stomach was heaving, sick bile was preferable to the loneliness without him.

Chapter Ten

Geoffrey sat in the riverside inn and threw a pouch across the table. It was taken by fingers smelling of tar with black and broken nails.

'He needs money and 'as no love of England, he'll do what you want. I wouldn't mind doin' it meself, as it's gold yer offering.'

'If this information is false, I know of someone who will find you. Now get out of here, but remember, if you want your other guineas . . .' Geoffrey let the sentence hang.

The sailor backed away. 'Oh, it's true alright and I'll be back, *m'lord*.'

His drawn out *m'lord* made Geoffrey rise from his chair. How dare scum like this question his status? But looking round at the sawdust-covered floor, rough tables and the clientele – men from the docks, harlots with their painted faces – made him eager to leave. Tossing a few coins down, he followed the departing sailor. The hackney coach he had taken from Oxford Street was waiting and he instructed the driver to take him to Chelsea.

'Is everything going to plan?' Lucille took Geoffrey's coat and wrinkled her nose as the smell of the waterside inn wafted from the cloth.

'All is well, my love. Come here, I have a little trinket for you.'

Lucille's growing shape was beginning to show clearly under her dress and her full breasts were squeezed tight into the high bodice. 'I need to buy new dresses. My old ones are showing my condition too much. Why do you want me to keep these on? They are making me look ugly. Do you not want me to look appealing for you, my sweet?' Lucille pouted her lips. 'Why, Geoffrey?'

'I have my reasons. Turn round.'

Lifting a circle of pearls from a velvet case, he slipped them over her fair hair and down round her neck. 'Your reward,' he whispered, kissing her bare shoulder, trailing kisses to her neck. He turned her round, pulling her towards him. 'Now it is time for my reward.' Her rounded bulge brought Lucille to a halt and Geoffrey looked down at the gap between them. 'Good lord, are you growing this fast that I cannot get near you now?'

'Of course I am. Surely, you of all people should know what is happening to me. I cannot change just to suit your visits. I am having your child, Geoffrey, and you will have to make allowances until I have come full term and delivered this . . . this . . .' Lucille burst into tears and covered her face with her hands.

'A brat conceived and born out of wedlock; it will never have my name.' Geoffrey's face was impassive as if he were discussing the weather. He picked up his jacket and handed it to her. 'Help me on with this. I don't think I want to be fondling around that bulge tonight.'

'Geoffrey, please, don't go, we can still make . . .'

'No. Just remember to be ready when you are wanted again.'

He left, slamming the front door. He looked for the hackney. Fool, he had let it go, the waiting cost would have emptied his pocket. He started walking, began thinking and his sluggish gait became a sprightly stride.

Alex sat in his study looking at the glass of brandy in his hand. The clock chimed ten. The evening was early for the *ton*, but he had no inclination to go anywhere. The door opening broke his thoughts and Saunders announced that Lord Wainwright wished to see him.

Willy was dressed for a night out. 'Good evening, Alex. I haven't seen you at the club, so I thought . . . good grief, man, you look terrible . . . is anything wrong?'

'No.' Alex cursed inwardly; company was the last thing he needed.

'I came to ask if you would accompany me to Lady Goodchild's musical evening.'

'I think not, Willy. Squeaking sopranos and ill-timed notes do not appeal to me tonight.'

'You have to talk about it, Alex. Isabelle heard from her maid that . . .'

'Good God, is that all women have to do – repeat everything they hear?' Alex sprang from the chair, spilling his brandy onto the carpet. 'And I suppose she sent you to find out if it is true?'

Willy stood his ground. 'Then talk to me about it.'

In truth, the mystery of the night intruder had been playing on his mind. 'I don't believe in ghosts, but I heard one in this study. How this "phantom" person got out could only have been when I stepped further into this room. In the poor light of one candle she slipped past me. But it doesn't answer the question – why?'

'No, it doesn't. Why are you back from Whitecliffs? Don't fob me off with business. Remember, I've known you for over thirty years – the real reason, if you please?'

Alex sat back down and waved Willy to sit in the chair opposite.

'Fear, Willy, plain simple fear of the woman. Oh, not Grace, but what she represents. My wife! She deserves love, loyalty and respect. All of which I have failed to give her. Liddy sits like a judge over me. Look at her portrait, those eyes follow me round the room, sometimes loving, at others condemning. I have to solve this problem myself before I can face Grace again.'

'Isabelle had a letter from her today.'

'Of course, the second reason you are here. Is everything alright?'

'All is sunny and rosy at Solitaire according to Grace. What the hell is wrong with you both? You here, looking like a dead man, and bubbly words from Grace, which we know are a lie. Go back, Alex.'

'You make it sound so easy. I can't even write a letter and I certainly don't expect one from her.'

Alex sat thinking about the note he had left. Perhaps she never wanted to see him again. This thought brought him up short; is that what he wanted?

'Come to Lady Goodchild's evening soirée; the company might cheer you up.'

'You think so?'

'Yes, get your cloak, my coach is outside.'

Alex got up. 'I put my sad, miserable self in your hands, Willy. Let's hope she has a talented entertainer.'

It was a small gathering and Alex was surprised that he enjoyed both the singer and the company. After supper several of the men left for more bawdy entertainment at the inns, or Madame Chastain's gambling tables.

Alex sat on a sofa and looked about the room. It was a family room and the pale pink, embossed wallpaper reminded him of Grace's bedchamber at Kilbraith House. Her delight of the rose-patterned pink walls, her pleasure riding across Kensington and their decision to marry.

Willy was deep in conversation and looked settled for another hour. He got up and went over.

'Good evening, Lord Hinlock. Willy, may I use your coach to take me home?'

'Home! The night is young, I thought we might take a turn at White's, win or lose a few guineas at the tables.'

'Not tonight. I'll send your coach back immediately.'

Alex found Lady Goodchild sitting in a chair by the fire.

'Thank you for accepting an uninvited guest. It has been a most pleasant evening.'

'Let us call it a return pleasure for your wonderful ball to celebrate your betrothal to Miss Matthews. I look forward to inviting your wife to tea when she returns to London.'

Alex wasn't sure how to answer this, so he bowed, smiled and said, 'I will pass on your felicitations.'

Outside the rain fell like a shifting veil, making the row of coaches shine from the lighted lamp hanging above the doorway.

Signalling Willy's coachman, Alex got in and gave instructions to take him home. For the first time since arriving back in London he relaxed, the wine and brandy dulling his thoughts and when the coach stopped, he got out and waved it away.

A woman's voice came from behind him. 'Alex, where have you been? Why have you left me alone?' Swinging round, Alex could see only blackness beyond the light shining down from his own doorway.

'Go away. I know you're an impostor. What do you want?'

'You are mine for always. She cannot take you away from me.'

Alex stepped into the darkness, his arms thrashing from under his cloak, grabbing right, left and centre. Knowing that whoever was playing these tricks was there.

'Come to me, my love, I'm here waiting for you.'

'What the hell is the meaning of this? Come into the light so I can see you.'

In his anger, he did not hear the sound of the wheels or the rattling harness. Then out of the dark, two horses and a coach raced towards him.

'Liddy, look out!' Alex whirled in a circle. 'Liddy, run,' and he followed on into the black night. Something hit his shoulder and he pitched forward, the coach wheels running past within a few inches of his back. Then his foot caught in a pothole, sending him face down on the road. He lay still, the breath knocked out of him. It was the sound of another coach in the distance that made him get up. His ankle gave way as he stepped forward and he limped to his front door.

Where the hell was Saunders? Alex banged with his fist. 'Saunders, open this door, where the devil are you?'

Within seconds, the door widened and the butler rushed to help his master.

'My lord, what has happened?'

'Stop blabbering and get me into my study.'

Saunders lowered Alex into an armchair. 'Will I call Miles, you need attention.'

'Yes, but first pour me a brandy.'

Alex rested his head back and closed his eyes. Who was this mystery woman who spoke to him? In his panic he had called her Liddy, but he knew this was not so.

Saunders said, 'Your brandy, my lord.'

Opening his eyes, Alex's vision was blurred, but he took the glass and downed the liquid in one gulp. 'Another, Saunders, before you fetch Miles.'

Miles insisted on getting the doctor after he had examined the ankle. 'Just a precaution, my lord, I don't think it is broken.' Supported by Miles, he went up the stairs to his bedchamber.

John Winter arrived, bleary eyed at three o'clock. Testing the ankle for movement his verdict was positive. 'My medical attentions are unnecessary, Alex. It is only a swollen muscle and will heal on its own. A bandage would help and your man can put on one of his herbal concoctions.'

'Thank you, John. Miles fusses, but I indulge him.'

Later, left to sleep, Alex began wondering who was gaining anything from this fantasy of Liddy's ghost. But one thing had come out of it. He wasn't going anywhere until he could approach Grace as her fit and able husband.

Time did little to improve Alex's frustration. He refused to stay in bed and hobbled around his room. The space seemed to decrease with each hour and at five o'clock he summoned Miles to help him dress, so that he could go to his club. When he arrived, the news of his accident seemed to have spread like fanned fire on heathland.

'How's the leg, old man, too many tipples at the inns?'

'Don't let her ladyship know where you went to get that gammy foot.'

'Heard you were seeing things, Rossmore? Nasty accident, that ankle wound.'

Alex turned on the last remark.

Sir Quentin Baines raised his glass in a salute. 'To your recent marriage, Lord Rossmore.'

Alex schooled his face into a smile. 'Thank you, Baines. I will pass on your good wishes.'

Tension was mounting in Alex. It seemed he was becoming the talk of London, both by the tabbies and the toms. Just then Willy came in and the jokers moved aside.

'Thank God you've come. I feel like the prize bull on show. Let's go in to supper, a full stomach may improve my temper.'

'The solution is in your own hands, but I agree, food may improve both your manner and your looks.'

Willy had persuaded him to come to The Blue Parrot, a tavern down by the river in Blackfriars. Lanterns lit the room, some hanging from beams, others placed on the tables. Smoke from sailors' pipes spiralled to reach the caged parrots that hung from the ceiling. They squawked and flapped, their cries mingling with the accented Irish and foreign tongues. The elite *ton* at the gambling tables were being plied with tankards of beer by the serving wenches in readiness for the gaudily dressed, painted faced women offering their services for a romp in the rooms upstairs.

Alex hadn't indulged in this sort of escapade since he took over the earldom. He shouldn't have come. He sat on a chair by the wall next to a shelf, where he placed his glass. His eyes wandered from table to table – cards were the tavern's main choice. Nearest to him were four foreign sailors, their guttural voices loud and they were playing for high stakes – captains, no doubt.

One of the men said something that amused the others. Alex leaned forward and concentrated on his stilted English.

'. . . The *Clementine* is being repaired. He just made Weymouth. I hear his crew fought bad storms in the Atlantic and the damage is great. They were lucky not to be down with ol' Neptune. He's rented a house. I wonder what that's about.'

There were mutters and the game ended. A new hand was dealt. 'I hear he might be bedding a titled lady.' They banged on the table in support of the declaration. 'A victory for Norway, gentlemen.'

113

Alex picked up his glass and sipped.

The pipe smoke now hung low around the tables, cloaking the men in a fog. The prostitutes' laughter came over shrill and forced as they coaxed the beaux to drink rum instead of the cheap ale. When they were drunk enough, they guided them to the tables set apart from the rabble to be fleeced by the cardsharks.

Again, the accented voice. 'She lives at a place called Solitaire, fitting for a lonely lady, don't you think?'

One of the men slapped a card down with a triumphant call, 'Mine, gentlemen.' He scooped up the pile of guineas. 'Off to my bed. See you another time.' Before any of the other players could move or speak, he was making for the door.

Alex could feel every muscle in his face tighten. He fought for control and calm but failed and threw the remaining liquid down his throat.

He found Willy playing whist in a private room and bid him goodnight. In his coach he exploded in a stream of oaths and hammered his stick on the floor. In the past week his life was the talk of the town. Whichever way he turned, there was mayhem: Liddy, his marriage and now Grace with some foreign captain.

When the coach stopped, Alex was still cursing. To hell with women; why hadn't he remained as he was – unattached and sane?

The servants in Kilbraith House retired early when the master went out for the evening. Only Saunders and Miles would be up.

A knife slid between the two half-paned pantry windows and pushed the lock open. A small thin boy opened the bottom half and climbed in. He crept through the kitchen and took a key from a hook and unlocked the outside basement door. A man came in and handed the boy a bundle, then crossed to the inside door that led to the passage and went through. The boy crouched in the darkest corner and waited, clutching his reward in his arms. He waited an hour. The passage door opened and the man returned and left. The boy locked the door and replaced the key on its hook. He departed the way he had come in.

At the end of the square they stopped. The boy held out his hand and the man took a pouch from his pocket.

'This is to keep your tongue tied in your mouth. My master has a long arm should what we have done reach a magistrate's ears.'

'Don't fret yerself, if you've kept yer promise.'

'*The Farthing* sails on the morning tide. The bo'sun is expecting you. There are a few extra pennies for a ferryman to row you out.' He dropped the pouch into the boy's hand. 'Be off with yer now. Make sure you get to the docks by dawn.'

'Could yer maybe spare an extra sixpence for good luck?'

The man cuffed the boy round the head. 'Go, before I change me mind and dump yer body in the river.'

The boy ran off.

The man walked away in the opposite direction.

The sounds of London had ceased, yet Alex could not sleep. He sat in a chair and mulled over the foreigner's remarks about a sea captain and Grace. He reasoned it could not be true. She was his wife. Such rumours could harm her position, especially in London. He had a strong standing in the *ton* but the old tabbies loved to bring down a lady, even if it was only for a short while. Grace did not deserve that. He was the one who had thrown her into a state of bewilderment and revenge. The word revenge sat on his tongue; it did not fit her nature. No, he wiped that from his mind. He looked at the connecting door to Grace's bedchamber. He had not been in there since his arrival from Whitecliffs. Without her being here there was little point. But now he had a desire to be where she had set out her combs and brushes, oils and scent pots. Bury his face in the clothes she had left in readiness for her return after the honeymoon. Lie on the bed they should be sharing. It was an over-whelming need.

He stood and picked up a branch of candles from a table and went to the door. The brass handle felt cold to his touch and sent a shiver down his back. The room was dark except for a narrow strip of moonlight from the partly closed curtains. In its beam, Alex could see dresses strewn on the floor. He walked forward, bringing the candlelight to the middle of the room, shoes and undergarments were tangled together. The dressing table was covered in powder, bottles half-emptied and there was a strong scented smell. He bent and ran his fingers over a satin gown.

Alex held his candle to the wick of those on the dressing table. In the added light he could see they were Grace's clothes. Alex flung open the door into the corridor. Turning right, he went to the end, lifted a door catch hidden in the panelling and climbed the narrow stairs to an attic. Holding the candle branch high, it made a circular halo around him as he moved in the darkness of the windowless room. Four wooden trunks stood side by side along the back wall. He placed the candle branch on a round marble table and knelt down in front of the first trunk. His shirt was damp and it clung to his body; bile rose in his throat as he pushed the lid open. Liddy's clothes were there, as neatly folded as when he had packed the trunk, allowing no one else to touch them. Alex fingered the top dress. Why had he come up here? Why had his first thought been that Liddy had ravaged Grace's room? Who was playing with his mind? And why? This was the recurring thought that plagued him.

He raised his head and called to the room, 'No, Liddy, you are not doing this. Someone needs me to think it is you, but I will not be drawn into such a nightmare.' His breathing was harsh, his shoulders rising and falling as he fought to control his grief. He closed the lid and got up and, taking the candle branch, went back down to the corridor. The silence was uncanny. Breathing slowly, he went back into Grace's bedchamber. With the initial shock over, he saw a white nightgown spread full length and the sleeves crossed over the bodice on the counterpane. Alex willed his mind not to see Liddy, but she was there, with her fair curls and blue eyes, flushed cheeks, waiting for him. Alex tore his eyes away from the bed and turned away. He went out into the corridor shouting, 'Saunders, Saunders, wake up. Get the household up, get everyone up. I want to know what's going on.' He went down the stairs, his copper hair glinting with golden highlights in the candlelight, the white evening shirt open at the neck, his chest straining at the buttons as his breath came in great gulps. 'Saunders, wake up, man. How the devil is someone getting into this house without you knowing?'

The sounds of the house stirring did little to appease him.

Saunders appeared buttoning his jacket, his hair uncombed and as short of breath as his master. 'My lord, have we been invaded again?'

'Yes. By evil spirits that are bent on driving me mad so that I will end up in Bethlem. I want every door and window checked. I want the staff interviewed. I want . . . get me a bottle of brandy. When everything is checked, come to my study.'

Alex opened the door to the one place he had always considered his refuge from the outside world and stopped. What would he find in here? He held up the candles and walked to his desk, the light not strong enough for him to see far. The expected villainous message scratched in blood across his papers was not there. He dropped down into his chair, put his elbows on the desk and ran his fingers through his hair. Slowly his tangled thoughts settled.

Saunders came in with a tray, placed it on a table and then began lighting the other candle branches. Alex glanced around; there was nothing amiss in his study.

'I shall return as soon as possible, my lord. The kitchen door is locked. The footman assures me he secured all the doors at ten o'clock.'

'What has happened here tonight was planned. Will you please fetch Mrs Fielding? I need to speak to both of you.'

Alex poured a glass of brandy and sat in the chair facing Liddy's portrait. He studied her features, something he hadn't done for a long time. There was no malice in her eyes, no cruel twist to her lips and no hatred for him. They had loved and created a son. And in truth both had known the risks.

The accident in the road had been no careless handling of the reins by a coachman, it had been deliberate. What he didn't know was whether the incident meant to maim or kill?

Fifteen minutes later Saunders and Mrs Fielding arrived. The housekeeper was dressed and presentable. Saunders had also taken the opportunity to attire himself likewise.

Alex stood up. 'An unearthly hour to be called upon, but the sooner the house is back to normal, the better for all. The intruder tonight has vandalised Lady Rossmore's bedchamber. I would like this to be your priority this morning, Mrs Fielding. I want all the toiletries replaced, if any of the gowns are damaged, see they are re-ordered, not repaired. And I impress on you both the importance that this evil act must not be spoken of outside this house. Any, and I repeat, any person from this household will be dismissed instantly, should I hear it become gossip in the houses, clubs or taverns of London.'

Saunders spoke. 'That will be conveyed to everyone, my lord. Please be assured not a word will pass through these walls to the gossips.'

'Thank you. Now back to your beds, the morning light will soon be upon us.'

Saunders bowed and Mrs Fielding curtsied and left.

Alex poured a large draught of brandy and sat down behind his desk. He looked at his first wife's portrait.

'What is it that I have, and they want?'

Chapter Eleven

Grace pulled on the reins to bring her mount to a halt. She had discarded her jacket, letting the warm sunshine seep through her dress onto her skin. Her face had taken on a colour that her London cousins would abhor. There had been no message from Alex and she found her feelings becoming more rebellious. She dismounted and stroked Chestnut's muzzle. 'Did I so misjudge him?' In a mute reply, the horse moved closer to her. 'No, of course not. I must be patient, let him sort out his troubles, but it is very hard for me.' Grace let her gaze roam over the grassland and out across the sea. A perfect day and alone, with space and time to think unhappy thoughts, *what did she really know about Alex, about his deep inner feelings – nothing. He had presented her with only what he wanted her to see. But hadn't she done the same? Evaded any mention of Simon, her lover, from her past?* She turned and looked back towards the village, nestled in the valley between the two headlands. The square house of Captain Olsen stood out impressively above the cottages and a coach was standing outside. The front door opened and the Captain escorted a man down the path. He was not a local squire by his dress and their stance and mannerisms did not speak of a friendly parting when the coach pulled away up the hill. The Captain watched until it was out of sight, then pulled his shoulders square and returned to the house. A few minutes later, two other men left, this time from the back entrance. These were local fishermen; a strange mixture of guests.

*

A sealed letter was on the hall table when Grace returned to Solitaire. It was what she had been waiting for, yet she could not touch it. Was it good or bad news? When she reached out to pick it up, her hand trembled.

After luncheon, Esther helped her change into a light muslin dress for her afternoon tea in the garden. The letter lay on the bed, still unopened. Should she read it now or take it with her? Better now, if it was to be bad news . . . She ran her finger under the seal.

Dear Grace,

My apologies for not writing sooner, but my engagements have been many.

Unfortunately, I have had a slight accident to my ankle. I shall return to Whitecliffs soon.

Yours Alex

What sort of message was this – non-committal, and how serious an accident?

Grace threw it back on the bed. Anger and relief mingled together. The message said nothing, except that he would return soon. Was there really an injury? Were these few words an excuse for him not to return? Why didn't he ask her to go to him? What was he hiding? With each new thought, she saw how much he didn't want her. Well, that suited her; two could play at being evasive. She sat down at a small table by the window and snatched a sheet of paper from the rack.

My condolences, Alex. I hope your injury is healing. I am quite happy here at Solitaire, please do not hurry to join me. I am getting reacquainted with the local society and enjoying my walks along the beach and riding across the headlands.

Grace.

She sealed and addressed it as the teardrops splashed onto her hand. The tension in her shoulders moved to her head. A pain, like an iron helmet squeezing tight, made her close her eyelids. She wanted to go back to London, but pride would not allow it. He had not asked.

To fill her lonely days, Grace had sent out tea invitations and Solitaire House and its garden had buzzed with ladies' chatter.

Now, in the small sitting room she was replying to Lady Culver, accepting her offer to attend an afternoon garden party. She had been very wary of accepting evening soirées since her embarrassment with Captain Olsen. In fact, she had seen little of him, although she knew from Esther's gossiping that he was attending nearly all the social functions. She pondered the Captain. He was very handsome with his fair hair and blue eyes and his accented English speech, and it gave him a mysterious aura. Perhaps he would be there? For all his disregard of protocol, she found him quite enjoyable company.

Grace offered a small curtsey to the Dowager Lady Culver. 'Good afternoon.'

'Lady Rossmore, a delight to see you. Lord Rossmore is still indisposed?'

Grace saw the raised eyebrows and made a non-committal murmur, allowing Lady Culver to take her arm and steer her further into the garden. It was set out in a festive mode of small circular tables with serving maids and footmen dressed in matching colours of blue and green.

'Mrs Clive is sitting alone, would you care to join her?' Grace was given no time to reply as her ladyship walked her over to the table, beckoned for refreshments, then left them to welcome another new guest.

'May I sit down?'

Despite the warm afternoon, the rector's wife was dressed in a dark brown, long-sleeved dress with a high neckline. Her face flushed. 'Of course, Lady Rossmore. How are you?'

'Very well, thank you.'

Two glasses of lemonade were put before them, and the silence lengthened.

Grace was aware of the discomfort the other woman was experiencing. And she had no intention of smoothing the ripples of dislike between them.

Mary Clive cleared her throat. 'Do you stay much longer in Whitecliffs, Lady Rossmore?'

'Maybe, the weather is very fine at the moment.'

'The Reverend and I are planning a little dinner party soon. May I send an invitation?'

Grace wanted to laugh; the woman had got herself into deep water and was thrashing to get out. 'Yes. Please excuse me; I see Mrs Willmott has arrived.'

Grace was so intent on escaping she did not see Captain Olsen until he stepped in front of her. 'Good afternoon, Lady Rossmore.' He clicked his heels and bowed low.

'Captain Olsen.' This man was like a ghost who seemed to appear from nowhere. 'I would not have thought afternoon tea parties were a sea captain's brew?'

'When a charming guest such as you is on the list, how could I refuse?'

'Your tongue has not improved since last we met. Will you let me pass?' He did not move. 'Please.'

In response, the Captain took her hand and placed it through the crook of his arm. 'I must show you the countryside views; they are quite stunning from the bottom of the garden.' It was not a question, but a statement. Grace knew all eyes would be upon her if she made a scene, but looking towards Mary Clive, she saw the woman staring at them. The damage was already done. Let the spiteful old crones tittle and she squeezed the Captain's arm and gave him her best flirting smile.

The path led through a walled rose garden and a few of the bushes were beginning to open their buds. At the end was a wooden door. The Captain opened it and led Grace through to a view of the countryside spread to the horizon. Under the blue sky farmhouses and barns clustered together. Carts, horses and the figures of men and women were dotted in the fields, their voices unheard in the still air.

'It is like the calm of a sea with no wind, when the sails are furled and the men sit on the deck, mending their clothes, humming a tune. We see two different environments, but with the same soothing peacefulness.'

Grace felt the calm. It eased her turmoil. 'Yes, a moment I would like to keep with me forever.'

'Grace, I cannot keep calling you Lady Rossmore. I know you feel this is improper, for I have not yet met your husband, but we have a bond, a loneliness that we can dispel for a few hours. Will you allow me to call on you as a friend?'

No, this is not what she wanted. She wanted her loneliness dispelled with Alex, either here or in London, but that was not what *he* wanted. This behaviour was not in keeping with her social standing and could ruin her reputation; it could damage Alex. But he was not here . . . so why not? 'Yes, you may, within the proper daytime hours. My maid will be with us at all times.'

'Thank you . . . Grace. Will you call me Hugo?'

Friendship meant a familiarity between them, so there would be no point in keeping it formal. 'Thank you . . . Hugo . . . We must return to the party now.'

A satisfied look came into his eyes and he said, 'Excellent. I'm sure his lordship will not call me out for this.'

Grace raised her brows. 'You are afraid of my husband, sir?'

'Certainly not. Although I am sure Lord Rossmore is a fine shot. I will return you to the party; I'm sure you have many ladies to chatter with? I have an appointment in Weymouth tonight, so I must take my leave.'

They returned to the party and Grace noticed Mrs Clive had joined several ladies and went to find Mrs Willmott, as had been her original intention.

*

The following afternoon, Grace sat in her usual place under a tree on the lawn, the circle of rose bushes were now showing colour and would soon be in full bloom. Hearing the rattle of china, she lowered her book and stared at the man following Mrs Gillett and carrying the tea tray.

'My lady, I'm sorry about this, but Captain Olsen will not wait in the hall to be announced.' Red faced, Gillie cast a look over her shoulder. 'Now wait right there on the spot, until Lady Rossmore says you can see her.' She took the tray from him and put it on the table beside Grace.

Grace felt annoyed, then flustered. Everything this man did was unconventional. Gentlemen did not follow servants about until presented. Norway must have some form of manners. She looked past Mrs Gillett and her chagrin waned; he looked like a naughty schoolboy with his hat rim clenched tightly in both hands and his blond head bowed. But there was nothing schoolboy about the jacket that fitted his broad shoulders, the breeches that disappeared into the riding boots . . .

'Does my lady wish to see Captain Olsen?' Gillie stood by the table looking at Grace with a frown wrinkling her brow.

Grace stood up, conscious of what she had been doing. 'Yes, Mrs Gillett, please ask Captain Olsen to join me, and bring another place setting.'

Mrs Gillett turned and walked up to the Captain. 'Her Ladyship will see you.'

'Thank you, Mrs Gillett. I'm sorry if I have offended you.'

The apology did not soften her blazing eyes, or the pressed lips. 'I will bring more china for your tea, Captain Olsen, but perhaps you will not be here when I come back'

'Teatime is one of my favourite pastimes, Mrs Gillett. I will be here when you return.' Battle lines had been drawn.

Grace watched them with growing bewilderment. She was becoming like a pawn in a chess game. The Captain knew he was overstepping the mark. But why?

'Captain, will you join me?' She sat down at the table. 'Thank you, Mrs Gillett.' The dismissal broke the tension, and the combatants moved in different directions.

'Grace, you look lovely, white muslin with rosebuds. I'm sure you radiate the same scent.' He stood before her and bowed, then smiled. 'Beautiful, as ever, my dear.'

'Really, Hugo, you are trying my patience to the limit. Now you have upset Gillie and I shall have to reprimand her for her insolence, but you did deserve it.'

'You might have changed your mind about our friendship and I could not accept a refusal, especially on such a perfect day as this. Besides, I am thirsty for a cup of tea.'

As if on cue from stage right, Mrs Gillett came across the lawn with a tray and laid the extra china. 'Will that be all, Miss Grace?'

'Yes.'

Mrs Gillett nodded. 'Miss Grace.'

Grace held her tongue between her teeth and waited for her to enter the house. 'My, now I know why my mother kept Gillie on after my governess arrived. I hope you have taken note, Hugo; I have a lioness in the house. She will protect her cub to the death.'

'Only if you promise not to abandon me.' Hugo took a small leather-bound book from his pocket. 'I have a gift for you to seal our friendship. It is English poems of the sea, for you to remember me, when you are back in London.'

'Hugo, that is so very kind of you.' Grace stood up and took the book from his outstretched hand. As her fingers touched his, a tingling sensation went up her arm, jumped to her throat and then to her cheeks. She knew her face crimsoned like the budding roses behind her. 'Please, sit down, the tea is getting cold in the pot.' It was a breathless command and she plumped down, very unladylike, onto her seat.

She took several breaths before arranging the cups on saucers and then pouring the tea. She felt proud of her composure, as not a drop was spilled as she handed it to him.

They sat drinking, only the sound of china tapping, bees buzzing and the gulls squawking over the headland.

'Shall I read you my favourite poem, Grace?' Hugo put down his cup and saucer and picked up the book. 'The poems are scripted in English, but the first page is written in Norwegian. I will translate.' Opening the cover, Hugo waited.

'Yes, I should like that.'

Hugo stood up and moved to stand behind Grace's chair. His voice was soft, just above a whisper.

'The sea is my partner, the ship my friend
Together we ride the waves
But whichever ocean of our world I'm in
Your memory will forever be mine.'

'Who wrote it?'

'Hugo Olsen, Captain of the *Clementine*. I gave this book to my wife the day we married. I took it from her cold fingers the day she died and I have carried it with me ever since. I would like you to have it, Grace, as a token of our friendship.'

'Hugo, I can't take it.'

Grace watched as he came to stand before her.

'Please, my gift, remember. Helga would like you. You have the same temperament. Perhaps you and she were forged with the same willpower. It is what happens when the wife is left behind.'

'I'm not left behind in the same way. Alex has not gone to sea. Our separation is completely different. He will return soon and I will go back to London.' As she uttered the words, she realised that perhaps Hugo was asking more than friendship. 'Are you asking me to be your mistress, Hugo?'

His face changed from the gentle, playful man she had come to know into a cauldron of boiling rage. 'Mistress! What are you saying? That I want to take you to my bed! By the thunder god Thor, are you nothing more than a harlot wife of the elite *ton* that I've heard about?' His anger was so intense that he swung his hand down on the table, the china jumping into the air and clattering back.

Grace stared at him, her face draining to the whiteness of her dress. Then she began to laugh, hysterical laughter that she couldn't stop. 'That's the second time the table's been thumped because of a first wife. Oh Hugo . . .' sobs were rising in her throat and her voice became rasping, 'go away; go home. I don't want to see you again.'

Hugo stepped towards her; he attempted to take her in his arms, but she fought him off. 'Grace, I'm sorry. How could I have said those words to you? Of course I don't think you are a . . .'

Her hand slapped across his cheek, stopping his words. 'Go away. Now! Or I will have Gillett throw you out.'

'Grace, please, let me . . .'

Grace turned her back on him. He didn't move for several seconds. Then she heard his footsteps go up the stone steps and fade away.

She reached to sit on her chair. Her legs were weak and her heart pounded. But her eyes were dry, although the lump in her throat had grown to the size of an egg and she fought for air to pass it. How could this have happened a second time? Could so many men have first wives tucked away in their hearts? She had wanted Hugo's friendship. Was that now impossible? Were men worth all this heartache? Her grandmother had been right; a haven by oneself could be a much better choice.

Chestnut pulled at the grass.

Grace lay nearby looking at Hugo's poetry book raised and held in both hands.

After their heated row she had flung the book into the drawer of her writing table. She wanted to destroy it, wanted to fling it back at him, wanted to read it, wanted to know what his Helga had read. The confusion deprived her of sleep and her appetite. Then she had relented and took the book down to the beach and read it with the sound of the waves and the tang of salt in the air.

They were poems that touched her heart. They told from page to page of a sailor's hopes and dreams, of fear and peril, and tears had blurred her vision. Several had made her laugh. But mostly they told her of the sea. How the breeze could whisper over the swell as calm as a pond, then blow into a hurricane that could rip a ship in two. Sonnets told of deserts, jungles and ice, of spices from the east and tobacco from the west. She had walked along the beach and wished that Hugo had been with her. She wanted to hear his voice, the accent giving flavour to his tales, but she had challenged him about his intentions and ruined everything.

Grace lowered the book and stood up. The air was so clear. She gazed past the headland to the horizon. It seemed very close today and even the gulls were silent as they soared on outstretched wings.

She turned and walked towards her horse. 'Well, Chestnut, I must make amends for my behaviour.' The mare raised her head from the grass and snorted. 'I agree,' she replied, 'not something a lady likes to do, but it is my fault and he is a foreigner after all.'

Grace rode down from the headland on to the road and down the lane. The same coach as she had seen before was outside Hugo's house. Still in the saddle, she took time to look more closely at the vehicle. It was old and the paintwork dull. The dark red inside was faded with pink patches and the fabric was thread-bare. On his seat, the coachman was asleep.

Voices from the open front door caught Grace's attention. 'I have her eating out of my hand. You must leave me to deal with this in my own way.'

'Time is running out, I suggest you move it along. The Excise men would like to know about you, Olsen. This house has a deep cellar, what's it full of?' The laughter that came from the man was not humorous, but vindictive.

Grace kicked Chestnut to move on. She did not want to be caught eavesdropping, although the mystery visitor seemed to have a control over Hugo about something.

After luncheon, Grace wrote her apology and had Gillett deliver it at once, before she changed her mind. Within the hour, while she was in the garden, he arrived to see her.

This time, Mrs Gillett announced his request. 'Captain Olsen asks if you are at home, m'lady. He also says he won't go without seeing you.'

Grace tried not to smile, but it was very difficult. 'I'll see him, Gillie. Please bring a tray of tea.' This was the second time he had called unexpectedly and Esther was not with her. Still, they were in the garden and one could not be compromised here — could one?

Hugo Olsen walked down the steps with a stern look on his face and stopped before her.

Grace watched his eyes narrow and his lips thin as he pressed them together.

Finally he said, 'So, you think by sending words of apology, I will fall to my knees and kiss your feet?'

'Don't talk such rubbish. I realise that I have offended you . . . with my implication . . . that you wanted . . . oh, I cannot do this.'

Grace made to pass him, but he barred her way with his arm. 'I accept, Lady Rossmore.' And he swept her into his arms. There was no kiss, no intention of intimacy, but he held her close for several seconds then whispered, 'I accept, Grace, I am very sorry that we quarrelled.' He loosened his hold and stepped back. 'I now apologise for hugging you.'

His smile washed away the hot words she was about to say. Instead, Grace smiled back. 'Your conduct is unforgivable; but I will not reprimand you today. I will accept it as a gesture of our friendship. Will you have tea with me?'

He had that boyish look again and Grace knew she had set things straight between them. She took the book from her skirt pocket. 'Hugo, I cannot accept your gift.'

She saw his linen shirt rise with each breath; saw the happiness leave his face. 'Why?'

'Because it is not right, that you give it to me. I have sat on the beach and the headland reading the verses; they are touching and frightening, sometimes together in the same poem. They made me understand why a seaman loves the sea. But I cannot keep it. I am married to Alex, and although our separation may give the impression that we are estranged, my vows to him are steadfast to the day I die.'

Grace lifted her hand and placed it on his chest. 'I would like to be there as your friend. I can make that gift to you, only if that is enough.'

Hugo placed his large calloused hand over her small one. 'Thank you, Grace. I fear I overstepped my place and I accept your offer.' He raised her hand and kissed her fingers. 'Friendship, it is.'

Mrs Gillett came across the lawn with the tea and Grace moved away from Hugo. Friendship also required propriety.

Grace put the book on the table. 'Please put it in your pocket, Hugo.' He seemed reluctant to further the conversation, so she busied herself pouring the tea.

They sat opposite each other and Grace decided to probe a little about the conversation she had heard and the people who Hugo allowed in his house.

'Mrs Gillett has excellent quality tea, would you agree, Hugo? If my memory serves me well, it is much stronger than on my last visit. Does it have the same flavour that your manservant uses?'

He did not answer, but kept the cup to his lips.

'Oh, I see. Ask no questions – receive no lies. I fear that is a dangerous occupation, especially along this coast.'

Hugo placed his cup back in the saucer. 'I don't know where it comes from, my crew deal with the everyday tasks of housekeeping.' He would not meet her eyes, but spoke to the china on the table.

'It is none of my business what you do. Let us speak of something more pleasing to the mind. How is the repair to your ship coming along?'

The mention of his *Clementine* changed his features immediately. 'She is about three-quarters done. The new sails should be ready soon and there is a little carpentry work. Then, we shall go to sea.'

His remark made Grace realise how stupid she had been to think that Hugo wanted a more permanent liaison. She smiled, feeling a lightness come to her heart. Everything would be alright; she had what she wanted, a friend.

'What have I said to make you look happy all of a sudden?'

'You have given me the solution to my dilemma, Hugo.'

The following evening, after dinner, Grace sat with Esther playing whist.

Although the sunset did not come through the window, rays of gold filled the room, matching Grace's satin dress. She had let Esther pile her hair high with curls and ringlets, leaving her neck unadorned of any jewellery.

A knock interrupted their game and Gillett came in to announce that Captain Olsen wished to call on her.

Grace was lost for words. It was way past visiting time, unless one was officially dining out. 'Has he a reason, Gillett?'

'No, your ladyship, but he has a large parcel with him.'

'Oh. Well . . . I suppose . . . oh, show him in.'

Grace glanced at Esther. Thank goodness she was here.

Hugo manoeuvred his way through the door with a triangular package.

'Good evening, Grace. Where can I put this down?'

'Down where? On the floor or a table?'

'Table, of course.' And without waiting for her answer, set it down on a small table in front of the window.

'Hugo, good evening, this is a most unexpected visit. Could it not have waited until the morning?'

'No. I want you to have this now. I have just finished it and I shall not rest until you have seen it.' Stopping only to take a breath, 'Come, look.' He began to unravel the protective cloth from whatever was beneath.

Grace got up and moved over to him. As his fingers lifted the linen away, a model ship, rigged to full sail, appeared. The deep hull rested on a stand of blue waves.

'Hugo, it's beautiful.' Admiration for his skill burst from her. 'Look at the planked decking, the miniature sails, and the fine twisted rope. I had no idea you were such a talented man.'

''Tis but a pastime, should I have any free hours for myself at sea. It was badly damaged in the storm, but I could not throw it away. She is of the *Clementine*. I want you to have her, Grace.' He squared his shoulders as he looked at her. It was an unspoken challenge.

'This is most generous of you, but I don't . . .' Her words were cut off.

'I will not take no for an answer, not this time. Think of it as a late wedding present, Lady Rossmore. I am sure your husband will appreciate my humble efforts.'

Grace realised that if her friendship was to continue, she had to meet him halfway. 'Thank you, Captain Olsen. I accept on behalf of us both.'

Hugo stood to attention, clicked his heels and bowed. 'It is *my* pleasure, Grace.' The wicked smile that creased his face as he straightened told her she had been duped.

'May I offer you a glass of brandy?'

'Aye, brandy will do if you have no schnapps or the Englishman's rum.'

He was playing the rough sailor with her now and she laughed. 'Lady Rossmore only has brandy, rum is for the taverns, I believe.' She went over to a cabinet and took out a glass and a bottle, poured a full measure.

He was still standing by the model as Grace handed it to him.

'To our friendship continuing, *my lady*,' and he raised his glass.

Grace let his emphasis go and responded with a smile.

Esther still sat at the card table, keeping her gaze anywhere other than at the two people by the window.

'Esther, would you go to his lordship's study and bring the magnifying glass? I believe it is on the small table by the winged chair. On the way back collect my shawl, I would like to show Captain Olsen my new sundial before he leaves.'

Alone, Grace and Hugo bent over the model.

He touched the top sail. 'There are so many details that you will be able to see in the morning light.'

'Yes.' It was a whisper. Grace turned her face towards him and felt his finger touch one of her ringlets. Watched him put down his glass and take her hand, lift it to his lips. He pulled her close. In the fading light they were silhouetted against the window, a cameo of two lovers.

The door opened, yet neither moved.

'A most touching scene, *Lady Rossmore*. Captain Olsen, I presume?'

Alex walked into the room, his face as dark as the thunderous storm that had slashed the *Clementine*.

Chapter Twelve

Alex saw them jump apart. He held on to his temper and walked towards them.

'Good evening, Grace. I think a little light is called for and then you can introduce me to your guest.'

Esther came into the room at that moment and Alex turned. 'Would you ask Gillett to light the candles and your mistress will not need you again until later.' The sharp dismissal sent her wheeling round and back out through the door.

Hugo said, 'Lord Rossmore, may I . . .'

His words were silenced by Alex's raised hand. 'We will wait for Gillett to leave before . . .' His words were halted as the servant came in with a lighted branch and placed it on the card table. He moved from this with a flaming taper to the other candles already in the room.

'Thank you, Gillett. I will see Captain Olsen out. My coachman and manservant need help before you retire.' His authoritative manner seemed to terrify the old man and he scurried from the room.

Alex turned to Grace, who had now found her voice. 'Lord Rossmore, may I present Captain Hugo Olsen, a neighbour. He has just brought us a late wedding present. This beautiful model ship is of his own vessel, the *Clementine*.' Her voice gained momentum with each word.

'A most unusual gift, since we are not acquainted with you or your ship.'

Hugo once again clicked his heels and bowed. 'It is a pleasure to meet you, my lord. Perhaps my present does seem a little odd to you, but Lady Rossmore and I have been neighbours now since you arrived for your honeymoon.'

Alex saw the trap that the Captain was setting and smiled. 'Yes. My untimely return to London on urgent business does mean that both of you have the advantage over me.'

'Do come and look at it, Alex. It is truly a wonderful model of a wonderful ship.'

Her admiration did the exact opposite to what was intended. The two men's eyes met, clashing like weapons of steel.

'I think I would prefer to see it in the daylight. I have spent two days journeying from London; therefore, I'm sure Captain Olsen will not think me rude if I see him out.'

Hugo took his dismissal with flair by bowing to Grace. 'Thank you for your hospitality, Lady Rossmore.' He then turned to Alex. 'My lord, I bid you goodnight.'

Alex opened the door and looked at Grace. 'Please, do not scamper off to bed, but wait here until I return.'

Closing the front door, Alex breathed deeply. How was he going to handle the next few minutes; the whole of their future hinged on it? He had not expected to be confronted with them together, so his prepared speech was now useless. Admittedly, they had not been in an embrace, but they had been standing close enough to make his blood boil. He moved across the hall and stopped outside the drawing-room door; he would have to take each second as it came, but was determined not to let his anger take over his tongue.

Grace was looking out of the window into the dark night. Her back was pulled stiff and Alex wanted to go to her. Instead, he noisily cleared his throat, giving her time to turn round.

'Why did you not send word that you would be arriving today? The Gilletts would have had everything ready for you.'

'I have been waiting to finalise a business deal. Then I decided to leave immediately. Miles grumbled about not enough time to prepare, but good lord, this is Dorset, I don't need dozens of out-fits. I have enough here already.'

His words seemed to ease her stiffness and she smiled. 'I can see that we shall be spending very little time here, unless I come alone.'

'Rossmore Manor is far more convenient, in size and distance from London. You may come and play here with my full consent, Grace, whenever you want.'

'Thank you, my lord. Have you come to take me back to London?'

'Yes and no. Grace, there are things happening that I do not understand. Something I must resolve before I take you back. It concerns Liddy and I need . . .'

Grace's calm countenance changed to a wildfire of emotions that took Alex back a step. 'How dare you come down here with her name on your lips? I thought that when we met again we would start anew. You've had weeks to sort this out, Alex. I want a straight answer to a straight question. Do you love me?'

'Grace, it's not that simple. Liddy will always . . .'

'No. That will not do. When you came into this room tonight, I felt guilty that Hugo was here, that we were standing close; that you would read into it more than there is. But I should not have. He is only a neighbour, but has more feelings for me than you ever will.' Tears welled into her eyes and spilled down her cheeks, her voice becoming a gurgle of jumbled words. 'You have wasted your time in coming here, Alex. Go back to London. I will stay here.'

Alex moved to her and tried to take her in his arms, but she hammered at him, on his chest, his shoulders, even trying to hit his face until he caught her wrists.

'Grace, listen to me. It's not what you think, it's . . .'

'I don't want to hear your lies. Leave me alone.'

With strength he did not think any woman could have, she wrenched herself away from him and ran for the door. Before opening it she stopped and turned. 'Our marriage was a mistake, Alex, a terrible mistake.' Then she left.

Alex did not follow.

He thought that by not mentioning Olsen and how he had seen them, they could whitewash the past and talk calmly about the future. But he had failed. He had said the one word that she had not wanted to hear. *Liddy.* Alex saw the half-empty glass near the model ship and picked it up, downing the brandy in one gulp. Where was the bottle, he needed something tonight to blot out his bungling?

Grace couldn't stop the tears. They were like a waterfall with a never-ending source. How could Alex come back with Liddy still claiming first place? She paced from door to window, like a caged animal. The nightgown's hem dragging on the floor made her stumble. She lifted it and stopped at the window.

The moonlight on the garden had paled the grass and rose bushes to a greyish hue and the trees behind stood like dark soldiers in the shadow. Watching this vista seemed to quiet her anguish and the sobs ceased. What were they to do? As her mind began to probe, so the tears returned. Grace turned to the bed; she needed to sleep. She went to the bedside cabinet and opened a secret drawer in the side and took out a small bottle. A few drops of laudanum would work; it had long ago when she had heard of Simon's death.

Alex had picked at his breakfast, dealt with his post from London and asked Esther twice if Lady Rossmore was available. To which her replies were that Grace was still in a deep sleep. Well, that proved one conclusive point. She wasn't as upset as she had seemed last night, if her slumber was going on past the noon hour. He had not slept at all, except the dozing moments sitting in a chair, with that confounded model ship in his sightline, reminding him of Olsen's cunning games.

Now, well past three o'clock, he pushed the lunch tray away and wondered what to do next.

He went into the hall and stood still, listening. There was not a sound to be heard. A worrying niggle began to squirm in his mind, was she alright, she hadn't done anything silly, like . . . Alex made for the stairs and raced up, the beating of his heart hammering against his ribs. Without knocking he rushed into her room.

Grace looked up from her tray and stopped spreading preserve on a piece of bread. Her face was white, not a hint of colour shading her cheeks, and dark shadows beneath her eyes made her look ill.

'Would you please have the courtesy to knock before coming into my room?' Her voice was a croak, as if her throat had not tasted water for days.

Alex slowed his pace and went to the bedside. 'I was worried about you and it is now mid-afternoon, are you not well?'

'Do I look well, Alex? I have a hammering headache, my eyes hurt and I should like you to leave.'

'Grace, about last night—'

'Now!' Her shout caused her to start coughing and she waved her hand in frantic circles for him to leave.

Esther appeared in the doorway and rushed to her mistress. 'There now, m'lady, drink a few drops of water.'

Alex felt the unwelcome atmosphere like a cloak. 'I'll see you later, Gra . . .' The look on Esther's face made him turn and leave. As he closed the door, the click echoed through the silent house.

Grace sent a message that she would be staying in her room for dinner.

Alex sat alone, depressed and angry. He had come to Solitaire to make amends with her, not begin another tussle that seemed to have no ending. If he was not careful, she would turn to Olsen for comfort and he had no doubt that the Captain would offer it with open arms. He pushed the food around the plate, his appetite gone. He came to a decision. Tomorrow he would tell Grace everything that had happened in London, even if he had to tie her in a chair and force her to listen.

He went into the study. For the first time, he noticed the feminine touches. Grace's own styles of paintings, flowery cushions, spindle-legged chairs and table. He had taken this from her without a word, taken it for granted that he had the right. He was beginning to see that he had lived on his own too long. He ran a finger along the bookshelf and selected one; maybe it would occupy his mind until the light faded and he retired to his room.

It was almost midnight and Alex stood looking out of his bedroom window. The sound of thunder rumbled and a flash of sheet lightning lit up the garden. 'Come on, rain, what are you waiting for?'

The next flash was brighter and Alex leaned forward, his eyes fixed on the path below him. Grace was hurrying by, her dark cloak pulled together across her middle, leaving only a pale patch of underskirt showing. The light faded, but his eyes followed her silhouette as she climbed the steps leading to the wood. He turned and left the room.

Dressed only in trousers and a shirt, he thanked providence that he had waved Miles away earlier. Passing through the hall he left the house through the study door into the garden. He ran up the steps into the wood and stopped. The moon had been shining bright a short time ago, but now it was only lighting his way through streaked cloud. Grace was out of sight. At the fork, he stopped. Left to the beach or right to the cliff? Stones rattled and he cocked his head – left. In contrast to the white light that had lit up the sky, now a jagged line of fork lightning splintered across the dark heavens. The brightness lasted only a few seconds and he did not see her ahead. Then, further down, the sound of more slipping stones and Alex hurried on. He reached the wooden platform just as another flash illuminated the beach.

Grace was standing close to the sea. Chased by an increasing wind the incoming tide of black water rose in a monstrous swell and broke in a crescendo of noise and spray, almost reaching her. She did not move and on the next swell, the creeping water covered her feet. She waited, the cloak released and billowing out behind her. But she was as still as a carved statue. Then the moon disappeared completely behind the storm clouds.

Alex hurried down the wooden steps and looked up and down the beach. The weather was worsening and he saw the spray lifting with the wind, the droplets being driven inland onto the beach. It would prick her skin like needles and damage her eyes. Who was she waiting for? Olsen? This was madness. Surely, if he were coming, he would be here? Questions with no answers raced through his mind. But the only one that repeated over and over was that it was his fault. God, how could he have been so stupid? All the London fiasco had driven reason out of his mind. Grace was the only one that mattered to him. Why hadn't he told her so?

Sizzling lightning followed immediately by thunder clashed overhead in an ear-splitting boom and the spray became a curtain hiding Grace from his sight. He ran towards her as the first drops of rain dotted his shirt. He shouted to her, but his voice was lost in the roar of the sea. She wouldn't deliberately let it take her, would she? Another flash, but she had stepped back. Now the rain soaked her hair, her cloak, yet still she waited.

Alex reached her and swung her round. 'Grace, what are you doing? He's not coming; Olsen isn't coming. Do you hear me?'

She looked at him, but he could see she did not recognise him.

'It's me, Alex. Grace, come back, this is insane.'

The storm was now like a ferocious animal, its teeth ripping at their clothes. Alex's shirt was another skin showing every muscle and curve of his shoulders and chest. The once pristine trousers clung to his legs like breeches and his shoes sank into the gritty sand.

'Alex? What are you doing here? I came . . . I came . . .'

'It doesn't matter why. Come away from here, please.'

'The sea, the poems, I wanted to see it, feel it. Hugo was right, I love . . .'

Her words were snatched away by the wind and he caught only a few: sea, feel, Hugo, love. Alex tried to pull her into his arms, but she pushed him away. Not even his comfort meant anything to her now. He looked, once more, along the beach. Olsen had deserted her. 'You must come back to the house, your clothes are drenched.'

There was no reply.

Alex pulled her into his arms and lifted her. He expected Grace to struggle, but she laid her head on his shoulder and he felt her relax against him. Wind whipped into his face and he narrowed his eyes, but the rain was easing and the lightning and thunder was moving away inland.

As he carried Grace up the beach, the sound of the sea lessened and by the time he reached the platform he felt more in control. Grace had her eyes closed and now was not the time for questions. The rain had made the path slippery and he tested his first step with caution. By the time he was halfway up, water was running down like a stream and each step splattered mud in all directions. Fragments of rock pierced into the soles of his shoes and brambles scratched his hands. Grace muttered several times about being put down, but Alex ignored her. She was wet and cold and time wasted in arguing would only put her in danger of catching a chill. When he reached the woodland fork that led down to the house the rain had stopped and the moon was peeping through the tail end of the storm clouds.

Alex could see her white nightgown was dyed brown to the knees and splattered mud had dotted her neck and face. She was shivering and he pulled her cloak tighter around her.

'Grace, can you hear me?' There was no reply and he cursed. If they didn't get out of their wet clothes soon they would both die of a fever.

Alex flexed his shoulders to ease the stiffness that was settling in his muscles. Like Grace, he was covered from head to foot in mud. He looked at the path leading to the garden. It was less slippery where the thick foliage had sheltered it and he cradled her closer and went down the track leading to the garden. Reaching the house he went in through the study door, leaving clods of mud all the way to her bedchamber.

Alex laid Grace on the bed and pulled the edges of the counterpane round her, but she flung her arms out, fighting it away.

'Grace, please, you need to take your wet clothes off.'

'I'm comfortable as I am, go away.'

'No. Let me help you. Lie still, close your eyes.'

'Why? Let me up, I can manage.' Grace tried to push up on her elbow, but a groan left her lips and she sank back down.

Alex brushed the dark wet hair from her forehead. 'Now, do as I say. Close your eyes and go to sleep.'

'Um, sleep.' And she accepted his command.

He gently rolled her back and forth, stripping away the wet cloak and nightgown. Then he removed her shoes still covered in sand. In the light of a single candle he filled a bowl with cold water and bathed her face, working down her neck and body to her cold feet. His saw her womanly beauty, but any desire was over-ridden by the urgent need to clean and wrap her in the warm bedclothes. As he tucked the sheet around her shoulders, under her chin, she opened her eyes and looked directly into his. For a few seconds they were sightless; then they flamed into life.

'What are you doing?'

Alex stilled. He chose his words carefully. 'Making sure Lady Rossmore does not catch the fever and die.' He straightened up and stood by the bed.

'You're wet and filthy, where have you been?'

'Your memory is still hazy. I must go and change. Think about the last hour while I am gone.' He walked over to the dividing door between their bedchambers and went through.

Alex returned within fifteen minutes. He could see her shivering before he reached the bed. Grace was turned on her side and curled into a ball. She needed more blankets. Summoning Esther was the last thing he wanted to do so he returned to his own bed and pulled off the blanket.

The extra warmth did nothing to help Grace.

He pulled back the covers and got in beside her.

Her feet were like ice-blocks against his thighs and he lifted her head and slipped his arm beneath, so he could cradle her close into his warm body. She did not speak or move away, but pulled his arm from her waist up between her breasts, cuddling deeper into his belly. He drew in his breath, let it out slowly, then moving his hand a few inches he cupped one of her soft breasts. As time passed her tremors lessened and Alex could feel her skin return to a warm womanly softness. He slipped his hand down to her hip, across her belly and down to her parted thighs where his leg crossed over them. She moved her head and the damp hair brushed his chin; a sigh left her lips.

'Do you feel warm now?' There was no reply. 'Grace, answer me.'

'What are we doing in this bed together?'

Alex touched her shoulder and pulled her round. 'You do remember the beach and the storm?'

'Yes, and the mud path and the brambles.'

He showed her one of his hands. ''Tis not a laughing matter.'

As if everything came back in a flash, Grace looked away. 'Did Esther . . . who called her?'

'I did what was needed.'

'But I have nothing on. You cannot have done . . . cannot have seen . . .' Her words dried up and she covered her face with her hands.

'Grace, it is not shameful. I am your husband—'

'You are not . . . that is . . . not until we have . . .' She turned away from him.

Alex knew that this would happen, but she had needed his warmth, his protection and that was all he had given.

'Grace, please, nothing has happened between us.'

He put out his hand and stroked her tangled curls. He touched her ear, finger and thumb caressing the lobe. She did not pull away and Alex continued his stroking down her neck across her shoulder. He kissed and tasted where his fingers had been and touched his lips to her back, trailed kisses down her spine. And still she did not pull away.

'You are so soft and warm and my desire grows for you, Grace.'

Alex let his fingers encourage her to turn to him. When she did, her eyes looked into his. He moved towards her, taking her lips in a soft kiss. His hand held her waist and as their kisses deepened, his

143

tongue stroked across her lips, the tip running along her teeth, delving deeper to savour the sweetness within. Fire ignited in him and he let his hand slide to her womanly parting and felt the moistness come as his other hand fondled her breast. He left her lips and sucked upon each nipple, until she cried out.

Grace lifted her hips to draw his hand deeper into her warmth; she wanted his manhood, but he knew she must wait a little longer. He moved over her, kissing her belly, moving lower to her moist opening and trailing his tongue slowly up and down. Then he lowered his own manhood onto her and retook her nipple in his mouth. She lifted to him and Alex took her head in his hands. Grace was panting, her body circling under his, but he needed to know this was what she wanted.

'Is this what you want, Grace? Do you want us to be one?' Of all the foolhardy things he had done since their wedding day, this was something she had to agree with. Would he be able to stop, if she said no?

'Oh, yes. I want this now. Alex, you cannot stop now, what are you saying?'

'Only, my sweet, that I do not want you to regret this moment one hour from now.'

His answer was her cry of need and he lay full on her, his shaft sinking deep. They moved as one. Her fingers bit deep into his flesh and he pulled her up to him, holding her into his chest so that their two hearts beat as one. In a shuddering crescendo of passion they sank and lay with arms and legs entwined.

Alex pulled the covers over them and Grace into his arms.

'We are one now, Alex. My child will be ours, no matter what happens.'

It was what Alex feared. He had let his love for her flow, but at what cost.

'Sleep now. The dawn will soon be here.'

Alex watched her drift into slumber and then moved slowly away.

He pulled on his robe and stood by the side of the bed.

Grace. From the Latin meaning *gratia; favour.* But she had bestowed that honour to Olsen, because she was not the untouched virgin bride he expected. A growing despair brought bile into his throat. He despised her and hated himself. Both were like vines, twisting and tightening around his heart.

He tucked the sheet into her back, wiping out any sign of where he had been lying. In his room he locked the connecting door and threw the key into the fireplace.

Chapter Thirteen

The clink of china woke Grace.

Esther was arranging a place setting on the table by the window.

'What time is it, Esther?'

'Good morning, m'lady, just past the noon. His lordship said to leave you sleeping, then bring your luncheon to your room.'

'Noon!' It was not a question, just an exclamation of surprise. Grace struggled to sit up. She forgot she was naked and the sheet slipped to her waist. Snatching it to her chin, she saw Esther was keeping her eyes fixed on the tray.

'I can manage, thank you. Will you go and ask Mr Gillett to heat some water? I would like to bathe and wash my hair. Come back when it's ready.' A pink blush was changing to crimson, creeping down her neck and chest. 'You may go.' It was a command and the servant woman hurried to the door, opened it and was gone.

Grace pushed back the covers and got out of bed. She had never slept without a nightgown in her life. Then she saw her mud-splattered cloak crumpled on the floor. Her knees weakened and she sat on the bed. Every second of the previous night came rushing into her memory: the vivid image of the beach, the storm, Alex and their lovemaking.

She looked at the connecting door, then at her nakedness. Like the speed of the previous night's lightning she grabbed her robe and scrambled into it, tying the belt tight. Her throat was dry and she went to the table and poured a cup of coffee. She drank the hot liquid in one go and refilled a second cup. Sitting down at the table she picked up a slice of bread and bit a piece off.

Everything about yesterday seemed unbelievable. She had stayed in her room. Had barely touched her dinner and by the late evening the oppressive atmosphere had become a cloying pressure and given her a headache. The desire to be down on the beach had reached obsessive proportions. She had thought the house asleep, even listened at the connecting door, but not a sound had come from within.

Standing on the beach close to the surf, she had let Hugo's poems come to life as the raging sea and storm strengthened. It had mesmerised her and only when Alex had turned her round did she come back to reality. The sea had become a maelstrom, and the wind so strong it drove everything before it inland. Alex had carried her up the cliff path and into the house and up the stairs to her room. He had bathed her, warmed her and loved her.

She finished the bread and reached for a fruit. She remembered his fingers in her hair, his mouth and lips on her skin and then his rhythmic strokes in her body. They had become one at last.

Grace loosened the belt and let the wrap fall apart. She placed her hands on her belly and smiled. 'Perhaps?' she whispered.

A knock on the door and Esther peeped in. 'Your bath is ready, m'lady.'

The rain from the previous night had softened the ground and the grass looked lush. Grace sat in her usual place under the tree, embroidering the linen stretched over a small hand frame, working at the initials APK.

She had chosen her gown with care. Alex had said on more than one occasion that he liked her in pink, so she had on rose muslin, matching the flowers behind her.

When Mrs Gillett brought the tea tray, Grace was disappointed that Alex had not come. 'Is Lord Rossmore at home?'

'No. His lordship ordered his horse directly after luncheon. I have not heard him return.'

Mrs Gillett looked as if she was about to say more, so Grace forestalled her. 'Oh, yes, I had forgotten. He won't be back until dinnertime.'

Her lie did not deter her old nurse. 'Miss Grace, I will speak out of turn and you may reprimand me, but is everything alright? His lordship instructed that any clothing of his and yours soiled with mud is to be put out. Is this . . . I mean . . . shall I do it?'

Grace coloured a lighter shade of her dress. 'Yes. Or wash and give them to the church for distribution. And that is the end of it. No more words or I *shall* give you a telling-off. Now, let me have my tea in peace.'

Mrs Gillett pursed her lips, but gave an answering nod and left.

Where was Alex? She had expected him to come into her room earlier. What was so important that he left without a word? As if by magic, he came from the woods behind the house, leading his horse. Tying it to a post at the top of the steps he came down to the terrace and then to the garden. 'I am just in time. Do you have an extra cup?'

Grace felt her heart begin to race. 'Yes, I ordered tea for two.'

'Has Captain Olsen come to tea?'

The question was asked politely enough, but Grace didn't want to answer.

'Everyone is invited to tea. I've had Lady Culver, Mrs Willmott and, of course, the Reverend's wife, Mrs Clive and . . .'

'That was not what I asked.'

'Yes, Hugo . . . I mean, Captain Olsen, has visited for tea.'

'How pleasant, my dear. I am pleased to hear you have entertained your friends in my absence.'

'Well, I cannot sit at home fretting, wondering where you are, Alex. Reading and needlepoint become very boring after weeks alone.'

'I apologise, Grace. Please, I would like a cup of this excellent Dorset tea.'

She gave him a startled look. 'That is a very peculiar remark.'

'I have been taking an interest in the village and shoreline today. A few well-distributed coins have loosened tongues to my advantage.'

Grace saw that he was watching her from narrowed eyes and a feeling of apprehension crept down her spine. 'I don't know what to say to that, Alex. Are you suggesting that this tea has something wrong with it?'

'On the contrary, quality such as this would fetch a high price for the salons of the *ton*.'

She handed him his cup and they sipped in silence.

Grace wondered why he did not mention last night. His manner was distant, polite to the extreme. What was wrong now?

'Alex, thank you for last night . . .'

His angry voice interrupted. 'Your escapade on the beach was foolish and unfruitful. I did what any sensible man would do and brought you back to safety. Roaming the woods and beach in the middle of the night, on a coastline like this, is asking for trouble. Smugglers, English and French, outrun the Excise men and neither would think twice about shooting first and asking questions after. *And*, my duty as a husband has been fulfilled, Grace.'

Banging his fist on the table with one hand and almost throwing the china onto the tray with the other, Grace wondered if her tea-times with men were destined to always be a fighting match.

'I'm sorry.'

'Sorry! Is that all you have to say?'

Alex pulled her from the chair. 'You look like a delicate rose, as if a puff of air could blow you away, yet last night you had the strength of a soldier. You make me angry, but all I want to do is kiss you. I know it is too late for us, but I will have one more moment with you.'

He bent his head and touched her lips. It was a soft melding that deepened and he wrapped his arms tightly round her. She parted her lips and it was a kiss that lasted and lasted, until they were both breathless. When he let her go, he stepped back. 'I made a misjudgement – I should have asked – but a lord expects his spin-ster wife to be a virgin, Grace. At least my heir would then be a true Kilbraith. Sailors' tales of a woman in every port seem to be true. I hope I came up to Olsen's expertise. Now, if there is a child, whose will it be? Until we meet for dinner; my faithless wife.' And he was gone, collecting his horse and walking back into the woods.

Grace didn't move. She had done wrong. She should have told him about Simon. Told him she had had a lover. But it was ten years ago. Now he thought she had betrayed him with Captain Olsen. And she knew he wouldn't believe her even if she tried to explain. The gossip he had purchased in the village and how he had found her and Hugo together in the drawing room the night he arrived, clearly pointed to a liaison between them. What a fool she was. But one thing she had learned about Alex in the month before their marriage – he was a proud man and would not be made to look like a cuckold.

There was a strained atmosphere between them.

Grace picked at her food. She had drunk two glasses of wine and now raised her empty glass. 'May I?' She wagged the stem between finger and thumb.

He hesitated, then filled it halfway. 'Full, please, Alex.' The decanter was tilted and he complied. 'It helps our little silences, don't you think?'

'I think you have had enough.'

'I've heard said that in the brothels of London the harlots encourage men to buy them wine; or is it champagne? Have you ever been to a house of ladies, Alex?'

'That is none of your business and not a question *Lady Rossmore* should be asking.'

'Why?' Grace sipped continuously and the glass swayed in her hand.

'Grace, watch what you are doing. Give me that glass.'

He got up and went to her, but she swung the glass away as he went to take it, slapping at his hand. 'Go away.'

'Give it here, now. You're acting like a tavern wench from the village.'

'Is that the type of woman you like, full of wine and pliable? Shall I be like that for you?'

Grace watched the anger flare in his eyes and his lips thinned to a line.

'I like a woman who is faithful and honours her vows before God.' The words were spat like venom.

'Like me? I am, you know. I should have told you I once had a lover. I was a spinster lover. Does that make things right between us?' He was never going to believe her. It was too late for confessions.

Alex leaned towards her, the wineglass forgotten and he took her head between his hands. 'I wish.' And he kissed her with such force that the chair tipped and the wine shot from the glass onto the shoulder of his coat.

Grace's mind raced round and round, chased by too much wine and making her giddy. She gripped his lapel with her free hand but he wrenched it free and straightened up.

'Go to bed, Grace, and sleep the wine off. Sweet dreams of the sea and ships.'

He didn't wait to see how she fared.

Grace sat at the table with the empty wineglass still in her hand. Tavern wench was she? Picking up the decanter she filled her glass to the top, and kept refilling it until the crystal-cut carafe was empty.

The following morning, Grace walked her horse into the village. Fishermen were unloading their catch into carts and the smell made her stomach retch. The idea that fresh air would clear her headache proved untrue.

Added to her discomfort was the noise being made by the innkeeper as he rolled a barrel towards the Smugglers Inn shouting, 'Open the trap door into the cellar, boy.' Without a doubt, a tavern wench must have a stronger constitution than she did.

What was to be done? Alex and she were like two fighters, sparing with each other, never coming to an end of their conflict. Everything should have been alright between them after their

151

lovemaking. Instead, because of her flouting social tradition and her position as Lady Rossmore, things had gone from bad to worse. Infamous gossip would be a bitter pill to swallow.

She saw Hugo coming towards her and wished she could avoid him. But there was nowhere to hide.

'Good morning, Grace.'

She looked at his fresh complexion and clear blue eyes. 'No, it is not, Hugo. I have a headache and my stomach churns.'

'You need egg-milk, my mother's remedy for all stomach disorders.'

His light-hearted manner made Grace laugh, which in turn made her head worse. 'Oh, don't make me laugh, Hugo. Take pity on a poor wretch.'

'Come home with me and Erik will make the cure.' Without waiting for a reply, he took Chestnut's reins.

'I can't. Really, Hugo, do you have no sense of propriety? My husband is here and you dare to ask me to your home, un-chaperoned?'

His manner changed, became challenging. 'You care what a heartless husband thinks? Do you know what he has been doing in London? Business commitments can be very loosely applied to all sorts of things and to all sorts of people . . .' he paused, 'ladies, for instance.'

'What are you saying, Hugo? What do you know?' Grace felt the wine that still lay in her stomach rise to her throat. 'I don't believe you.' Yet she could not completely dispel a niggling doubt. What did she know about Alex's return to London? Only what his letter had said. And she had questioned his 'accident' excuse.

'Would I tell a mistruth to you, Grace, after our declared friendship?'

Rebellion surged once more. Stronger than when Alex had left her abandoned here in Whitecliffs. Why shouldn't she give him something to really paint her a faithless wife?

'Thank you, Hugo. Egg-milk sounds just what I need.'

There had been a tension to Hugo, but it left him when she

152

agreed. He gave her a smile. To Chestnut he whispered, 'Eating from my hand,' and led her horse along the road.

In the quiet of his drawing room, Grace relaxed and sipped the concoction Erik gave her. 'It doesn't taste very nice.'

'All good medicines taste the worst. That's a saying of my mother.'

Hugo held up a sweetmeat. 'And I say you may have this afterwards.'

Grace drained the last of the egg-milk. 'Now I like you both.'

Hugo held out his hand and helped her from the chair. He placed his arm around her waist, trapping her and held the sweet-meat to her mouth.

Grace felt his nearness, but did not move, taking the morsel and savouring the flavour. 'Um, delicious.' She closed her eyes, feeling the tension ease from her forehead. 'You are good for me, Hugo. The best friend I have.'

'I hope so, Grace.' His kiss was soft against her lips.

His arm loosened and she opened her eyes. She wished she hadn't. The look in his was not what she wanted. But by Alex . . . it would send her to heaven on the wing of an angel.

'I must go. Thank you, Hugo.'

'I am here, anytime, my Lady Rossmore.'

Hugo untied her horse from the post at the bottom of the path and helped her to mount. Taking her hand he kissed her palm; then tapped Chestnut's rump, signalling her to move off.

Hidden by a turn in the road, Alex watched her leave Olsen's house.

His fears were founded; there was an affair between them. The vines twisted tighter in his chest. Was he partly to blame? This nagging question had kept him awake for the past two nights. Did he want her any more? Yes, he did. But he was not prepared to cross that connecting door again. So it was stale-mate. He mounted and turned the horse away from the village and Solitaire.

★

'You look charming this evening. Red is becoming your colour.'

Alex slid the chair back for her to sit at the card table. 'Shall we play backgammon?'

'If you so wish.'

'You do not sound very enthusiastic. Is anything the matter?'

'I've had a bad headache and my insides have been a little queasy.'

He raised his brows and his voice held no sympathy. 'Playing the harlot has its consequences.'

She looked at him, ignoring the reprimand. 'I'm better now since . . .' She stopped speaking and smiled.

'Please, share the moment. I would like to know what can make you smile. My conversation only makes you angry.'

'If you must know, Alex, it is egg-milk.'

'What the hell is that? Some sort of baby slop?'

'No, a stomach remedy.'

There was not an answer to that, so he handed her the dice. They started playing.

'You are not concentrating, Grace. That's the second time you have let me win with your carelessness. Where has your competitive spirit gone?'

The truth of the matter was, he knew about egg-milk and who had given it to her. Jealousy wormed its way into his head. He wanted to make her laugh, like she had when they played cards. When there was trust between them. Was it only a few weeks; it seemed a lifetime to him?

'I've played enough. I'm going to bed. Goodnight.'

Before he could rise from his chair, Grace was going out through the door.

He replaced the counters in their box, then went to the cabinet and took out the brandy bottle and a glass. He chuckled to himself. 'Grace, last night, with the wine, me tonight with the spirit. This won't do, my dear. We cannot endure this and survive. It is better that I go back to London.' Alex sat down and raised his glass to the model ship. 'To Grace.'

Two days passed and Alex was still at Solitaire. He knew he

should leave, but he could not go. It would be the end for him and Grace. So, they played out the polite lord and lady; had dinner together and sat waiting for the light to fade when they went their separate ways to bed.

It was gone midnight, yet Alex lay awake, looking at the bed canopy. The recent rain had done little to reduce the night temperature and his naked body had rejected even the sheet in the past few minutes. She was next door, the faithless wife, for she was truly that. He was entitled to go to her at any time, but did he want to be what she would consider second best? Hugo Olsen was her choice. The Captain's name beat inside his brain like a hammer. What was so special about the Norwegian? There was little difference in their ages; they were both fit and healthy. He had far more to offer than the Captain – title, land, money and protection by the English gentry.

Alex could not stay on his bed another minute. The image of her beneath him after the storm, when he had thought her his virgin bride, tore an oath from him, comparing her with the alley ladies of the night.

He listened at the connecting door – not a sound. Was she in there? Or was she away again, racing down to the beach to meet him? Alex turned the handle, but the door did not open. He was the one who had locked it. He was the one who had vowed never to go through again. It was time to leave.

Grace handed Chestnut to Jenkins and went into the house through the kitchen door. Mrs Gillett was kneading dough and the smell reminded her of when she was a little girl sitting at the heavy square table, asking questions about food, loving the stories about Mr Carrot and Mrs Cabbage.

'Ah, this brings back memories, Gillie. Is that bread dough I smell?'

'Yes. And it is your favourite. It will go well with the soup for luncheon.'

155

'Well, I missed breakfast. The morning was so beautiful, I got Esther out of bed at five, so I could ride with the rising sun.' Grace's cheeks were pink and her eyes sparkled. 'Is his lordship up yet?'

Mrs Gillett kept her gaze on the dough. 'He's gone. There's a letter for you in the drawing room.' She raised her head, tears spilling down her cheeks. 'Oh Gracie, why did you marry him? He will bring you nothing but heartache.'

Grace stood dumbfounded. Her colour drained. 'No. He cannot have done this to me again.' Then she ran from the kitchen.

It was on the mantel in front of the clock.

Grace stared at it.

He had finally decided he didn't want a faithless wife. She should have begged him to understand that she wasn't. She should have told him everything about Simon. But she had played her cards all wrong. She had stupidly thought that after ten years he wouldn't know. What did she know of the bed antics? She had made love with Simon just one night. What a fool she was. Alex had loved her. They had broken the taboo of Liddy. Something must have happened in London for him to leave without seeing her first. She took it down and broke his seal.

Dear Grace,

I find myself unable to remain with you.
 I will seek advice on our situation and have my solicitor contact you.
 You have found the love and peace you deserve.

Yours, Alex.

From a whispered reading her voice rose to a shout. She whirled round. 'No, you can't have gone.' She ran from the room, up the stairs and into his bedchamber. Every polished surface was bare. She opened the clothes cupboard and stilled. He really was gone. Grace sank to the floor and covered her face.

Grace was still sitting on the floor when Mrs Gillett found her. The old woman eased her arthritic bones down next to Grace, rubbed her rough thumb over the soft white knuckles of her mistress.

'Come to the kitchen and have your soup, Gracie. He isn't worth your tears.' Mrs Gillett put her arms around the shaking shoulders. 'You're cold, come away from here, the kitchen is warm and I'll make you a pot of tea.'

Like the child she had once been, Grace went with her to the kitchen and sat at the table waiting for Mrs Gillett to comfort her. After the tea and a bowl of soup, Grace began to think for herself. She got up and prowled round the kitchen.

'I won't stay here any longer. I shall go to London and see him.'

'Is that wise?'

'Maybe not, but I am going. I will write immediately and ask Saunders to have my arrival prepared for.' Now that the decision was made, Grace was fuelled with energy that was fanned by anger and hurt. 'Find Mr Gillett for me. I want the letter sent this afternoon.'

Esther was put into a fluster as she was ordered to pack and prepare to leave for London in two days. 'But your ladyship, many of your gowns needs laundering and the ironing takes forever. There's only Mrs Gillett and me! To do everything! Two days is impossible.'

'Then don't wash them. They can be done when we reach Grosvenor Square. We leave the day after tomorrow, at six o'clock sharp with the call of the birds.'

Grace had misjudged the journey time and they were forced to spend three nights at wayside coaching inns.

Preparing to make an early start, Grace and Esther were in the courtyard waiting for Jenkins to bring the coach. Suddenly, the sound of hooves and wheels on cobblestones coming through the archway heralded the stagecoach bound for Bristol. The coachman was shouting and the gentlemen passengers sitting on the outside top seats were waving their hats and yelling, 'Victory! The Duke of Wellington has bested Bonaparte!'

From inside the tavern passengers waiting for the London stage-coach raced out, their excitement matching those revellers outside. One young man added, 'At Waterloo, south of Brussels.' It had taken only a few seconds to turn a quiet posting-inn to a continuous din of cheers and hoots.

'Oh, your ladyship, England has won! Isn't it wonderful?'

Grace hugged Esther. 'The best news possible. London will be triumphant when we ride in today. Tell Jenkins to hurry. I want to be there to celebrate.' She didn't add, with Alex, but her pulse raced as she imagined the joy he must be feeling and she wanted to be there with him. Then the innkeeper came out with a tray of tankards full of ale for everyone and this delayed their departure a little longer.

They arrived at London just before noon. Hundreds of merry-makers were filling the roads. Carriages, vendors' horse carts and loaded hand-barrows were brought to a slow crawl. Dirty faces with blackened teeth and matted hair peered inside and Esther banged on the window, raising her fist, scolding, 'Be off, scally-wags, and clear the way.'

Then their coach came to a stop.

'Ask Jenkins what is the matter, why are we not moving?'

Esther opened the door and leaned out. 'Her ladyship wants to know what is wrong?'

'Wrong! Bodies are what's wrong. Ask her ladyship does she mind if I try another way?'

Grace heard the exchange. 'Yes, any way. Just get us to Grosvenor Square.'

Jenkins turned into a side street and the throng thinned out. Turning and twisting along unfamiliar roads, they unfortunately then turned into another busy thoroughfare. It seemed that there was no avoiding the mêlée of coaches and people.

Stationary again, Grace looked out of the coach window. The impulsive decision to come to London worried her as she got nearer to Kilbraith House. Would he be glad to see her? Mentally shaking her thoughts away she watched the crowds and noticed several red-haired children; then one adult head stood out, copper coloured. The man was getting out of a coach, appeared to be checking the pavement right and left, and then bent back inside. He helped a blonde woman out, who was noticeably with child and she leaned on his arm for support. As they moved away from the coach Grace saw his face.

Alex!

She watched them walk to a well-presented mid-terrace house and he opened the door. Before going in the woman said something close to his ear and he laughed. Then the door closed.

Grace's eyes couldn't focus; her senses were frozen in that moment of time. Alex was with another woman.

The coach started to move forward but she banged on the side. 'Where are we?'

Esther was dozing, but sat up at the shouted question. 'Where are we? I don't know, I'll ask.'

Jenkins sounded irritable. 'Somewhere in Chelsea, that's all I know.'

'Ask Jenkins to wait, I mean stop. I have to think.'

Alex was betraying her. He wasn't running from her, he was running to another woman. The blonde woman was his mistress, carrying his child. So why had he married her? All that talk about Liddy was a sham. Nothing made sense. She couldn't go to Grosvenor Square, couldn't face him knowing what she had just witnessed.

Then she remembered their rides to Kensington. She had praised him for his knowledge of London. What had he said? 'I have a business need to come through Kensington on my way to Chelsea.' Hugo had been right; business covered a wide range of activities. Well, Alex's was adultery.

'Tell Jenkins to turn around. Go back to Solitaire.'

'Your ladyship, why? We're nearly there. We've been travelling four days. You're tired, I'm tired. Please, let us go on.'

Grace was not listening. Perhaps Solitaire was not the place to go. She couldn't go to Aunt Matilda and it was not the done thing to arrive unannounced at an acquaintance's residence. There was Isabelle Wainwright, but then Willy was Alex's cousin. Where, where could she go? Rachel was at Hawthorn Hall. It was not too far a distance north of London. 'Tell Jenkins we are going to Hawthorn Hall. I'm sure he knows the way.'

Esther looked horrified, her eyes wide and she started to cry.

Grace was in no mood for melodramatic outbursts from servants. 'Pull yourself together and give my order to Jenkins.'

Grace heard raised voices, but she didn't care. They would do her bidding. After all, she was the wedded Lady Rossmore.

They reached Hawthorn Hall just before dark.

Grace got out of the coach as soon as it stopped. Rachel was nearing her confinement and she didn't want her upset.

The front door opened and Jessop, with the expertise of long experience, welcomed her with a formal bow. Rachel appeared in the hall and hurried forward with outstretched arms.

'Lady Rossmore, what an unexpected surprise.'

The understatement made Grace smile. 'Mrs Kilbraith, good evening. I must apologise for my appearance at this late hour and without invitation, but I . . .' And Grace burst into tears.

Rachel looked at Jessop. 'Can I leave you to arrange accommodation for Lady Rossmore and her staff?' She fluttered her hand in the air like a wand. 'Thank you, Jessop.'

Taking Grace's arm she led her forward. 'Come into my sitting room, I do not use the drawing room when Geoffrey is not here.'

Although it was now summertime, there was a fire warming the room. Grace had felt a chill creeping into her bones during the last few miles of the journey, so she crossed to the fireplace and held her hands out to the flames. Without turning to look at Rachel, she said, 'I don't know where to begin. I'm so tired, so confused. Can we talk in the morning, Rachel?' She turned. 'May I stay until I know what to do?'

'My dear, you may stay as long as you wish. We are now family, although I have been, shall we say, banished to the country until after the birth. I look forward to your company. And I need to know nothing, unless you wish to tell me. Now, I shall ring for a light supper for you, after which time your room will be ready.'

Chapter Fourteen

The staff at Kilbraith House had gone into a flurry at the news of Lady Rossmore's pending arrival from Whitecliffs.

Alex, on the other hand, wondered what it was all about. He had left her free to follow her heart, so why was she coming?

Her letter had said she would be arriving yesterday. Given the distance, he had not overly worried when she had not reached Kilbraith House.

All day he had been expecting her. He sat at his desk drumming his fingers. It was now four o'clock and still no sign of her. The revelling throughout the day celebrating Wellington's victory might have caused some delay, but his concern was mounting with each minute. Thieves and vagabonds found crowded occasions prime pickings to the unsuspecting. This thought made him more anxious. Sitting doing nothing was wasting valuable daylight time. He pulled the bell-rope and immediately the door opened.

'Have my horse brought to the front, Saunders. I'm going to look for Lady Rossmore.'

The streets were crowded. Rich silks and poor cottons made a rainbow of colour. Voices rang out in song, and music flowed from fiddles and pipes. Drinkers at alehouses spilled into the street with tankards held high. Alex had to weave amongst them and the shouts from coachmen to move out of the way made his horse skittish.

He pulled in at an eating house and dismounted. Riding on was impossible.

A man, already half a sheet to the wind, shouted, 'Waste of time sir. They won't be goin' 'ome until the dawn. Take a seat and drink a toast to The Duke.'

'I agree. Order me a tankard then I'll toast Wellington with you.'

Several tankards later, Alex was as merry as the crowds. He was certain that Grace would be at Grosvenor Square by now and Saunders would have them all settled in by the time he returned. He relaxed for the first time since leaving Solitaire and wondered if it was the victory celebrations, or the thought that she had followed him to London.

It was near on midnight when he was helped onto his horse to return.

The front door opened as soon as he dismounted.

'My lord, are you alright? It is getting late; I was worried, after all that has happened recently and her ladyship not arrived . . . well . . .' Saunders' voice trailed off.

'I'm well; met a few well-wishers and raised a tankard to . . . she's not arrived? You're telling me her ladyship is not here?' The jubilant Alex couldn't comprehend that. He had been so sure. 'But that's impossible. Even the crowds, taking a slower pace . . . where can she be?' Alex gave the reins to a footman and hurried into the house. 'It's too late for a search now. Have my horse back here at six sharp. Saunders, tell Miles to pack me a small valise to strap onto my saddle. I'll have supper and something to clear my head. The cheap ale was strong and it's lying like lead in my gut.' He closed the study door without waiting for an answer.

The dawn light strengthened as Alex rode out of London and stopped at the first inn. The negative shake of the innkeeper's head that no lady had boarded there spurred him on. At Hammersmith and onwards he visited three more inns along the London to Bristol road. At the fourth hostelry, the courtyard was empty and he dismounted. 'Ahoy there, stable boy, where are you?' A boy came out of the tavern door and ran to take the reins. 'Water and feed

163

him while I speak to the innkeeper.' He tossed a coin into the air that the boy caught with expert grace.

Inside the smell of ale tinged with vomit hit Alex. So much for yesterday's merrymakers, no doubt still lying in beds and wallowing in their own mess. The stench made Alex taste bile. He also feared another negative answer to his question. 'Innkeeper, are you abroad?'

A red-faced, pot-bellied man came from the back room, his soiled apron good evidence of the night before. 'What can I get you, sir? Most of the kegs are dry, but I can offer wine.'

'I'm not after food or drink, only information. Did a coach halt here overnight the day before yesterday? It was a gentle lady, with a maidservant and coachman.'

Alex did not want to use Grace's name, Lady Rossmore. It would make him look as though he were chasing a runaway elopement.

'You expect me to remember after the day we had yesterday?'

'Look at your books, man. She would have paid you.'

'Well, those still here on the morning the news arrived about The Duke's victory, their celebrating, and I was giving out trays of ale, for free mind you, I, um, forgot to . . . well, you can understand, sir, things got a bit muddled.'

'You mean you pocketed the money for yourself.'

'Well . . . I could ask the wife, she would have had more to do with ladies than me.'

Alex's frustration at the man's indifference came out on an angry shout. 'Then move to it, man, I want an answer now.' The innkeeper fled, shouting for his wife at the top of his voice.

The room was small and claustrophobic and Alex couldn't stand the smell any longer. He went out into the yard and sat down on a bench. The morning sun was warm; he tilted his face up and closed his eyes. She danced behind his lids, her dark ringlets bobbing as they side stepped between clapping hands down the aisle in the cotillion. She was laughing at him, enjoying every moment.

A voice interrupted his thoughts. 'The wife says, "yes," there was a party as you describe, sir. They were still here when the news came and joined in for my free ale.'

'Alex opened his eyes. 'Thank you. I'll have meat and bread with a jug of wine.' As an afterthought, he called to the retreating back, 'Out here in the yard, the air is sweeter.' This was her last stop.

He was hungry. The beef was good and the wine acceptable. As he ate he wondered what to do next. She hadn't stopped at the inns he had already enquired at. Those were the most likely, if the coach had sustained any damage. The chaos on the roads, with every kind of vehicle pushing for space, and the crowd so dense in town, no one would remember a specific coach. It seemed an impossible problem to solve. Still he now knew in which direction to search.

For the rest of the day he stopped at every public resting house, but the answer was always a shaken head. No.

When he arrived back, Saunders had the same reply. No.

'Hell, Saunders, where can she be? After I found her last overnight stop, I searched every rest-place and eating house for miles.'

'If your lordship will allow, I should like to say on behalf of myself and the staff that we are most concerned with Lady Rossmore's disappearance.'

For the first time, Alex accepted that fact. Grace had disappeared, along with his coach, coachman and her maid. Impossible! She had to be somewhere.

'I . . . thank you.' What else was there to say? 'Ask Miles to get me a bath ready, and I will have a supper tray.'

Alex sat in his study, thinking what to do next. The clock chimed three. Through the window the night emphasised the fear that was racing round in his head. He was reluctant to have a private agent look for her, especially if Olsen was involved. Her reputation was at full gossiping height now; the affair would be the crowning glory.

She had left Solitaire, travelled within striking distance of London and then, poof, gone like the magician's dove. Did she change her mind and go back to Whitecliffs? This was the most logical explanation. If, nearing London, she had come to a decision not to . . . not to what? Love him? The word suddenly filled him with dread. No, that he could not bear.

He looked up at Liddy's portrait. Every muscle in his body was rigid and the quill pen he was toying with between his fingers snapped in two halves.

'I won't give her up.'

When had he decided this? As he lay awake, twisting and turning until he couldn't stay in the bed any longer? While he paced his room until he could go out looking again? But go where? Her relationship with her father was strained, so she would not go to Woodford Hall. If she were with Lady Crowmarsh he would have received correspondence from her. It would be her duty to inform him. So he must go to Solitaire and beg her to come to London.

He pulled the bell-cord continuously and waited. When Saunders arrived, he said, 'Regardless of the hour, please tell Miles we are going to Whitecliffs. Have Benton ready the coach immediately.'

Geoffrey sauntered up St James's Street intending to go to his club when he saw Sir Quentin Baines sitting in the bow window of a coffee shop. With a light step he went in and slapped Baines on the shoulder. 'Congratulations, Quen,' he said and sat down in the seat opposite.

'For what, may I ask?'

'She's disappeared. Gone like a puff of pipe smoke.'

Baines looked away from the window and raised his eyebrows. 'Well, well, now what?'

'I thought a spot of lunch at Madame Chastain's and a round of the tables. I feel lucky today. Then I shall leave you to your own little romp and go to see Lucille.'

'You're a callous scoundrel, Geoffrey. But I admit, I shall miss the excitement of our adventure.'

'Oh. I don't think it is over yet. I hear Alex is quite perplexed and has been searching for her. He thinks she has gone back to Whitecliffs. Will you get your man to find out?'

'All in good time, Geoffrey, your schemes take money, and if you lose at the tables today . . .' he pointed his thumb downwards, 'I have already warned you, I cannot be your banker at the moment.'

'Stop trying to be my conscience. I deserve a bit of merriment; this has all been quite a strain, you know.'

Quentin threw back his head and laughed. 'That's the tallest lie I've heard. You think of no one but yourself. But so be it, merriment it is. It takes time to find someone, especially someone who doesn't want to be found.'

Several hours later and a purse full of winnings, Geoffrey tapped five times with his cane on Lucille's door. He liked to think of this as his secret code. He heard the lock move and then she stood before him and his mood changed.

'When are you going to buy something to hide that?' And he pushed past her.

'Do come in,' she said to his back, 'and hello. You don't want me to buy new dresses, in fact, you insisted.'

'Well, that was then. Now you can go and get your dressmaker to make something more suitable.'

He pulled her towards him and kissed her. 'Um, you taste good.'

She grimaced and put her hand across her nose and mouth. 'You taste of wine and your jacket smells of pipe smoke.' Her shoulders heaved and she turned away. 'You are making the bile rise in my throat.'

Geoffrey took a drawstring purse from his pocket, held it between his fingers a moment then threw on the table. 'A cut of my winnings, Lucille. More than enough to satisfy your seamstress and my desires, don't you think?'

Lucille hesitated, but he knew her well enough to know he would get what he wanted.

Chapter Fifteen

Grace opened her eyes to a shaded room, only a crack of sunshine coming through the top of the curtains. She wondered what the time was and looked for a clock. It was on a table where ink and writing articles were laid out. Two o'clock! Surely that must be wrong? She looked to the side of the big double bed and saw a bell-pull. She rolled over and gave it several tugs.

When Esther arrived she looked pale and tired, with a worried tone to her voice. 'Your ladyship. At last you are awake. We were beginning to wonder if you are ill.'

'No, I am not. Could you bring me tea and toast, please? Esther, you look rather wan, are you not feeling well?'

'It's just the travelling, m'lady. Are we staying here long?'

'I'm not sure . . . perhaps a few days. I have not discussed it with Mrs Kilbraith yet.'

The maid opened the curtains and left, leaving Grace to lie back and think.

No, she was not ill. She had lain awake for hours, churning over and over the events of the past weeks since her marriage and Alex's troubled behaviour. About Liddy's ghostly power over him and his blonde mistress who was with child. And above all, Alex's disgust that she was not a virgin bride. That he had accused her of having an affair with Hugo. True, their friendship was improper, but after seeing Alex in Chelsea, how could he paint her character so black? All of this had faded in and out of her mind until she couldn't think any longer and had finally fallen into a dreamless sleep.

Rachel must be wondering what all this was about. She and Grace had only met socially one afternoon, as Rachel spent most of her time in the country. This had made it difficult to keep in contact. How much should she tell her?

A knock and the door opening interrupted her thoughts.

Rachel came in with a tray. 'Good afternoon, Grace, are you feeling better?'

Better! That was an understatement for her chaotic thoughts. 'Yes, thank you.'

'While you take your refreshments, I thought I could sit with you.' She walked to the writing table and put the tray down, then sat on the high-backed chair. 'The cosy fireside one is most uncomfortable now. I shall be so glad when this delivery is done.'

Grace felt inadequate to answer. She was older than Rachel yet this woman was about to deliver her fifth child and approached it with such confidence. She wasn't sure she could.

'It is very kind of you to have me, Rachel. I owe you an explanation for my untimely arrival . . . you see . . .'

Rachel held up her hand. 'No, Grace. I want you to think about this before you tell me anything. I know what one Kilbraith is like, so I would ask that you consider this first. You are welcome here at Hawthorn Hall for as long as you wish to stay. Geoffrey seldom comes to visit, he hates the country, so we have the estate to ourselves and I shall enjoy your company for as long as you think it necessary to hide from Alex.'

This long speech left Grace both happy and distressed. Rachel could read the situation without a word being said. She could feel her face heating and let her gaze drop to the counterpane. 'You are very understanding. Thank you.'

'Now, let me pour your tea, I'm sure you have a great thirst.'

Rachel brought the tray and put it across Grace's lap. 'I'll let you have it in peace. I promised Nurse that I would visit the children this afternoon.'

When the door closed, Grace thought, *I suppose I am in hiding from Alex*. For in truth, she could not face him and let him see how much she loved him; could not bear to have it thrown back in favour of his breeding mistress.

Grace did not rise until well into the afternoon, yet she felt lethargic. She sat in the sitting room and a niggling cough irritated her throat, causing a pain in her chest. As another spasm began, she saw Rachel put aside her sewing on the window seat. 'Can I ask Nurse to get you something for your cough, Grace?'

'I cannot think why it is? I am so sorry, Rachel, this must be very annoying for you.'

'I am more concerned with your health, my dear. I will ring for tea, the hot brew will help.'

But it did not and by early evening, Grace was persuaded to go to her bed.

'Really, Rachel, I am never ill, this is most unusual.'

Rachel smoothed the sheet and put her fingers to Grace's forehead. 'Not so unusual, when one has travelled the distance you have over the last few days. Your poor Esther is completely worn out. I sent her to rest for an hour after tea. We ladies are more delicate than you think. Have you always been so strong willed?'

'Do you mean determined? If so, then yes. Just because one is female doesn't mean we have no horizons to reach or desires of our own.'

'My, if Geoffrey heard you speak like that he would be furious. He is such a . . .'

Rachel stepped back as Grace began to cough again. She buried her face into a linen towel that was more practical than the little cotton square she normally used.

'I'm so sorry, Rachel.'

'Try to sleep. You will feel better tomorrow.'

But as the hours passed, her temperature rose and the fever began to dampen her forehead. Esther bathed her face with tepid water and pulled the covers close to her chin.

'No, take them away.' Tearing at the sheet, she clawed the covers down, the lawn nightgown wet and clinging. Grace thrashed her arms aimlessly, as though boxing an unseen opponent and the cough had become a continuous bark.

At midnight, Esther asked for Rachel to be woken.

In the dim bedchamber, Rachel could see that Grace was near delirium.

'Esther, raise Jessop and ask him to send for Dr Morton. Wake Tilly and tell her to come and help me dress. Then come straight back.'

Grace was starting to shiver.

Rachel was pulling the counterpane over Grace when Esther returned.

'Keep the covers on her. I must dress before Dr Morton arrives.'

Rachel insisted that Esther remain in the bedchamber during Dr Morton's examination. He was a tall man with thinning hair and long fingers and he prodded and poked Grace's neck, chest and back. Listened with his ear at her ribs and tut-tutted several times. Ignoring the maid, he left when he had finished.

Downstairs, in the hall, the doctor spoke to Rachel. 'Lady Rossmore is very ill with the fever. Keep a maid with her, bathe her body with warm water and give her water to drink. I will return in the morning.' His face had deep lines around the mouth and his manner was grave.

'Are you saying that Lady Rossmore could die?'

'Fever and coughing reduce one's strength. But she is strong and I do not expect such an extreme outcome. How are you? It is not the time to be using your strength; you will need that yourself soon.'

'I am very well, Dr Morton, thank you. Esther is Lady Rossmore's maid and I have sufficient staff to cope.'

He looked up at the fanlight and a smile lightened his face. 'I bid you . . . good day.'

As the morning light strengthened, Grace's fever continued.

'My lady, will you drink.' Esther held a glass to her lips, but Grace refused. 'Please, just a little. Dr Morton said you must, it will make you better.' Esther pressed the glass between Grace's lips and forced them open, tipping the liquid into her mouth. The effort to swallow made Grace cough, and the water dribbled down her chin. 'Oh, my lady, do drink.'

In the end it was Rachel who persuaded her. She cradled Grace's shoulders and lifted her. Swept the damp hair from her face and talked to her until she opened her eyes. 'Come, you must drink. For me, please?'

'Alex.' The voice was a whispered croak from her dry lips.

'Shh.' Tears welled in Rachel's eyes as Grace finally sipped at the water.

All day Rachel and Esther cajoled her to drink and take a little broth. She drifted between a delirious sleep and a fuddled waking. She muttered names that meant nothing to Rachel except her calls for Alex.

In a choked whisper Rachel muttered, 'What has gone wrong between them? Surely it could be straightened out; they have only been married a few weeks.' She sighed and continued talking, as though Grace could hear. 'Geoffrey is not the easiest person to live with, but even we have managed to stay together, of sorts. A woman's life is a hazardous path to tread.' Rachel stood up and took a cotton handkerchief from her dress pocket and dabbed her eyes, then went over to the washstand to refill the bowl with water.

During the night Grace made a turn for the better. She opened her eyes to see Esther sitting on a chair near the bed, her head bent forward and her arms crossed over her chest.

'Esther, can you hear me?'

There was no reply. Grace closed her eyes and drifted into a natural sleep.

'I cannot stay in bed any longer. You have had me coddled for three days and it is time for me to come downstairs.' Her bravado words were a contradiction to her weak voice

'Only two really, your ladyship, the first one you were so ill we all thought . . .'

'Thought what? That I would die? Oh, come, Esther; do not be

172

so melodramatic. You sound like one of those actresses on the stage at Drury Lane.' But her raised voice was followed by a bout of coughing.

'Mrs Kilbraith has not said you can get up. Please, m'lady, stay in bed until I can find her.'

Grace relented as she saw her maid's distress. 'Oh, very well; ask Mrs Kilbraith to visit me as soon as it is convenient.' Satisfied, Esther left.

Pulling the pillows up, Grace levered herself into a sitting position. She found that the effort was making her breathe deeply and have a great desire to cough again. 'I won't stay here another day, I don't care what Rachel says.'

A knock on the door presented Dr Morton and not Rachel. 'Ah, the patient is sitting up. That is a good sign. How are you today, Lady Rossmore?'

He walked to the bed and took her hand. 'Warm, not over hot.' He placed his palm on her forehead. 'Good, not hot either. How is your breathing?'

Grace wanted to lie, but she didn't. 'I suppose I am a little weak and the cough is still with me.'

'Um . . . perhaps you need another day or two in bed? We can't have you taking the fever again.'

'Two days! Oh, no. I want to get up.'

'A compromise then; you may get up tomorrow, but you must not exert yourself in walking up and down the stairs. Your meals are to be served in your room here. I will advise Mrs Kilbraith that you may go down the day after.'

'But I'm . . .'

Dr Morton raised his hand. 'No, Lady Rossmore. You will do as I say.'

Grace felt like she had when little, with her father giving out orders that were never to be disobeyed. A rebellious retort was on the tip of her tongue, when the door opened and Rachel came in.

'Dr Morton, good morning. I am to assume that you have a fiery damsel who wants to get up?'

173

'Yes, indeed. But I do not recommend such action yet.'

'Leave it to me. Lady Rossmore and I will come to an agreement.'

'Thank you. I do not think it necessary to call again.' He turned to Grace, wagging his finger. 'Unless her recklessness brings the fever back. Good day, Lady Rossmore.'

He walked to the door, followed by Rachel. She looked at Grace. 'I'll be back immediately,' and she winked.

As a compromise, Grace agreed to stay in bed until after luncheon.

Later, sitting in the winged chair with a blanket over her knees, she could hear the birds singing, feel the light breeze that came through the open window and hear the duck calls from the lake. The summer sounds made her long to go riding. She closed her eyes and thought of Whitecliffs and the headland, the soaring gulls. Recalled the sea and how it crept up the beach and darkened the shingle. Hugo came into her mind with his blond head and tall stature. Yes, he was a very handsome sea captain. Then he was pushed away by Alex; she loved his copper hair, strong features and determined mind, even though it had turned against her. Her memory saw him getting out of a coach, furtively looking left and right along the pavement before helping the fair-haired woman out. It all pointed to secrecy and deceit. She started to cough. That's what he did to her, made her ill. She must learn to stop loving him, or she would never be well again.

On the fifth day, Grace was allowed down to luncheon.

She would not admit to anyone how weak her legs felt. Using both hands on the banister for support she descended one tread at a time down the stairs, keeping a watchful eye below, praying that a servant would not come into the hall. Stepping off the bottom tread, she smoothed her dress before going into the dining room.

Rachel was already there. She came to Grace with outstretched arms. 'Well done, my dear.' Then took both her hands and guided her to the table. 'Now, come and eat, we must build your strength back. I have ordered a light meal and a delicious pudding for after.'

Sitting at the offered chair, Grace realised that her defiant words over the last few days, were just that. *I'm as a newborn lamb on spindly legs, very much dependent on its mother, and Rachel is surely taking that role.* 'You have been very kind to me . . . I don't know what I would have done, had I not thought to come here.' She reached for the glass of water and sipped, keeping her gaze lowered.

'Grace, I want you to think of this as home, for the near future at least, until you make up your mind what to do. Now is not the time to worry about anything. When you are stronger, we will discuss it again.'

It is the weakness, she thought and burst into tears, snatching the napkin from the table and burying her face.

'That is exactly what I mean. You are too weak even to be down here.'

Grace controlled her crying and looked up. 'I won't go back to bed. I'm alright now. You are so kind; it touches my heart, Rachel. Thank you.'

Nothing else was said, as the door opened and Jessop supervised the serving of luncheon.

Left alone in the afternoon, Grace needed something to do while Rachel went with the children and Nurse for a walk by the lake. Going into the library she ran her eyes along the rows of volumes. Shakespeare's *Romeo and Juliet* caught her attention and she took it down. Such a tragic story: of families and feuds, young love and death. Not the book to cheer one up after illness, yet she could not put it back. She went to a chair by the window and started to read. She was there with them through the pages, smiling and frowning, feeling their emotions, feeling their frustrations. When the sun moved from the page and the room fell into shadow, Grace realised she had been sitting there for several hours and not once had her troubles or Alex entered her mind. She smiled and closed the book. 'Thank you, Shakespeare, for a pleasing and restful afternoon.'

Crossing the hall to the stairs, she saw Rachel's sitting-room door open and heard Dr Morton's voice. 'Your time is very near,

Mrs Kilbraith. I must advise you to rest as much as possible. Is your husband aware of your delivery time?'

'He is in London on business, but I will write to him tomorrow of your observations, Dr Morton, and thank you for coming today. You will be pleased to hear Lady Rossmore is improving.'

There was movement as though the doctor was leaving and Grace went up the stairs out of sight before they came into the hall. She went into her bedchamber and sat in the winged chair, wondering if her presence at Hawthorn Hall was a help or hindrance to Rachel. Still, she had said to stay and it was a large house; she would see to it that her visit was not overlong.

The days were growing hot and the flowers at Hawthorn Hall were an abundance of colour. Grace was back to full health and strength.

Today, she had been riding on the estate, through the woods, across the parkland and finally to the lake. She saw the swans, swimming slowly near the reeds, the pen trailing her eight soft bundles of brown cygnets in her wake, the cob circling, constantly on guard, the defender of his family. Grace reined the mare to a stop – what a wonderful scene. Then the haunting scene of Alex and the fair-haired woman was there; they were always lurking in her subconscious to torment. She turned her mount and used her whip more forcefully than intended, so that the mare shot forward, back into the park.

Later, still dressed in her riding clothes, Grace joined Rachel for tea.

'Did you have an exhilarating ride, Grace?'

'Very much, thank you. The woods and grassland are beautiful, Rachel. Geoffrey is lucky to have such an excellent manager.'

'I love to ride, especially in the country. Unfortunately, confinement prevents the pleasure. Wait until it is your turn.'

Rachel's remark stabbed like a knife into Grace. 'I think not. Alex and I will never have children.'

'But you cannot be sure. Goodness, you have not been married two months yet. I know all ladies cannot be like me, breeding every year, but have faith, Grace, you will hold a son in your arms one day.' Rachel tried to lean forward and take Grace's hand, but she couldn't reach. 'Oh dear, this one is exceptionally big.'

Grace did the leaning instead. 'Time will tell, Rachel. Now, I must go and change.'

Through the sitting-room window the sun sank in a halo of orange and indigo.

With several branches of candles lighting the room, Grace and Rachel were playing whist. Into the peaceful aura of the room, noise and commotion came from the hall. Rachel put her cards down. 'Whatever is going on out there?' Leaning heavily on the table, she levered herself out of the chair, then went and opened the door with Grace following.

In the dim hall, lit by only one branch of candles, statuette shadows danced over a man wearing a full-length cloak and hat.

'Geoffrey! What are you doing here?' Rachel was evidently shocked at the sight of him.

'I live here, remember. It's been one hell of a journey, so I don't want an inquisition now. I just want . . .' He ceased speaking, his gaze fixed on Grace. The scene froze, no one moved. Finally he found his voice, but it was little more than a whisper. 'What, in God's name, is *she* doing here?'

Everyone in the hall turned to look at Grace.

Rachel was the first to speak. 'Lady Rossmore is staying for a while. She has been ill and is recovering . . .'

'I can see who it is. I thought she would be miles . . .' He didn't finish, but turned to Jessop. 'Get my rooms ready. I'm starving; the food at the inns is appalling. Rachel, I will see you in the morning.' He looked again at Grace. Seeming to remember his manners he said, 'Lady Rossmore, goodnight.'

The next moment he turned and went into his study.

'Oh dear.' Rachel's moan had Grace going to her.

'Are you alright? It isn't the baby, is it?' The shock of Geoffrey's arrival and his peculiar behaviour could easily cause her to begin.

'No, my dear, it's just Geoffrey. By the look of things we are in for a thunderous visit. But, then, I am used to that.' Rachel gave Grace's hand a tap. 'It is time to go to my bed. Goodnight.'

Grace watched her go up the stairs, then went back into the sitting room and tidied the cards. She sat on the window seat and looked out into the night. What should she do now?

Before the dawn broke, nothing mattered except Rachel.

Rachel woke with a pain in her lower back and didn't need Nurse to tell her what was happening. Reaching for the bell-rope she pulled, yanking it several times before the first cramping sensation in her groin made her pull her legs up and roll into a ball.

Minutes passed and she cried out, 'Tilly, where are you?'

Was everyone sleeping so soundly they didn't hear the bell? A fear greater than she had ever known engulfed her. She called again, 'Tilly, anyone, please come and help me.' Her head was spinning and she heaved vomit into her throat. She knew, from her past labours, that each time had been quicker to deliver than the last. She couldn't be here alone, in the dark, to deliver her baby. Closing her eyes the dizziness slowed and she moved to sit on the edge of the bed. Using her arms like crutches she tried to stand up.

The door opened and Tilly rushed in.

'Oh! It is time, my lady, please don't try to stand.' The maid was in her nightgown and carrying a candle. She put it on the bedside cabinet and then pushed Rachel back onto the bed, lifting her legs. 'I'll get Nurse and tell Jessop to send for the doctor. Oh my, it is too soon, my lady. What shall I do?'

Rachel felt her rapidly beating heart slow and the fear lessen. 'Do as you have just said and then wake Lady Rossmore and ask her to come here. And tell Jessop to wake Kilbraith.'

Tilly flew from room to room and within fifteen minutes the whole household was awake and in motion for the arrival of a new life.

Grace did not wait for Esther, just put on her simplest dress and hurried along to Rachel's room.

There was an atmosphere of tension.

Rachel was pale and sweat beaded her forehead. The counter-pane had been taken away and the sheet showed her extended shape, so much more than her loose dresses.

Grace went to the bed and took Rachel's hand. 'Everything will be well. Nurse is here and the doctor has been sent for. Can I get you anything? I'm afraid, with no siblings of my own, I am quite untutored in what to do.'

This seemed to amuse Rachel. 'As I said, your turn will come. But for now, I am grateful you are here. I want to ask you a very important . . .' Her words were turned into a groan and her fingers squeezed Grace's hand as she leaned forward, a cry of pain escaping from her lips. Nurse hurried over, but Rachel waved her away. 'I need to finish talking . . .' She lay back, seemingly too crippled with pain to continue. She closed her eyes, then opened them, looking directly at Grace's worried face.

'Promise me, Grace, you will take my children with you if any-thing should happen.' Her breath came as short pants and she fought to finish. 'Geoffrey would be useless. He has never taken any interest . . . this baby is so large, I don't know if I can deliver it this time . . .'

The pleading in her eyes tore at Grace's heart. Rachel thought she was going to die? That she would never see the light of day. 'Don't speak of such things. Of course you will see your children again. You have been strong and come through this before. Oh, Rachel, don't ask me to promise what will not be necessary.'

'I can't do both, Grace. I can't bring this child into the world and worry about who will look after my little ones. Geoffrey has no patience, no love, he will send them away . . .' Rachel heaved a great gulp of air and stiffened as the pains strengthened. This time Nurse would have no more dismissal signs and motioned for Grace to leave. 'Please, Grace, promise me.' And her fingers clawed at Grace's dress, forcing her to lean over the bed. 'You must, Grace, for me.' Now tears were running down her face and Grace recog-nised true fear, not for herself, but her family.

'Yes, Rachel, I promise. But it is not necessary, everything will be alright.'

'You'll take them with you to Rossmore Manor, and Nurse Thompson. They would like that. It is so beautiful there. I have your promise.' Rachel closed her eyes and let go of Grace's dress. 'Thank you. Will you spend the waiting time with the boys? Thomas is the only one who will be frightened; the others are too young. Go now, or Nurse will be carrying you out.' A weak smile touched Rachel's face. 'Goodbye, Grace.'

Outside in the corridor, Grace felt distraught, Rachel's fear now her own. She had never been in a house where a birth was due and the tension was making her head pound and she was trembling from head to foot. She went to the head of the staircase in time to see the front door open and Dr Morton hurry in.

Geoffrey Kilbraith opened the study door and spoke to him.

Grace could not hear the words, but both men parted with just a nod, Geoffrey going back into his study and the doctor coming up the stairs.

'Good morning, Lady Rossmore.' He tried to smile, but there was no humour in his eyes. 'Is Mrs Kilbraith coping with everything?'

'She is very distressed, Dr Morton. In fact, she believes she is dying. That can't be so; she is young and has delivered well in the past. It's not possible . . .'

'It is always possible, Lady Rossmore. We can only do our best, she and I. I must go to her.' Nodding to Grace, as he had Geoffrey, she watched him go into Rachel's room.

Food had no taste. Grace sat in the small sitting room and nibbled on a slice of bread, but gave up and just drank the coffee. She must go to the children, keep her promise to look after them if . . . there was no 'if'. Rachel would be alright, she had to be, there were four sons to rear and a fifth, God willing.

Grace went to the nursery and found Tilly with the boys.

'I will look after them now, Tilly. Go to the kitchen and get yourself some breakfast. Tell Cook I said you are to have an egg with fresh bread. We will all need our strength today.'

The children were dressed for the day and Thomas sat curled with his legs under him in a low, over-stuffed chair. He didn't take his eyes from the page of a book as Grace walked towards him. The two younger ones were sat in a wooden pen, playing with coloured bricks and the youngest was asleep in a cot. A tranquil scene compared with the writhing agony that was taking place in a room on the floor below.

Grace sat down on the floor by Thomas. 'Is it a good book?' There was no reply and he continued to stare at the page. 'Everything will be alright with your mama, Thomas. It just takes a long time. Would you like me to read to you?'

'She might die. Nurse says that many boys are left alone and that their papas marry again. I don't want another mama.' He swallowed hard on a tear-clogged voice.

A lump rose in Grace's throat and she wanted to hug the boy in her arms. But she didn't know him that well and refusal would make a rift between them. 'Your mama is strong and she has you to think about. She wants to see you grow tall and become a man, like your father. Soon you will be able to see her, and a new sibling. Shall we ask Cook to send up some biscuits and milk?'

Thomas looked at Grace. He had the Kilbraith eyes; they cut deep into Grace's soul. Had Alex's eyes looked like this all those years ago when he lost Liddy? Had she judged him too harshly? Without thinking she reached forward and took the small boy into her arms and pulled him down onto her lap. There was no struggling, only his small arms clinging to her, his release of tears wetting the bodice of her dress. She rocked back and forth until they ceased, waited until he fell asleep.

Grace put Thomas onto his bed and then went to the other children. They were so young and vulnerable; the two middle ones content with their toys and the youngest still asleep.

She went over to the window and looked out over the parkland.

Although it was still quite early, the morning sun was dispelling the mist and, as it strengthened, made the room bright and cheerful. She went over to a large wooden rocking horse, painted brown with amber-colour eyes and ran her fingers across the stirrup scratches along its side. Had they been made by generations of Kilbraiths? Had Alex sat on it?

Sitting on the chair that Thomas had used earlier she waited.

When Tilly came back she left her in charge of the nursery.

Hours passed and only Rachel's labour cries echoed down the corridor.

No one saw Geoffrey Kilbraith. He stayed in his study and only Jessop was allowed to go in.

Grace paced round Rachel's sitting room until she thought a threadbare trail would appear. Then voices in the hall sent her flying to open the door. Geoffrey was racing up the stairs and she feared the worst. Her heart started to beat with such force she thought it would break her ribs, and her mouth went so dry there was not a drop of saliva to swallow. Without thinking she ran up the stairs, giving no thought to what she was going to do, only knowing that she had to find someone to ask. Yet asking could result in tragedy and grief. Her answer was the sound of a voice from the open doorway.

Rachel's voice!

'We have two little girls, Geoffrey.'

The silence that followed was broken by just two words. 'Two, Rachel . . .'

Grace heard the incredulous disbelief in his voice, but she smiled. It wasn't what Rachel had feared, one very large baby, but two little girls. Oh, my, she had better go tell Thomas he still had a mama *and two sisters.*

Chapter Sixteen

Mrs Gillett was passing through the hall when a knock on the front door surprised her. The day was grim and rain fell from a leaden sky.

The caller wore a cloak and a naval hat. 'Good afternoon, Mrs Gillett. Is Lady Rossmore at home? I should like to call on her, please.'

Captain Olsen removed his hat and the polite manner was regarded suspiciously. 'Lady Rossmore is not at home.'

'I see. When will she be home? It is not a day to go riding.'

'Lady Rossmore has left residence to go to London.' Mrs Gillett paused. 'To her husband, Captain Olsen.'

His face did not change expression, except for his eyes and they looked past Mrs Gillett and seemed to be searching beyond.

'She did not mention going to London.'

'Her ladyship does not have to inform neighbours of her decisions. If there is nothing else . . .' Her unfinished sentence informed the gentleman that it was time to go.

Affording Mrs Gillett a nod, he replaced his hat and hurried down the steps, out of the gate and onto the road. Unseen by Mrs Gillett, he checked the coach house, then went into the village and tossed a few coins on the inn counter, buying a tankard of ale for anyone with gossip about her ladyship.

Alex left London as dawn lightened the sky.

He stopped for food and drink only twice during the day, and stayed overnight at a coaching inn. Now, after another long day, and the hoof beats of the horses thrumming in his head like a hammer, the coach turned south onto the road that would lead him to the village and Solitaire House. Would she refuse him entrance? No, she wouldn't do that; he was her husband. She might ask him not to stay. He came to the spot where he had watched her leave Olsen's house. Was she in there? He had blocked out this thought until now. Jealousy swept through him. He wanted to confront this man, but logic beat his anger to the top of the ladder. Now was not the time. Alex flexed his shoulders and they passed by the red-brick building.

Solitaire House looked black and deserted, like a residence not in use and a shiver ran down his back. The coach stopped and he immediately got out and ran up the steps, banging on the door with the knocker and then his fists. A light brightened in the side windows and the door bolts were drawn.

Mr Gillett, his shortness emphasised by holding the candlestick high, peered cautiously round the gap as the door opened. 'Yes. What do you want?'

'Gillett, it is the Earl of Rossmore. Open the door and let me in.' There was a shuffling of feet and the doorway widened.

'My lord! We have had no news of you . . .'

'Don't worry about that. I want to see Lady Rossmore, at once.'

'Lady Rossmore? But your lordship, she is not here. She went . . .'

Alex slammed the door with his fist and it shot back and quivered on its hinges.

'Where has she gone? No matter, go and fetch her at once. Tell her I wish to speak with her. Now!' Alex's temper was rising. He had visualised her in the drawing room, sewing or reading, beautiful in a satin gown, the dark curls framing her face.

'Lady Rossmore left for London. She is not here.'

Gillett stood still, the candle slowly lowering to his waist and the flickering light picking out the features of his master: pale, the lips parted and the eyes looking black as coal.

Neither man moved, until the sound of footsteps came from the back of the house and Mrs Gillett came into the hall.

'Mr Gillett, who is it calling at this late hour?'

'It is his lordship. He has come to see Lady Rossmore.'

Alex could hear Mrs Gillett's intake of breath. 'But she is in London. This is impossible. She was going to Grosvenor Square, to see his lordship, to . . .'

'But she didn't come to me, Mrs Gillett. Where has she gone?' Alex was unable to grasp that Grace had disappeared from the face of the earth. He walked across the hall, then stopped, and said to Gillett, 'Miles will bring the luggage, Benton will deal with the coach. I'll be in my room.' And he walked away up the stairs.

Mrs Gillett set to preparing him supper while he washed the dust from his hands and face. He ate little and sat at the dining table without a neck cloth, his shirt open and the sleeves rolled to his elbows. The copper hair was uncombed and its thickness waved down to his collar line. He raised the wineglass to where Grace usually sat.

'To wherever you are, may you be safe.' He downed the red liquid in one go and reached for the decanter. He laughed, remembering how Grace had offered to be his tavern wench. Like a tavern wench, she had given herself to a sea captain and then a lord. Yet he could not let her go. He needed to know why. But first he had to find her.

Mrs Gillett came in to clear the table. Her manner to him was civil, yet he sensed a simmering anger that flashed from her eyes.

'Would you stay a moment, Mrs Gillett? Please, will you sit down?' He motioned to Grace's chair.

She looked quite bewildered, but sat down.

'Mrs Gillett, I know you have a great loyalty to Lady Rossmore. It is understandable. You have known her since a babe, but now is not the time to be shielding her from what might be a dangerous situation. Do you know where she is?'

'Her ladyship was very upset. She decided to leave for London directly after you left.' She lifted her gaze from her lap and looked at Alex. 'She is truly missing, isn't she, my lord?'

'Yes, she is. I don't know where to look. I was putting all my hopes and prayers that she would be here. Now my fears run around in my head, beating a pain in my eyes, yet if I close them, I dread what I might imagine. So, I ask again, do you know where she is?'

'No. I only wish I did.'

Alex had to accept her answer. He knew that Mrs Gillett must have a very bad impression of him as a husband. In the little time he had spent here, he saw how close Grace and her old nurse were and she was very protective of her.

'Thank you. I will retire now and leave you to tidy away.' Alex stood up and reached for the glass and wine. 'My night-cap.' But there was nothing jovial about the remark.

As he left, Mrs Gillett muttered, 'And may the demons haunt your dreams, until you find my Gracie.'

Demons did indeed haunt Alex, but not red-faced, horned devils. No, his were highwaymen, robbers and Chinese dens, who snatched young girls and high-bred women to sell in the opium hellholes in the slums. Chained them down and let vile-smelling men have them for a high price. He woke in a sweat before the dawn and lay letting his heart slow. He couldn't stay in this room any longer; to close his eyes again would bring more anguish. He dressed and let himself out of the house through the study door. Even this was a torture, as he remembered the night of the storm.

The morning was fresh, but not cold. He climbed the path through the wood and took the right fork that would take him to the cliff. The trail had narrowed where ferns had thickened on either side and then he stepped clear and walked on grass to the edge. Here he had kissed her. Alex stood with his face tilted to the sky and gave in to his despair. He had lost Liddy, but had been able to grieve at her grave. Now, he had nothing and it was worse, because he didn't know where to start looking. Finally, he sat down and forced his mind to think. He would go back to London and engage an agent. They had men at their disposal, informants who ran with the lower life of the streets. They could find her.

This settled him and he lay down, listening to the sea lap across the rocks below and slept.

The journey back to London was excruciating. The weather turned wet and made every mile a torment. Alex was forced to spend an additional night at an inn where the smell from rotting horse manure was nauseating, the food meagre and the bed unclean.

When he reached Kilbraith House, Miles immediately set about cleansing his master of the fleas he had picked up and told Saunders to burn every scrap of his lordship's clothing or the house would be infested.

Sitting up to his shoulders in hot water, Alex asked, 'Tell me, Miles, have you ever had a master that comes home with such appalling guests hopping over him?'

Miles hesitated and looked uncomfortable. 'I do not think it quite right, to repeat their names, my lord. Although your circumstances are a little different.'

'You mean they came from the dens and hellholes no decent gentleman would frequent?'

'Quite so. Young bucks and old stags alike. Never would they learn.'

'Well, make sure they are all gone. I don't want to be barred from my club. Not just yet, anyway.'

The conversation ceased as Miles dipped his master completely under the bath water for a third time.

Alex looked at the man sitting on the other side of his desk. He was short and had a girth that bespoke good living, advertised by the spots of dried food on his lapels.

'I have taken much trouble in seeking you out, Mr Beesell. You have been recommended as a man of discretion. Perhaps you would tell me about your agency?'

A face smiled through a halo of grey hair covering his head, down the cheeks and over the chin. 'Your lordship is very kind. I run a good show, with more results than failures. I have a gang of boys, very trustworthy, my lord, and they know about keeping their tongues in the mouth. Loose tongues means no more work, see.' He winked at Alex, indicating his knowledge of the *ton*. 'So, what is it you want me to do?'

Alex sat silent, not sure this was how he wanted to proceed, but how else was he going to find Grace? 'It is a rather delicate situation . . .'

'No need to be over cautious, my lord, is it the usual?'

'The usual, what do you mean?'

'Well . . . is she cavorting with a young buck?'

'No, she is not! The fact of the matter is my wife is missing.'

'Oh.' That one word implied the agent was surmising again. 'Perhaps, you can give me the details . . .' He left the sentence hanging.

Alex leaned forward onto his desk, linked his fingers and began to explain how Grace had gone missing between her last inn stop and Grosvenor Square. These were the only facts needed. What had happened between him and Grace before then was not necessary for the agent to know.

'That is a very strange happening, Lord Rossmore. The difficulties are that the celebrations, the hundreds of revellers who came into town, the ale flowing, will make it, perhaps, a very long search.' He paused and a pair of bushy eyebrows rose, wrinkling a line of flesh in his forehead. 'The cost could be high.'

Alex moved back from leaning on the desk. The little man was overstepping his station.

'The cost is not the issue. Finding Lady Rossmore is your only concern. But mark my word, your bill will be scrutinised by me in great detail. If I find undue expenditure, you may have to wait a very, very long time for payment.' With that Alex rang the bell on his desk and immediately Saunders opened the study door.

'Good day to you, Mr Beesell. I await your findings as soon as possible.'

Geoffrey was tired. He had travelled yesterday from Hawthorn Hall.

Now he felt conspicuous waiting on a path in Hyde Park, cursing Quentin Baines for being late. He couldn't believe that Grace was with Rachel. To see her standing behind his wife had thrown him into a panic. Then the birth of twins! He didn't know whether his senses would ever recover.

Crowds strolled in every direction and Quentin emerged looking as though he didn't have a care in the world.

'You're late. I've been standing here for fifteen minutes. Have you no sense of time?'

'Oh, dear. Do you have another problem, Geoffrey?'

'Rachel delivered twin girls two days ago, Baines! Now I have six children.'

'Congratulations. How are mother and daughters?'

The frown that had been on Geoffrey's forehead smoothed and he smiled. 'To tell the truth, Quen, it was such a shock, I am finding it difficult to accept. Rachel is very weak and the babes are tiny, but Nurse is confident they will survive. But time will tell. I would like at least one to live; Rachel so wanted a daughter this time.'

For once Geoffrey let his emotion show and he plucked a white square from his pocket and dabbed his eyes. 'How foolish, tears are not a normal emotion for me.'

Baines slapped him on the shoulder. 'Do I see a spark of gratitude for Rachel? Not going soft, are you, Geoff? Lucille is next, perhaps she will have three?'

'Speak not in jest. At least Alex will increase my allowance twofold, which will help.'

'Money! That is all your life seems to revolve round. So, what is the meaning of this clandestine meeting in a park?'

'Lady Rossmore is at Hawthorn Hall.'

If the news of twins had not thrown Quentin, then this news did. 'Good lord, at your country estate?' If passers-by had taken the trouble to look, they would have wondered why the two men stared at each other without a muscle moving. Quentin was the first to speak. 'She didn't just run off then, like we hoped. What is she doing at Hawthorn Hall?'

'When I arrived it was late evening and I just hid in my study, meaning to speak to Rachel in the morning. But then, everything went mad. Before dawn Rachel was in labour and . . . I couldn't think straight any more.'

The two men walked across the grass and found a wooden bench in the shade of a tree.

'Yesterday morning, I left before the household was awake. I wrote a note to Lady Rossmore, asking her if she would stay for a while, to give Rachel comfort and support. I said there was import-ant business in London and I must return immediately. So we know where she is at the moment. Odd, now I think of it, she didn't even congratulate me on my daughters' births. Maybe she was hiding from *me*.'

'Well, this gives us time to make new plans.' Quentin stood up. 'I think White's is the place for us now. No doubt the news has arrived, via the downstairs gossip line, and they will be expecting a toast to your new additions.'

'There you are, that's where my money goes. The married man is constantly paying bills for an expanding family.'

Alex heard the news when he went to White's that same evening. Geoffrey was not there, but from accounts he had been almost car-ried out to Sir Quentin's coach and taken home.

It was a pity they were not compatible. As half-brothers they had the same father and Catherine, Geoffrey's mother, was a pleas-ant and happy woman. On the rare occasions they were all together, she often spoke of their uncanny likeness, which made the other man's behaviour disappointing and Alex always came back to the same thought: Geoffrey was a throw-back to a more unsavoury ancestor.

He found a seat in the reading room and reached for *The Times* on a side table. Picking up his brandy glass he silently toasted the health of his two new nieces. This set him thinking of Grace. Could she too . . . ? But then who would be the father? This ques-tion hurt. He felt his insides tighten and his heart hammer within his ribs. They had never spoken in depth about a family – because he had been unsure and frightened of the outcome. Grace because she probably took it for granted that children would be part of their married life. He tipped the glass high and emptied it, then waved it for attention and a refill.

As each glass was finished, Alex sank deeper into despair. He remembered her in the church, slipping his wedding ring on her finger. Saw her at the beach, the storm and then their coming together with such passion and love; he could not believe that she had betrayed him. He wanted to cry out to the room that she was gone and he didn't know where. Where could he look? Had Mrs Gillett lied? Had she gone back and was with Olsen, hidden in his house? The torment was driving him to drink. He knew it was wrong, but he waved his glass again and had it filled.

The sunlight was fierce. From his bed Alex squinted through puffy eyes at Miles pouring something into a glass from a small square bottle.

'Pull the curtains, Miles. Are you trying to blind me?'

Miles obliged by pulling just one, then went to the bed. 'I have a little medicine for your headache, my lord.'

Alex did not move to take the glass.

'Lord Wainwright has sent word that he will call on you this afternoon at three. It is now noon. I think you will need all that time to bathe and eat something solid.' His face was expressionless, but his eyes looked at the glass and then at his master. 'Drink it now, if you please.'

Alex sat up, took the glass and sipped, his furred tongue barely tasting the vile syrup.

'Have you brought me coffee?'

Without answering, Miles went to the table and poured out the steaming dark liquid and returned. 'Your bath is ready when you have finished. Please ring, my lord, when you feel able to rise.'

'Don't be so impertinent, Miles. I can always replace you.'

'Yes, my lord. But who else knows your whims, your little, ah,

191

peculiarities, even before you do? Enjoy your coffee, my lord, your luncheon is on the table.'

With a bow, he left.

Alex was in the drawing room standing by the window, trying to sport a hearty countenance. 'The countryside is blooming, Willy. The weather is holding fair and I should like to be at Rossmore.'

'So, why aren't you? I would have thought Grace would like it too.'

'If only we could be. I don't know how to say this, Willy. I suppose the only way is straight out. Grace is gone.'

'Gone! What in heaven's name are you saying, Alex? Gone where?'

'I don't know. She just disappeared somewhere between her last inn stop and here.'

Willy Wainwright crossed the room to Alex and gripped his upper arm. 'You mean she has been kidnapped? But who . . .'

Alex pulled his arm away and stepped back. 'No. She has just . . . left me. If she had been kidnapped, I would have received a demand for payment.'

'What are you doing to find her? Damn it, Alex, anything could have happened to her.'

'I've searched London, gone to Dorset. The trouble is it was the day of the celebration. Everywhere was so crowded. Anyone I asked couldn't remember her coach – anything! I engaged an agent yesterday.'

Willy sat down in a chair and ran his fingers across his forehead. 'This is unbelievable. Surely your relationship didn't sink so low that Grace would run away? You're not telling me everything, are you? There were rumours this morning in White's. Are they true?'

'If you mean that Grace has not been in London since we were married, then yes. There was the strange goings on here, involving Liddy. I went to Grace at Whitecliffs, with the intention of explaining everything. When I arrived, there were complications and I

192

managed to bungle my words, then things just went from bad to worse.'

Alex paced the room, running his hands through his hair, the copper shading to bronze as he passed through the sunlight coming in the window.

'Well, without sounding like a preacher, you only have yourself to blame. I want to help, but evidently there is nothing to do until your man finds a lead. In the meantime, you will have to occupy your mind with something other than the brandy bottle, or you will end up a gibbering wreck. Isabelle is in the country, so I have plenty of time. Now, get your hat; a spell of swordplay will tone up your paltry-looking face. Then to the theatre; Drury Lane has a new play, can't remember what, but I hear it's worth seeing. Finish off with a supper and a few hands at cards.' Willy opened the door.

'No. I must be here when Beesell calls. Every minute . . .'

'We'll leave our plans with Saunders; he can send a message to you. Where is the man I knew, a man of decision and purpose? Is love addling your brain?'

Alex stopped midway across the room. Yes, that was exactly what was wrong. She had captured him from the first dance, but he had let fear override his feelings. And when they had made love, his whole being had been given to her. For the first time Alex began to understand the meaning of moving on.

'Yes, I believe it is. I'm in your hands, Willy. Can you guide a lost friend through this tangle of emotions?'

'Not really. But knowing you, you'll succeed. Now come on, I've missed our crossing swords these last few weeks.'

When Alex returned later that night, Saunders informed him there was a letter waiting from Mr Beesell. In his study he skimmed over the words; it only confirmed what he already knew, that Grace had not gone home to her father, or aunt. Beesell was widening the search.

Alex's feeling of goodwill that had prevailed when he was with

Willy, vanished. With his hopes dashed at Whitecliffs, he was back in the black hole of fear.

'Can you help me find her, Liddy? Waiting is driving me mad and the brandy bottle is taking me down the road to ruin.'

The portrait, in the flickering candlelight, seemed to shimmer. The love that he had once thought he saw was gone and only her painted blue eyes looked back at him. Turning away, Alex left the room.

Saunders had left one branch of candles in the hall and Alex picked it up and climbed the stairs. In the halo of light his shoulders began to heave and tears ran down his face. Stopping in the corridor outside Grace's door he stretched out his hand and turned the handle. Inside, he smelt the mustiness and saw how bare everything looked. Hanging in the wardrobe were all her refreshed gowns. The powders and scents replenished. Coolness touched his face, even though it was summertime. He walked to the bed and ran his hand over the counterpane. Putting the candles on the side table, he pulled back the cover and lifted the pillow to his wet, closed eyes and inhaled. But her scent was not there, only the impersonal laundry wash. With both arms he hugged the pillow tighter and cried until there were no more tears to flow. Beesell's face came into his mind. Where else could he look? It all depended now on his boys, those alley urchins who ran the lanes like ferrets and picked up any piece of information going.

Alex lowered the pillow and put it back on the bed. He stood as a statue and a fury fired in him, a bitter jealousy of Hugo Olsen. That he should have his wife. Picking up the candle branch he walked stiff, his back rigid, uncontrolled anger seething through him, to the connecting door. This one would never be locked as long as he lived. If they found her . . . no, when they found her . . . he would plead for a second chance. Until then, he would instruct Saunders to have fresh flowers put in her room every day.

Chapter Seventeen

Grace sat with Rachel in her bedchamber.

'You are looking quite the contented mama. Is that Deborah or Clarissa?'

'This is my little first-born, Deborah. Isn't she the most beautiful baby you have ever seen? Oh, Grace, my dream come true, although two was a shock to both mind and body. Dr Morton was quite perplexed; apologising profusely at his lack of diagnosis.'

Grace nodded. 'He is quite the serious physician. It must have been a blow to his pride.'

'And poor Geoffrey . . .' Rachel's voice rose to a giggle, as she changed over sides for the babe to suckle again. 'I thought he was going to faint, he went so white.'

'Has he sent word when he will be returning?'

'Not as yet.'

Grace wondered when Geoffrey would tell Alex she was at Hawthorn Hall. She was expecting a letter, or worse, to see him ride up the drive. But there was nothing, so he must be quite content with his mistress. What had he thought when she had not arrived? Was he relieved? An unwanted wife in Kilbraith House could hamper his liaisons with his child-carrying paramour. She looked down at her own belly hidden under her dress; could there be a growing child, so tiny that no one, not even herself, could see? What would Alex say? Would he be angry, banish her to Rossmore Manor as Geoffrey did Rachel? Lost in her thoughts, Grace jumped when Rachel spoke.

'Grace. Can you ring for Nurse? It is time for Clarissa.'

Grace got up and pulled the bell, then waited beside the bed.

'Where were you, you looked so unhappy? What are you going to do about Alex?'

'I don't know. I can't stay here indefinitely and I won't go home to Father, to be subjected to his unbending rules again. I could go back to Whitecliffs. Perhaps that is the best solution.'

Rachel's eyes watered. 'I'm so sorry, dear, that after such a short time your marriage has failed. Yet I would venture to say it is not on your part. You do love him, don't you?'

Grace wanted to deny it, not let Rachel see how much she was hurting, but honesty had grown between the two women and she answered truthfully, 'Yes.'

'Then fight for him. Go to London and talk to Alex.'

'That was what I had intended, but on the way something happened . . .' She hesitated; this was something she just couldn't bring herself to tell Rachel. 'I can't see him now. That is why I came here.'

'You know there is a place here for you, Grace. I will be spending more of my time at Hawthorn Hall than in London. Six children need space and our town house would be too small. Besides, Geoffrey has little time for the children; he leads a very busy life when in town.'

The subject of the two brothers seemed to send both into a thoughtful mood and wasn't broken until Nurse came in with Clarissa.

Grace reached to take Deborah and cradled her close. Walking to the window she rocked the tiny babe, marvelling at the creation of a new life, at the pink face, the eyes shut but her bow-shaped lips still sucking. Tears welled in Grace's eyes and overflowed down her cheeks. What was to become of her and the life she had left? She couldn't turn and let Rachel see her despair, so waited until Nurse tapped her arm.

'Shall I take Miss Deborah back to the nursery, Lady Rossmore?'

Grace didn't want to part with the warm bundle. With Deborah in her arms, she felt a bond of love, a protection so fierce her words to Hugo about Gillie being a lioness she now understood with a clarity she hadn't before, and she wanted it for herself. A child conceived with Alex, to love and cherish. The thought of his adultery pierced her heart, yet like Rachel a feckless husband could give her a gift to love, their children.

'I think I shall go for a ride,' she said, and passed the babe over.

The summer air was hot and Grace rode without a jacket and her hair tied with a ribbon. She was finding at Hawthorn Manor that Rachel did not adhere to the strict rules of dress and manner, much like she did at Solitaire. The concentration of riding and jumping over fallen tree trunks cleared her mind and she let the sounds of the birds and farms take over. She stopped to rest on a hillock and looked at the landscape. Here was a tranquil country estate, a place where she could live with a family. Whitecliffs had the sea and cliffs but offered only loneliness. A choice she would have to make soon, but not now. Taking the reins, she used a tree stump to help her mount and this brought Hugo back into her mind. She knew that if she allowed him, he would comfort her and this would lead to an affair. She did not want that; besides, he was a sea captain and that was where his heart lay, out challenging the ocean, at the mercy of wave and storm.

The path through the wood was shaded and the unexpected gunfire made her horse break its trotting gait and veer sideways into the bushes. A second blast sounded. The horse reared, pawing the air and Grace fought for control as the mare came down onto all fours, then charged forward. Two men stepped from the undergrowth and barred the way. She gripped her leg round the pommel and brought the horse to a slithering halt. In the chaos her neck was jolted and her vision swam dizzily before her eyes. She closed her lids and took a deep breath. Hands unhooked her leg and she was pulled from the saddle. A sack was rammed over her head and pulled down. The tug of a rope pinned her arms to her sides, then her ankles were tied and she was lying on the ground.

A voice shouted, 'Get her on the horse.' The next moment she was hauled upright and lifted. She tried to scream, but the suffocating cloth smelt of farm manure and she gagged. Everything went spinning as hands hoisted her up over a saddle, her head dangling and making her feel sick.

Ropes cut into her back, which in turn forced her breasts and middle down hard against the leather of the saddle. Her legs, acting as a balance weight, tilted upwards and she screamed, this time a piercing cry of panic as she felt herself sliding head down.

'Shut the screamin', or we'll gag tha' pretty mouth wid somethin' more smelly than sackin'.'

Fear made her heart pound and she cried out, 'Let me go. What do you want?'

The sacking was pushed into her face and something was jammed into her mouth. She tried to push it out with her tongue, but a rope was bound round it and knotted at the back of her head. Grace could hear voices and she thought there were three of them. The horse started to move and her breasts chafed against the saddle and the harness pressed into her ribs.

Every yard was a nightmare. They moved fast and Grace fought the desire to give in to a blackness that would relieve her of the constant rubbing of her skin. This was kidnap! But who would want to do it? She wasn't royalty. Alex wasn't even a duke. Questions came and went; but uppermost in her mind was fear. This, surprisingly, forced her to keep calm and she closed her eyes and tried to relax, hoping this would help the ride.

When they stopped, Grace was taken from the saddle and immediately put into a vehicle. A dim haze had been penetrating the sacking, but now it had gone dark. The swaying and sound of several horses' hooves made her assume it was a coach. Keeping upright on the seat was difficult. Despite her arms being tied to her sides she could use her hands a little, but as time passed any feeling numbed. Everything became meaningless.

The jolting stopped and Grace heard voices. Someone shouted, 'Open the gates,' and then the sound of bolts being drawn. Judging the length of the ride, the driveway was long and Grace felt the swing into a circle before it stopped. The door opened and she was lifted out. No attempt was made to untie or remove her hood. Her throat was parched and the gag was making her retch. Fear flared; if she was sick she couldn't spit it out, and it was said that one could drown in the bile. She breathed deeply through her nose, forcing herself to control the heaving desire to vomit.

A curt command came from a woman. 'Take her to the top floor, Room K.'

Grace was lifted and an arm buckled her knees and she was hoisted over a shoulder. The man's shoulder bone dug into her middle and she was carried up several flights of stairs.

Another juggling and she felt a mattress. She had come to the end of her journey. A key turned in a lock and there was nothing but a blessed silence. A burning sensation lined her throat and the taste of bile kept rising. She knew she couldn't hold it down much longer. Silently she prayed, '*Please, come and take this out of my mouth. I don't want to die.*'

Grace heard the key turn, the door open and then re-locked.

Fingers loosened the ties on her ankles, then around her body. The gag was pulled out and the sack withdrawn over her head. On a cabinet beside the bed a single candle glowed, but even this light made Grace's eyes hurt and she closed her lids.

Asking, her voice a whimper, 'Water. *Please,* do you have water?'

She tried to sit up. Her hands were numb and tingling, but she forced through their weakness and pushed down, shuffled backwards into a sitting position against a wall. A beaker was put into her hand, but she had not the strength to hold it, so her captor pressed it to her lips and she sipped.

'Welcome to Greensleeves, Mrs Temple.'

Grace forced her half-opened eyes wide and stared at a woman. Woman was hardly the correct word. Her features were angular, eyes deep set, and the black eyebrows and short hair seemed very mannish. Her dress was black linen, high-necked, long-sleeved and cut with a bodice to the waist.

199

'I am Mrs Norris, the supervisor. Betsey will come and help you settle in.'

Grace still stared, not believing what she heard. The water had helped, but in a rasping voice she said, 'There is a mistake. I am not Mrs Temple. I am Grace Kilbraith, the Countess of Rossmore. What is the meaning of this? Why have I been brought here? I demand you release me immediately.' The dryness was back in her throat and she started to cough. She was offered the beaker and took it, using both hands.

'There, there, Mrs Temple. Everything will be alright. Fantasies of grandeur are a common symptom of your ailment. The nurses at Greensleeves will make your stay as pleasant as possible. Do not fret so.'

'Fret! I have been kidnapped, brought here against my will and you tell me not to *fret*.' Grace coughed again, and sipped more water.

'A little light supper should make you feel better. I shall send it up at once.'

The woman was speaking to Grace as though she was simple-minded.

'Who owns this place?' Grace was beginning to have a different kind of fear creep into her mind.

'Dr Palmer. You will meet him on his next visit. Until then, Betsey and I will look after you.'

Grace eased her legs to the floor. They were trembling as she tried to stand, but determination not to show how weak she really was forced her up; her height two inches taller than the *supervisor*. A small mental victory, but a triumphant physical battle won over her jailer.

'I don't want looking after. Do you think I have gone simple in the mind?'

'No, no. But you have been acting a little strange and your husband thinks a spell here will do you good.'

'My husband!' Grace fell back onto the bed. 'Alex wouldn't do this to me! This is a mistake . . .' Her words trailed off as the horror of where she was sank in.

'You all say that. Just do as he wishes, and then you will enjoy your time here.'

Grace was speechless. So astounded that she made no attempt to get out of the room when Mrs Norris unlocked the door. The scraping noise of the key being turned from the outside proved she was being regarded as dangerous.

Ten minutes later the girl, Betsey, came with a supper tray.

'Mrs Norris says I am to be your maid. I have to take the clothes you be wearing. You will put on those in the closet.'

In the space of time since Mrs Norris had left, Grace was feeling more herself – strong bodied and most definitely in full control over her mind.

'Get out! I have no intention of staying here or giving you my clothes. First thing in the morning, I want to see Dr Palmer to get this sorted out.'

Betsey curtsied. 'Yes ma'am.' The girl left and locked the door, the grating sound festering like a sore on Grace's nerves.

The room was small and had the barest of furnishings: a bed, washstand and the clothes closet. The wooden floor was smooth, but they had not provided even a rug to put one's bare feet on. Blue curtains covered the window and Grace walked over to pull them back. Shock hit her like a blow to the head as she saw vertical bars secured to the window frame. The fear of her kidnap paled in the face of this new threat. She had been brought to an asylum.

Her heart started to pound and a prickly sensation, like being stung with nettles, began in her hands, crept up her wrists. She reached out and clung to the bars, laid her forehead on her hands. 'Alex, what have you done?'

Grace was too shocked to cry, but her eyes hurt and the dryness had come back to her mouth. She pushed away from the window and staggered like a drunken wench to take the beaker of water from the bedside cabinet. Her hand shook so much that the metal rattled against her teeth and only half the water found its way down her throat, the rest wetting her bodice. Sitting down on the bed, she stared at the floor, not seeing the planking, only Alex, with the face of a devil, his lips twisted into a bitter smile.

Who had told him she was at Hawthorn Hall? There were only two people: Rachel and Geoffrey, the half-brother. So much for her thinking they were at loggerheads. Family ties were a chain that was hard to break.

Grace looked at the tray. She had not eaten since luncheon and although she had no appetite, picked up the bread and put the slice of ham on top. Chewing was painful; the harsh treatment to her mouth had made her tongue thicken and her jaws hurt as they moved, but she forced the food down her sore throat and drank more water.

Tiredness came over her and she could feel her eyelids closing. She lay down on the bed, remembering only how Alex had deserted her and she was alone.

Grace woke to light coming in through the curtains. The blue made it seem like sky and the room less dreary. Pushing up, another shock awaited her. Gone were her riding clothes and she was dressed in a white cotton nightgown. How had they managed to complete such an act without her waking? She gave a bitter laugh. How naive could she be? Betsey; she didn't make a fuss when she refused to change her clothes. The girl had known the supper was drugged.

Grace lay back down. Her head hurt and she was thirsty again.

The key turned in the lock and Betsey came in, carrying another tray.

'Good mornin', Mrs Temple.'

This time Grace pulled herself from the bed and stood up.

'I am *not* Mrs Temple. I am the Countess of Rossmore and you will address me as such.'

'As you wish, ma'am.'

'I am "your ladyship" to you.'

The girl blushed. 'I can call you anythin' you like, Mrs Temple.'

Grace realised that nothing, short of showing her the marriage papers, would convince the girl otherwise.

'Is that another drugged meal?' Grace pointed to the tray. 'I won't be caught a second time.'

'Oh no, ma'am. Most visitors are a bit upset when they arrive and Mrs Norris finds it better to cope if they have a good night's sleep.'

'And take away their clothes and put them in this.' Grace fingered the poor quality cloth. 'This makes me look like a peasant from France. When can I see Mrs Norris?'

'She gone out and won't be back till tomorrow. She left instructions for you to stay in your room today.'

Grace went over to the window and pulled the curtains. 'And what is the meaning of this?' She tugged at the bars. 'Why am I a prisoner here?'

Betsey put the tray on the cabinet and stood fidgeting with her apron. 'Please, I not allowed to answer any questions, you wait for Mrs Norris.'

Grace was in no mood to be kind. 'I refuse to be held here a moment longer. Go and find me someone of authority, who can speak.'

Betsey bobbed and without replying left, locking the door.

Grace picked up the plate, smelt the food. It was a bowl of greyish gruel. If she was to maintain her strength she would have to eat it; she just hoped it was not going to make her sleepy again.

Ten minutes after eating the breakfast Grace washed and then looked in the closet. Gone were her fashionable clothes. A solitary grey linen dress hung on a hook. In place of her boots were black slippers, suitable only for indoor wear. One consolation, they had left her personal undergarments. She had no choice but to use what was there.

Grace sat on the bed thinking about her life since she met Alex. The over-riding question was: *why had he married her*? He had never said he loved her, but she had been prepared to take the risk that it would grow between them. *Why had she married him?* She was lonely and wanted a family. And, sometime, somewhere, somehow during their betrothal she had fallen in love with him. She could forgive him his fears and Liddy, but not a breeding mistress, who must have been well into her term when he married her. So, she was back to the question of *why marry me*? The answer was because a bastard son could not inherit his title. This left Geoffrey, even though the half-brothers had seemed to be obvious enemies.

Trying to piece together a reason, Grace could only come up with one thought. If she should be with child, Alex would be forced to accept it as his. If it were a girl, perhaps yes. A boy: a bastard to be his heir and the next Earl of Rossmore? No. Greensleeves was a gentlewoman's home of convenience with barred windows, locked doors and drugged food. No wonder there was always a place for a new unwanted relative – boredom and poison saw to that. She must find a way to escape from here.

No one came except Betsey and the day dragged by. She was given a book describing the wildlife held in the Tower of London. This only made her compare the poor creatures with herself. A trapped animal held in a cage. The meals were poor and even though Grace suspected the evening food was drugged, she ate a little.

She slept very well.

The following afternoon, the door was unlocked.

Grace was sitting on the bed and watched a middle-aged man come into the room. He walked with a limp and had thinning grey hair that barely covered his scalp.

'Good afternoon, Mrs Temple, I am Dr Palmer.'

'I am not Mrs Temple. I am the Countess of Rossmore. As this seems to be a place for the simple-minded, how many more times do I have to repeat it?'

Dr Palmer inhaled a deep breath and let it out as a sigh. 'Very well, good afternoon, your ladyship. I thought we might take a little walk round the house and garden.' He held out his hand.

Grace's instinct was to refuse, a sarcastic reply on the tip of her tongue, but if she went meekly, it would be a good opportunity to see the layout of the place.

'Thank you.'

There were three flights of stairs and Grace assumed that she was in the servants' quarters. Both the second and first floors had evenly spaced doors, each with a letter of the alphabet painted on it. When they reached the hall, Dr Palmer led her into a large room, where about twenty ladies murmured a greeting. The only thing that distinguished them from her was their bodily shape and height, for each had on the grey shapeless dress.

'Ladies, may I present Mrs Temple. She has come to join us.'

Several were stitching needlepoint, others reading and one plump soul sat strumming a harp, a fixed smile on her face and a far-away look in her eyes. Then, one of them, with a face like a china doll and her white hair set in frizzed ringlets, lowered her book.

'Do come and join us, Mrs Temple. How nice of you to come visiting, we seldom have visitors, do we, Mrs A? We call her that because she can't remember her name and Fanny there, the one with the harp, can only play five strings so we want to hear a song. Can you play, Mrs Temple? Fanny, move away, let our visitor play.'

Fanny, who had looked so placid, swung her head round and shouted, 'No. This is mine; I won't let anyone touch my harp. See, I have nails, I'll scratch her eyes out.' She clawed her fingers and flayed the air like an enraged cat.

Grace's fear returned ten-fold. She took in the shabby furnishings and the bars on the windows. If she were forced to stay with these women she would end up going mad. Her eyes searched for a door that would lead into the garden, but there was none, or if there had been, it was walled in now.

'You said you would show me the garden, Dr Palmer. Shall we continue?'

Grace could feel her inside churning; she was frightened of these people. The tranquil scene covered an insanity that boiled beneath the surface.

'As you so wish, m'lady, it is this way.' His fawning attitude was a sign of how he manipulated his very wealthy clients.

The front door was solid and heavy. Grace noticed several bolts as well as the key. Outside, the grounds were extensive, but she had no doubt there was a secure boundary wall. This gave her little comfort, remembering the sounds she had heard at the gate when they arrived. Escape would be very difficult indeed.

Dr Palmer chatted as they circled the central flowerbed of the driveway. 'It is very quiet here, Mrs Temple, a soothing balm for the mind. Our other guests are quite content, as you will be after a while. Mrs Norris is an exceptional nurse.' Cupping Grace's elbow, his voice swelled with pride. 'She trained at the Westminster Hospital in London.'

Grace felt as though she were in a dream, being pulled deeper and deeper into a black well and as every hour went by she would not be able to climb out. She looked into the face of the doctor and saw that he really believed what he was saying.

'I'm afraid I must disagree with you, sir. I am not in need of quiet or Mrs Norris's administrations. I require that you release me at once and have me taken back to where your kidnappers found me.' Like the doctor, Grace's voice was rising, not with pride, but frustration and anger.

'When we feel you are ready, then of course, you shall return.'

His hand had tightened on her arm and Grace looked at his fingers. 'Please, let go of me, Dr Palmer. I think you and I both know there is nowhere for me to run.'

He smiled. 'Ah, you see my point. It is such a pleasure to speak to someone who understands.'

'Oh, I understand well enough. My husband wants me out of the way. This looks to be the perfect place.'

The doctor gave a nod of acknowledgement. 'Tea will be served in the salon. Come and join your companions.' And he steered Grace back into the house.

Drinking the tea, Grace again wondered if it was drugged. She watched the others. There was little conversation; they seemed not to have any energy, as though the action of lifting the cup to their lips was a routine, a set pattern. Thinking back, when she had been introduced earlier, apart from the one lady who had spoken, the others never looked up. They had continued with their stitch-work and she wasn't sure if those with books were reading or just staring at the pages. Not sure whether to break the silence, she finished her tea. When a maid came in to clear away the china, she moved to a seat near the window. It was a devious action to put the bars on the inside, for it made the house look normal, in comparison to Bethlem Hospital where they were on the outside. There were no clocks. Only the passage of the sun shifting the shadows of the bars gave any indication of the hour.

Now, a gong sounded and the room came to life.

'Supper, ladies, put away your pleasures.'

Everyone moved in different directions, books were put back on tables, needlework into a wooden trunk near the window. Cushions were plumped and tidied, chairs moved a few inches as though they had an accurate spot on the carpet. Then they lined up in single file, each pushing into a position, as if they were numbered.

Grace knew she was sinking deeper into the black well as she watched them walk out into the hall and enter another room opposite. She followed into a room identical to the salon, except there were two long tables with stools placed down both sides. Each sat down in turn, leaving a vacant place at the end of one table, which Grace assumed was for her. Sitting down, she waited and watched.

Grace had mentally named the lady who seemed to be the leader as Chatty and saw her rise and steeple her fingers under her chin. 'Ladies, please stand.' There was a shuffle of feet and they all stood and copied Chatty for prayer. 'Thank you God and Dr Palmer. Amen.' More shuffling and they sat down.

The soup was hot, but the bread dry and Grace feared to eat, remembering last night. She wound her spoon round the liquid.

'Don't you want it?' A pair of eyes moved from Grace to her bowl. 'I'll have it if you don't.' A hand with bulging blue veins waved in the air between them. 'I always sleep better on a full belly. Not that it's difficult to sleep and we all go to bed after supper.'

207

Grace licked her lips; she was hungry, but not enough to be drugged again. Lifting the bowl, she passed it over. 'You can have it.' And the frail old lady tipped it into her own bowl. Grace was now fearful of even drinking a glass of water, but her thirst was so great that she had to give in before they left.

There was no attempt to go back into the salon. Like a flock of birds nesting for the night they went up the stairs and into their rooms. Grace found that she was the only one on the top floor and wondered what would happen if she just turned round and fled back down the stairs, out the front door and kept running? The urge was like a torture, but she knew now was not the time. She had to make a plan.

She lay on the bed hearing her stomach rumble. She had been thinking for ages and come to a decision. She needed help to escape. Betsey was her only chance. Somehow she must persuade the girl to let her out at night.

The door opened.

'Oh, you still awake, Mrs Temple.' The surprise in her voice confirmed Grace's suspicion that the supper had been tampered with.

'Yes, Betsey; I am not yet tired. Do come in, we can talk a while.'

Betsey hesitated. 'Like I said, I'm not allowed.'

'Just for a few minutes, I have been very lonely today. Please.' Grace got off the bed and went over to the girl and closed the door. 'How long have you worked here?'

Betsey fidgeted with her apron, something Grace had noticed every time she was in the room. 'Two years.'

'Then you must know the household very well. Do the servants live in this house?'

'No. Only Mrs Norris, Cook, an' me.'

'Where do the others live?'

'Beyond the kitchen garden, there is a wooden house. They sleep in there.'

Grace felt her hopes rising. She returned to the bed and sat down. 'Are you walking out with a boy?'

Betsey blushed. 'Yes.'

Grace patted the space next to her. 'Come and rest your feet, Betsey. It has been a long day.'

The girl didn't move, although the mention of her feet made her raise one and rest it on the back of her other ankle.

'What is his name? Does he live nearby?'

'Joseph. He lives at Mr Freeman's farm. He works the fields.'

'Are you going to marry soon?'

Betsey started fidgeting again. 'Yes, when we have enough money. There room for me at the farm and I could still come 'ere every day . . .' She looked down and when she raised her head a few seconds later, there was wetness in her eyes. 'But we will never have enough; I will die an old spinster.'

There was anguish in her voice and Grace pressed her questions quicker. 'How much do you need?'

'Joseph needs money for my wedding ring; and the church fee. I have a pretty dress and Joseph a fine jacket. We don't need a wedding breakfast; I just want to be married. Joseph says we can pretend to be wed, and we could . . .' her face went crimson, 'but I can't . . . do what he asks.' Now the tears ran down her cheeks.

'I could help you, Betsey, if you will help me.'

'How?'

'I can give you some money, enough for your wedding and something to put away for a rainy day.'

Betsey stopped crying. 'How, Mrs Temple? You have no money. I was 'ere when Mrs Norris took your clothes. There was no money.' She started to step back towards the door.

'No, wait.' Grace jumped up. She couldn't miss this chance; it might be her only one. What did she have to give the girl? Looking down she saw her wedding ring, Alex's ring, which he had placed on her finger with his vows before God. How she had believed in those words. Empty words, so why shouldn't she use it for her freedom? She pulled it from her finger and held it out to Betsey.

'Here, you can have this. It is worth a lot of money. You can sell it. It will fetch more than enough for you and Joseph.'

Betsey stopped. 'What you want me to do for you?'

'Come back and let me out of the house and grounds when everyone is asleep.'

'I can't. Mrs Norris would dismiss me. Then your ring wouldn't help us at all.'

'The ring will fetch more than you and Joseph earn. You could leave here. Help Joseph on the farm. Be a wife to him all day instead of working for Mrs Norris. And soon you would have a family, a little baby to look after.'

Betsey was shaking her head. 'I can't . . . your husband would come and Dr Palmer would beat me . . .'

Grace was becoming desperate. The girl was frightened of the consequences.

'Has anyone else left here?'

'No. Well . . . only those who die.'

'How often is that?'

'About . . . once a month or so.'

Grace swallowed the panic that was rising; the situation here was more disturbing than she had thought. 'Then I think you should leave here, Betsey. Take my offer and get married to Joseph.' Grace held out her ring on the palm of her hand, keeping it steady, willing it not to tremble.

Betsey didn't move. Her eyes fixed on Grace's hand. 'How much is it worth?'

'Many, many guineas; a very wealthy man gave this ring to me.'

As much as Grace wanted to escape, it was breaking her heart to give Alex's ring away. 'I trust you, Betsey. Take it now and promise me that you will come back later and let me out.' If she took the ring and didn't come back . . . it was a gamble Grace had to take.

Still the girl hesitated.

'Very well, forget I asked.' Grace started to put the ring back on.

'Wait!' Betsey moved forward. 'I'll do it. But I want the ring now.'

This time Grace hesitated. If the girl went to Mrs Norris and betrayed her, goodness knows what the woman would do to restrain her. There were horror stories of Bethlem, where they handcuffed and chained the inmates, men and women. Or Dr Palmer could drug her until she died. She held out the ring. 'I shall be waiting for you, Betsey. Please come back.'

The girl took the ring. 'I'll be back when they all go asleep.'

Grace watched the moon travel across the sky through the barred window. It was hours since she had bribed the girl, hours since the moon had risen and was now sliding towards the end of its arc.

Betsey wasn't coming.

Grace had gambled and lost. Leaning her head against the bars, she let her despair flow out in tears. Then the scraping of the key sounded and she turned, hoping with every ounce of her being that it was Betsey and not Mrs Norris.

The girl held a candle and beckoned urgently.

Grace needed no second bidding.

Together they crept down the narrow wooden stairs leading to the second floor and along the corridor, the sounds of snoring amplified by the quiet of the night. Grace feared every plank she stepped on would creak. Feared that a door would open and Dr Palmer or Mrs Norris would snatch her back. When they reached the hall, Betsey ignored the front door and made for the back stairs.

As they walked across the kitchen a black shape rose from a chair and a scream filled her throat. She clamped her hand over her mouth as a cat arched its back, stretched and curled up again.

Betsey was moving quickly, familiar with the layout.

Grace tried to keep up with her, but in the darkness didn't see the corner of the table and hit her leg; an excruciating pain speared through her thigh, making her bend over, rubbing it through the thin fabric.

'We can't stop,' Betsey whispered.

'Just for a second.'

In the candlelight, Grace saw how scared the girl was. 'Go on.'

Blowing out the candle, Betsey slipped the catch and they were out into the night. Grace felt the warm summer air and breathed deeply, then whispered close to the girl's ear, 'How do I get out of the grounds?' Without answering, Betsey led the way along a path close to the house.

Grace looked up at the numerous windows. Which ones were the household rooms? She hoped they were not having a sleepless night, but no shouts sounded behind them and then they were going into the walled kitchen garden. Skirting round the plots they left the vegetables and moved through an orchard. The grass was damp and the thin shoes Grace had been given were soaked within seconds.

Betsey slowed and they came to a brick wall.

'I can't climb over *that*; it must be eight feet high.'

The girl put a finger to her lips and called, 'Joseph.' Then there was a scraping noise, followed by grunts and oaths. A face peeped above the wall; then a ladder was heaved over and dropped down. 'Joseph will help you from here. I must go back. I hope they not seen me.'

'Shouldn't you come with us?'

'No. It better I am doing my duties when they find you gone.'

Grace took the girl's hand. 'Thank you for keeping your promise.'

Between them, they propped the ladder against the wall and Grace climbed up. At the top the young man helped her over and down a second ladder. Then he heaved the first ladder back. Hoisting both of them onto his shoulder, he signalled Grace to follow.

Chapter Eighteen

'Tilly, pass my robe.'

Rachel pushed back the covers and swivelled to the side of the bed.

'No, Mrs Kilbraith, you cannot get up. It is too soon.'

'Nonsense. I must speak to Jessop at once. How long ago did Lady Rossmore's horse come back rider-less?'

'About half an hour. He is organising a search of the estate. You cannot go down the stairs, my lady, Nurse will not allow it.'

'I'm not going down. Ask Jessop to bring Brownsmith to the spare room opposite mine here.'

Tilly stopped at the door and looked round. 'Wait until I come back to help. Please, my lady, I could be dismissed for letting you get up.'

'Don't talk such piffle, Tilly. I engage and dismiss the female staff at Hawthorn Hall.' Rachel went to stand, wobbled and sank back down. 'Oh alright, I'll wait. Now hurry.'

Rachel sat in a chair by the window, listening to Brownsmith's account of the frothing, frightened horse that had come galloping into the stable yard.

'How many men and farm workers can you find to search before it is dark?'

'About twenty, ma'am.' He stood looking at his feet, a cap twisting in his hands, his rugged features overly red at being asked to see the mistress in an upstairs room. 'But most will be on foot. I know Lady Rossmore likes to ride through the woods to the hill. I have told them to start there.'

'Good. Thank you. Please keep me informed. I want to know the minute Lady Rossmore is found. Will you please ask Jessop to come in?'

Brownsmith nodded and took several steps backwards.

Rachel laughed. 'I'm not royalty. You may turn round to go.'

'Ma'am.' In two strides he was gone.

Jessop's knock was soft, discreet and he stood just inside the open doorway.

'I'm going to give you an order, Jessop, and it is to be obeyed without question.'

He nodded and waited.

'No matter what the time, day or night, I want to know the minute Lady Rossmore is found. Nurse will fuss, but you have my authority to see me at any time.'

'Very well, ma'am. I will see to it that Nurse is notified immediately.'

'Thank you. Will you ask Tilly to come in now?'

Rachel sat thinking. Grace could be walking home right now, or she could be lying injured. She refused to go beyond an accident; a fatality was unthinkable. Should she send word to Alex? No. She would wait to see how serious this was before sending a message.

The late afternoon passed into evening and Grace was not found. Rachel took the decision at dawn to send a message to Lord Rossmore.

Kilbraith House erupted into chaos when Jenkins arrived.

Alex was finishing a late luncheon when Saunders, followed by the coachman, burst into the dining room.

'Your lordship, it is Jenkins, your coachman. He has a message.'

For just a moment, Alex stared at the two men; then bolted from his chair.

'You have her here? Where the devil have you been? Bring her in at once.'

'No, my lord. Jenkins has a message from Mrs Kilbraith, at Hawthorn Hall.'

This stopped Alex in his stride.

Jenkins held out a leather pouch. 'From Mrs Rachel Kilbraith, my lord.'

Alex took the message and nodded to them. 'Thank you. That is all.'

Saunders ushered the coachman out, but hesitated in the doorway, then said, 'You will call, your lordship, if there is . . .'

'Yes, Saunders, I will call if I need you.'

When the door closed, Alex sat back down at the table. He did not open the package. If Jenkins had brought the message, then that meant Grace did not wish to come to the house. It spoke ill that there would be good news inside. He turned it over in his hands, the leather warm from being in the man's pocket. Taking a deep breath, Alex untied the pouch.

If he had been asked what to expect, he would never, in a hundred years, have guessed what he was reading.

Dear Lord Rossmore,

I feel that it is my duty to write that Grace has been staying with me.

She has been a great comfort before and during the birth of my two beautiful daughters.

But it is with regret that I have to say, this afternoon, she went riding and her mount returned alone.

A search has not found her, at the time of this despatch.

Your sister-in-law,
Rachel Kilbraith.

Alex re-read the message. Found and lost in one moment of time. Utter shock caused him to sit still; then he exploded into action. Rushing into the hall he saw Saunders standing at the bottom of the stairs. 'Where is Jenkins?'

'He is waiting in the kitchen, my lord.'

'Did he bring the coach?'

'No. He came on horse.'

'Then get him a fresh mount and one for me. I am going to Hawthorn Hall.'

'Is her ladyship there?'

'No. Well, yes, she was, but there may have been an accident. Tell Miles I want a small saddlebag ready in ten minutes.' Then Alex was racing up the stairs.

The butler hurried towards the below stairs kitchen. 'This house becomes more like a coaching inn than an earl's residence.' Uncharacteristic of Saunders, he slammed the connecting hall door.

Alex rode with unrelenting speed, giving little thought to the horse under him. Questions came and went in his mind. Why had she not come to Grosvenor Square? What had happened to send her to Hawthorn Hall? Why was she staying, why was Grace ignoring him, why was she tormenting him so? He slowed his pace. The answers came like knife stabs: Grace-didn't-love-or-want-him-any-more.

He arrived at Hawthorn Hall as it basked in the mellow, fading light of the day. The front door opened before Alex had dismounted and the butler hurried out to meet him.

'Have they found her, Jessop?'

'No, my lord. We have searched all day. Lady Rossmore has just disappeared.'

Alex felt a coldness creep over his skin. His control was slipping. At every turn he was just too late; she kept fading like a ghost. Where would she reappear next time?

'Mrs Kilbraith would like to see you at once.'

'Then lead the way.' Remembering his position as the twins' uncle he asked, 'How are my two nieces?'

'Nurse has great hopes that they will both survive, my lord.'

Rachel was again sat in the spare bedchamber. She held out her hands as he went in.

'I am so thankful to see you, Alex. This is truly a devastating situation.'

'Rachel, how are you?'

'Very well, considering what has happened to me over the last few days.'

He squeezed both her hands and held on to them tightly. 'Are they still searching?'

'No.'

He let Rachel's hands go and moved to the window, keeping his back towards her.

'The whole of the estate has been gone over. Brownsmith only found one thing that struck him as strange. In the woods, where Grace likes to ride, there are a lot of different hoof marks and churning up of the soil. When the horse came back it was frothing and very frightened and had dirt marks on its rump. I am so sorry, Alex, my letter must have been a shock.'

Alex turned back into the room. 'She was on her way to Kilbraith House. Why did she change her mind and come here?'

'We did not speak of it. She arrived and was in need of a place to stay. My home is always open to my relatives and friends.'

'Things have been difficult between us . . .' he paused and began pacing the room. 'It is my fault, Rachel. I thought when Jenkins arrived today . . . my hopes rose, but this disappearance again . . .' He pulled at his neck cloth, as if it was choking him. 'I don't think I can take much more.'

'Alex, you are the strong one. Geoffrey is in London and I cannot cope with this additional strain. My duty lies in looking after my two new babes. Please, stay as long as you need. Jessop will prepare you a room. Cook will see you have supper.'

Alex frowned. His sister-in-law looked pale and tired. 'Forgive me, of course I will see to whatever is needed. Shall I call your maid?'

'Thank you. Tilly will be in the corridor waiting like a protective terrier. I will see you in the morning. Goodnight, Alex.'

Bowing, he left.

In the morning Alex ordered a mount to ride and look at the estate. It was not large, but brought Geoffrey a good income, if he would only spend it wisely. He thought about his half-brother's six children and the fact that he had none. Could Grace be carrying his heir? Or Olsen's child? How many times had he been tormented by this vision? *Too many*, he felt, and he kicked the horse into a gallop.

He rode to the spot that Brownsmith had mentioned. It was possible that a struggle had taken place here, but the searchers had trampled the ground so much it was difficult to be certain. There was nothing to be gained in staying at Hawthorn Hall. The best course of action was to go back to London and give Beesell the information he had.

It was the not knowing that was driving him crazy. Why had she changed her plans and come here? Rachel was very weak and he should not force her to tell him anything that had been a confidence between them. But this was an emergency. Grace's life might depend on what decision was made here today. Alex turned his horse and returned to the house.

Rachel sat by the window looking at Alex with raised eyebrows. 'I've journeyed across the corridor so many times this past two days, I think I shall turn it into a sitting room.'

'My apologies for causing you so much inconvenience, Rachel, but I must know why Grace came here instead of Kilbraith House? The answer may be of considerable importance. I am asking you to break a confidence, but I must know.'

'There is no confidence to break. I offered my home to her for as long as she wanted. I did not ask why and she did not tell me.'

'But she must have hinted; all women gossip and tell their secrets . . .' Alex stopped when he saw Rachel raise her hand.

'There is nothing to tell. Except that Grace was ill after she arrived, the fever took her for several days and in her delirium she called for you many times.'

Alex was leaning against the fireplace, but straightened at her words, a feeling of elation surging through him. 'My name? Did she really call for me, Rachel?'

'And why should she not? You are her husband.'

'Did she call for anyone else? Did you hear . . .' He paused,

218

should he mention names? What the hell, he had to know. 'Hugo Olsen, for instance.'

'I don't know. Her voice was a rasping whisper and her words unclear. What is wrong with the two of you? You look gaunt and exhausted, Grace is unhappy. Have all Kilbraith men been cursed with black hearts?' Rachel's cheeks coloured and looking down she twisted the cotton square into a rope. 'I'm sorry, my lord, for such an outburst. Please put it down to my being in child-bed.'

Alex came and knelt on the floor in front of her. 'You have nothing to apologise for. I am going back to London this afternoon. I have an agent looking for her, although this was the last place I would have thought of. Grace and I have . . . a few problems to sort out, but I swear that I will find her, Rachel. No one can just disappear into the air. I will send word the minute I have any news. You must regain your strength . . .' He took her fingers away from the handkerchief. 'My two little nieces are depending on you.'

Rachel looked at him, a direct look into his eyes. 'She needs you. Please find her, Alex. I can't bear this terrible uncertainty. Who would want to harm her?'

'I don't know. But when I find who has done this, I'll . . . I'll kill him.'

The tears that had been held back trickled down Rachel's flushed face. 'No you won't! Grace wouldn't want to be a widow, especially of someone who is hanged for murder.' Her outraged comment eased the tension and they both laughed.

'I'm sure you're right. I'll horsewhip him instead.'

Alex got up. 'I'll take Esther and Jenkins back to London.'

'What if Grace returns here? Will you leave her wardrobe?'

'No. Without a maid and her clothes she can't run away again.'

'A cunning thought, Alex. I admire your strategy.'

'I must go. I'll call Tilly for you.' He turned before opening the door. 'Thank you for looking after her. Goodbye, my dear.'

Esther was thrown into a panic at the news she was to pack her mistress's wardrobe and be ready to travel in the coach by mid-afternoon. However, the other maids rallied to help and Esther left, waving her farewell, on time.

Alex left immediately after issuing his orders. He rode back to Grosvenor Square and immediately sent a message for Beesell to call within the hour.

Fifty-five minutes later, Alex told Beesell, 'I have found where Lady Rossmore has been staying; at Hawthorn Hall, with my sister-in-law.'

The bearded face nodded up and down. 'Quite a coincidence, your lordship. My boys found information that a coach, with your lordship's crest, was seen travelling north from the city. So it would have been only a matter of time before I found her too.' Beesell puffed out his chest. 'Like I said, my little rats rarely have a failure. My bill will be quite small, my lord, nothing on it that will displease you. Can I look forward to settlement within the month?'

Alex looked at the man. He was going to have to put his faith in him once more.

'You can withhold your bill, Beesell. Unfortunately, Lady Rossmore has disappeared again. Except this time, there is a more sinister plot for you to unravel.'

The agent listened to how Grace had gone riding and vanished without a trace. 'May I give my condolences, my lord? Her ladyship found and lost in such a short time. It is a most distressing situation. But, fear not, like I said, I have more successes than failures. My boys . . . well, older boys since it will be travelling further afield, will be on the trail at first light tomorrow. Of course, the expenses will be a little more . . .'

'Oh, for heaven's sake, Beesell; I'm not quibbling about the cost. Find Lady Rossmore. That is your priority, not your confounded expenses.' Alex couldn't stand the man's wheedling voice or the smell of him another minute. 'Find her. That's all I care about.'

Chapter Nineteen

It was dark, though a faint hue lightened the sky to the east.

Grace followed Joseph along a path. He did not speak or lessen his pace until they came to a farm.

'Is this Mr Freeman's farm?'

'Yes.'

His attitude and curt reply made Grace wonder how willing Joseph had been to help her. Betsey must have very persuasive powers.

'Where is this?'

'Camden.'

'How far is it to London?'

'I don't know.'

Grace gave up trying to talk to him and concentrated instead on what she was to do next. She had no money, nothing to sell.

When they reached the farmyard a man was loading a cart. He did not stop working but asked, 'This your friend that wants a ride to the market?' He was a stocky man with brown hair curled tightly to his head and in the half-light his face was almost a coffee colour.

'Yes, Mr Freeman. Are we ready to go?'

'Pass those two baskets and we can be off.'

Grace sat in the cart with Joseph. They were going to Covent Garden Market.

She could see vegetables and fruit and this made her inside rumble.

'Your hunger sounds very loud. Would you like a carrot to eat?'

Joseph leaned past Grace and took two from a basket. She wondered how old he was. When they had walked along the path, his long stride had forced her to almost run to keep up, but his youthful build suggested he was no older than Betsey and he had a clean smell about him, unusual for a farm worker.

'Thank you. It is a long time since my last meal.'

The crunch of them both biting sounded very loud in the rising dawn.

She had no option but to go to Kilbraith House. The thought sent a shiver down her spine. What would Alex do when he saw her? Have her taken back to Greensleeves? It would be difficult to whisk her away once she was there. The staff would gossip. Or was he past caring what the *ton* had to say any more?

Whilst she was thinking, the light had strengthened and the sun was warming the early morning chill. As they rode into the London streets, the horse-drawn cart rumbled over the cobbles and passed local barrowmen setting up their stalls. This was a world that Grace had never seen: houses so narrow and small they didn't look big enough for a dwarf to live in and ragged humans unfolding from huddled balls in doorways. The aroma of fresh bread baking made her feel hungry again, but this was overlaid with an odour of rotting vegetables and gagging smells from open sewers. Such unfamiliar sights increased her worries.

'I need to get to Grosvenor Square, Joseph.' The boy did not answer. 'Do you know the way?'

'No.'

'Would Mr Freeman?'

'No.'

Grace did know that the Covent Garden was not a place to be wandering alone. 'Perhaps one of the other farmers could help.'

He shrugged his shoulders. 'Maybe.'

'Joseph, you have my ring, surely a little help would not be too much to ask?'

He sat with his legs tucked up to his chin, his eyes fixed on his feet. 'Betsey 'ad no right to get involved. She'll lose 'er job.' Raising his head, his lips were pressed together, accusing fire in his eyes. 'I can't give it back. We need the money now. She only had to wait a little longer; I almost have what we need.'

'I do not expect you to return it. Just give me a few minutes of your time to find someone who knows the way.'

He looked towards Mr Freeman. 'When we have unloaded, he goes for a draught of ale. I'll see what I can do.'

Grace accepted Joseph's resentment, but was thankful for his consent.

The cart continued through the streets and as they neared the centre of the city it became crowded with street sellers and carts that were coming in from all directions. Mr Freeman slowed and turned into Covent Garden Market. Neighing horses and shouts filled the air. Some farmers were setting up stalls while others were selling direct from their carts and flower sellers arranged their blooms to attract the buyers. Somewhere out of sight the smell of cooking food wafted into the square.

Mr Freeman found his pitch and pulled to a stop. Climbing down he shouted to Joseph, 'Get to it, lad, and use the woman to 'elp. Get some work out of 'er for the ride.'

Grace went to stand up and found her legs had the cramps, but she was not going to give any cause for the farmer to complain and steadied herself on the side to get out.

Joseph was already placing baskets on the ground along the side of the cart.

'What do you want me to do?' He motioned her to hand the baskets to him.

Grace strained with the weight as she lifted one off the back and dropped it. There was no way she could carry it the few yards to Joseph and began to drag it over.

'Don't do that. You'll damage the basket bottom. Old Freeman will deduct the repair from my wage.' And he elbowed Grace out of the way. 'You arrange 'em and I'll unload. Be quick, customers are coming. They come this way first.'

Joseph heaved and Grace pulled. Her back began to hurt and her arms felt they would be wrenched from her shoulders. 'How often do you come to market?'

'Twice a week.'

Mr Freeman put a nosebag on the horse and then spoke to Joseph. 'I'm going for a bite. Remember that we have the best, for a fair price. Don't go taking less.'

'Yes, Mr Freeman. Can the woman go now?'

He looked at Grace. 'Might as well. She don't have the looks of a worker, too thin, no muscle.' He waved his hand in dismissal and walked off.

The market was filling fast and shouts started, voices bellowing.

'See my fine vegetables, best in the market.'

'Come and smell my roses, red as your fine mistress' lips.'

'A bargain today, my dears, and our eggs are cheapest by the dozen.'

Grace stood to one side and watched Joseph trade and laugh with his customers; heard his practised chant, 'Freeman's, the best country veg and fruit, the best price this side of the Thames.' He had many customers, obviously regulars, for the boy was confident, his manner bold and he sold every time. But, watching the antics of the market was not getting her to Grosvenor Square.

When a lull came she went over to him. 'Can you ask for me now? I would like to go.'

'You'll 'ave to stay with the goods.'

'What if someone wants to buy? What do I do?'

'Sell, of course.' And he walked off leaving Grace horrified at such a thought.

The throng of customers was thicker than ever. She stepped back, avoiding any eye contact with the people who passed, wishing Joseph had asked her to do anything but sell his wares. Grace knew she didn't stand out, as would the fashionable Lady Rossmore, clothed as she was in the asylum dress and her hair falling loose round her shoulders. But if she had to speak, any servant would know she was not a farm maid and there were many cooks

224

here, because this was the preferred market of the big houses. Should she follow one of them, could she find Kilbraith House? But on a second thought, what if she *was* recognised? Unlikely, but . . . a woman stopped and felt a carrot. Grace's mouth went dry. What should she say if asked a question? But she was saved; the maid was not satisfied and walked on. Grace let her gaze roam over the crowd; where was Joseph? Then she spotted him coming with a man whose hair covered not only his head, but cheeks and chin. He looked like an owl and his dark eyes were moving constantly.

'This gentleman can help you. He knows the way.'

Grace began to tremble inside. He was a stranger. Although Joseph had been unknown to her, she had felt safe with the country lad, perhaps because he was Betsey's spoken for. Even the ride into London had a certain comfort, but now . . . this area was notorious for the lower life . . . he might be a thief, a murderer . . .

'Good morning.' His voice was polite.

'You know the way to Grosvenor Square?'

'Indeed I do.'

What should she do? If he knew the way . . . 'Will you take me? I have no money to pay you now. But I can give you a shilling when we arrive.'

'A shilling? That be a good sum for any guide.' The man showed his yellow teeth in a stretched smile. 'I have a . . . nephew who can go. He would appreciate such a fine coin.'

Grace had a nasty feeling that there was a hidden meaning in that reply. Turning he whistled three sharp blasts and a boy ran up. The man took him aside and whispered close to his ear. There were several nods and he pocketed a coin that the man gave him.

'All settled. Don't let me keep you.' Giving a bow he pushed the urchin forward. 'Get moving, rat. I have a little business to do with young Joe here before Mr Freeman returns.'

Grace hesitated. She had no knowledge of this part of the city; how would she know they were going in the right direction? Would it be better to ask the man to loan her the carriage fare? She almost laughed aloud. Would anyone believe that she was Lady

Rossmore? That she could pay for as many fares as she wanted. It came home to her how sheltered her life was, that money was always to hand. 'Are you sure you know the way?'

The boy nodded and pointed to her shoes. 'You'll 'ave sore feet by then,' and he laughed. 'A shillin' could buy me a pair from Sally Shaw with beta bottoms than yours.' He thumbed towards Grace. 'Follow me.'

Grace wanted to thank Joseph, but he had his back to her and was listening to something the owl man was saying. Well, he hadn't wanted anything to do with her so she turned and saw the boy disappearing into the crowd. She ran forward, afraid of losing him, but he turned every few yards and waited for her to catch up.

'Not used to walking far, are you? Me an' me sisters would be there by now and half way back.'

'What is your uncle's name?'

'Uncle? Oh, you mean fuzzy face. Nah, he not me uncle – is that what he said? I work for him.'

'But he has a name.'

The boy put several yards between them, then waited. 'No names, just fuzzy face.'

This underworld frightened her: men who got paid for kidnapping, boys who worked for a nameless employer. She looked at the street they were in. She didn't recognise it, but it had uniform-style houses, nothing like the small hovels she had seen from the cart.

'How much further have we to go?'

'Not far. How's yer feet?'

Was it the area they were in, or was she taking a liking to this ragged boy? He was thin and dirty, but his face was a mass of freckles and he had emerald green eyes.

'I shall not be able to walk for a week.'

Admitting her discomfort seemed to please him and he pointed. 'Just to the end of here an' round the corner.' Grace started to count the steps, anything to take her mind off her sore feet. Then the boy stopped and pointed. 'Grosvenor Square, ma'am.'

The house was half-way down on the left hand-side. Forgetting her damaged feet she ran along the pavement and stopped at the bottom of the steps. *She was really here.* After all that had happened, she was at Kilbraith House.

Tears sprang to her eyes as she knocked on the door. When it opened, Saunders' face hardened and his lips thinned. 'How dare you come to the front door? The kitchen is below.' And it was shut in her face. Grace just stood there. Didn't the man recognise her? She hammered again. When it opened this time, she didn't give the butler a chance to speak.

'Let me in at once. I may look like a servant, but I am certainly not one.'

Pushing past a shocked and speechless Saunders, she turned and said, 'I promised the boy a shilling. Pay him, Saunders.' With her head held high, she marched through the hall, up the stairs and into the bedchamber that had been readied for her prior to her marriage.

Grace sank onto the bed, stretched full length and covered her face with trembling hands. She was safe. How safe, remained to be seen when Alex found out she had escaped from Greensleeves. If the truth was told, she was frightened. If he could do that to her, he would have no qualms in getting rid of her again. It wasn't until she arrived at the house and Saunders hadn't recognised her that she realised putting her trust into a stranger and the urchin boy had been foolhardy. She could only thank her Maker that it had turned out well.

A knock on the door brought Esther running into the room. 'Oh, your ladyship, wherever have you been?'

'It's a long and complicated story, Esther. One I am not going to tell. I want a bath, a very hot bath. A large lunch and a footman put outside my door, day and night. No one, and I include his lordship, is to come in here except you.'

Grace sat up and her head went dizzy. 'I'm very hungry, Esther, please get me something to eat.'

Esther just stood and stared. 'But, his lordship has been so worried. He has searched . . .'

'Enough, my orders are clear.'

'But, Mr Saunders will not take those orders from me, your ladyship. Please don't ask this of me.'

Grace relented. Of course Saunders wouldn't take such orders. 'Please ask him to see me in the drawing room immediately.'

With that, Esther left and Grace followed her down the stairs.

Saunders came into the drawing room and closed the door. He bowed and began speaking immediately. 'Your ladyship, I am so ashamed not to have recognised you. May I profusely apologise for such insulting behaviour?'

'Good afternoon, Saunders. It is good to be here at last. Your mishap is well understood. Let us leave it at that.'

'Thank you. Welcome to Kilbraith House. I hope everything will be to your satisfaction. His lordship is out, but I expect him back shortly.'

Grace felt awkward. There must be questions he wanted to ask, but dare not, which gave her the opportunity to say very little. She wondered what character of man became a butler. Saunders was so calm and smooth on the surface, but must be boiling with curiosity inside.

'I'm sure you have seen to all that is needed. I have something I want you to do, and I insist that it is done immediately.' She saw his eyes blink. 'I require a footman to be outside my bedchamber door, day and night. No one, not even his lordship, is to enter; only my maid, Esther.'

A look of alarm came over the old man's face. 'But . . . I have sent for his lordship. He has been so worried about your disappearance, you cannot mean to . . .'

'I mean every word. You will see to it at once. I will take all my meals in my room and shall require a footman with me every time I go out. That will be all.'

Saunders did not go. 'May I enquire what I am to tell his lordship when he returns?'

Grace was beginning to feel sick. Her nerves were at breaking point. She felt dirty and the hunger pains were getting worse.

'Whatever you like, I am going to my room.' She moved forward and Saunders opened the door for her.

'Thank you.' Grace went directly to her bedchamber.

Alex lowered his sword and signalled Willy to stop. He went over to where one of his footmen stood waiting by the hall door.

He was handed a sealed note. 'A message from Mr Saunders, your lordship.'

Alex scanned the sheet and felt as if a hammer had been slammed into his middle. All the emotions that he had been holding back came flooding through at the good news. She was safe; in Kilbraith House. A lump blocked his throat and his eyes watered.

Willy hurried over and took the sheet from his fingers.

'Grace is home, Alex. Everything is alright. I'm so relieved.'

Alex said nothing, just stood there, unable to believe that after all the worry, searching, imagining every kind of horror, Grace was safe.

'Tell Saunders I will be home within the hour.'

He passed his foil to Willy. 'I'll see you later.'

There was a buzz in Kilbraith House when he arrived. Yet Saunders looked strained as he took Alex's hat and cane. 'Is there anything wrong?'

'No, your lordship. Lady Rossmore has bathed and had luncheon. But she has given the strangest instructions. Could I have a word in private?'

Alex indicated his study.

Saunders followed him and after closing the door, stood just inside, as he had when summoned by Grace to the drawing room.

'Her ladyship arrived late this morning, quite unrecognisable by her appearance. I'm afraid I mistook her for a servant and much to my chagrin, my lord, closed the door on her. I have apologised and I'm sure she understands my . . . how can I put it . . . disrespect. She went straight to her room and has stayed there, except for summoning me with these . . . extraordinary orders.'

Alex didn't want to waste time listening; he wanted to see Grace. 'Well, out with it, man.'

The butler looked uneasy and cleared his throat. 'She has asked that a footman be stationed outside her bedchamber door, day and night and that no one, except Esther, be allowed in.'

Alex frowned. What in heaven's name had happened, to make her act like this? 'I'll speak to her at once.'

'My lord . . .' Saunders coloured red and a sweat broke out on his forehead, 'it includes you.'

'Me!'

'It is all very . . . unsettling for the staff.'

The elation Alex felt knowing Grace was here evaporated in one breath. What was she trying to do to him? Send him into an asylum? Whereas Saunders had coloured, Alex went white. A smouldering anger began to rise and his chest heaved with each intake of air. 'Thank you, Saunders. I will deal with this. You may go.'

The butler bowed and was out of the door in a second.

Alex's chest muscles tightened and he felt as though his lungs would be squeezed empty of air. He sat down at his desk and stared, seeing nothing. He needed a drink and forced his body to rise. The few steps to the brandy decanter were like a mile and his hand shook as he poured, spilling it down the outside of the glass. He went back and sat at his desk and tipped the fiery liquid down his throat, then slammed the glass on the desktop. Whatever terrible things had happened to Grace, they must have turned her mind. He would go and see her and hope she had come back to normal.

He crossed the empty hall and went up the stairs. In the corridor he saw the footman straighten and step in front of the door. Alex walked up to him and stopped. 'Cooper, isn't it?'

'Yes, your lordship.'

'I will only ask you once to step aside. Do I make myself clear?'

'Yes, your lordship.'

Alex could see the footman's indecision. Then he said, 'Her ladyship has said no one, your lordship.'

Alex held back the reprimand he so wanted to spit out. 'I am glad to see that you take your post seriously.' And Alex walked on to his own bedchamber.

Inside, he walked across to the connecting door and turned the handle. It was locked. Now a smile showed his teeth, but the look on his face was not one of humour. He walked to the desk in front of the window and opened the central drawer, took out a key and returned and slipped it into the lock. The well-oiled mechanism moved and he opened the door.

Grace was asleep.

All his anger and frustration melted at the sight of her. She looked like a sleeping princess; but she did not want to be awakened by her charming prince. He moved over to the bed. Alex watched the lace trimming on her nightgown flutter with each breath. Her dark hair was damp and spread across the pillow, but she looked pale and her eyelids flickered as though she was dreaming. Dreaming of the ordeal she had endured?

Alex wanted to know what had happened and how she had arrived at the house. But to wake her would give away his secret: that he could come through the connecting door. Bide your time, he told himself. Let her come to terms with whatever was troubling her. He had her here; it was all that mattered for now. The scent of roses gave him a moment of pleasure. He wanted to stay, but that would be dangerous. Leaving, he closed and locked the door, then put the key back in the desk drawer.

Alex sat alone in the dining room. His appetite was not tempted by the beef and vegetables, but sated with wine. He had been drinking steadily and the decanter was almost empty.

A knock sounded and Saunders came into the room. 'I am sorry to disturb your dinner, my lord, but Mr Beesell wishes to see you. He says it is urgent.'

Alex pushed the plate away and got up. 'Show him into my study.'

Saunders held the door open for him and in the hall beckoned Beesell to follow.

Alex sat down at his desk. 'Well, Beesell, what bit of wisdom are you going to impart tonight?'

The agent came and stood opposite. He almost purred when he spoke. 'Lady Rossmore arrived safe and well?'

Alex, lounging back in his chair, sat forward. 'What do you know of Lady Rossmore's arrival here?'

Beesell did not answer. He took a scrap of cloth from his jacket pocket and laid it on the desk, unwrapped a ring. 'Is this Lady Rossmore's?'

For a moment Alex just stared at her wedding ring, the Rossmore ring. The gold band inlaid with five emeralds spread equally round the circle. By tradition, a new one was made for every earl's bride.

'Where did you get this?'

Beesell started to wrap the ring.

Alex shot out of his chair, clamping the agent's wrist with an iron grip. 'The answer is yes. Where did you get it?' His anger rising at this seedy, fat little man.

The agent looked at him and gave a forced laugh. 'It is rather a long story, but if your lordship would let me sit down . . .' He paused, looking down at their hands.

'Leave the ring on the desk.' Alex took his hand away and sat down.

Beesell withdrew his hand and did likewise. 'I am working on another case that took me to Covent Garden Market this morning. It was opportune, indeed. A country lad was making enquiries about Grosvenor Square. This struck me as odd and I asked what he was about. It appeared that a lady wished to be escorted there. I went with him and although I only have your lordship's description of Lady Rossmore, it was apparent to me who it was. Her dress was poor, but taking into account the circumstances of her ladyship's disappearance, I was able to make a calculated guess.'

Alex got up from his chair. 'A snifter of brandy?'

'Your lordship is very kind, thank you.'

Settled back in his chair, Alex raised his glass, signalling Beesell to continue.

'I had one of my boys bring her here and report back. It confirmed my deduction. I took the country boy, Joseph, aside and questioned him. He was very wary. I believe he does not know the full story, as he kept referring to her ladyship as Mrs Temple. However, he was anxious to sell a ring and asked my advice.' Beesell grinned and sipped his brandy. 'I have a very honest face. It always amazes me how trusting they are.'

'Where has she been? I want those responsible brought to justice.'

'Patience is the word in my profession. I offered to buy the ring. He was very happy to take my guineas, although I have to admit, it was way below the value of such a jewel. I shall have to put this on your lordship's bill . . .' He paused, raising his bushy eyebrows. 'I take it that is acceptable?'

'How much did you pay?'

'Ten guineas. I thought your lordship would want me to compensate him for his help to her ladyship.'

Alex said nothing.

In the silence that followed, the agent lowered his eyebrows and returned to sipping the amber liquid.

'Do you have any idea how much that ring is worth?'

'Oh yes, I certainly do. It was obvious that the boy did not. He would have been in grave danger had he shown it to any of those undesirables that frequent the Covent Garden. Including, I might add, her ladyship. She would have been a prize object for ransom in the wrong hands.'

Alex listened and with each word his skin chilled. 'How did she get to the market?'

Beesell put his empty glass on the desk. 'Here I would like to stop. You have your wife safe. I do not want to speculate on the events of the past few days. There is much investigation to be done and I shall need to keep the ring for the time being. May I take it?'

Alex reached and took the ring from the cloth. 'I am reluctant, Beesell. This belongs on Lady Rossmore's finger. But, under the circumstances, I shall agree.' He put it on his little finger and held his hand up, his thoughts going back to holding her cold hand and slipping it on her ring finger. Who had taken it from her? Was it taken by force? He looked at Beesell, trying to gauge the man. He had been recommended, but . . . 'I want it back as soon as possible.'

Beesell opened his palm. 'Of course, my lord.'

Chapter Twenty

Grace remained in her room, refusing anyone admittance and taking all her meals alone.

By the third day, Alex's mood was one of frustration and anger. He had tried to be patient with her, but this had gone far enough. He left his study and started up the stairs, when he was brought to a halt. Grace was coming down dressed to go out.

Taken completely by surprise, he blurted out, 'Grace. What are you doing?'

She stopped, two treads above him. 'Good afternoon, my lord, I am going out.'

'Out! What do you mean? Out where?'

'It seems my return to London has leaked out to Society. I have an invitation from Lady Gilworth to visit her this afternoon. No doubt I shall be offered tea.'

'Tea?'

'I think a lady's social afternoon is something his lordship would not be interested in.'

'You can't go. I have not seen or spoken to you since you . . . returned from your ordeal. Please, Grace, come into my study.'

Alex saw her eyes flash with an emotion he did not understand, but he held out his hand to her. She did not respond, but when he took a step up, narrowing the space between them, she placed her hand in his.

He led her in and closed the door, leaning back against it. 'How are you?'

Grace walked over to the window and stood looking out, keeping her back to him.

'Better, thank you.'

'Are you able to tell me what happened?'

Alex couldn't believe she looked so frail. 'I don't want to force you, but something must be done to apprehend those who took you from me.'

Grace turned and he could see anger had replaced the strange look that had been in her eyes earlier. 'You wish to *apprehend* those responsible. Come, my lord, let us not fool with words that are false. I am here and you are here. We will live under this roof together, but I do not want pretence that we are husband and wife. You have your pursuits and I will have mine. Now, if you will please stand away from the door, I shall be late arriving at Lady Gilworth's home.'

'What the hell are you talking about, Grace? What did they do to you?'

Alex took a step forward into the room, but Grace put out her arm to fend him off. 'Don't touch me.'

'I have been patient, knowing that you must be confused and frightened. You must talk to me about your kidnapping; it's the only way that I can help you. These brutes must be brought to justice.'

'A fair act of indignation, you would do well on the stage.'

'On the stage? Has your mind gone addled? I will get the doctor to you.' Alex feared for her sanity. This nonsense she was spilling out, she couldn't be in her right mind.

'This reaction is just as I expected. You want me taken away. Not again, Alex.' She walked towards him and stood within two paces of where he barred the door.

In her lavender-coloured muslin dress and dark hair piled high with curls cascading down her back, he thought he had never seen her look lovelier. But there was fear in her face and she trembled, waiting for his reaction.

'I don't understand you or your words. I withdraw my offer of

236

Dr Winter. Will you join me for dinner?' She hesitated and expecting a refusal he rushed on. 'Please, Grace.'

'Very well. Now may I go?'

'You have Cooper to accompany you?'

'Yes. I will have Cooper as my protector at all times. Remember that.'

Alex moved and opened the door. 'I will order dinner for six o'clock.'

In her bedchamber a few hours later Grace didn't want to go down to dinner with Alex. She felt tired and the thought of dressing in an evening gown, having her hair fussed over, was just too much trouble. But she had to face him. Look at the man who had betrayed her, not only with his lies, but his wickedness in having her kidnapped and put into an asylum.

The news that she was now in London, the first time since her wedding, had brought in immediate invitations to morning visits and evening parties. This made her strategy to protect her life simple. The more engagements she accepted, the more difficult it would be for Alex to have her removed. The thought of being put back into Greensleeves was unthinkable.

But this first outing today had been difficult. The endless questions, especially from Lady Gilworth, had made her feel like an object put out for display. But she had rehearsed her patter well. The good weather in Dorset, his lordship's busy business engagements, visiting Rachel and being there to comfort and support her after the birth of twin girls, satisfied them. It provided plenty to gossip about in the days to come.

A deep green dress was laid out on the bed and this reminded her of the stones in her wedding ring. Somehow, this lifted her spirits instead of plunging them into despair. She had worn cotton gloves instead of a light lacy pair and had kept them on at tea. The thought that the nosy ladies would have been observing her attire and every move, brought a smile to her lips.

There was a light knock at the door and Esther came in. 'Are you ready to dress, m'lady?'

'Yes, but not the green. Find me something simple and light.'

An hour later, Grace entered the drawing room. It was empty. She had deliberately come down late, hoping to have Alex at a disadvantage, have him wondering if she was going to come. She stood waiting, undecided whether to sit down, when the door opened and he came in.

'What were you doing? Spying on my door to see when I came down?'

'Yes.'

The blunt reply took her by surprise and the sarcastic reply she was going to make died on her lips.

'Would you like a drink?'

'No.'

'Well, I do.' He went over to the table and poured one glass of spirit. Alex sat down in a chair and lifted the glass to his lips.

Grace didn't know what to do, so she went and sat on the window seat and looked out at the square.

'How was your afternoon?'

'Pleasing. Lady Gilworth has a wide circle of friends. Several asked if they could send a calling card to visit.'

'I can see that Kilbraith House will soon become a hive of activity. You must warn Saunders so that Cook can have plenty of tea and cake ready.'

Grace's nerves were on edge and her throat was dry. She should have asked him for a glass of lemonade, but if Alex came close, it would make her limbs tremble, not with desire and love, but distaste and fear.

She was saved answering with Saunders coming in to announce dinner was ready.

They sat at one end of the table, neither eating much of the fine food before them.

Alex broke the silence. 'I asked that the table be set as at Solitaire. Does it please you?' Grace glanced at him, then back to her plate. 'You look charming in your afternoon dress. Pink suits you so well. I am far too formal for this homely occasion.'

'No doubt you will be going out later, so it is not wasted.'

'Why should I go out, with such a delightful lady sat at my side?'

'Flattery is not your style, Alex. Save it for . . .' she stopped, he did not know that she had seen him with his mistress, '. . . your party, that no doubt you are going to.'

'Grace, if I am going to any parties, you will be coming with me. Cooper can be your bodyguard during the day, but I will be the one during our evenings out.'

Her plan to be out of Alex's reach was, by Society's etiquette, impossible. Cooper could not escort her around the houses and ballrooms of the *ton*.

'I think I shall not be attending any evening soirées or parties. There is no need for you to bother yourself.'

Alex pushed his chair back and came round to her. He stood behind her chair and leaned over and whispered close to her ear, 'It is no bother, Lady Rossmore. No bother at all.' Then he moved to her side and picked up her left hand.

Grace tried to snatch it away, but he held it tight. He rubbed his finger across her knuckles. 'Cotton gloves, my lady, a little cumbersome for the evening,' and he let her hand go.

'If you have eaten enough, shall we retire to the drawing room? Perhaps a board game, backgammon?'

Grace could not keep up with him. He was darting from one subject to the next, flitting like a fly, making her head dizzy. 'Not tonight, Alex. I am tired. I shall go to my room.'

'As you please. Goodnight, Grace.'

He bowed and left the room.

She sat there astounded. Where had his manners gone? A gentleman should see his wife . . . but she had told him that they were not going to be husband and wife. What seemed to be a simple plan when she had arrived at Kilbraith House was turning into a nightmare. She couldn't stay hidden in her bedchamber. That was only exchanging one prison room for another. She didn't want to go back there now; it was far too early, although she could write to Rachel. A letter had arrived in response to one from Alex, wishing her well and telling how Nurse was still fussing and that the twins were improving in strength daily. Grace envied Rachel, for she was a good mother and quite content to be in the country with her children.

Grace foresaw her future empty without Alex and his love, empty without his children, the futility of it all crushing her dreams. She stood up. It was best she hid away in her room; she would rather die than let Alex see her tears.

During the next week, Grace kept to her plan. She entertained and visited during the day, taking Cooper everywhere she went.

Grace had been grateful to hear through Esther's gossip that Aunt Matilda was not in London. She and Lord Crowmarsh had gone to his Norfolk estate for a few weeks. A letter was her only requirement, full of half-truths, except about being with Rachel during her confinement. The second surprise was that Isabelle was with child. And she too was residing in Herefordshire. The letter to her was harder to write, because their friendship had grown strong during the month of her wedding preparations. But the truth of her kidnap was not to be told and so she filled the page with best wishes and seeing her when she returned to London.

Now, mid-morning, she and Esther were shopping in Bond Street.

Without warning, Cooper stopped and indicated a chocolate shop. 'I believe we are being followed, your ladyship. Please go in there while I try to find out if my suspicions are founded.'

Grace's heart started to hammer and her breath caught in her throat. 'How long has he been there?'

'Some time. I noticed him about half-an-hour ago. Please do not come out into the street.' Cooper waited until the shop door closed behind his mistress.

Grace circled the tables, looking at the pretty wrapping on the boxes. Unfortunately, there were no other customers and she noticed the assistant was hovering with the expectation of a purchase.

'Esther, would you please choose a box for yourself and one for the staff to share? I think you all deserve a little luxury this evening.'

Her maid stepped forward from where she was standing by the door. 'Thank you, your ladyship.'

To continue the charade, Grace picked up and put down several boxes. 'I'm looking for a present. I think the blue box will do nicely.' She handed it to Esther to add to her chosen gifts.

Where was Cooper? He said not to leave the shop, so she slowly placed one coin after another on the counter until the exact purchase money was paid. Now there was no reason to linger. Grace started to walk to the front door, when Cooper arrived.

'He's gone. I've looked around; there seems to be no one else. If your ladyship has finished shopping, I think we should go back to Kilbraith House. The coach is outside.'

'Very well, I have finished, thank you.'

Leaving the shop, she glanced around; but she would never be able to recognise her kidnappers. In the woods at Hawthorn Hall they had attacked her and pulled the sack over her head so fast, the only clue she had was of their sweaty smell, and that was a common odour, especially in the streets of London.

Grace fixed her gaze on the crowds while the coach journeyed through the busy roads. The threat made her feel sick. Was it real or just Cooper's protective imagination running away with him? She closed her eyes, but this only brought back her ordeal at the hands of the kidnappers who took her to Greensleeves. She had been sleeping better the past two nights, her nightmares fading. Now they rolled round her mind non-stop.

When they reached home and she was safe in her bedchamber, Grace wrote a note to Mrs Chamberlin, declining to visit that afternoon due to a headache. This was the truth, but she also didn't want to leave the sanctuary of Kilbraith House.

Grace lay down on her bed and tried to think calmly, not let the panic that was gaining hold escape in screams of terror. A knock came at the door and assuming it was Esther, she called for her to come in.

It wasn't her maid, but Alex.

'Are you alright, Grace? Cooper has been to see me about . . .'

Grace swung her legs from the bed and stood up. Then, without a sound or word passing her lips, crumpled to the floor.

Alex was not quick enough to catch her and picked her up and laid her back on the bed. Going to the washstand, he poured cold water into the bowl and soaked a small towel. Wringing it tight, he went back to Grace and, placing the cool cloth to her forehead, dabbed her face and ran the cloth down her neck. She was as white as the sheet she lay on, but then her eyelids fluttered and her grey eyes looked straight into his.

'Lie still. You fainted and need a little time to settle.'

Grace ignored his words and tried to sit up. 'No. What are you doing here? Cooper shouldn't have let you in.'

'It is a little late, my dear, for that order. I've sent Cooper to the kitchen. You're a hard taskmaster; the man is quite upset about this morning's mystery follower.'

'Are you surprised?' Grace saw her words made him look away. 'I see.'

'Do you? I doubt it, Lady Rossmore. You are seeing only what you want to see and I have no idea what that is. When are you going to talk to me, Grace? Holding this secret is damaging your health. Why can't you *see* that?'

Grace turned on her side away from him. 'I would like to sleep now. Would you ask Esther to come? Now, please.'

She heard Alex give a heavy sigh. 'Remember your promise that you would accompany me to Lord Barlow's mansion for their summer ball this evening. I won't give your excuses, Grace, especially as it is our first formal occasion in London together since our marriage. The Barlows are close friends of mine and Lady Elizabeth is looking forward to seeing you.'

Grace knew he stood looking at her, she could almost feel his eyes boring holes into her back; then there was a click and the door opened and closed.

Alex waited for Grace in the hall.

She appeared at the top of the stairs in the deep green gown. Her hair was swept high, leaving her neck free to show the full beauty of the Rossmore emeralds. She came down slowly, her eyes watching each step. Alex took full advantage of this to study her face. She was still pale, only a little rouge giving a glow to her cheeks. He had decided that nothing was going to spoil this evening. He wouldn't take his eyes from her, nor leave her side even to fetch refreshments. He was her protector. Woe betide anyone who came within an inch of hurting her.

'You are the most beautiful of all ladies. I shall be the envy of every bachelor and married man in London.' As he took her hand in the cotton glove, he was reminded of her wedding ring. There had been no news from Beesell, but at this moment he didn't care. She was here with him, albeit under strange and disturbing conditions. But time would heal what was wrong. He would have to be patient, play a waiting game.

Grace smiled. 'Then I must see if I can make you jealous. There must be many young beaux who I can tempt a dance with me, fill my card.'

'There you are mistaken. I shall fill your card, on every line. Let the tabbies talk. You are mine, Lady Rossmore.' Alex pulled her hand through the crook of his arm and Saunders opened the front door for them to leave.

Bertie Barlow was dancing with Grace.

Alex had warded off any suitor other than his old friend. He stood, now, watching the crowd. Crowds were dangerous. It would be easy to lose sight of her if she should wander amongst them. Was it possible they would try again? He was putting a lot of faith in the agent's ability to track down these villains.

The music stopped and Bertie brought Grace back.

'I am out of breath, but this young woman is as fresh as a daisy. I suggest you take the next dance, Alex; I shall head for the nearest chair.' Bowing to Grace, he moved on.

'Fresh as a daisy, I think not. My toes have been trodden on several times and they hurt.'

'Ah. But this next dance is a waltz. May I have your hand, my lady?'

Alex led her into the dancers and opened his arms. He saw her hesitate, said, 'Dance with me, Grace.' He stepped forward and drew her into the circle of his arms, his hand slipping to her waist and coaxed her to him. He could smell her scent and it set his senses hurtling back to their first waltz. How she had captivated him, and, he realised now, started to fall in love with her. The music dipped with the beat and he twirled her round and round, holding her closer and closer. He forgot everything; there was just them and the music. When it stopped, he didn't let her go. He looked into her eyes and saw unshed tears.

'I think we are causing just a little tittle, Alex.'

For the first time since she had arrived at Kilbraith House there was normality to her voice, even a little humour, and Alex prayed that this was her turning point.

'Is that a challenge I hear? Shall we indulge them or just disappear home?'

'Home sounds wonderful. I am feeling very tired.'

Alex took her arm and led her to where Bertie and Elizabeth were standing. 'A wonderful party, Elizabeth, but Grace is tired, so we are leaving. Goodnight.'

He kissed Elizabeth's cheek and turned to her husband. 'Maybe see you at White's soon, Bertie. Goodnight.'

In the coach, Alex sat next to Grace and within a few minutes she was falling asleep. He put his arm behind her and drew her head down onto his shoulder. This was the nearest he had been to her since the night of the storm and he wanted that nearness again. Not for just one night, but always.

She was still asleep when they reached Grosvenor Square. Alex waited for the coach to settle and the door to be opened. Grace stirred when he removed his arm, and he helped her sit up. 'We are home, my dear,' but she was only half-awake. Getting out he leaned back in to guide her through the doorway. Then he scooped her into his arms as Saunders opened the front door.

'Is her ladyship ill, my lord?' Concern tinged the butler's voice.

'No, Saunders, just sleepy.'

When he reached her door, it opened. Esther looked startled and backed away as Alex carried Grace in and laid her on the bed. He wanted to order Esther out of the room, so that he could be alone with his wife. Alone and close, to undress her sensuous body, one garment at a time. Stroke each new layer of skin until she was naked before him. Rip his own clothes from his heated body and lie with her. Kiss and fondle her breasts, trail his tongue down her ribs, suck the dimple in her belly, sink into her warm body and love her.

Esther sniffed.

Alex let out a deep sigh. 'Help your mistress into bed. She is very tired.' He left, going to his own room next door.

A little later Alex heard Esther leave and the sounds of the household go silent. He took the key from the drawer and unlocked the connecting door.

The curtains were pulled three-quarters across the window and in the darkness he could see very little. But the essence of her scent filled the room and he knew where she lay. He crossed the carpet and sat on the padded box at the bottom of the bed. It was a warm night and she had no covering, except a nightgown. Her sleeping shape lay curled and he remembered how he had drawn her cold, shivering body into him at Solitaire. She was not shivering now, but lay as a child, secure and content.

Whispered words passed Alex's lips. 'When are you going to tell me what happened?'

Her breathing rhythm changed and he knew she was awake. Her voice sounded uncertain. 'Alex, is that you?'

He got up and moved to the side of the bed. He lay down beside her. 'Yes.'

Her voice was throaty, almost tearful. 'Where's Cooper?'

'I've sent him to bed. I admire his loyalty, but the man is sleeping on his feet.'

'Oh. Have I been very selfish?'

'Yes. You have kept me away, like the unwanted plague.'

Alex touched her shoulder. 'Is that what you really want, Grace? Never to feel my touch, never lie in my arms?' She didn't answer and Alex fought the urge to turn her to him. 'Grace?'

'I don't know. I know I shouldn't. You will use me . . . then go to . . . but I don't want to be alone. Don't send me back . . .'

Alex pulled her over and silenced her lips with his finger.

'Shh. There is much to talk about, but not now,' and he replaced his finger with a gentle kiss, that acted as a spark from a flint stone. Circling his arms round her he pulled her close. The kiss deepened, making his body fire into a raging inferno. She opened her lips and he plunged deep inside, feeling her teeth tighten, gripping him in anticipation of what her body could soon be doing.

Her cotton nightgown was a barrier between them and, remembering his earlier musings, he found the hem and slid it up her legs. When it reached her buttocks she stilled his hand. 'Grace?' With her other hand she pushed against his chest, parting them.

'I cannot do this, unless I know you love me, just a little. That you won't send me back to that place . . .'

Alex smothered her face with kisses. 'I love you, Grace, nothing will come between us, ever. Your mind is confused. Let me help you through this nightmare. We will talk about this tomorrow; let me show you my love now.' He pulled again at the cotton hem and she raised her hips, her arms and the nightgown was thrown to the floor. He felt her fingers beneath his robe, rubbing the hair on his chest, sliding down to the belt; it was tied loosely and fell apart with one pull. Grace followed the lapel and pushed it from his shoulder. With one shrug it slipped to his waist and he released one arm at a time to discard it next to her nightgown on the floor.

Alex shivered, as though he was cold, and she pulled him towards her. Wrapped her legs around his hips, her arms round his shoulders, and he could feel her warm breath. He covered her lips, capturing that breath and pulled her onto him. Her legs slid either side of his hips and she braced her hands each side of his head. She broke the kiss and threw her head back, and her breasts dropped. He took one nipple slowly into his mouth, teased it with his teeth and sucked deeply. She pushed down on his shaft and he was drawn into her and a moan of pleasure left her lips. Grace pushed upright above him, sinking her weight down and a pulsing sensation exploded into ecstasy. Alex spread his hands and held her ribs, lifted his shoulders and retook a nipple, pulling hard. Together they moved as one. Together they reached a climax of such rapture that Alex shouted her name over and over.

Alex waited until Grace sank down onto him and then he held her close and turned onto his side. He could feel his heart pounding, hammering an echo in his head, and felt Grace's quick breathing on his chest. The warm summer night and their heated passion had made their bodies glisten and they slid into a comfortable embrace. He wrapped his leg across her thigh and tucked her head beneath his chin. He didn't speak. He was afraid to speak. Words could break the spell, for he still could not fathom Grace's strange utterances. She spoke of him as a villain. When had he ever given her that impression? Perhaps when he had left her at White-cliffs? There was much to straighten out tomorrow. The household had been instructed not to talk about the strange happenings in Kilbraith House or the intruder. He had not wanted Grace to be burdened with his troubles; she had enough of her own. But, if she were at a turning point to recovery, it would be a wise decision to tell her.

Grace stirred and everything other than loving her left his mind.

'You are a beautiful lover, my dearest wife.' Alex kissed her head, then tilted her face up with a finger. 'There are still a few hours until the dawn, hours we should not waste sleeping.'

Grace tilted her head further. 'Then let us not waste them talking.'

Alex had a light step and a smile for everyone in the morning.

He spent an hour in his study checking his ledgers and then sent a message to Willy, saying he would be going for an hour of fencing at noon. He was not expecting Grace to rise until after midday. Perhaps they would dine at home this evening, retire early. The secret thought had him leaving the house with a sparkle in his eyes.

When he returned to Kilbraith House mid-afternoon, there were servants everywhere. Trunks were being carried down the stairs and placed in the hall. Esther was waving her arms directing and bewailing, 'Don't crush those, they're her ladyship's hat boxes.' And Saunders stood looking aghast.

'What the devil is this?'

'Her ladyship is going to Whitecliffs, my lord, tomorrow morning.'

Alex exploded into action. He threw his hat and cane towards the butler. 'We'll see about that.'

Cooper was outside her door. 'Go downstairs, Cooper.'

'But, her ladyship has said . . .'

'I am the master in this house. Move out of the way. Now!'

Cooper hesitated, but stepped aside.

Alex didn't knock, but turned the handle and walked in.

Grace was sitting on a stool before her dressing table. Their eyes met in the reflection of the mirror and he closed the door with deliberate poise. He walked towards her, seeing the white face, frightened expression. 'Will you tell me what is going on?'

She lowered her gaze. 'I am going to Solitaire. It is the best thing for me to do.'

'For you, Grace, maybe. What about me?'

'You have a life here and your other . . . pursuits.'

'Grace, these mad statements of yours, they leave me bewildered. I thought we were going to talk everything through today.

248

You were going to tell me what happened during your ordeal. Was it so bad that you cannot speak of it to me?'

She got up from the stool and pushed past him, going to the window. 'It may seem a long time ago, but you did say I could go to Solitaire anytime I wish. Well, I wish tomorrow.'

'Then I will come with you.'

'No. I must go alone.'

'After all the wickedness, the crime that has befallen you? You are not thinking with a clear mind. What about last night, I was with you, loving you? We have to settle our differences, Grace. There is so much to discuss.'

'Not with me, Alex. It was my weakness, last night. It won't happen again.'

Alex could see no solution to this dilemma. She had gone back into her own world of fear. Fear of him, it seemed. Would the country life and sea air help bring her back to him?

'Then Cooper will go with you.'

'He will not be necessary at Solitaire.'

'It's either Cooper or me, Grace. Or you stay, here in London.'

'So you can make me a prisoner again?'

'You have never been a captive.'

'Very well, Alex. Cooper it is.'

He looked at her, his heart breaking into a thousand pieces. 'Then, my dear, I agree.'

Turning, he left her stroking the petals of fresh pink roses.

Alex had not slept all night.

With his unshaven face, puffy eyes and dishevelled clothes, he could not let her see how distraught he was. Imprisoned in his study, it offered him no other option but to watch through the window as her coach drove away.

He couldn't understand her swinging moods. He wanted to help her through this hellish nightmare she seemed to be in. Without any communication between them, how was he going to succeed now they would be miles apart again? He was beginning to hate the name Solitaire. It was turning into her fortress, where she could hide from everything, including him.

He went to his desk. Looking at the bills that needed his attention he picked them up and crushed them in his hands. Bills for trivial items, things he did not really need. There was only one thing he truly wanted, and that was Grace. Grace, as he had known her, eager to wed him, eager to love him, eager to spend the rest of her life with him. What demons had taken hold of her? He had no answer until Beesell's digging came up with some names.

It would be a good time to settle his bills.

Chapter Twenty-one

During dinner a message was delivered from Beesell; could he call on his lordship late that evening?

Waiting in his study, Alex heard the clock's rhythmic ticking. It was dark outside and he was beginning to think the agent wasn't coming. Voices sounded in the hall, and a moment later Saunders opened the door and announced the agent had arrived.

Beesell came straight to his desk and stood silent until the door was closed. 'May I make sure there are no listening ears, your lordship?' Without waiting for permission, he went back to the door, opened it with a sharp pull and went out into the hall. Returning, he closed the door and checked that it was secure. Only then did he return and take the seat opposite the desk. 'Thank you. One cannot be too careful.'

'I should hope my household is secure. Saunders was with my father; I have every confidence in his ability to manage the staff.'

Beesell made no reply, but took a sheaf of papers from inside his coat. 'My enquiries are now complete.' He placed the papers in front of Alex. 'This report will enable you to decide what to do next.'

Alex noticed that Beesell was uncomfortable. The man kept his eyes averted, not looking at him and there was moisture trickling down the centre of his nose. He had licked his lips twice.

'A brandy, while I read?'

'Thank you. It will help to clear my throat.'

Alex got up and went to the cabinet, poured two large measures. When he gave Beesell his glass, the man gulped half in one go.

Alex took his time sitting back down. Sipping the spirit, he didn't take his eyes off the agent then, placing the glass to one side, he picked up the report. The writing was difficult to read. But the content was unbelievable. He put the papers back onto the desk and looked at Beesell.

The man cleared his throat and waited.

'Do you expect me to believe what is in here?' Alex's voice was calm.

'This is why I wanted to come late, why I checked the door, your lordship. Family . . . ah, disputes . . . can be very awkward to deal with.'

'Would you explain in your own words what all this is about?'

Beesell coughed and downed the remainder of his brandy.

'A refill first.' Alex held up his own glass, and the agent nodded. Standing at the cabinet he put the glasses down, but did not refill them. He went over to the window and looked out into the night. He needed a few minutes to grasp the implications of the report. Family! How was he going to handle this? When he turned, he saw the agent was staring at him. 'This is a complete shambles, Beesell. You may begin.' Refilling the glasses he sat down again.

'I went backwards, beginning with the lad Joseph. With a little persuasion and a few extra guineas, tinged with a hint that he was in deep trouble, he told me how her ladyship came to be at Covent Garden Market. He knew her as Mrs Temple. The wedding ring was a bribe to his intended, a girl called Betsey, who worked at the Greensleeves Home for Ladies.' Beesell took a sip of brandy. 'I then went to this home. The ladies I saw seemed a little strange . . . there are bars on the inside of the windows. I would venture an opinion that they didn't know where they were.' The man paused and reached for his glass.

Alex felt a shudder run down his spine; Grace had been held in a place where there were mentally ill patients. He looked at Beesell and nodded for him continue.

'I found Betsey at the farm. The girl was terrified when I showed her the ring, saying Mrs Temple had truly given her it in exchange for helping her escape. When I asked how her ladyship had arrived she said by coach at night, trussed up and taken to the attic room. She said that *Mrs Temple's husband* had put her there.'

At those words, Alex slammed his fist on the desk and bolted out of the chair. He leaned heavily on both hands and looked Beesell straight in the eyes. 'Don't even think it for one minute. I had nothing to do with this scheme.' Alex's breath was coming in gasps. 'Who was masquerading as her husband?'

Beesell shifted back in his chair. 'I don't know. One of the kidnappers I presume.'

Alex sat back down. 'Carry on. We have solved the mystery of how she disappeared from Hawthorn Hall.'

'Enquiries around Hawthorn estate led me to a farm worker. A man of quality had paid him for information about where her ladyship went riding. I traced him to an inn, thence to London. He has lodgings in Bury Street.' Beesell paused again. 'Then there is the matter of . . . your first wife's . . . apparition or ghost in this house. A little something your lordship forgot to mention. The lady concerned was very helpful when reminded what a prison cell would be like; especially carrying an unborn child . . . I will say no more.' The man shifted to sit more upright in his chair. 'I am finding this very awkward, your lordship, there is a conspiracy going on concerning both yourself and her ladyship. This is very much outside my normal investigative commission. As you know, kidnapping is punishable by imprisonment.'

'I am well aware of that fact. Go on, I need the names that you have left blank in your report.' Alex was beginning to shake; he too realised what could happen to those yet to be named.

'Sir Quentin Baines is the . . . how shall I put it . . . organiser. Then there is . . . my lord, may I recheck the door.' Beesell got up and opened the study door into the hall. He disappeared through the doorway and came back a few seconds later. He was as cautious as he had been the first time. 'Then there is your half-brother . . . who I believe, at this moment, is your heir?'

Alex got up and paced between his desk and the window. 'Are you absolutely sure about Geoffrey?'

'Yes, my lord. I have been doubly careful with this investigation. I am sorry that this has turned out so badly.' Beesell stood up and took something from his coat pocket and laid it on the desk. 'Her ladyship's ring. I will not need it any more.'

Alex stopped at his desk, but did not touch the piece of cloth. His mind was full of the terrible and pointless acts that his own flesh and blood had been party to. He now knew that Geoffrey was behind all the tricks that had been going on at Kilbraith House. He couldn't comprehend that title and money meant more to Geoffrey than his family. That Geoffrey would risk going to prison or being deported to such continents as the Americas or Australia. That he had given no thought of leaving a wife and six children to bear the shame of his criminal act.

Beesell took a paper from his coat and put it next to the ring. 'My account, your lordship. If you need me for anything else, you know where I am.' He didn't wait to be dismissed.

The click of the closing door broke into Alex's thoughts. Beesell had not finished telling all. He picked up the report and turned to the last page.

From London my investigations led me to Dorset and to a blackguard who is backing the smugglers. Then on to Whitecliffs Bay and a Norwegian sea captain named Hugo Olsen, whose name has been linked with Lady Rossmore.

Alex threw the report back down.

He had let her go to Solitaire House, thinking it was the best course of action. Instead, he had let her walk into the lion's den. Olsen was now the most dangerous person she could be with.

He pulled the bell-rope. Throwing open the study door he saw his butler entering the hall from below stairs. 'Saunders, send a footman to find me a hackney carriage, now. Have my horse tethered outside this house by the time I return. I will be going to Solitaire.'

★

The carriage drew up outside Geoffrey's town house in Lincoln's Inn Fields.

Alex sat pondering his actions. This late hour was the best time to confront his half-brother. He pulled a watch from his waistcoat pocket. Half-past the hour of two o'clock. He knocked on the roof with his cane and the coachman opened the door. 'I will be about an hour and keep a sharp lookout for footpads.'

A moment after knocking, the front door opened. 'Is my brother at home?' Alex did not wait to be invited in, but walked past the butler, assuming from his spluttering words that he had been expecting Geoffrey.

'The master has not yet returned, my lord. I do not know how long . . .'

'No matter, Harris, I will wait in his study until he arrives.'

The man hurried to open a door. 'I will inform him of your presence as soon as he comes home.'

Alex saw the study was well lit, so Geoffrey must come in here for his supper. Well, he wouldn't get food tonight, more likely a doctor. The cabinet held a good supply of spirits and Alex helped himself to a small brandy and sat down in a winged chair by the fireplace.

Ten minutes later the voices in the hall told him that Geoffrey was home. Another few seconds and his half-brother came in. He was, as usual, flamboyantly dressed, having the finest of cloth and leather. God, they could be twins. Quirks of fate, that they both resembled their father, with not a trace of their different mothers in face or limb.

Geoffrey closed the door. 'What are you doing here at this hour?'

Alex got up. 'You would do well to check that your man is not listening at the door, Geoffrey. What we have to discuss is for our hearing only.'

Alex's terse words made Geoffrey stop mid-stride.

'What piffle is this, Alex? I'm tired and ready for my bed; the tables were not my friend this evening.'

'More nights than not, so I hear.'

'What business is it of yours? You have enough to lose every night and not let it dent your pocket.'

Alex held down his anger. Geoffrey's gambling habit was not the reason he was here. 'Your stupidity is not my concern. What is my concern is your treachery to my wife and ultimately me.'

These words made Geoffrey's face go crimson and he returned to the door and looked out into the hall.

'What are you talking about? Is all the scandal, *I hear,* turning your mind into pulp?'

'That would suit you well, brother. Being my heir would give you full control. Oh, no. My mind is working well. It is your mind that has taken a turn to insanity.'

Geoffrey's forehead beaded with droplets of sweat.

'I know it all. I have a full written report by an investigating agent. You are minutes away from being thrown into Newgate Prison unless we sit down now and bring this lunacy to an end.'

As expected, Geoffrey went straight to the cabinet and poured a large brandy.

'Sit down at your desk, Geoffrey. I do not think a cosy chat round the fireplace is for us this night.'

Sat facing each other Alex took the report from inside his coat. 'On these pages is everything you have done. Your own hand may not have committed all of them, but they were your instructions.'

'No! You have it wrong. It is Baines; he organised everything. I just happened to mention something about . . .'

'Do not compound your villainy with lies. Or do you wish me to go and see Baines now? I'm sure he will tell all when the threat of a prison ship is put to him.'

'Alex, it all got out of hand. I'm not lying. It all started out as a simple idea, but Baines became dogmatic in separating you and Grace. He saw it as the only way . . . hell, I don't know what I was thinking . . . to secure my position . . .'

'As my only surviving heir?' Alex finished for him.

'Yes.' It was a whisper and Geoffrey paled to a deathly white.

256

Alex got up and went to the cabinet and poured himself another brandy. Returned and sat back down. 'What you have done is criminal. The evidence I have could mean years in prison or deportation to a penal colony. Our family name ruined. Did you not think of Rachel, of your children? And your mistress's yet-to-be-born bastard child? By God, Geoffrey, we may look alike, but we are miles apart in character. Our father must turn in his grave with your irresponsible acts. Have you anything left from this quarter's allowance?'

'Well, no . . . but you haven't paid me for the twins . . . yet.'

Alex rose from his seat and leaned across the desk, forcing his half-brother to push his chair backwards. 'You sink so low, to rely on increasing your allowance by using Rachel as your means?' Alex banged on the desk with his clenched fist. 'All this ends now. Is that clear?'

Geoffrey had slipped down in his seat, raising his arms over his face as a defence against Alex's rage.

'I have two instructions for you and I want them carried out immediately.'

Alex sat back down in his chair. 'First. You will personally go and see Baines and give him a message from me. His game playing is over. If anything happens to either Grace or me, no matter how insignificant, this report goes from my solicitor's holding safe to the magistrate. I will not raise a finger to help you.

'Secondly . . .'

Geoffrey interrupted. 'But Baines is in Bath, pandering to his mother. It will take days for my valet to get ready and the travelling will need at least one overnight stop. Alex, this is asking too much, surely a letter will do?'

'Not one word of this is to be put in writing. Go by horse with a saddlebag. And to continue, secondly, you will go to my estate in Ireland until I recall you . . . or not recall; it will be at my pleasure.'

'You can't . . . do this. What about Rachel, she would hate living in Ireland? And the children . . . ?'

Alex was losing control of his temper. 'You mean *you* would hate Ireland. Rachel stays here in England. I will look after your family. She can stay at Hawthorn Hall or come to Rossmore Manor. If you want a woman, take your mistress.'

Geoffrey began to splutter incoherent words.

Alex got up. His half-brother was a stranger. A man he did not want to see again for a very long time. 'I'll have my solicitor draw up the papers for your management of Craigkillie, and, of course, an allowance. If you make a success of the estate, you can keep the profits. A little incentive . . . it will help you pay the gambling chits. If you are still in England fourteen days from now, I will . . .' Alex waved the report at Geoffrey before putting it back into his coat pocket.

Alex turned and left the study; left the house.

In the carriage he started to shake. He had wanted to throttle Geoffrey, kill Baines and any other low life who had been party to harming Grace. He ran his fingers through his copper hair and cursed his ancestors.

Arriving at Kilbraith House, Saunders had the staff preparing for his departure. He should rest, but Grace filled his mind too much to sleep.

Chapter Twenty-two

Grace leaned forward and looked out of the coach window. They were bumping along the narrow road to Whitecliffs and she would soon see Solitaire House.

Had she done the right thing in coming here alone? But she could not continue to live in London. As each day passed she realised she had only exchanged Greensleeves for Kilbraith House. If she wanted to live a fearless life she had to leave. So, she had decided to enjoy her last evening with him at Lord Barlow's party. Their night together had not been planned and it was her only moment of weakness. She loved him, no matter what he had done.

A wheel tipped over a large stone and as Grace steadied herself, Solitaire came into view. Here was her haven: a home, where she could start her life anew.

Grace looked past Cooper's shoulder as he helped her from the coach. Mrs Gillett was opening the door. The old retainer rushed forward with her arms wide. 'Miss Grace, I am so glad to see you.'

Grace felt a lump rise in her throat as she ran up the path, 'Gillie, I'm here, safe and well,' and she let her old nurse wrap her in a hug. When they parted, Grace cleared her throat and smiled. 'I'm very thirsty, Gillie, will you bring a jug of lemonade into the garden?'

'Yes I will and a bowl of your favourite sweetmeats.'

Behind her Mr Gillett was taking instructions from Esther about their luggage and a feeling of relief spread through her. Here, at Solitaire, she could be herself: no pretences, no social delicacies of the *ton* to observe and no fear of what Alex might do next. It was hard to come to terms with what he had done to her.

Grace went into the hall and into her study, then out through the glass door into the garden. The summer air was warm, the scent of the roses and flowers wonderful and the call of the gulls a reminder of the sea. The sunken garden's carpet of grass, set with the table and chairs, calmed her frantic thoughts. She must not let Alex bring her to the point of insanity, not let what he was doing drive her, in truth, into the hands of Dr Palmer and Mrs Norris. There would be no second chance to escape. The sound of Mrs Gillett's footsteps encouraged Grace to go down the steps and sit under the shade of a tree.

Waiting until the glassware was on the table, Grace asked, 'What is the gossip in the village? Have the Excise men found any smugglers of late?'

'No, Miss Grace. But there will be two marriages before the harvest and God willing a few births for the Reverend Clive to baptise.'

'Is the captain still here?' Grace kept her gaze lowered, but she could sense Mrs Gillett's manner change.

'I believe so.' The short reply left Grace in no doubt about her disapproval.

'Thank you, Gillie. I will pour when I am ready.'

Grace watched her go back to the house.

Alex had informed her that he had written to Mrs Gillett after her arrival at Grosvenor Square. She wondered now what lies he may have told. Poor Gillie, she must be very confused about everything.

Grace's thoughts began to snatch at ridiculous scenarios: was it for the thrill of a secret alliance? That this woman was going to bear him a child? But, she could give him an heir. Why, why, why?

Grace poured her lemonade and sipped slowly, letting her thoughts wander to Hugo Olsen. She was surprised he was still here. When she had left for London his ship repairs were almost finished. Still, it would be nice to see him again, if only to say goodbye. Grace replaced her glass on the table and closed her eyes. The familiar sounds of the garden were soothing, weaving a web of tranquillity, something she had not known for many weeks. Resting her head against the seatback, she went to sleep.

Grace looked at the blue satin dress laid on the bed.

'I think not, Esther. Something lighter, please, my pale green muslin.'

'But, your ladyship, that's a day dress.'

'So, who is going to see me? I'm sure Mr and Mrs Gillett will not be shocked by my choice. Leave my hair loose and fasten it with a bow.'

Later, in the dining room, a sad smile curved her lips as she ate at the single place setting at the head of the table. It was where her mother had always sat, only relinquishing it should her father be in residence. Had her mother ever wanted him to come? Probably not, he had little time for the women of his house, except to demand obedience, without question. But Alex had agreed to spend their honeymoon here. Had asked what she wanted to do, where she would like to go. He had been so kind and caring, wanting to please her. Was it all an act? She pushed her plate away, most of the food untouched. She was letting him into her thoughts again.

The door opened and Mr Gillett came in. He looked very butler-like, his attire and manner no doubt the command of his wife.

'Please tell Mrs Gillett that the dinner was excellent, but I have a headache. The travelling was most tiring. I am going to take a walk before the sun dips into the sea.'

'Shall I call Esther or Cooper?'

'No. I am quite safe here at Whitecliffs, and I want to be alone.'

Grace left, going out through the study again. Climbing the steps into the wood, the path was dry under her feet and the sunlight passing through the branches was like threads of gold interwoven in a dark cloth. Birds sang their pre-bedtime songs before the night predators arrived. Coming to the fork, Grace hesitated, but took the

261

left track to the beach. Stepping onto the platform, no wind lifted her hair or the surf's gentle ripples creeping towards its full tide.

Hugo was standing with his back to her. Against the evening sky, he darkened to a silhouette of a man, boots only inches from the water's edge, breeches tight across his thighs and a wide-sleeved linen shirt loose about his body.

Grace walked down the steps onto the beach. Could he hear her footsteps on the shingle? As if her steps acted as a command, he turned and opened his arms. Grace stopped just for a moment and then ran forward. He gathered her to him and held her close; she could feel his kisses on her hair and the tenderness released the tears she had been holding back since walking out of Kilbraith House.

'Grace. Oh, Grace, don't cry.' He pushed them apart, but did not release her. 'What can be so bad to make you weep so?'

She looked at his face and saw the frown pushing his fair eyebrows closer together.

'Oh, just seeing you after such a long time. Really, it is so silly of me. It has been a long journey from London and I am tired. Tomorrow, I shall be myself again.' Grace took a step back, pulling herself away from his hold. 'This is wrong, Hugo, please, can we walk awhile?'

Hugo dropped his hands and put them behind his back. 'Yes, of course.'

They walked side by side along the water's edge, his boots being lapped by the sea when it surged to creep higher. Words did not seem to be necessary, the silence between them acceptable. Each lost in their thoughts.

Grace was the first to speak. 'Thank you.'

Hugo turned his head. 'Aye, there are times when only a friend can give comfort. And I am your friend, Grace, whatever you may hear about me . . . someday.'

'I make my own judgements, Hugo. Tittle-tattle I leave to those who have nothing better to do than bend and exaggerate gossip to suit their own twisted minds.'

Hugo quickened his step to stand in front of her. 'Lady Rossmore!

Such heated words from a lady of the English *ton*.' He took from his head an imaginary hat and bowed low. 'Bravo. I sail away from your shores knowing that there is one woman who has the spirit to rebel.'

Grace began to laugh, but stopped at his words. 'You are leaving, Hugo? When?'

He turned his head and looked out to sea. 'Damnation. I should not have mentioned it now.' He looked back at her, his face muscles taut. 'The repairs are complete. My cargo is to be reloaded . . .'

Grace cut into his speech. 'Where?'

'Home. To Norway. When that is delivered, I will take on another cargo for . . . who knows, the Americas?'

Grace held her breath for a moment. 'Of course. Whitecliffs was only a stopover for you. I wish you a safe voyage.'

'Grace, I'm sorry. I should have kept this evening happy between us. I saw your coach come into the village. I knew Lord Rossmore was not with you, so I was reluctant to call at Solitaire.' He gave a bitter laugh. 'Your confounded social rules! So, I came to the beach, hoping that you might come. When I saw you, I just opened my arms for you . . . and . . .'

'And I ran into them. I'm sorry I used you for my own comfort. Nothing has changed since before I went away. Alex is my husband. I love him for better or worse. And at the moment it is worse. I've come back because I don't know where else to go. I want your friendship, Hugo, but nothing more.'

'Then it is best that I am gone.'

'We will part as friends?

'I shall remain your Norwegian captain and friend, always.'

Grace felt her tension ease a little and smiled at him. 'Thank you, and my gallant sire, I think it is time for you to show some chivalry and escort me back.'

When they reached the steps leading to the garden, Grace stopped. 'I think it would be wise for you to find another way back to your house. I may be a rebel, but it would not be proper for you to come with me any further.'

Hugo gave an exaggerated sigh and bowed. 'Goodnight, Lady Rossmore. Perhaps I shall see Grace riding tomorrow?'

He had regained his good humour, much to Grace's delight. 'You may find me riding tomorrow, Hugo, after the noon hour I think. Goodnight.'

She descended the steps and walked to the study door. Turning, she saw Hugo was gone.

Alex rode relentlessly, changing horses several times at coaching inns, but still had to make an overnight stop. His head was filled with all the evils Grace could be enduring and the report lay like a lead weight in his coat pocket.

This time, Grace and he would resolve their differences.

He turned his mount down the lane and halted outside the captain's house. It looked so ordinary. Yet the man inside . . . a vagabond, a smuggler and seducer of his wife. Alex wanted to tear him apart, throw him back into the ocean where he had come from. But Grace was his first priority. He rode on.

The afternoon sun was on the wane and he expected Grace to be taking tea. He didn't knock on the front door, but went round to the garden. She was not there and the disappointment stabbed into him. He saw the study door open and went through, and on into the hall calling for Mrs Gillett.

Mrs Gillett came from the kitchen, her hands floured and flustered. 'Your lordship . . . we were . . .' She was lost for words.

'Unexpected. I know. It's becoming a habit. Where is her ladyship?'

'She is out riding. She did not say you . . .'

Alex cut her off. 'Do you know where she rides?'

'No, not really, she loves the grass on the headland . . . but she never says . . .' Mrs Gillett started cleaning her hands on her apron. 'Shall I ask Mr Gillett . . .'

'No. I shall go and look for her. Ask him to get my room ready. Later, my horse will need attention; I have ridden him hard today.'

Without waiting for any reply, Alex left by the front door.

'Well, I don't know what this house is coming to. Her late lady-ship would be most put out with all his lordship's coming and going. What sort of a husband has my Gracie married?' And she returned to her kitchen, tutting and calling for Mr Gillett.

Alex circled the village and rode out onto the headland. Apart from the gulls, their wings spread wide, soaring on the uplift of air and his horse's hooves pounding the earth, no human or animal was to be seen. In the past half-hour the sun had lost its brilliance and hazed over. There was a change in the temperature and a slight clamminess to the air. Spreading in from the horizon, clouds were building into white balls, some already flattening and darkening beneath.

Alex pulled to a stop. There were many headlands and Grace could have returned to Solitaire by now. He nudged his horse and prompted by an uneasiness he couldn't explain, he headed back to the village.

Grace was not home.

Mrs Gillett frowned as Alex questioned her. 'Is this usual, her not returning for tea?'

'No. After she rides, her first words are "Is tea ready?" If she is out visiting, she always takes the coach.'

'Has Captain Olsen been here?' The question was direct and he held Mrs Gillett's gaze.

'No, my lord. But he is still living in the village.' Her cheeks reddened and she lowered her eyes.

'Thank you. I presume my room is ready and hot water is there?'

'Everything is as you like it, my lord. I'll tell Jenkins to see to your horse.'

As Alex went to the stairs a loud explosive sound penetrated the walls.

Mrs Gillett called out, 'What is that?'

'I don't know, it sounds like a thousand cannons firing as one.'

Alex opened the front door and went out, looking to the sky. From the west a rumbling crescendo filled the air and black smoke was being blown inland by an increasing wind.

'Does her ladyship ride in that direction?' A terrible fear was gripping him.

'Perhaps, she loves riding along all the cliff tops. It sounded like a rock fall, but surely, she wouldn't be that close to the edge? Oh, where is she?' Mrs Gillett raised her hands to her lips and muttered through the fingers, 'I can't take much more of this. Please, go and find her.' As if a floodgate had been released, Mrs Gillett burst into tears.

In turn, this spurred Alex into action and he ran to his horse tethered at the gate.

Men, women and children were running towards the plume of smoke rising into the sky. On his horse Alex reined left and right, until he was ahead of them and urged his mount across the headland. He dismounted well away from the cliff edge, moved cautiously forward and lay down to look over at the beach below. The incoming wind whipped his hair back from his forehead and dust filled his eyes. To his right, the cliff had broken away and was like a small mountain cutting the beach into two halves. The bright afternoon was gone, grey rain clouds raced overhead and the first drops of rain splattered onto his coat. As the rain increased, he heard voices calling for help.

Grace was feeling restless. She would go as far as saying irritable. Snapping at Gillie during breakfast, demanding Mr Gillett attend to her garden, because she had seen a few weeds and had unnecessarily pulled the bit into Chestnut's mouth. It was so unlike her. Solitaire House was not giving her the peace of mind she had hoped. She feared villainy in every male villager and personally had gone round the house last night checking the locks. Alex was constantly in her mind: she hated him, she despised him and she *loved* him. What sort of fool did that make her?

Grace gave the mare her head and together they let fly across the headland behind the village. She had refused to wear her riding-habit jacket or hat, unconventional as it might be; she was not ruled by the London *ton* here. The sun warmed her shoulders through her muslin shirt, soothing away her troubles. In their place came memories of her mother's dark hair and pale face. She had been so elegant in her tea dresses entertaining at Solitaire. Grace cherished those precious months living from under the restraints of her father. How she had enjoyed helping to plan the rose garden with Gillett and talking with guests taking tea on the lawn during those August afternoons.

Without any conscious intention, Grace had circled round and come to the cut in the cliff where a steep zig-zag path led down to Crescent Bay. She dismounted and looked out to sea, remembering this beach had been a forbidden place. But her mother wasn't here now. No one was here, not even Hugo. She hadn't seen him, although he knew she would be riding. Rebellion rose within her. If she were to be deserted by husband and friend, she would make her own decisions. She tethered Chestnut to a few twigs of spindly bush and stepped cautiously onto the steep cliff path.

Halfway down she was having second thoughts; perhaps Mama had been right. Her skirt kept catching on the rough, white, chalky outcrops and her boots, although good leather for riding, were not suitable for this. But sheer defiance made her carry on and even though it was hotter than ever, she made it to the beach.

The triumph of her adventure was awesome. She spread her arms and circled, like she had as a child, and waved to the gulls overhead. 'I'm here, gulls. I'm going to walk to the end and back. Watch me, gulls. I wish I could fly.'

Beyond the shingle, sand lay dark and damp the full length of the beach. She walked towards it and the water's edge. She sat down and, taking her boots off, stretched her legs and put her feet into the sea, watching her silk stockings cling and wrinkle with each surge.

She looked along the beach. It was deserted, yet there were sounds. Ignoring everything but the pleasure of the afternoon, she got up and started walking along the tide line.

The water felt cold yet the sensation of the sand under her toes was a joy she had almost forgotten. The end of the beach seemed never to grow nearer and the distance was more than she had reckoned. When she did reach the end, her shirt was damp with perspiration and she was tired. There was nowhere to sit out of the sun except beside a jagged rock near the base of the cliff. Stretching full length, she closed her eyes and wished she wasn't so thirsty.

It was the wind that woke her. Grace sat up feeling cold and shivered. She looked at the sky; the sun was gone and clouds were building on the horizon and she wondered how long she had slept. Standing up she brushed her skirt. It had been an unwise thing to have done and she picked up her boots and started back.

'Hey, gulls, why didn't you wake me up? It must be way past teatime. Gillie will be worried.' This thought made her run, but she was soon out of breath and stopped as a pain stabbed in her side. 'Really, gulls, I haven't had this since I was little. And my, it's making me dizzy.' Grace unrolled, letting her head settle. 'Remember you're a grown-up now. Walk, Lady Rossmore, don't run.'

Mysteriously, the sounds she had heard earlier came again. But this time, they were more distinct. Voices? Yet the beach was clear. She looked along the cliff and saw a round opening about a quarter of the way up. She was sure it hadn't been there before, and curious, she walked towards it.

An explosive sound ripped through the air and a flash of fire leapt from the hole. The cliff above seemed to shudder and then break away, falling down towards the beach.

Grace froze in terror; the cliff was coming towards her. It was the shower of small stones that spurred her to run for the shelter of the cliff base as rocks hurled around her head. She dropped her boots, arching her arms like a hood. A massive piece of cliff dropped into the sand a few feet in front of her and she couldn't miss running into it. The impact catapulted her back. As she fell, she saw a second rock coming towards her. She screamed, but it was too late to get up and run.

There was blackness and water. Grace couldn't move; her skirt was tight over her thighs and when she tried to lever herself up, the pain in her chest sent her gasping back down. She couldn't see anything, not even her own hand. Swinging her head from side to side panic surged in every nerve in her body. Reaching up, her hands touched rock no more than twelve inches away. She searched sideways and found more rock – uneven, sharp, gaps only the size of her thumb, and slits the width of a knife blade. Worse than all this was the sea rising round her.

She was in a rock coffin, except underneath her was wet sand. Her mind wouldn't clear and her eyes hurt. She rubbed them, but the stinging continued. Holding her breath, she tried again to sit up, pushing hard on her elbows. It still hurt and she lay back down. Part of the trouble was her skirt. It was caught under the side stone. She tugged at the cloth; it didn't budge an inch. Grace lay still.

She thought there were voices, but they seemed a long way off. She filled her lungs with air and called out, called again, then again. Her throat was dry and her call came out as a croak. She'd been thirsty at the end of her walk along the beach – then falling asleep. She hadn't had a drink since lunch and then only a glass of lemonade. She thought of her missed tea. Oh, she so wanted a drink.

Fear was spiralling like a mountain road. The sound of the sea was getting louder. The water was still rising along her body. She had survived the rock fall to be drowned in this cavernous grave. The sand was a sponge releasing its water with nowhere to go. It was so dark, and terror welled up and gripped her entire body. She started to shake. She was going to die, going to feel the sea rise little by little until it covered her face, filled her mouth and washed the life out of her. Grace screamed and kept on screaming. She was alone; no one knew where she was. Her hands were going numb and she put them over her face, pushing her fingers through the damp, matted hair. The horror gave her strength to raise her voice. 'Someone, help me, please. I'm here under the rock.' She listened, hope soaring, but it ebbed away like the tide, only the roaring sea answering.

She calmed, it was useless. Her breathing slowed, and in that moment Alex filled her mind and she whispered, 'I love you. I always have.'

The voices didn't get any closer. Why didn't they? Perhaps she wasn't calling at all, only in her mind. She cupped her hand and washed her face with the seawater that was now halfway up her body. Soon she would have to lift her head. She gulped in more air and this time concentrated on calling. 'I'm here. Under the rock, the water's rising. Help! Help me!'

Only the dreaded silence followed.

Grace tugged at her skirt again. This time there was a little movement. Why? The rock was as large. Then she thought how one could scoop wet sand away and she dug with her fingers, clawing the sand from under the skirt and pulling the cloth with her other hand. Tug by tug it came free.

There was no room to sit in her rock coffin, but she pushed herself up onto her elbows. This triumph gave her new energy and she shouted and shouted. Someone must come; she didn't want to die. Sobs choked her but she called out, 'Where are you? I don't want to drown.'

This time there was a voice nearer and Grace thumped on the rock in desperation, knowing, yet not caring, that those outside could not hear. 'I'm here. Help. The tide's coming in faster.' Water now reached her waist and each time there was a surge, it rose higher than the last. Grace knew she had only a few more minutes to live unless she was rescued.

A voice and the sound of scraping filled the void above the seawater. She screamed with fear and frustration. 'I'm here, I'm here, hurry.' A surge filled her prison and hit the walls, slapped back and washed over her face. It filled her nose and she choked. 'Now,' she screamed, 'or you're too late.'

The sea swelled again and washed over her head. Grace called one more time, 'Remember me, Alex. Dear Lord, take my soul in to Heaven, Amen.'

They were so near, but too late.

Then the rock above her head moved and a rod slid in. A faint glow spread across her tomb as the rock was levered away from the hole. The night sky spread above her and she could feel heavy droplets pit into the water round her, then felt pressure under her armpits, strong hands pulling her free.

Grace stood in the lashing rain and wind, soaked, shaking and uncomprehending, while her rescuer hugged her, calling her name over and over and thanking God for His mercy.

Grace opened her eyes. She was lying on dry sand, shivering. Over her wet clothes she was wearing a coat. A few feet away Hugo knelt, blowing at some twigs, coaxing them to take the flame.

'Where . . . are . . . we?' She could only say one word at a time through teeth that clattered like castanets. It looked like a cave, but Grace couldn't remember anything after being lifted from beneath the rock.

'A cave; it's a deep cleft in the cliff.'

'Why can't we go home?'

'The tide is in and to get round the rock fall we would have to go out to sea. I've no boat. We can walk round at low tide.'

'Why can't we climb over?'

The fire flared and he put on some wood. Grace struggled up onto her elbow. 'How do you know about this place? And you have dry wood.' Her teeth had stopped chattering quite so much, and she pushed up until she was sitting, sand clinging to her sodden skirt. She looked beyond the circle of firelight, but the darkness hid all.

Hugo did not look at her or answer. Instead he turned to a sack and took out two tin cups, then filled them from a small keg. Handing Grace one he said, 'This will help warm you. I come here quite a lot. I'm what you might call a Freetrader. I'm just a storekeeper.'

She sipped the contents. 'This is brandy.'

'You are making things very difficult for me, Grace. I have a ship that needs very expensive repairs. I lost a lot of my cargo to spoilage. I had to make some money, *fast* . . .'

271

'Hugo, stop going round in circles. Are you a smuggler?'

He looked away. 'I suppose so.'

'Did you have anything to do with the explosion?'

'No! By the Gods of Valhalla, no.'

'But it was to do with smuggling?'

'Yes. Some of the villagers were getting impatient about moving the . . . goods. Someone must have been careless, flame torches and spirits do not go well together.'

The fire was warming her and she had stopped shivering, but her throat ached and her voice was weak 'How many are hurt? Are there any missing?'

'Several were killed. I don't know how many are missing. But one survivor remembered a woman walking along the beach this afternoon. I knew you were . . . I . . .' he seemed unsure what to say, '. . . when I heard a voice, I prayed it was you, because time had run out. A few more seconds . . .' He moved to sit beside her.

'You saved my life, Hugo. What you do for a living is no concern of mine. But it is a dangerous occupation. You will be served well when you go back to sea.' She took his hand and raised it to her lips. 'Thank you.'

Hugo made no attempt to refuse her gesture. 'On the cheek would be more rewarding.'

She lifted her head and looked into his eyes. 'You make me feel guilty, that I should . . . oblige you but we agreed, just friends.'

'Yes, just passing ships in the night.'

Hugo stood up. 'Would you like a hot drink?'

'You store water here as well as brandy, smuggler man?'

'No. A trick of a sailor,' and he disappeared down a passage, returning several minutes later with a jug and wet trousers up to his knees. 'Rainwater.' He nestled the tin jug into the embers. 'I put it out on a ledge while you were . . .' he waved his hand above his head, '. . . not fully aware of here.'

'Thank you for lending me your jacket.' Grace didn't ask how he had put her into it.

'My pleasure, Lady Rossmore, the colour suits you well.'

Grace sipped the neat brandy. 'The cave that had the explosion, I don't remember seeing the opening in the cliff when I walked along the beach. Surely such a hole that large would be seen by the Excise men?'

Hugo shrugged. 'They are cunning, your village fellows. There is . . . was, a door to the cave. It would be difficult to define unless one knew where to look.'

'How do they get to it?'

'They climb down a rope from the cliff top. Then a ladder to the beach.'

'How clever, no wonder the Excise men cannot find them.'

Hugo smiled. 'I have been loaned this hidey-hole. It runs deep into the cliff, beyond the high-tide line.' He thumbed to some kegs stacked against a rock. 'This is my last run.'

'I'm glad to hear that. When do you leave for your ship?'

'In two days.'

Grace felt a sadness that she knew she shouldn't, yet was glad to hear this dangerous game he was playing would be finished. 'Were you going without saying goodbye?'

'No. I would have called.' His face brightened. 'Without an appointment, no visiting card and demanding tea no matter what the time of day.'

'Oh, poor Gillie. Have you no thought for the proprieties of an old servant? Or, may I add, that of a Society lady of the *ton*?'

'Friends do not need such formality. We dispensed with that when I called you Grace. See, I am finally grasping your peculiar customs now that I am leaving.'

The water began to bubble in the jug and Hugo used a piece of sacking to take it from the fire. 'Give me your cup. A hot toddy will quench your thirst and help you to sleep.' Filling both cups he then added brandy from the keg. Building the fire with more wood, he sat next to her again. 'Put your hands round the cup and sip slowly. Are your clothes still very wet?'

'My skirt, yes. But my shirt has dried under your jacket.'

'Take your skirt off. It will dry quicker by the fire.'

'Hugo! I cannot. It would be quite improper. Even before a friend.'

'You would sooner die of the fever? Then I might as well have left you to drown.'

Getting up, he went over to the sack, pulled out a pair of trousers. 'Will your ladyship deem to wear these? I would hasten to say, they are not mine. I found this sack the first time I came here.' Anger tinged his voice and his eyes glinted in the firelight. 'I will go to see what the weather is like.'

Grace stripped off her riding habit skirt, but kept her personal underwear on. No way could she drape them near the fire for Hugo to see. The trousers must have belonged to a lad, for they fitted very well. Sitting back down, she had to admit that the dry clothes, warm jacket and her feet toasting by the fire was making her feel sleepy. She lay down on the hard ground. It should have been uncomfortable, but her head had a floating sensation. The hot toddy was doing its job and she closed her eyes.

Grace woke, still curled up on the ground and every muscle hurting. She sat up, rolled her shoulders and arched her back. She rubbed the back of her neck and was relieved the pain in her chest had eased. She looked round the cave, the darkness of the night now tinged with daylight from the passage. 'It is morning?'

Hugo was stooping by the fire, stirring the embers and adding wood. He seemed reluctant to look at her, his manner strained and he didn't lift his head. 'Yes. Dawn has arrived. The tide is going out. Would you like another hot toddy?'

'What is wrong?'

'What is wrong, we have been in this cave all night. Alone! Do you think they will believe we just slept by the fire? When the villagers see us walk round the cliff-slide they will know you were not drowned and that I rescued you. This cave is not secret to them. I should have gone back and told him. He was frantic, searching for you . . .' he ran his fingers through his hair, tugging at it, '. . . but this accident fulfilled a requirement that I use these

274

hours alone with you. Now, scandal will erupt the minute they see us. The only way out is the path you came down.'

Grace licked her lips. 'So be it. I am alive.' Then as an after-thought, 'Who should you have told?'

Hugo did not answer. Instead he asked, 'What of your husband? What will his reaction be?'

Grace got up and rubbed the backs of her legs. Still bent she said, 'Alex could divorce me, a stigma worse than death to the gentry. I would be painted the worst; it is always the woman's fault. But more likely he would banish me to Rossmore Manor. Society's estates or an asylum are a very handy places to put unwanted wives.'

She picked up her skirt. It was dry, although stained by the sea-water and stiff with sand grit. 'Will you please turn away while I dress?'

Hugo turned his back to her.

Grace took off Hugo's jacket. Then she struggled into the skirt which seemed to have shrunk, but she breathed in and forced the loops over the buttons. It felt heavy and uncomfortable. She put the trousers next to the jacket. 'Hugo, you can turn round now.'

He turned.

She pointed to the tin jug. 'A little early in the day, but a hot toddy is just what I need to face the world.'

Chapter Twenty-three

The rain had stopped and the wind had lessened to a brisk breeze.

Alex sat on a rock and put out the lantern flame as the dawn washed the sky with its pale light.

He had dozed on and off since the search for any survivors ended. He couldn't accept that Grace was somewhere under this mountain of chalk cliff. He hadn't been in time to tell her about the plot to separate them that would secure Geoffrey's succession to the earldom. He would have to live the rest of his life having not put things right between them.

He thought back to yesterday. The explosion and the cliff-slide had been devastating. He had found Grace's horse tethered to a bush and assumed she was searching for survivors. He had joined the villagers as they scrambled down the steep cliff path. By the time he reached the beach, the sky was black and slashing rain was being driven inland by the wind. The mixture of chalk dust and wet skin turned into a cloying grey paste on the faces of the rescuers.

He had scrambled over the rubble, looking for her, asking everyone. No one had seen Lady Rossmore. When his first fear surfaced, he paid the children to check again. Then the ultimate fear filled his head. If she was not searching then she must be a victim.

When men shouted that they heard a faint voice from below, he had clawed at the rocks, levered boulders until he thought his muscles would break through the skin, but each time it was someone else. Children were sent for lanterns as night approached and still the rain pelted down and the wind blew. Then someone shouted those horrifying words. 'The tide is reaching the edge of the fall.' Time was running out.

The women had banded together to supply the men with food and drink. Mrs Gillett had tried to insist that he stop for a while, but he had drunk the water, pushing the food inside his coat and eaten the ham and bread as he worked, calling and calling Grace's name. But the tide won. Little by little it crept forward, covering the rocks and anyone that was under it. When the villagers went home, exhausted and defeated by the sea, it left only those like him, praying for a miracle to save their loved one.

Later, cold and beaten, even they bowed their heads and left. He watched their lantern lights zig-zag up the cliff path until they reached the top, then fade away.

Climbing the rock as the sea forced him higher he could hear nothing but the rain and the wind. His clothes were torn almost to shreds and covered in white mud. His boot soles slipped and his legs and hands were so bruised he could no longer touch another stone. Yet the pain kept him awake and he used the rain to wash his face and cleanse his hair. But he could not leave her. If it took a thousand men he would move every rock on this beach until he could hold her in his arms one more time.

In the stronger daylight Alex watched the men from the village arrive in small groups. There was no rush now, for it would only be lifeless bodies to recover.

Alex got up and stretched, every muscle from neck to foot ached. He went towards them; at this moment they were his equal, men mourning for family, friends and neighbours. They stopped talking when he arrived and looked at him, almost as though he would take charge.

Alex cleared his throat. 'Good morning. How many are . . .' He couldn't finish, the words refusing to pass his lips.

'Four and . . .' the tallest man looked at his companions, but they lowered their eyes to the beach, 'her ladyship.'

'Do you have a plan?'

'No, my lord. It is an impossible task. We must leave them where they are.' He pointed behind Alex. 'They are coming to pay their respects.'

Women and children were carrying bunches of flowers and the Reverend and Mrs Clive walked amongst them. Stopping in front of Alex, the Reverend Clive stepped forward. 'Lord Rossmore, we have come to bless our Children into His hands. May I . . . may we . . . say how sorry we are about Lady Rossmore.' He bowed his head and stepped back. Taking a Bible from his coat pocket, he opened it at a marker ribbon, but before a word left his lips one of the women pointed towards the sea.

'There, my lord, it is she.'

Everyone turned towards where the receding tide had left the beach clear.

Grace was walking beside Olsen. Not as a ghost, but a living, breathing person.

Alex's red-rimmed eyes widened; the gritty pain forgotten he started to run. 'Grace! Grace, you're alive. Grace, I'm here, I'm here.'

Grace stopped. When he reached her, those grey eyes he loved looked dazed. 'Alex?'

Taking her in his arms, he kissed her hair, her forehead, her eyes and finally her lips. Releasing her he held their bodies apart. 'Oh, Grace, I thought you were dead; buried under the rubble, drowned by the sea. Where have you been?'

Olsen took several steps away from Grace.

'Hugo rescued me. The tide was high and we had to stay in a . . . a cave. But, Alex, what are you doing here? You are in London.' She twisted to look at Hugo. 'Am I seeing things?'

Hugo shook his head. 'No, Grace.'

Alex looked at Olsen. At last he was face-to-face with the man he had come to confront. This man was her enemy, yet also her saviour.

'You have been in a cave with this man all night?'

278

Grace looked from Hugo to Alex; then beyond, at the villagers clustered round the Reverend Clive. 'What are they doing?'

'Answer me, Grace.'

She seemed in a trance, uncomprehending. 'What?'

'Have you been in a cave with this man all night?'

'Yes.'

It was a simple one-word answer, yet plunged him into the depths of despair. 'And I suppose he comforted you, gave you his warmth, gave you . . .' Alex could not continue. A mental picture of Grace and Olsen, lying together, crowded out everything. Slowly, it was replaced with hatred for a man who could seduce his wife at the command of his half-brother. A red rage engulfed Alex and he stepped towards Olsen. Their eyes clashed. Alex could not hold his anger any longer. It made him blind and deaf to reason. 'You knew I was here, searching for her. Why didn't you come and tell me?'

'I couldn't leave her . . . I . . .'

'Liar! It was the chance you were waiting for . . . a chance to fulfil your orders.'

Hugo did not reply.

Grace looked at him. 'What is he saying, Hugo? I don't understand. What orders?'

'Grace, it's a complicated story, but not so black as your husband believes . . .'

Alex cut in. 'You have seduced my wife and lied to her. I demand satisfaction from you.'

Olsen stood as though turned to stone.

Alex flung the age-old offer at him. 'You may choose the weapons.'

Olsen came to life. 'So, the Lord Rossmore demands satisfaction by duel. I accept. Weapons will be pistols. The meeting place, on the beach, below Solitaire House, tomorrow at dawn.' He bowed to Alex and then went over to Grace. Taking her hand he raised it to his lips. 'I think tea will be inappropriate, Lady Rossmore. I bid you goodbye.' He turned and walked away, back in the direction they had come. He left behind a tableau of stunned villagers with Lord and Lady Rossmore as far apart in their reconciliation as they had ever been.

Alex spoke to the Reverend Clive and left them to continue their prayers. Without a word to Grace he took hold of her arm and escorted her along the beach to the cliff path.

Climbing, she stumbled over a rock and he saw her feet. 'Where are your boots?'

'I lost them in the rock fall.' She stopped and turned round. 'Your concern overwhelms me, Alex. If it hadn't been for Hugo, I would be dead.'

He shuddered. He hadn't even asked about her rescue. His blinding rage with Olsen swamped every scrap of decency and manners he had.

'Sit down. I'll bind your feet to give them some protection.' Her lips pressed into a thin line. 'Please, Grace.' He moved up, taking her elbow. 'You'll be thankful later.' She wrenched her arm free, but sat down.

Alex took off his coat, waistcoat and shirt. He ripped the shirt in half, binding one piece round each foot. 'Does that feel better?'

'Yes. Thank you.' The reply was given through pursed lips.

Alex put his clothes back on, held out his hand to Grace. 'What happened yesterday?' She ignored him and pushed with her own hands and stood up.

'Not now, Alex. I'm alive and that is all that matters.'

He wanted to press her into telling him. This was another incident that she was refusing to speak about, a second horror, to go hand-in-hand with her kidnapping. Would they ever tell each other their deepest secrets?

Grace took a step and stumbled again.

'You should have used the time in the cave to sleep.'

She stopped and half-turned. 'Alex, have you gone mad? Hugo is nothing more than a friend and neighbour. He is a sea captain.

He joins his ship tomorrow. Where have you got all these wild accusations?'

'They are not wild, but investigated truth. How can you love this man?'

'Any love he has is for me and me alone. Not like you . . . you have used me for your own ends.'

'None of that is true. We have to talk about it. I have papers for you to read and Beesell brought proof.'

Grace waved her hand. 'All rubbish. You are a . . . a rake, yes, that's what you are.'

Alex took her arm. 'This is not the place for our discussion. We will speak of it later. Now you need a bath, food and sleep.' He picked her up before she could speak. 'Don't vex me, Grace. You must be exhausted. Lay your head on my shoulder. We will soon be home.'

He felt all the fight drain out of her and she relaxed against him. By the time he reached Solitaire, she was asleep in his arms.

Mrs Gillett heard the thumping on the front door and dried her eyes with her apron. She heaved her plump figure out of the chair and went into the hall. The sight of Alex carrying Grace sent the old woman into floods of tears and she followed them up the stairs calling for Esther in a hysterical voice.

Alex laid Grace on her bed. Her face was colourless, even her lips. He touched her hair and wondered what horror she was dreaming of now? Still, he would put it all to order later. Now, he too, needed a bath, food and sleep.

Grace sat in bed, with a tray balanced over her thighs. The yolk of the egg made her stomach turn. She picked up a slice of bread and nibbled off a small piece. Chewing it slowly, she let it go down her throat, settling the queasy sensation.

It was hard to believe what had happened in the last twenty-four hours: a carefree stroll along the beach, an explosion that nearly killed her and Alex and Hugo battling over her like two rampant stags. Then this duel at dawn! She had to stop this folly. Fired with determination, Grace pulled the bell-rope to call Esther.

When the tea hour arrived, Grace was sitting in the drawing room. Although the sun was out, she felt too tired to walk the extra distance to the garden. Alex was missing, no one knew where and her frustration with him deepened. It was only fourteen hours before he and Hugo met. Although she did not feel like laughing, a chuckle left her throat. Now her life was being determined by the cycle of the moon.

There was a noise in the hall, voices and the front door closing. Alex walked in, his boots marked with mud. He stopped when he saw her.

'You are up? I thought you would remain in bed until dinner.'

'Staying in bed is not the answer to the problems you have. What in heaven's name are you thinking of, Alex? You have to stop this duel. *Now!*'

His features hardened. 'No.'

Tiredness forgotten, Grace got up and went to stand within an arm's length from him. 'You could both be killed. Hugo is a sailor; he is used to fighting. Have you dismissed the fact that England was at war with Norway until last year?'

'I am well aware of the war.'

'Then withdraw. Please, Alex.'

'Is your concern for me or Olsen?'

'It is for you both.'

'No. What is done is done. Do not meddle in what is not a woman's business.'

'Not my business! I could be a widow before breakfast. I will go to see Hugo, ask him to . . .'

Alex stepped forward and took hold of her arms in a grip that made her wince. 'You would dishonour me. Make it look like I am hiding behind your skirt. How dare you, Grace, consider such an act? Does Olsen mean more to you than I do?'

'Alex, I didn't mean . . . it's just that . . .'

'I can see clearly enough for myself what you mean. If you will

282

excuse me, I have preparations to make.' His face flushed with anger, he turned and left the room.

Grace did not move. She had overstepped the mark. Alexander Peter Kilbraith was the Earl of Rossmore, his honour was paramount.

Alex stood in the open study doorway, looking at the garden. He wished Willy were here, he needed a second who could perform the duty competently. Instead, he had asked Jenkins. The coachman was reluctant, until Alex pointed out that he required a loyal man at his side.

He sat down at his desk and drew a sheet of paper towards him. How was he going to explain to Grace all that had happened since their marriage? He could not write Geoffrey's name, for although the villain, he was family. In the end he wrote a short note, requesting her to contact Beesell. A letter to Willy and, finally, a letter addressed to Geoffrey. He placed all three in the desk drawer. The report he sealed in a package addressed to his solicitor.

The dining room was empty when Alex went in to dinner. The white folded paper at his place setting was a note saying she was tired and would remain in her room. She wasn't even going to give him the pleasure of her company on what could be his last night alive. He screwed the note into a ball and threw it across the room.

He needed a brandy, but didn't go to the decanter. He had no intention of giving Olsen one inch of an advantage. Instead, he went to the table and poured water into his wineglass. Damn her, damn Geoffrey and damn his own stupidity.

He looked at the clock. Less than twelve hours to go till he faced the Norwegian.

He would retire now, have a tray sent up and try to get some sleep. Sleep? Knowing she was next door loathing him? But she hadn't loathed him that night in Kilbraith House. He could find the connecting door key he had thrown into the fireplace . . . how would she react if he used it? No. He couldn't face this duel with her rejection hammering in his mind. If he survived, there would be plenty of time to sort out their problems. He rang the bell for Gillett; he would need the man an hour before dawn.

Grace had lain awake all night: first hating him, then fearing his death and then anguished that she might never feel his hands caress her body again. She heard movement in the connecting bedchamber. Alex was getting ready.

She got out of bed and went and pulled back the curtains. It was still dark. She couldn't stay in this house, this room, waiting to know what had happened.

Grace lit a candle and looked for a dark dress. Her fingers found the grey smock she had been forced to wear at Greensleeves. Esther had wanted to throw it away, but she had refused. She didn't know why, but it was just what she needed to merge into the grey dawn through the woods to the beach.

Dressed and wearing ankle boots, her hair tied back with a ribbon, she listened once more at the connecting door. Voices were muffled, but she was sure he was ready to leave the house.

Grace left by the study door and in the faint light tingeing the sky she ran up the steps into the wood. It was darker under the foliage, but she knew the path like the back of her hand. At the fork, she went left and, coming to where it started to descend to the beach, she moved off the path into the ferns. There were fronds big enough for her to hide behind and Grace knelt down, pulling a grey cotton shawl over her head. Through the thin material she felt the undergrowth graze her knees and the wet morning dew dampen the skirt of the dress.

Within minutes, she heard voices.

Jenkins came along the path with a lantern held high, followed by Alex. As they passed, Grace could see he was hatless and held a cloak tight around his body. Her mouth went dry and she swallowed to moisten it with saliva. Her whole being wanted to run out and beg him to stop. She was not worth fighting over. He had so much to live for, a babe soon to be born, even if he would never acknowledge the bastard child of his paramour. But she remained kneeling, silent, as they disappeared down the path to the beach.

Grace followed and saw them going down the steps, then onto the shingle. As she walked on, loose stones slid under her boots and she stopped and crouched down, praying her grey clothes blended with the cliff. But neither man looked back and she moved on to the wooden platform.

The tide was low. Hugo and Erik were waiting on the firm sand. A third person stood apart, but Grace did not recognise him. There was a long delay and she strained to catch any word that would give her hope that this duel would be abandoned. But when the voices stopped, Alex took off his cloak. Hugo did not have a topcoat, but was wearing his captain's jacket and both men wore boots.

Erik stepped between the men with a case balanced across his forearms. Hugo unclipped the lid and raised it to Erik's chest.

Jenkins now moved forward. He spent several minutes inspecting the contents, then turned and said something to Alex.

Grace watched Hugo step back and wave his hand, giving his opponent first choice of weapon. Alex reached forward and took a pistol. Hugo then took the other. Both men waited until Erik closed the lid, stepped away and walked up the beach a few paces. The glow of pale yellow was rising from the east. It was the first brush stroke onto the sky's morning canvas. She could now see their faces, their grim expressions and tightly closed lips. The pistols held against their sides. A breeze came in off the sea and raised Alex's copper hair from his forehead and their words carried to Grace.

'A fine pair of Mortimer pistols, Olsen.'

'They were left at the house in the study by my predecessor, my lord. Otherwise, it would have been the pirates' cutlasses.' Olsen gave a humourless laugh. 'An advantage to me, I think.'

'Then my heartfelt thanks to him.'

Erik called out, 'Gentlemen. Twenty paces; turn and fire.'

Alex and Hugo nodded to each other and positioned themselves, back to back.

Grace felt her skin prickle and perspiration break out on her fore-head. They were going to do it! They were going to kill each other. She left the platform and ran down the steps onto the beach. She had to stop this. But as each step took her towards them, so their steps took them one pace nearer the turning point. She knew she was not going to get there in time. Mentally she was counting . . . seventeen, eighteen, nineteen, twenty! She stopped. Their pacing ceased and she watched as they turned, each raise their arm and she saw the pistols kick upwards as the triggers were pulled and she heard the deafening crack of gunfire. The sound faded away and in the strengthening light, Grace waited for Alex and Hugo to fall onto the sand.

She stood there for a timeless ten seconds, waiting, yet neither fell and a hope began to rise within her. Her legs wouldn't move and her heart was thumping so hard, her ears hurt. Yet, they stood there, seemingly unhurt. Adrenaline flowed into her blood and Grace started to run. Run and stumble towards Alex.

He was like a stone monument, his arm by his side, the pistol in his hand.

'Alex, Alex. I'm here. You're alright, oh you're alright.'

Alex raised his head, as though her words broke into his mind. 'Grace?'

She was within a few paces of him, when the crack of another gun rang out and Grace lurched forward. Something had hit her in the back, throwing her down onto the beach. Then a red patch spread through the grey shawl.

Alex watched Grace coming towards him. She was running to him, calling *his* name, not Olsen's. He couldn't believe it, but it was so.

Then the gunshot sounded. She was falling, falling in front of him.

Alex sank to his knees and pulled her into his arms. 'Grace, Grace.' They were the only words that would come into his numb mind. 'Speak to me, Grace, open your eyes, please, Grace.' As he cradled her to him, rocking backwards and forwards, he saw blood spreading across her back. 'No. You can't take her away from me. Help, Jenkins.' He looked up; three people were running towards him.

Hugo was the first to drop to the sand. 'Grace. Grace.' His voice was a broken croak, and he touched her arm with tenderness. 'Doctor Humphries, here, come here.'

The third person who had been on the beach, knelt. Alex's coat sleeve was now red with blood.

'My lord, your cloak, we must lie her down.'

Jenkins pushed forward and spread it out then Alex laid Grace onto it.

Dr Humphries turned her over and removed the shawl. The thin material of her dress was soaked with blood and spreading. He took a knife from his case and slit the cloth. A bullet wound was in her back, just below the right shoulder. He felt her pulse and grunted. 'She is alive, but not for long unless I stop the bleeding.'

Alex saw her eyelids flicker and he bent to whisper in her ear. 'I'm here, Grace. Lie still, my love, and let Dr Humphries deal with your wound.'

The doctor took a thick pad of cotton and a bandage from his case. He placed it over the bullet hole and then circled the bandage several times round her body.

'We must get her to the house. My lord, can you and your man carry her in your cloak?'

Alex nodded. 'I'll find the strength of ten men, to save her.'

The doctor stood up. 'Jenkins, take the end, make a stretcher.'

But it was Olsen who gathered the cloth. 'I will. We will need Jenkins' help climbing the path.' He turned to Erik and spoke to him in Norwegian. 'I have asked my man to go to Solitaire. The doctor will want Mrs Gillett's help.'

Alex didn't want this man near her, but knew he was far more experienced in a situation like this. 'Very well. Are you ready to lift?' Olsen nodded and both men stood, then lifted Grace cradled in the cloak. As they moved away, the rising sun cast elongated shadows reminiscent of a battlefield.

From the platform onwards, the narrow path was difficult and progress was slow. Grace cried out with pain several times as they twisted and turned the cloak to avoid the jutting rocks and bushes.

Jenkins could do little to help until they reached the wood. 'May I take a turn, my lord?'

'No. I will carry her. Take a turn from the captain.'

But Olsen, too, refused.

Under the foliage of the trees, the only sound along the path was shuffling feet, as the two adversaries carried Grace. Then the early morning light signalled a lone bird to sing and it ran through the scales calling for the chorus to join in.

Reaching the house, they went in through the study door. Alex had been numb until now, all his energy channelled into carrying Grace. But walking through this doorway brought him back to reality. Brought him back to how he had carried her that night, when the man behind him had left her alone on the beach. A seething anger started to grow. Who had fired the shot? It wasn't Olsen; an associate? In the horror of what had happened, everything except Grace had gone from his mind. Now he wanted to strangle the man with his own hands. He should have killed him down on the beach.

In her room, Mrs Gillett stood waiting, her face pale, but not a word passed her lips.

They lowered the dark cloak onto the white bed linen. Alex pulled the edges over her. She looked so cold and white. He bent and kissed her forehead. What right did he have to kiss her lips? She had taken the bullet meant for him.

Dr Humphries waved Alex and Olsen out. 'I have a doctor's work to do.'

In the corridor, both men looked at each other.

Olsen walked towards the stairs and stopped at the top step, turned, saying, 'I am a very good marksman, my lord. But I would never put Grace's life or love for you into jeopardy.' Then he was gone.

Alex went into his bedchamber. The blood on his coat was like a badge of guilt. He took it off and threw it on the floor, followed by his waistcoat and shirt. The shot was intended for him, aimed at his heart. What had she been thinking, coming to the beach? Pouring cold water into a bowl he bathed the wound on his upper left arm, touching a bruise that was darkening his skin round a scratch. His mouth tightened; what indescribable pain must Grace be going through as the doctor took out the bullet? Olsen's words spoken on the landing came back, 'I am a very good marksman; Grace's life and love . . .' Was that why he too had aimed high? Not to kill the man she had feelings for?

Alex found a clean shirt and put it on. Ignoring his soiled breeches and boots, he went out into the corridor. What was the doctor doing? He couldn't wait outside, not knowing. As he reached for the handle, the door opened from inside. Dr Humphries looked startled, but stepped round Alex and closed the door.

'Lord Rossmore . . . I am reluctant to take out the bullet.' The doctor ran his finger round the inside of his neck cloth. 'I would prefer to have your own surgeon come. I don't think I can take it out.'

'Can't take it out, what do you mean?'

'I can't take the risk.'

'And if you leave it in?'

'Lady Rossmore . . .' Dr Humphries' voice trailed off.

Alex went spinning back ten years. He was going to lose her like Liddy. 'Then do it, man. You have no alternative.' Alex was now shouting at the doctor. 'You've got to save her; do you hear me? I won't let you stand here and refuse.'

The doctor took a step back. 'I need your permission, my lord. A bullet in a woman . . . Lady Rossmore is a delicate lady and she has lost a lot of blood. I will not take the decision.'

Alex grabbed his lapels and brought his face to within an inch of the doctor's nose. 'I'll write it in my own blood, to give Grace her life.'

Dr Humphries nodded and Alex let him go. 'Lady Rossmore is conscious. I will proceed immediately.'

Alex went into her room and over to the bed. Grace lay flat, supported by a pillow at her back, keeping her injured shoulder raised. A single sheet covered her body and the soiled bandages looked unclean against the white skin above her breasts. The dark hair was brushed back and spread out over the pillow. Her eyes opened and Alex could see her pain. He knelt down and took her left hand, the hand that should have the Rossmore wedding ring on the third finger. He lifted it to his lips and then his forehead.

Grace spoke, but he could not hear her words.

'Fight for your life, Grace. Fight for me, I love you, so much.'

Mrs Gillett came into the room with clean sheets and towels, her face as white as Grace. 'Dr Humphries is ready, your lordship. He asks that you leave.' Alex started to refuse, but she laid her hand on his shoulder. 'It is best. I will be here to look after her.'

'I can't leave her yet, just another minute.'

But that minute was only a few seconds when the doctor came over and helped him rise and led him out of the door.

Alex sat on the top stair, waiting. As he had waited a decade ago, except then Liddy's cries had filled Kilbraith House. Now there was just silence. Downstairs he heard a door open and Esther came into the hall. She carried a tray and brought it up the stairs to him.

'Mrs Gillett said for you to have something to eat and drink, my lord.'

'I'm not hungry. A cup of coffee would help.'

Esther put the tray on the tread. Her hand shook as she poured and she sniffed, wiping her nose with the sleeve of her uniform. 'Will her ladyship be alright? Oh, there's been so much upset of late.' The maid handed Alex his cup, curtsied and went back down the stairs.

He sipped the hot brew, his eyes watching Grace's door.

The clock struck eight.

He paced the corridor. Everything was being repeated. He was re-living the nightmare. Something in him snapped and he rushed down the stairs and out of the front door. He ran round the side and down the steps into her garden. The sun was shining in a

290

cloudless sky and the gulls soared above the trees. Roses were in full bloom and their scent filled the air. Her table and chair were placed ready for tea. Alex didn't know what to do; he imagined her in every nook and cranny. This was her house, her retreat. Climbing the steps to the wood, he ran along the path and took the right fork upwards. The thick growth of ferns slashed against his boots until he came to the grassland and the cliff edge. Panting, he called out to the sea and rocks, 'Don't leave me alone. I can't do it again. I can't face the years without you. Live for me, Grace, live to share our future.'

Alex sank to his knees, bowing his head with tears streaming down his cheeks.

Dr Humphries removed his necktie and opened the buttons of his shirt.

He picked up a cloth and wiped away the perspiration running down his forehead. He looked across to Mrs Gillett. 'It is now or never, Josephine, pray for a steady hand.'

Mrs Gillett gave him a reassuring smile. 'You've taken enough lead from the men along this shore to mend the church roof. You're the only one who can save her, Oscar.'

'Men are not women. Especially, a lady brought up only to live a life of luxury. If this was a farmer's wife I would not be so hesitant, she would have the strength of an ox. To leave a bullet in is a sure way to . . .' He took a deep breath. 'Let us do it.'

The instrument in his hand probed into the wound in Grace's shoulder. 'I can feel it. I just need to get a grip each side.' Slowly, he began to lift the lead ball through the seepage of blood and drew it out, dropped it into a dish. He worked quickly to clean the wound, then padded and circled a bandage as he had on the beach. They made Grace comfortable and Mrs Gillett cleared away the soiled sheets and cloths. The room looked like a bedchamber again.

'That was a good job done, Oscar. Now she is in God's hands. I will pray for her.'

'She is very weak. If she is still with us tomorrow, there is hope.

I will sit here awhile, before speaking to Lord Rossmore. A breakfast tray would be most appreciated, Josephine.'

Mrs Gillett smiled; a little colour back in her cheeks. 'On a gold plate for what you have done this day.' She picked up the laundry and left the room.

Alex returned to the house and sat in the corridor. He leaned forward, placing his head in his hands. What was Humphries doing? It must be too deep; he wasn't going to be able to get the bullet out. His probing was making things worse. He got up to invade that sanctum he had been banished from. But, as before, the door opened as he reached it. His heart beat like a drum and his limbs began to shake. His mouth was too dry to ask the question.

Dr Humphries smiled. 'All went well, my lord. But I must warn you . . .'

Alex rushed past him into her room.

Grace lay with her dark head raised by only one pillow, her face drained of any colour. Alex knelt down by the bed and took her hand. It was limp, yet she was so strong to have endured these past hours. He placed it against his cheek, slid it to his lips and kissed her palm. He knew it wasn't over yet, but she had fought this far, she must fight that bit longer to help her wound heal and her blood return.

Dr Humphries came back into the room and touched Alex's shoulder. 'I will return in a few hours, Lord Rossmore. Mrs Gillett knows how to contact me should it be necessary.' He left as quietly as he had come.

Alex sat waiting. When the noon hour arrived, Mrs Gillett brought him a tray. 'I have a light luncheon, my lord.'

'I'm not hungry. Later.'

'You must eat. Your strength will be needed when she wakes.'

'Wakes, Mrs Gillett? Is she going to wake?'

'Oh, yes. Miss Grace will not let this take her. I know how strong she can be.'

'You sound very sure.'

'I suspect there is much she has not told you. She will in her own time.'

'That soup is tempting my stomach. Leave the tray, I will eat here.'

Alex pondered Mrs Gillett's words, mysterious meanings indeed. He ate with a hunger he had not realised and felt a renewed energy in his body.

He bathed her face with cool water and wetted her lips, hoping a few drops would find their way into her throat. He opened the window wide, letting the summer air fill the room, hoping that the scents from the garden would bring her back into this world. But she remained in the dark world of her own. As the afternoon sun passed across the window, Alex sat waiting for a sign.

Grace's eyes fluttered, then opened and a whisper passed her lips. 'Alex?'

'I'm here, my love.' He stood and kissed her forehead. 'Here forever.'

She licked her lips. 'Water.' Alex picked up the cup and with his right arm raised her head. 'Sip just a little.' Her hand moved to his upper left arm and he winced, a reminder of his own wound.

'You are alive? Really alive?'

'Yes. A duel of honour settled, but at what cost.' Olsen had clipped him. But the assassin's bullet could have killed her.

'I don't remember . . . I was running . . . you were firing . . . I tripped . . .'

'Not tripped. Someone fired at me from the dark, but you were there . . .' Alex buried his face in her hair, 'it should be me lying here, not you.' The anguish returned in one swoop and his fingers tightened on the cup.

'Hugo? Is he . . . alive?'

'Yes.'

'Then everything is alright.' She closed her eyes and he laid her head down on the pillow.

Alex pulled his chair closer. Sitting down he waited.

Chapter Twenty-four

Gillett lit the candles as the evening sun dipped low and the room dimmed.

Alex dabbed Grace's face and neck with a wet cloth. Lifting her head he scooped the long hair upwards and laid it across the pillow. Perspiration beaded her forehead and he feared the worst. Pulling the bell-rope he summoned Esther. 'Ask Gillett to go for Dr Humphries.'

Esther looked past him at her mistress. 'Oh, at once, my lord,' and she ran from the room.

When the doctor arrived he examined the wound. 'It looks clean, not infected. The fever could be many things. Hopefully it will abate in its own time.'

Alex felt so inadequate. 'Is that all you can do?'

'I can treat only what I see. I will have a word with Mrs Gillett. Call me if . . .' His words trailed off, the meaning clear. He picked up his bag and left.

Grace started to mumble and he leaned forward to hear the words. 'Papa. Please let me have a pony . . . you promised if I was good . . . Snowdrop, you are the prettiest . . . Mama, watch me ride.' Grace looked as if she was smiling. 'I love Solitaire . . . can we go, Mama . . . Papa won't come.'

She started to cry and Alex wiped away her tears. 'Papa you can't say no . . . Simon is leaving . . . Papa please.' She went still, her restlessness ceased. 'He won't consent . . . Simon I love you . . . we will say our vows.' Grace began to shiver.

Alex drew the counterpane up to her chin. Her words were meaningless. He looked for a clean cloth, but he had used them all. Pulling open the bedside cabinet drawer, it stopped halfway. Putting pressure on the handle he gave it a sharp tug and a hidden drawer opened at the side. Alex saw a Bible, the dark leather worn by many fingernail scratches. He took it out and opened the cover and read the inscription:

Second Lieutenant Simon Featherstone
To my only son, keep safe,
Deepest affection, Mama

Alex fanned through the pages, noticing they, too, were finger worn. A folded sheet fell out and he picked it up from the floor. A fear was reaching into his heart. He shouldn't read what was written, yet he had to know. Now, beads of sweat were showing on his forehead, a wetness that had nothing to do with the hot summer night air. He moved away from the bed and went over to the dressing table and sat on the stool. He began to open the sheet, but then stopped. This was prying into Grace's life, a part that she didn't want him to know. But how could they start anew if there were doubts? He pushed away the guilt and opened the single page.

Dear Grace, my daughter-in-law,

For you are the wife Simon wished you to be.
It is with sadness in my heart, that I write telling you
he was killed with our great Lord Nelson at Trafalgar.
I send you his Bible that he carried always.

Martha Featherstone.

Alex looked into the mirror at his reflection. There was disbelief in his eyes. Why hadn't she told him? It was almost ten years since Trafalgar. She had been eighteen. Did she think he wouldn't understand? He looked back at the bed and his heart ached for them both. There were so many questions that needed answers. Refolding the sheet, he replaced it amongst the pages and went back and tucked the Bible into the hidden drawer, pushed it closed. Pulling open another drawer he found several cotton squares.

The mumbling went on, often incoherent, until Alex gave up trying to listen.

Just before midnight, Esther came to ask if he would go down to supper. 'Mrs Gillett says she will not take no for an answer, my lord.' The girl blushed at giving such a command to her master.

Alex wanted to refuse, but he knew he needed food and rest for a while. 'You will fetch me immediately, if there is a change.'

'Yes.' Esther curtsied as Alex got up from the chair. At the door he stopped. 'Immediately, Esther,' and left.

The dining room looked desolate, the one place setting intolerable. He turned and left. Alex had never been to the kitchen and when he entered, Mrs Gillett was sat in a rocking chair, sewing along the hem of an apron.

'May I . . . have my supper in here?'

The sight of her master sent Mrs Gillett into a fluster. 'In here? But this is the kitchen.'

'Yes. But the dining room is so lonely, I thought . . .' He was going to crumble in front of a servant. Alex squared his shoulders, 'I'm sorry, of course, in the dining room.' He turned to leave.

'Please, your lordship, stay. Her ladyship used to have her meals in here, when her mama was out visiting.' She pulled a chair from the table, offering it to him and he sat down. Her hands trembled as she spread a cloth and laid a place.

Alex ate hungrily; the hours spent with Grace were a strain far greater than he would own to.

'How is her ladyship?'

'No better, yet no worse, Mrs Gillett. I must get back to her. Thank you for the supper.'

'She deserves a life. He never cared; she was not the son he wanted.'

Alex looked over to the old woman. It was as if she could not hold back her words any longer. 'Who?'

'Her father, he ruled with a rod of iron. Her only freedom was here, at Solitaire. Her mama tried to help, but she had no say.' Mrs Gillett was now red with anger; so much bottled up that her words spilled out, without any thought to the propriety of such an act. 'She was so happy when she met him. They were the perfect match, but he refused.'

Alex still sat at the table. 'Who are you talking about?'

'Simon Featherst—' Mrs Gillett stopped speaking. She looked down at the floor. 'I beg your pardon, my lord; I have spoken out of turn.'

'Yes, Mrs Gillett, you have. We shall forget the indiscretion.' He stood up and left.

In the early hours, Grace slipped into a fretful sleep.

Alex hoped it was the sign that the worst was over. He walked round and lay down on the bed beside her. It was to be for only a few minutes, to ease his aching back, but within seconds he was asleep. A knocking on the door woke him. 'Come in,' he called, as he carefully got off the bed.

Mr Gillett waited in the doorway, looking agitated. 'Captain Olsen is downstairs to see you, my lord.'

'Olsen! What the devil does he want?'

'He asked me to say that it is very urgent and please, not to refuse him.'

Alex went over to Grace. She was now calm and asleep.

'Wake Esther and tell her to come here and sit with her ladyship. Keep Olsen in the hall until I come down. I will see him in the study. Just one lighted candlestick on my desk, Gillett.'

When Esther arrived, he went into his own bedchamber and washed his face. He chose a clean shirt, tied a fresh necktie and put on a coat. He had no intention of facing Olsen looking like a tramp. It had also given him time to pull his thoughts together. The man downstairs was an enemy of both Grace and himself.

Olsen was dressed to travel.

Alex dismissed the servant and waved the captain towards the study.

The two men stood facing each other. Not twenty paces, but just two. 'Well.' Alex would give this man no homage.

'How is Grace? I could not leave without knowing.'

'You dare to ask!'

'Yes, my lord, I dare.'

Alex wanted to beat this man with his fists, but answered, 'She is alive and holding on.'

'May I sit down?'

Alex nodded and went to sit in his seat behind the desk. In the light of the one candlestick their shadows danced round the room.

'There are things that need to be settled before I sail from England.'

Again, Alex nodded.

'First, my name is Ludvig Hugo Olsen. My ship was badly damaged in a storm and I was forced to come into Weymouth for repairs. The cost was high. I could not pay. A man offered me the money I needed. The house here was part of the offer if I did a little smuggling for him. Soon after, he asked if I would . . .' Olsen hesitated and looked straight at Alex, 'would seduce a Lady Rossmore who was staying at Solitaire House.'

Alex shot up from his chair, but Olsen raised his hand. 'Let me finish. From the moment I met Grace, I knew she was not one of your English courtesan ladies that we Norwegians have heard about. We became friends. And that is all, my lord. Two troubled people needing a friend.'

Alex stared at the man with hatred in his heart. 'I hold you, and those who employed you, responsible for what has happened to Grace.'

'I have dealt with the weasel that fired from the dark.'

'Explain yourself?'

'I have done what your lordship has in his heart.'

At this admission, Alex looked more closely at the captain. There was no remorse in his tone and the deep lines etched down the side of his mouth had not been there at the beach. 'You have killed him? Who was it?'

298

'It is best that you do not have any details.' Olsen stood up. 'Assassins kill for gold. Why should they not be killed for revenge?'

These brutal words told more about the man than any written report.

'Then there is nothing more for us to discuss. I will deal with those who gave the order. Although not by your methods.'

Olsen took a letter from inside his jacket and placed it on the desk. 'I have one request. Would you please give this to Grace?'

Alex made no reply; his gaze fixed on the letter.

Olsen nodded. 'I shall not be returning to England.'

Alex heard the door open and close.

An hour later, Alex was still sitting in the chair behind his desk. Opening the middle drawer, he withdrew the three letters which he had written before the duel.

Throwing these letters into the fire-grate he held the candle flame to them. As the paper blackened into ash, the wax melted, running like Grace's blood from her wound.

He pinched the candle wick between finger and thumb.

The morning light strengthened and a lone birdcall sounded.

He sat back at his desk and picked up Olsen's letter. A moment of pity rose up in him. He understood Olsen's dilemma – skulduggery of an unknown countess for his ship and livelihood. But the heart has its own rules; Olsen fell in love with Grace.

Alex placed the letter in the drawer beside the report, closed it and turned the key. Taking a deep sigh he put the key in his pocket and left the study.

Alex could hear voices when he reached Grace's room. Inside, Mrs Gillett was drawing the curtains and Esther was tidying the bed.

'Has Lady Rossmore awakened at all?'

'No, my lord, but she has sighed many times.' Esther gave this information in a tone of hope. 'I'm sure she will wake up soon.'

'Will you take breakfast, my lord?' Mrs Gillett looked as tired as Alex.

'Bring me a tray: ham, bread and coffee.'

Both women left and Alex sat down on the chair beside the bed. Grace looked a little better. There was a slight pinkness to her lips and a touch of colour to her face. Dr Humphries had said twenty-four hours, which had now passed. If she made it through today, hope could turn into expectation. He lifted her hand and pressed her fingers to his forehead.

Grace stirred, her eyes fluttered and then opened. Now they were clear and she recognised him. 'Alex. You are still here?'

'I shall be here every minute of every day until you are well, my love.'

She tried to move, but winced with pain.

'Don't struggle, Grace, it may cause your wound to reopen. Would you like some water?'

'Please.' He sat and held her again, tipping the cup so tiny drops of water passed her lips. Laying her back, he said, 'I will ring for Esther . . .'

Grace shook her head. 'Not yet. Just sit with me.' Then she closed her eyes and drifted back into sleep.

Grace slept on and off all day. Every time she woke up, Alex was there, holding her hand.

At six o'clock, Dr Humphries called. Examined the wound, felt her forehead and gave her a smile. 'I think we can say there is no infection, but it will take some time for your strength to return. I recommend a week in bed, Lady Rossmore.'

Grace felt too weak to argue, so nodded.

'Good. I will speak with his lordship now. Good evening.' He left with the abruptness that was his manner.

Grace lay looking at the closed door. It opened and Esther came in with a tray.

'Mrs Gillett has sent a bowl of your favourite soup. I am to sit with you until it is empty. His lordship is dining downstairs.'

Grace didn't know whether to be pleased or sad. But the tempting smell of the soup made her hunger sharpen and Esther helped her to sit up. She used her left hand, finding it rather awkward, but when the bowl was empty, the maid smiled. 'Well done, m'lady. Will you finish the bread?'

'No, thank you, Esther, I am quite full, but a glass of lemonade would be very nice now.'

'I'll light the candles first.'

The task finished, she took the tray off the bed. 'I will be back immediately,' and her eyes watered, 'we are all so relieved you are going to be alright.' Then Esther hurried from the room.

Through the cotton nightgown Grace fingered the bandage circling her body. It was tight, but not uncomfortable. She closed her eyes, trying to remember what had happened, but it was hazy.

The door opened and Alex came in carrying a small tray. 'A glass of lemonade as requested.' He came over to the bed and handed the glass to Grace. 'Would you like me to hold you?'

Something was wrong, for he had been holding her during the day when she had requested drinks. 'No. I'm sure I can manage on my own now.'

Alex went over to the window, keeping his back to her. 'Are you feeling strong enough for us to talk?'

Grace knew this moment had to come. It was time for the truth. She was here at Solitaire and could stay forever. She sipped the drink, and then answered, 'Yes.'

He came back and sat on the bed, taking the glass from her hand. 'Where shall we begin?'

Grace felt confused. 'Begin?'

'Liddy or Simon?' Her downcast gaze flew to his face. 'You were delirious, mumbling. I was looking for a cloth . . .'

'Oh.'

'Oh, indeed.'

Grace wetted her lips and looked back down, then raised her head and lifted her chin. 'When I was eighteen, Mother and I were staying here for the summer. I met Simon Featherstone in Dorchester. He was a naval officer and was boarding in the town awaiting new orders. We fell in love. It was a fiery love that would not be held down. He travelled to Woodford Hall, asking Father for my

301

hand in marriage. And Father, in his usual unrelenting manner, refused our betrothal. I pleaded with him, but he said he had plans for my future, higher than that of a sailor's wife. Sneered, how I would be left alone at home for months, even years. He ruled every moment of my life. I hated him and Mother would not dare to disobey him. Our only relief was here, at Solitaire. Then Simon was recalled and I could not let him go without us . . .' Grace took the glass from Alex's fingers and sipped, '. . . Mother had been recalled to Woodford because Father had fallen from his horse and broken his leg.

'Simon and I went to the church on his last evening, here at Whitecliffs, and said our vows before God together. We have no written lines, but I was his wife and he was my husband. Gillie . . .' again Grace paused and sipped from the glass, 'Gillie knew and we stayed here, in my room, until the morning. Then he was gone and I never saw him again.'

Grace began to tremble and Alex took the glass from her and put it on the side cabinet. Moving to sit beside her, he cradled her to him, stroking her hair, kissing her temple. 'Cry, Grace, cry my love, for your lost Simon.' And at those words, Grace turned into him and let the tears flow.

Alex waited until Grace had no more tears to cry. He squeezed a cloth in the bowl of cold water beside him and bathed her face. 'Why didn't you tell me this before we were married?'

'I don't know. It has been my secret for ten years and I . . . and I just couldn't. I was a spinster, yet a widow in my heart. Father tried many times to have me married, but I had grown out from under his tyranny. When Mother died I spent a lot of time visiting relatives and friends. Then I have Solitaire. Father is now old and infirm. He had accepted that I would not marry. Then I met you . . .'

Alex saw her blush, the first real colour her face had had since the duel.

'You swept me off my feet. I was eighteen again, alive and in

302

love.' The colour faded from her face. 'But it is not to be. I know about your paramour and . . . and child, soon to be born. Is that not why you had me put into Greensleeves?'

Alex moved to sit in front of Grace. 'What are you talking about?'

'Alex, I saw you at Chelsea, on our way to Grosvenor Square. We had to detour because of the celebrations . . .'

He held up his hands in defence. 'No, Grace. Not me! It was Geoffrey. Everything that has happened was because of his greed for the earldom.'

'Geoffrey! No, it was you. Your hair, it is such an unusual colour.'

'Have you not noticed how alike we are?'

'Yes, but I've only seen him twice. Once at our betrothal party at the formal reception line, for he left soon after. Aunt Matilda thought it very poor manners. Then at Hawthorn Hall; but in the badly lit hall and with his hat and cloak on. . . .' she wetted her lips, 'he left the following morning before I was up. . . . Alex, how could I have been so stupid?'

Alex took her hands, squeezed them in his and looked directly into her eyes. 'Confusion, mixed with a little fury? I treated you badly, by leaving Solitaire House. Twice, remember! How can I ask your forgiveness?' He bowed his head and the candlelight made his copper hair glow.

Grace withdrew her hands, tilted his chin up. 'Love can forgive all, Alex.'

He leaned and kissed her lips, just a soft touch, then stood up, taking a turn round the room before sitting back down on the bed. 'It is my turn to do some confessing. In those years I was without Liddy, she had always been there, haunting me. I was the one who caused her death . . . her death was to give me an heir, but I didn't even have him to love. Geoffrey was, therefore, my heir. Our marriage would change all that. We would have a son. Geoffrey schemed to separate us.'

303

'Separate us? But how could he do that?'

Alex took Beesell's report from an inside pocket of his coat. 'Do you feel well enough to read this?'

'What is it?' Grace frowned as Alex unfolded several sheets.

'When you didn't arrive at Kilbraith House and I couldn't find you, I hired an agent. His report documents everything.'

Grace held out her hand. 'I would like to read it, Alex.'

As she started, he got up and went back to the window. The sky was a soft, washed-orange colour; it was going to be a glorious sunset and Grace would understand all by then. He heard many exclamations, but did not turn until Grace called his name.

'Alex, can this be true? Can people do such things?'

'I'm afraid they can; and much more.'

'Geoffrey had me kidnapped and taken to that awful place. Put me amongst those pitiful, insane women. A stranger pretended to be my husband?'

Alex went to the bed and sat down. 'There were mysterious happenings in Kilbraith House. All designed to turn my head and drive me away from you.'

'Liddy's ghost?' She waved the report.

'Yes.'

'What . . . what will happen to Geoffrey?'

'He should go to prison, but I cannot subject Rachel to such shame. Geoffrey has agreed to go to Craigkillie, my estate in Ireland. I have made him a fair offer and allowance.'

'Agreed? It sounds more like a command.'

'Maybe, he did rather splutter a lot when I told him. Especially after I said Rachel and the children would remain here in England. She can come to live at Rossmore Manor any time she chooses.'

'She loves Hawthorn Hall. I doubt she would move permanently from it. But I would love her to come and visit. We did so enjoy each other's company.'

Alex's good feelings faded. 'Then there was Hugo Olsen. He was used as a wedge between us, a paid accomplice . . .'

Grace cried out, 'No. I won't believe that. He was my friend; he saved me from the sea.'

Alex took Grace's hand and lifted it to his lips, feathering kisses over her fingers. 'On the night I returned to Whitecliffs, seeing you and Olsen together in the drawing room, silhouetted standing so close to each other, I feared you were having an affair with him. I was furious and my jealousy made me bungle what I had come to say to you. Then, when I found out you were not a virgin bride and I saw you leave Olsen's house . . .'

Grace stared at him, her eyes wide. 'When?'

'Egg-milk. Remember?'

For the second time, Grace blushed. 'There was never anything more than friendship. Well . . . not for me.'

Alex took Olsen's letter from his pocket. 'He left you this letter, Grace. I have to admit that I considered burning it unopened, but we need trust now, or we have no future together.'

Grace reached for it and her fingers trembled as she pulled the wax seal apart.

Dear Grace,

Your husband will tell you all that has happened.
I kept my part of the smuggling bargain, but not
the part about you, because you filled my heart with love.

Hugo

She looked at Alex. 'Will you read it?' She held the single sheet out to him.

'Are you sure this is what you want?'

'Like you said, there must be trust between us.'

Alex read the few lines and refolded it. 'Olsen will never return to England.'

He moved and took her in his arms. Grace lifted her head and Alex kissed her. 'All our secrets are secrets no more. I love you, Grace. We will have a wonderful life together.'

'Yes, Alex, we will.'

'There's one final thing I have to do.'

From his pocket he took a scrap of cloth and put it on the counterpane. Unfolding the edges, the Rossmore wedding ring lay inside. Taking Grace's left hand he slipped it onto her finger. 'Never take it off again, Lady Rossmore.'

'Never again, *my* Lord Rossmore.'

Epilogue

Autumn 1816

The nursery was bright with sunshine.

Grace cradled her son to her breast and he suckled her warm milk. She was a little plump still and had not yet ventured riding a horse in the parkland of Rossmore Manor.

So much had happened: Geoffrey's treachery, the misunderstandings, but so much happiness as well. She looked at the copper-coloured hair of her son, Daniel Alexander Kilbraith, heir to the Earl of Rossmore.

Grace gave him a shake. 'Wake up. You have much more to come yet.'

Esther came in. 'His lordship wants to know if you will be down for tea?'

'Of course I will. I never miss my afternoon tea. Tell him fifteen minutes.'

'Very well, m'lady, but he seems very impatient.'

'He is about to learn that his heir takes priority, even if he is only a baby.'

Esther laughed. 'Yes, indeed.'

Alex was waiting for Grace at the bottom of the staircase. He pulled her into his arms as she stepped off the last tread. 'This is our last chance to have a peaceful tea together; I want every minute of you to myself.'

'My, you are becoming a dutiful husband.'

'If it makes you happy as you are today, then I will have tea with you until the day I die.'

The noise of horses' harness and carriage wheels sounded outside and a footman opened the front door.

Grace raised her eyebrows. 'Too late, they're here.'

Two coaches stopped. When the door of the first coach opened, Rachel was helped out, with Tilly and Thomas following.

Grace ran forward, arms outstretched. 'Rachel, welcome to Rossmore.'

'Grace, how wonderful you look. Motherhood agrees with you.'

Alex came forward and kissed her cheek. 'Rossmore is your home for as long as you want to stay.'

'Thank you, Alex. But it will only be a visit.'

Rachel turned to direct the outflow of the other coach: Nurse, a young maid and six children. She waved her arm towards the drive. 'The luggage will be here shortly.'

Grace saw Alex take a step backwards and she slipped her hand into his. Putting her lips close to his ear she spoke a few words.

He grinned. 'When you're ready, my love, just whisper Solitaire in my ear.'

Acknowledgements

I would like to thank:

My manuscript editor, Jay Dixon, for her kindness and generous help in preparing my novel for publication.

Headline Publishing, and my editor, Faith Stoddard, for steering me through the channels of the complex world of novel writing.

Dorset History Centre, for their advice on the county name in 1815 – Dorset or Dorsetshire?

Liz Bartlett, at the Jane Austen Dancers, for her advice on public and private ballroom dancing.

To my husband, Tony, who has been my most devoted champion from the first word in my writing career.

I love researching about past times in history. But sometimes I need a little help. I give a basket full of thanks to my friends who gave their time so generously to this task.

Author's Notes

In the Regency era the marriage law defines a wife as '*femme covert*' meaning she is owned by her husband.

Upon marriage, the husband and wife then become one person under the law. This means that the wife's legal identity ceases to exist. She, her children and any wealth or goods at the time of marriage and afterwards belong to him. A wife cannot write a will.

Within the nobility and gentry a marriage settlement could be agreed. For example, a trust fund securing money: this was called pin-money for dress and personal expenditure.

Divorce was rare. Both Parliament and Church demanded stringent causes. The cost of such an action was extremely high, even for the nobility. Alongside this was the shunning by Society. The wife would be left impoverished, as the law deemed she had no rights from the marital purse.

Only a spinster, or a widow, was able to maintain her independence if she had sufficient funds.

Primogeniture: This is the right by law, or custom, of a firstborn legitimate son to inherit his deceased father's estate.

Research

2 March 2020

Married Women's Property Act 1870 Parliament of the United Kingdom https://en.wikipedia.org/wiki/Married_Women%27s_Property_Act_1870

Married Women's Property Act 1882 Parliament of the United Kingdom
https://en.wikipedia.org/wiki/Married_Women%27s_Property_Act_1882

Since 1882 there have been numerous amendments. The last that I can find is the Married Women's Property Act 1882 – 31st October 2016 The National Archives
https://www.legislation.gov.uk/cy/ukpga/Vict/45-46/75

The Marriage Law of Jane Austen's World: Martha Bailey, Professor of Law, Queen's University, Canada
http://jasna.org/publications/persuasions-online/vol36no1/bailey/